CASSIE EDWARDS

THE **SAVAGE**
S E R I E S

UNTIL DAWN

"*Nei-com-mar-pe-ein*, I love you so," Jae whispered in Comanche. She ran her fingers through his hair. She gazed into his eyes. "I wish tonight would last forever. I so fear tomorrow. What if you don't achieve what you have set out to do?" She drew his cheek down against hers.

"What if you don't survive?" she whispered, her voice breaking.

"I have not come this far to be defeated by the likes of Black Crow," Night Hawk whispered back.

"If anything happens to you, I would not want to live, either," she said, trembling inside at the thought of their parting in such a tragic way.

He placed a forefinger against her lips. He gazed into her troubled eyes. "Now is not the time to show doubts about what I have planned for my Comanche people," he said. He ran his hands up and down her spine, then slid them around, filling them with her breasts. "Now is not the time to think of anything but the joy of being together, of making love."

SAVAGE SHADOWS

CASSIE EDWARDS

LEISURE BOOKS **NEW YORK CITY**

A LEISURE BOOK®

August 1996

Published by

Dorchester Publishing Co., Inc.
276 Fifth Avenue
New York, NY 10001

Printed in the United States of America.

With much affection I dedicate *Savage Shadows* to Beverly Christner, Laura Mahdak, Tammy Yarbrough, Donna and Roy Combs, and Randy and Lupe Decker and children; also, Janice Bolin, Hazel Bedford, Judy Bohn, Velma Bobbitt, Nedra Barnes, Rosemarie Brown, Ann Blevins, Esther Bump, Eleanor Bird, and Millie Buxton.

Forever As One
Jacqueline Lee Holst

Our hearts so strong they're bound by Love
As if our souls were joined from Above

Oh Great Spirit up in the sky
I know our Love will never die

With your strength and guiding light
Our Love grew strong within your sight

There's nothing in this world alone
That can destroy the Love we hold

The good, the bad, the hurt, the pain
Can't change the oneness we became

A man whose skin is unlike mine
Has changed my heart forever divine

We love each other with all our heart
Forever As One we will never part

Our children will grow within our Love
Our children will learn the strengths from Above

We teach them how to love, to share
We teach them what it means to care

They will always know that the love we share
Will continue to grow because we care

We combine our love, our faith, our hope
We combine our beliefs and learn to cope

The words from others can not destroy
Our bonds of Love that bring us joy

It does not matter what others might say
It will never change our loving ways

Oh Great Spirit from Above
We were destined to be, Forever As One

Chapter One

The State of Texas, 1841

"Open the safe," the outlaw sneered as he held his pistol steady on Ralph Hampton. "Do it! Do it now!"

Tall and thin, his hair as black as his thick mustache, Ralph Hampton stood his ground behind the oak desk in the spacious office of his ranch house. He glared at the outlaw's sky-blue eyes as they peered at him over the bandanna tied around his lower face. His hand inched slowly toward the desk drawer, where he kept his pearl-handled pistol.

"Don't try it," the outlaw said, laughing unpleasantly, "or I'll blow your damn hand off. All you need is one hand to open that damn safe!"

"I know you," Ralph said, studying the blue eyes and the man's muscled physique. Although Ralph was a tall man himself, towering over most people with his six-foot height, this outlaw was at least four inches taller than he. The man held himself erect, his shoulders squared. "Yes, I know you even with your bandanna. You're Clifton Coldsmith. You have the reputation of being one of the deadliest outlaws in these parts."

Clifton chuckled. "You know me, all right," he said, taking a step closer. He glared at Ralph. "You idiot. Don't you know you just signed your death warrant by letting me know you recognize me?"

"You are the idiot. Don't *you* know that *I* know that I don't have a chance in hell of getting out of this alive, anyhow?" Ralph said, his hand still inching closer to the drawer. "You leave death behind wherever you go. Why would I think it'd be any different with me?"

"All I wanted was your money," Clifton said, his voice drawn. "I've never taken pleasure in killin'. I only do it when my hand is forced." He nodded toward Ralph's safe. "Now get that damn thing open."

"No, I don't think so," Ralph said. His lips curved into a sardonic smile beneath his mustache. "Why should I? I'm a dead man either way. So I'll just let you work for your money tonight. Figure out the combination yourself. If you're lucky, you'll be a rich man."

A soft voice spoke up behind the outlaw. "You're not getting your filthy hands on any of my husband's money," Penelope Hampton said.

The outlaw wheeled suddenly around and found a beautiful, redheaded woman standing just inside the door, a shotgun leveled at his stomach.

"No, Penelope!" Ralph shouted. He scrambled to get the desk drawer open. "Get back to your room! Lock your door!"

A sudden spattering of gunfire rang out in the room.

Paling and feeling suddenly faint, Penelope

dropped her rifle as she watched her husband crumple to the floor.

She then looked at the window behind the desk. The glass was shattered. Through the splinters of broken glass she saw another outlaw standing just outside the broken window, shadowed by moonlight, his pistol smoking.

Penelope stared again at the bandit who was only inches away from her. His intense sky-blue eyes momentarily unnerved her.

Then she ran past him and fell to her knees beside her husband, who lay on his side behind the desk, his eyes glazed over with pain.

"Oh, Lord," Penelope cried, seeing the blood seeping through his clothes. "Ralph, can you move? I fear the bullet is too close to your spine."

"Penelope, don't worry about me," Ralph managed to say in a raspy whisper. "Why . . . didn't you stay hidden in your room? Don't . . . you . . . know what might happen to you now?"

He winced when he tried to turn over, but found himself powerless. He knew then that he was partially paralyzed. He could move his fingers and arms, and even his head. But he felt nothing from his waist down. He tried to focus on his main concern—his wife and his unborn child!

"The child, Penelope. Good Lord, our child," he gulped out. He grabbed one of Penelope's hands. "Don't let the bastard know about the child."

Penelope slipped a hand to her abdomen. Tears came to her eyes at the thought of how long she had tried to become pregnant. Now she might lose her husband even her child, at the hand of a thieving, cowardly rapist.

She stiffened her upper lip. "Nothing is going to

13

happen to our child," she whispered loud enough for only Ralph to hear. "Nothing more is going to happen to *you*."

She eyed the desk drawer, which was partially open. Her pulse raced as she glanced up at the outlaw. She was taken aback at the way he was looking at her.

And again she noticed his eyes. They were almost too beautiful to be a man's. And they seemed too peaceful to belong to an outlaw!

But above all else she knew that there was no way for her to grab the pistol. Not with him staring at her so intently.

Her gaze wavered as her eyes locked with his, and, unnerved by his steady stare, she looked back down at her husband. "I've got to get you help," she said. She swept a hand over her husband's sweating brow. "Ralph, what am I to do?"

"Just cooperate," Ralph replied in a throaty whisper. "Do nothing to antagonize them. Then . . . then . . . at your first opportunity, *run*."

Clifton Coldsmith was taken not only by the woman's loveliness, but by her courage as well. She showed not even one ounce of fear. He had never met a woman like her before.

His gaze moved to the ripe, full breasts visible through the sheer fabric of her lacy, silk nightgown. His eyes followed her red hair as it fell in long tendrils over her breasts when she bent low to kiss her husband's brow. It was then that she broke into tears. He could feel her helplessness deep inside his heart and was moved to action by it.

Ignoring her despair and her tears, he went to her, grabbed her by one wrist, and gently urged her to her feet. He swallowed hard when he again found himself gazing into her eyes, ignoring the hate and defiance in their depths.

"Let me go!" Penelope screamed, trying to yank her wrist free. She kicked one of the man's legs, then cried out in pain, having forgotten that she was barefooted. When her toes came in contact with the man's leg, it was as though she had kicked something as solid as steel.

"Just settle down," the outlaw said, his voice no longer threatening. It was like honey in its softness. "I'm sorry about your husband."

"He's shot in the back!" Penelope cried, her struggles waning as she realized they were in vain. "Please let me go for a doctor. Please?"

"After I leave I'll send a doctor to see to your husband's welfare," the soft-spoken, blue-eyed outlaw said. "But first, ma'am, you've got to open that safe for me."

"If I do, will you promise to send a doctor for my husband?" Penelope asked, her eyes searching his.

"For you, yes, I'll make sure your husband is seen to," Clifton said. He reached up and slowly slid the bandanna down, revealing his face to Penelope.

Penelope gasped at the sight. His features were rugged, yet handsome. His voice and his eyes had already awakened strange feelings that she had never experienced before. And now to see that he was so handsome caused her knees to be suddenly weak and the pit of her stomach to feel strangely warm.

She had never had anything but sisterly affection for her husband. Their marriage had been arranged by Penelope's rich plantation father. Wanting to get away from her boring life in Louisiana, she had willingly married Ralph and come to live on his ranch in Texas, enjoying the excitement of living in a place that was wild and untamed.

The recent realization that she was with child had drawn her closer to her husband, yet there still was no thrill when he touched or kissed her.

This sudden rush of feelings in her now, a strange sort of thrill, frightened her. Ashamed at having felt anything but loathing for this outlaw, Penelope turned her eyes suddenly away.

"Is it a bargain, ma'am?" Clifton said, placing a finger beneath her chin and bringing her eyes back around to his. "Open the safe and I promise that a doctor will be sent soon to check on your husband."

Penelope searched his eyes again.

Then something came to her that made ice fill her veins. "You've shown me your face—that can mean only one of two things," she said, her voice drawn with fear. "You either are going to kill me to silence me, or . . . or . . . you are going to take me as a hostage!"

Clifton placed a gentle hand on her cheek. "Ma'am, I could never kill anyone as pretty as you," he said thickly. "And, ma'am, I certainly could never take you hostage. If I take you, it will be because you are going to be my woman."

"Oh, God!" Ralph managed to say loud enough for her to hear. "No!"

Clifton Coldsmith slid a slow look over at Ralph, then looked at Penelope again. "If you value your husband's life, you'll do as I say, *now,*" he said flatly.

Penelope stared at the outlaw a moment longer, glanced down at her husband, then rushed to the safe. Her fingers trembled as she turned the dial. When the door swung open, she slowly stood up and stepped aside.

Suddenly three more outlaws were in the room.

They laughed and jeered as they filled bags with jewelry, the diamonds gleaming like stars in the palms of their hands, and with huge stacks of bills and bags of jangling coins.

Then everything became quiet as they stopped their plundering and stood up to face their leader.

One of them smiled wryly at Penelope. His gaze slid over her, seeing her nudity beneath the sheer fabric of her nightgown.

Then he gave Clifton a leering look. "Can I have her first?" he said, almost choking on a lusty laugh.

"Get out of here, Flash," Clifton said, nodding toward the door. He looked at the other two men. "All of you. Get out. Secure the money in the saddlebags on our horses." He turned his gaze to Penelope again. "And grab another horse and saddle it. I'm taking the woman with me."

"No!" Ralph weakly cried. "Have mercy! Don't take my wife! Don't . . . harm . . . her!"

"I can guarantee you she won't be harmed in any way," Clifton said, reaching a hand out for Penelope. "Come on. You know you don't have any choice but to go with me. Go peacefully, okay?"

Penelope felt drawn to him; his eyes were hypnotic in their soft pleading. She swallowed hard, gave her husband a sorrowful glance, then reached her hand out for the outlaw and ran from the room with him.

They ran down the long hallway; then Clifton took Penelope quickly into a bedroom. She paled and sucked in a wild breath, her eyes filled with questioning as they stopped beside the large oak bed.

"Please don't . . . ," she pleaded. "Please don't rape me."

"Grab a blanket," he said thickly. "I don't want you to take a chill on the way to my hideout."

Penelope sighed with relief. She grabbed a blanket from the bed, then fled on outside with him.

The cold earth chilled the soles of her bare feet. She shivered as she gazed at the bunkhouse.

Then again she had cause for relief. Instead of having been shot, the ranch hands were tied up on the ground! Their lives had been spared as well as her husband's.

She turned with a start when one of the outlaws came running from the stables, a horse trotting along behind him.

She locked eyes with Clifton once again, then felt the strength in his hands as he placed them at her waist and lifted her onto the horse.

When she rode away with the outlaw gang, she knew that her life would never be the same again. She placed a hand on her abdomen, wondering what sort of life her child would be born into.

Chapter Two

Five Years Later

Sitting stoically quiet in the corner of a dark, dank room with several other Comanche children, ten-year-old Night Hawk stared over the heads of the others. His chin was lifted, proving his courage in the face of the saddest time of his life. Only a few days ago there had been a cavalry attack on his village.

The pony soldiers said they'd come to rescue white captives from the Comanche. But Night Hawk knew that they had used that excuse in an effort to annihilate his tribe. They had only succeeded at killing some of them.

During the attack, many of the Comanche people had escaped, among them their war chief, who was Night Hawk's father.

The fact that his father had not taken the time to rescue him made hatred soar through Night Hawk's heart. Tears filled his eyes as he thought of how his father had even left his mother to die!

He wondered if his father's cold-hearted behavior had been caused by the fact that Night Hawk's mother was white. She had been taken captive many moons before and had been forced to live as one of Chief Brown Bull's wives.

Had Chief Brown Bull left behind his only *son* because Night Hawk was not entirely Comanche? Although Night Hawk had never felt that his father was ashamed of him, surely that must be the case. Like his Comanche father, his skin was a reddish brown copper and his eyes were dark brown and slightly slanted. But it was obvious to everyone who saw him that he was a "breed," with the flaxen, straw-colored hair of his white mother.

Night Hawk's hands tightened into fists on his lap when he thought of the instant of his mother's death. It had not been at the hands of the white-eyed pony soldiers. It had been one of his father's warriors who had turned his rifle on Night Hawk's mother just prior to his cowardly escape from the village. So many of the villagers had seen his mother, with her beautiful golden hair and blue eyes, as an intrusion in their lives. They had only tolerated her because she was the wife of their war chief. And they had been forced to tolerate her child because he was the *son* of their chief.

Night Hawk quickly wiped the tears from his cheeks, for never did he want to appear weak in front of the other children or the white pony soldiers. But it was hard not to cry, for the soldiers had refused to bring his mother back to the fort for burial. She had been left behind with the rest of the dead, food for the coyotes.

He was filled with the need for vengeance, but to avenge his mother's death, he would not only have to strike out at the whites, but also at the Comanche.

He knew that he was fortunate in having been brought to Fort Phantom Hill along with the rest of the children, both white and red-skinned. Yet he felt so empty. Without his mother, what was his future to be? As long as she had lived, his father had seen to his welfare.

He hung his head and swallowed hard, still finding it hard to believe that his father had abandoned him. Brown Bull had taught Night Hawk how to ride a horse, how to shoot a bow and arrow, and how to hunt the small forest creatures. He had even given Night Hawk his name, chosen because of his piercing eyes and keen vision.

Night Hawk had thought that all of these things had been done with love! Now he did not know what to believe about his chieftain father, except that he was a false man who spoke with a false tongue to a son who could have adored him for a lifetime.

Night Hawk was born of two cultures, yet he felt as though he was a person without any people, white or red.

Light spilled in suddenly at the far end of the room as the door creaked open. Night Hawk saw the other children huddle together in a frightened manner at the sight of a white pony soldier as he entered the room.

The children gasped when a man entered the room in a strange sort of apparatus with wheels. A beautiful white lady walked behind it, pushing him.

But being a "breed," the presence of the white people did not make Night Hawk feel afraid. It only made his loneliness deepen, for the woman entering the room reminded him of the beloved mother whose arms would never hold him again!

He watched the flaxen-haired woman push the man in the chair with wheels closer. His pulse raced, for their eyes were on him. He seemed to be their purpose in being there.

"Hello, young man," Ralph Hampton said as he took control of his wheelchair and wheeled himself closer to Night Hawk.

The soldier lit a lamp, brought it over, and held it above Night Hawk's head so that the light would illuminate him, which allowed the two white people to scrutinize him more closely.

Night Hawk stiffened when the man in the chair with wheels stopped only inches away from him. He recoiled when the man reached a lean hand out for him.

"Don't be afraid," Ralph Hampton said, slowly drawing his hand back from Night Hawk's soft, copper face. "Young man, my wife and I have come to take you home with us. We would like for you to be a part of our family. We would like for you to be our *son.*"

Night Hawk's eyes widened. He gazed with utter disbelief from the woman to the man. He had understood every word that they had said. He knew both the Comanche and white man's tongue equally well. From the day of his birth, his mother had spoken English to him—to make him more white than Comanche.

"We truly would like for you to live with us," Lois Hampton murmured. "We are childless. We hunger so for the laughter of a child in our house. Night Hawk, if you will come with us, you will fill our house with such *joy.*"

Night Hawk was instantly drawn to the white woman. Not only did she look like his mother, but she also had the same sweet, soft voice—a voice that was filled with genuine caring.

He gazed again at the man, whose eyes were filled with a silent torment. He saw a man whose loneliness spoke from the depths of his dark brown eyes. And understanding many things inside his heart that others could not, Night Hawk could not help feeling this man's sadness.

He glanced at the strange chair with wheels, then looked into the eyes of the man again.

"I have never seen such a chair as that," Night Hawk said guardedly. "Why do you sit in it instead of standing beside your wife? Why are there wheels on the chair?"

Ralph patted the arms of the chair. "Son, this contraption is called a wheelchair," he said, his voice drawn. "Only people whose legs no longer function use such a chair as this."

"Your legs do not work?" Night Hawk said, his eyebrows rising. "You cannot walk?"

"No, I can no longer walk," Ralph said, battling the memories that assailed him.

But there was never any way to forget that damnable night, the night when he was not only shot and paralyzed, but also the night that he had lost his wife Penelope—and the child that had not been born to them yet.

He gritted his teeth at the memory of his wife being taken away, the outlaw having claimed her.

He gritted his teeth at the memory of having sent his men along with the calvary from Fort Phantom Hill to search for his sweet Penelope and the outlaws. They had scoured the land for days and nights without end, but they had found no trace of the outlaw or Penelope. It was as though they had disappeared from the face of the earth.

When Ralph had gotten strong enough to travel, he went to Penelope's parents' plantation in Louisiana and told them what had happened . . . that their daughter was missing.

It had been like a kick in the gut when they told him that she was dead. When he had asked how they knew, they said that word had been brought to them. When he had asked to see the grave, they had informed him that there was no grave, that her body had not been returned for burial.

He did not ask why, for he was afraid to hear the answer. Ralph did not wish to know the cause of his wife's untimely death.

Stunned, torn with grief over having lost Penelope forever, Ralph had returned to the ranch. He had lost his reason to live until a nurse had come to call one day. She had been assigned to his case by Ralph's doctor. She was to be his visiting nurse, coming daily to bathe him and to help him dress. She read to him for hours upon hours. An affection grew between them and their relationship progressed to the point that they began to eat their meals together by candlelight. She filled the void in his life. Even though she knew that he was not able to function sexually, she soon agreed to marry him.

Ralph feared that perhaps her affection was all pretense, that she truly was only interested in his money. But having her with him was all that mattered. It was the absence of children that they both felt so deeply. Adoption was the only answer, so when they had heard of this child whose white mother had recently been killed, they had both decided to adopt him.

"What made it so that you cannot walk?" Night

Hawk asked, becoming more interested by the minute in this couple.

"A stampede," Ralph said. He swallowed hard, even though the lie was getting easier each time he repeated it. He had never spoken of the truth of that unspeakable night to his new wife. She was not even aware that he'd been married before. When she came to him that first day, to care for his needs, he discovered that she was new in these parts and had no knowledge of the despicable acts of the outlaw who had crippled him, or that the outlaw had stolen his wife from him.

And he had instructed those at the fort not to discuss the tragedy in his new wife's presence. Nor were his cowhands ever to speak of it. To him the past was just that . . . something that he must learn to put behind him. Speaking of it would only make it all seem too real again. Thinking of it, being tortured by his memories, was bad enough, let alone having to explain it to everyone who ever became acquainted with him.

No, as far as he was concerned, the lie would suffice. He hoped that in time it would become so real to him that he would truly believe it himself.

"*Huh*, yes, I have seen men injured by stampedes," Night Hawk said, nodding. "I understand how it can take away the ability to walk." He slanted his head while in deep thought, then sat straight again. "Does it also mean that you can never ride a horse again?"

"Never," Ralph said, his voice breaking.

Feeling a sudden, deep empathy for this man whose life was filled with such pain, Night Hawk reached a slow hand out for him. He then took one of Ralph's hands and laid it above Night Hawk's heart. "My heart feels pain for you," he said softly.

Tears filled Ralph's eyes. He circled his fingers around the child's hand.

"Will you go home with us, Night Hawk?" Lois asked softly. She took a lacy handkerchief from the pocket of her dress and dabbed away the tears at the corners of her eyes. "We will love you as though you were *born* of our love."

"And, Night Hawk, out of all of the horses at my ranch, you can choose your very own special steed," Ralph said thickly. "You can choose your very own saddle. You can have anything that you want."

The mention of horses made Night Hawk's eyes brighten up. "You have many horses?" he asked anxiously. "You own a ranch?"

Night Hawk's pulse raced, for to the Comanche, many horses meant much wealth. To the Comanche, wealth *was* horses. Horses were the most valuable commodity to his father's people.

Ralph laughed softly. "Yes, I have many horses," he said, nodding. "And, yes, I own a ranch. A vast ranch. It is a place where a son is needed. Some day you will take over for me. You will be the one who hires and fires the cowhands. How does that suit you? You will be the most important man on my . . . on *our* ranch, Night Hawk, for you will be my *son*, my *heir*."

The words of this crippled white man were spinning around inside Night Hawk's head, making him understand the full meaning of what this couple was offering. He did not understand why he had been singled out to be the one to receive such blessings after having lost so much. Yet he had, and he was happy for it!

Suddenly he could see a future that was filled with much promise, whereas only moments before, he had been filled with such loss . . . with such despair!

Then he thought of his dead mother and knew that he could not be completely happy about anything.

"Night Hawk, you will be given anything your heart desires," Lois said, falling to her knees beside the child.

The boy gazed into her violet eyes and felt as though he was looking into his mother's!

Suddenly he flung himself into her arms and clung to her. "I miss her so much," he said, no longer holding back his tears. "My mother is dead! I . . . miss . . . her so!"

Lois held him close. She caressed his back with slow strokes. "I know," she whispered. "I'm so sorry, Night Hawk. You see, I understand such a loss. Not long ago my mother and father also died. That is why I came to Texas. I came to live with my uncle."

Night Hawk eased from her arms. He wiped the tears from his eyes with the backs of his hands and gazed at Lois. "I am sorry about your parents," he said, swallowing hard.

"It is this man here, my husband, who helped me forget my loss, as he will also help you forget yours," she said, sending a soft smile up at Ralph.

"Did he come for you as he has come for me today?" Night Hawk innocently asked.

Lois laughed softly. "No, that isn't how it happened with me," she said. "You see, Night Hawk, my uncle is a doctor. He is Ralph's doctor. I met my husband through my uncle."

"I see," the boy said, slowly nodding. He glanced up at Ralph. "Your name is Ralph?"

Ralph smiled and nodded. "Ralph Hampton," he murmured. He placed a gentle hand on his wife's shoulder. "And my wife's name is Lois."

27

"It is good to know your names—to know *you*," Night Hawk said, then grew quiet for a long, thoughtful moment.

"If you want me to live with you, I will," he then blurted out. "But for awhile, do not call me your child. My love for my true mother is too fresh in my mind, and my sadness over my father abandoning me cuts too deep into my soul for me to feel at peace calling someone else mother or father."

Lois broke into fresh tears. She grabbed Night Hawk into her arms and embraced him. "We understand," she whispered. "Oh, Lord, thank you, child. Thank you."

Night Hawk enjoyed the embrace, yet he could not help feeling sadness for those others in the room who were also without a home, or parents. He truly feared for them, for they were Comanche, through and through. Without any trace of white blood in their veins, they might not be as fortunate.

For once in his life he saw the benefit of being a "breed"!

Chapter Three

Twenty Years Later

The sun was high overhead. Except for a few fluffy white clouds, the sky was crystal blue. The wind was warm. The air was fresh. The land was flat and seemed to go on forever.

Night Hawk was dressed in sweat-stained buckskins with a wide-brimmed hat shading his face. He was now thirty, long-legged, strong, and sinewy. With the large, clear, and luminous eyes of a hawk, and with his long golden hair framing his noble shoulders, he was a striking sight. Night Hawk sat tall in the saddle on his big pinto as he returned home from a successful spring roundup.

He and his cowhands had driven 3,000 head of longhorns to the railhead at Fort Worth, from which the steers would then be shipped to Chicago. It had been a hard drive, but with his skilled cowhands, they had lost very few cattle on the way to the railhead.

Night Hawk smiled to himself as he thought of

other casualties that had occurred. He knew that no contingent of range hands ever reached home with their pockets as full of coins as they had been upon the sale of the cattle. Several men had separated from Night Hawk's crew and had stayed behind to have a whopping good time in the rowdy cow town, spending money on gambling, loose women, and whiskey.

Night Hawk glanced over his shoulder at the stragglers who had stayed with him after only one night out on the town. They had caught up with Night Hawk and the others the next night. They were all half broke, and some sported black eyes and broken limbs from brawls in the saloons.

Others wore hangdog looks from having been duped by pretty women in short, flashy skirts. The whores had lured them to their beds while their friends emptied the cowhands' pockets.

Night Hawk's gaze shifted. With pride and much love, he watched his very best friend and constant companion, who was riding a black mustang beside him.

"Crying Wolf, you have been quiet for the past several miles," Night Hawk said, edging his pinto closer to his friend's steed. He scrutinized the seriousness of Crying Wolf's expression as the old Indian turned his midnight dark eyes toward him and frowned.

Night Hawk tipped his hat back from his brow with a forefinger. "*Hait-sma*," he said, addressing his friend. "What is on your mind?"

Night Hawk was puzzled anew by that same quiet frown that his friend had been giving him ever since Crying Wolf had taken a fall from his horse a few days ago. It seemed to have changed him from the laughing, free spirit that Night Hawk had discovered ten years before.

He had found Crying Wolf on the trail, unconscious and bleeding profusely from a head wound. He had taken Crying Wolf to the bunkhouse at his father's ranch and had medicated the wound.

When Crying Wolf had awakened, he had been disoriented. Except for his name, he had not been able to remember anything of his past. He had no recollection of why he had been separated from his people. He wore no war paint. He was dressed in fringed buckskins. And much food had been in his parfleche bag, which meant that he had prepared himself well for many long days of travel while away from his village.

But he could not even remember who his true people were. Whether they were Comanche, Cheyenne, or Crow, he had left them to go on a long journey to he knew not where!

Night Hawk had gotten permission from his father for Crying Wolf to stay and live at their ranch. A close bond had sealed Crying Wolf and Night Hawk's friendship—they had become inseparable.

Night Hawk had wondered early on whether or not Crying Wolf might be Comanche, like he was. Although Crying Wolf's copper face was lined with wrinkles, he had the same skin and high cheekbones as Night Hawk. He also spoke the Comanche language well.

The younger man's gaze swept slowly over his old friend, and he smiled. Crying Wolf was a shaggy giant of a man. He looked like he had been put together with old planks. And like Night Hawk, Crying Wolf was a man seemingly without fear. To both of them, physical cowardice was an unforgivable sin. Neither had any fear of death, or of fate.

Yes, Night Hawk thought to himself, his old friend seemed to be Comanche. And Night Hawk had thought, the first time he had seen Crying Wolf, that there was something vaguely familiar about him.

He had wondered then if Crying Wolf might have been from his very own tribe, yet the idea seemed so far-fetched that he had never questioned him about it. Many long years had passed since Night Hawk had lived with the Comanche, and he had not seen any of his people since the cavalry attack.

And because his father had so cold-heartedly abandoned him during the attack, he had not made any attempt to find chief Brown Bull.

To Night Hawk, his true father was as dead as his dear mother. And he would never consider trying to enter that world again! If Crying Wolf *was* perhaps from his father's band of Comanche, Night Hawk was glad that he could not remember.

Still Crying Wolf said nothing. He stared at Night Hawk as though he was seeing him for the first time.

"Crying Wolf, have I done something to displease you?" Night Hawk persisted, returning Crying Wolf's frown. "Or is it that this long journey to the railhead has been hard on you? I did advise you not to go, you know."

"*Nei-chat*, I am well. Just because I am so much older than you does not mean that my body fails me," Crying Wolf said in his low, gravelly voice. "My *hait-sma*, friend, I do not mean to trouble you by my silence. It . . . it . . . is only since my recent fall that I have been recalling things of my past."

"You now remember which tribe you are from?" Night Hawk asked anxiously, glancing skyward when a sudden shadow fell over him and his elderly friend. He found himself gazing into the piercing eyes of a huge eagle as it glided lower and lower in the sky. It seemed to be an omen of sorts when the eagle peered directly into Night Hawk's eyes.

Then it swept on away and disappeared into a thick white cloud.

"The eagle tries to tell us something today," Crying Wolf said, also having seen the flight of the mighty, mystical bird. He shifted his gaze back to Night Hawk. "Just like my memory tries to tell me things that I have long forgotten. I do not wish to talk about them yet to you, Night Hawk. In time I will. *Huh,* yes, in time I will tell you everything. But first I must let myself become accustomed to the knowing myself. Then I shall tell you everything. But only . . . when . . . the time is right."

"You are behaving as though I am a part of your recollections," Night Hawk said, his pulse suddenly racing at the thought. Although he did not wish ever to see his father again, he could not quell the part of him that was Comanche. That part truly wished to be among his people again, if only to test himself as to his true feelings toward them.

Yet so many Comanche in this area were guilty of atrocities toward the white settlers. He had often prayed to himself that those Comanche were not from his band. He could not recall, as a child, whether or not his father ordered his warriors to ambush and kill whites. All of those orders were given in the privacy of council.

When Night Hawk had seen scalps swaying on poles outside his father's lodge, he wanted to think that they were from enemies of his father who deserved to be slain and scalped. Yet he could not deny having wondered, as a child, what it might be like to

33

own his own scalp pole, his own scalps.

"All right, if you think the time to share your recollections should come later, I will speak no more of them," Night Hawk said, glad that in the distance he could see the great expanse of his father's fenced-off land. Soon he would see the grand, two-storied adobe hacienda that sat in the middle of his family's magnificent spread.

His adopted father's ranch now sprawled across a valley with a huge pasture, a flowing stream, and a corral.

The nails in the new bunkhouses, cook sheds, and blacksmith shops had mostly been pounded there by Night Hawk's hammer. He had done this proudly for his father, whose failing health kept him inside his home, only able to dream of those days when he was virile and able to look after his own ranch.

Night Hawk was proud to be the son of Ralph and Lois Hampton. It was always good to return home to the loving arms of his adopted mother and to the secure relationship he had found with his adopted father.

He gazed over at Crying Wolf. "I wonder how father is faring?" he blurted out, concerned for Ralph, whose health was failing much too quickly of late. Due to his inability to exercise and the many years he'd been confined to a wheelchair, his weight had become immense, which had put a strain on his heart.

He had become so obese now that he was confined to his bed. The only way that he could enjoy his ranch was by looking out his bedroom window.

"I fear your father's lungs are his worst enemy," Crying Wolf said. "As he lies in his bed, they are not functioning as they should. I fear they are slowly filling with fluid. I can hear it when he breathes. I fear that one day soon his lungs will sound the death rattle of a man soon to die."

"When he goes, a part of my heart will go with him," Night Hawk said solemnly. "We could not have been closer in spirit had he been my true father."

"Prepare yourself to lose him," Crying Wolf said, flinching when the eagle dipped low from the sky again, covering them momentarily with its huge shadow.

Night Hawk lifted his eyes to the bird. "Perhaps the eagle warns me of my father's death," he said, swallowing hard. "Perhaps while we were at the rail-head making my father richer, he was dying."

He doubled a hand into a fist at his side. "What good has the wealth been to my father?" he said tightly. "He has not been on a horse since the stampede that caused his paralysis. His body cannot function as a husband. He cannot mingle with his men and laugh and joke with them! All he has known is the wheelchair and his bed."

"He has known the sunset, the beauty of the snows, the wonders of spring, and the love of a woman," Crying Wolf said, his gaze following the flight of the eagle as it again disappeared behind the clouds overhead. "From his window he has seen the wonder of the birds, perhaps even this very eagle that journeys with us today."

Crying Wolf smiled at Night Hawk. "Even though a man is disabled," he said, "there is still much that can fill his heart and soul with joy and peace. I have seen it in your father's eyes. He has been a content man. Only recently have I seen something else. I have wondered about it. It is a look of someone who is hiding a truth."

"*Huh,* yes, I have seen it also in how he stares at me while saying nothing," Night Hawk said. He frowned at Crying Wolf. "It is similar to your look, Crying Wolf, when I have found you staring at me." He paused and arched his brows. "Do you two have a joint secret that you are keeping from me?"

"If so, would I wonder what your father's quiet demeanor was all about?" Crying Wolf said, sighing heavily. "Huh, yes, your father seems to be a man carrying secrets." He laughed. "But believe me, my young friend, his secrets have nothing to do with this old Indian."

"I guess he'll open up to me in time if it concerns me," Night Hawk said.

Anxious to be home, he sank the heels of his boots into the flanks of his magnificent steed and sent him in a hard gallop through the hip-high, waving grass.

Crying Wolf caught up with him, leaving the cowhands to lag behind. As they had countless times before, Night Hawk and Crying Wolf rode on through the gate that led into the pasture of the "Wide Chaparral."

After getting their horses settled in the stable, brushed, watered, and fed, the two men went their separate ways. Crying Wolf went to the bunkhouse, while Night Hawk went to the adobe hacienda, where flowers were growing profusely in gardens in the front and on both sides, and where a long porch stretched out along the front of the house.

"Night Wolf! Son!" Lois cried excitedly as she ran from the house. She flung herself into his arms and hugged him just as he stepped up on the porch.

"You didn't give me time to tell you that I stink like a skunk," Night Hawk said, laughing as he felt her thick arms cling to him. He returned her hug. "Hi, Mom. I have missed you."

He pressed his cheek against her head, where she wore her long, graying hair loose and free across her shoulders. He inhaled the sweet rose fragrance of her hair. He knew that she used some special rose soap that she purchased in Abilene, not only for her hair, but also her skin. The soap make her always smell sweet and also kept her skin soft.

Neglect from her husband had caused Lois to spend most of her time eating. She was now almost double in size what she had been when Night Hawk had seen her that first time. But to him she was still the petite, sweet woman who had taken him into her heart and home that day she had come with her husband to get him from the fort to raise as their son.

"I've been so worried about you," Lois said, easing from his embrace. She ran her hands nervously down the front of her gathered cotton dress, which sported a high neck and long sleeves to hide as much of her bulky weight as possible.

She gazed up at Night Hawk and gently touched his dust-covered face. "It seems you've been gone longer than usual this time, son," she murmured. She ran her fingers over his cheek, across his chin, and then down his broad chest, as though testing to see if he was truly all right. "Did you have trouble? There have been reports of Comanche renegades ambushing people along the trail."

"I saw no Comanche," Night Hawk said, stiffening at the thought of someone of his own people murdering and killing innocent travelers. "And no, I had no trouble. I just had to slow down a mite as I waited for some of our cowhands to catch up with me. They needed to blow off steam in Fort Worth. I allowed it."

"I see," Lois said. She stepped away from him, blushing at the thought of what he was referring to.

Night Hawk looked past Lois, at the door. "How's father?" he asked guardedly. His thoughts returned to the eagle that had appeared to him on the trail not once but twice.

Lois wrung her hands as she followed his gaze toward the door. "He has worsened," she said, her voice breaking. "Doc Rose was here. He told your father to get . . . his . . . affairs in order. His lungs. They are scarcely working now, son."

"How long does he have?" Night Hawk asked, his gaze meeting his mother's.

"Perhaps a few days, perhaps a week, perhaps even months," Lois said softly. "This isn't something anyone can truly know. It's up to God, son. Only He knows."

Night Hawk stepped away from her and glanced down at himself. He felt tired and dirty from the long ride.

As though she could read his mind, Lois placed a gentle hand on his arm. "Son, your father is sleeping," she murmured. "Let me have hot water brought to your room. Bathe. Get into a change of clothes. By then your father might be awake. That will be time enough to go to him. Talk to him. He seems bothered by something these past weeks, and I don't believe it's concern for himself. It's something more."

"What do you think it is?" Night Hawk said, again recalling that strange stare of his father's.

"Do you recall several weeks ago when someone from Louisiana came to meet with your father? And then how your father sent someone to Louisiana?" Lois asked, her voice weary.

"Yes, he sent Charles Swainford, his attorney," Night Hawk replied, kneading his chin thoughtfully. "I thought it had something to do with business. Do you think it's something else?"

"It has to be," Lois said, sighing. "Your father has his moods. I know well enough about them. He ofttimes treats me as though I am only one of his hired hands. Sometimes his silence kills my very soul! But this time his silence seems different. It's in the way he looks at me, as though he truly wants to talk to me about something, but just won't let himself."

"*Huh,* yes, I have sensed the same thing about him since Charles came back from Louisiana and had that closed-door council with father," Night Hawk said, his interest piqued. What could be troubling his father? Night Hawk knew of no family business acquaintances in Louisiana, so it had to be some personal worry that was eating away at his father's insides.

"Find out what it is, son," Lois said, tightening her grip on his arm. "I feel threatened by his attitude, as though I am on the brink of losing everything."

Night Hawk gazed into his mother's eyes and saw a quiet desperation. In the way her grip tightened on his arm, he felt the same desperation.

"Mom, things are going to be all right," he said, suddenly pulling her into his arms. He held her close. "Do not worry. I will never allow anything bad to happen to you."

He closed his eyes and recalled someone else's desperation and fears, someone else's arms and sweet voice. He felt as though he was that young boy of ten again, being embraced by his true mother, just before . . . just before she had been murdered!

Lois's low sobs brought him back to the present.

He held her an arm's length away from him. Their eyes locked. "Mom, I promise you that no one will ever harm you," he blurted out. His jaw tight, he dropped his hands to his sides.

"Hurry, son," she said, wiping tears from her eyes. "Bathe. Eat. Then go and see what is on your father's mind." She grabbed his arm again. "Promise to tell me?"

"Everything," he said.

Chapter Four

The drapes were drawn at the windows; the room was void of sunlight. A faint candle glowed on the table beside the massive oak bed. The odor of medicine permeated the entire room.

Familiar with all of these things, Night Hawk stood over his adopted father's bed and gazed down at him as he struggled to breathe in his sleep. Seeing him so helpless made Night Hawk's heart ache. It was evident that his father had worsened while Night Hawk had been on the cattle drive to Fort Worth.

And although Night Hawk loved this man as though he were his true father, he knew now that Ralph Hampton would only find peace and rest in the afterlife . . . a life that would be without pain and suffering.

Night Hawk could almost feel his father's pain as his coughing became jagged and low like a series of hisses. He leaned low over the bed when his father's eyes slowly opened. "Father, I have returned from the cattle drive," he said softly.

"Son, did you make a good sale?" Ralph asked between his shallow, wheezing breaths. "Did we profit well this time? Did the prices go up? Or . . . down . . .? How much did you get per head?"

"It was nearly the same as the last roundup," Night Hawk said, wishing that he could have brought his father better news. But the War Between the States had changed everything in the country—especially the price of beef. "I received five dollars per head."

"I did not expect more," Ralph said, closing his eyes to rest for a moment. Then he slowly turned his gaze up to Night Hawk. "In truth, son, those who gave you five dollars a head will get forty or fifty dollars in Chicago. It's downright thievery."

"I would not worry myself about it," Night Hawk said, smiling down at his father. "Father, your safe is bulging with your profits. Let us hope that no outlaw gets wind of how much you are truly worth."

Night Hawk winced when he saw a sudden anger enter his father's eyes. "What did I say?" he asked, arching an eyebrow. "It seems that I have angered you. Why?"

"Nothing, son," Ralph said, his wheezing worsening. "You said nothing. But, son, we do have something to talk about besides business."

"What is it?" Night Hawk asked. He dragged a chair up beside the bed and sat down on it.

"Lean down a mite closer, son," Ralph said, reaching a trembling hand toward him.

Night Hawk leaned his face close enough for Ralph to touch it. He felt the love flowing from his father to him as Ralph slowly traced his facial features.

"I'll never forget that day I saw you the first time," Ralph said thickly. "My little forlorn waif. A 'breed.' I felt so much for you. You had suffered so much.

You had *lost* so much. Have you been happy here at my ranch? Have I given you enough to help lift the painful past from your heart?"

"You know that you have," Night Hawk said, straightening in the chair as Ralph took his hand away and slid it beneath his blanket. "You have given me more than I ever could have imagined having in a lifetime. Thank you, Father." He swallowed hard. "I just wish there was something more that I could do for you. I owe you so much. So . . . very . . . very much."

"Son, there is something I do wish to ask of you," Ralph said, his voice guarded.

Night Hawk saw something appear suddenly in his father's eyes, a strange sort of guardedness that puzzled him. It looked as though his father might be afraid of what he was about to say.

As far as Night Hawk knew, his father had always been honest and open with him.

What, then, could be so hard to say *now?* he wondered. It was surely something that troubled his father if he was so hesitant to mention it.

"Father, whatever is bothering you, you know that I am always here to help you," Night Hawk said. "Whatever you want done, I will personally see that it is done."

"What I have to ask of you will take several days, perhaps weeks," Ralph said. He lowered his eyes. "I . . . just . . . hope that I last long enough to . . . see . . . her."

"See her?" Night Hawk asked, arching an eyebrow. "Who, Father? Who are you talking about?"

Ralph inhaled deeply, then let out a quavering sigh. He gazed intently into Night Hawk's questioning eyes. "Son, I hope you understand what I'm going to tell you," he said, his voice breaking. "You see, for so long now, I've been living a lie. I've forced you and Lois to be a part of that lie. I . . . I just never wanted to be bothered with the past. I never wanted to talk about my first wife or . . . or . . ."

"First wife?" Night Hawk interrupted him. His eyes widened. "You have been married twice?"

"Long ago, Night Hawk, I was married to the most beautiful woman in the world," Ralph said, closing his eyes as Penelope's ravishingly beautiful face formed in his mind's eye.

Then he gazed up at Night Hawk again. "Son, I loved her with all of my heart," he said, his expression pained. "And we wanted children so badly. Shortly after we discovered she was with child, a . . . a damnable outlaw came and tore my world apart. He took my wife! In taking her, he also took my unborn child!"

Tears streamed from Ralph's eyes. He glanced down at where his legs lay lifeless beneath the blanket. "One of his outlaw buddies stole my ability to walk!" he cried. "The dirty coward shot me in the back. It was his bullet, not a damn stampede, that paralyzed me for life!"

His father's confession made Night Hawk's head spin. He shook his head in an attempt to clear his thoughts, to sort out the truth from the lie that he had been told!

"You had a wife, and she was abducted? And you weren't paralyzed during a stampede?" Night Hawk said, nervously kneading his brow. "Your wife was carrying a child when she was abducted?"

"I know this is a lot to take in all at once," Ralph said, eyeing a pitcher of water on the table. "Son, my mouth is parched. Please get me a drink of water."

Glad to have something to do while trying to sort through all of these new revelations, Night Hawk poured a glass of water. He placed one hand beneath his father's head and lifted his lips to the glass. His father's eyes stared up at him, silently pleading.

When his father began to choke, Night Hawk slipped the glass away and eased his father's head back down on the pillow.

Stiffly he set the half-emptied glass on the table beside the bed, then peered into his father's eyes again. "Why are you telling me this now?" he asked. "Why would you want to tell me something that you kept from me for so long?" Night Hawk paled suddenly. "You not only kept this from me, but also Mother, didn't you?" he gasped out.

"Indeed I did," Ralph said, sighing. "I saw no need to let her know about my first wife, nor how I was injured. It was best left unsaid."

"But her uncle is your doctor," Night Hawk said. "Surely he told her."

"Her uncle wasn't my doctor at the time of the accident," Ralph said, pausing to take another deep, wheezing breath. "And I paid the previous doctor a large sum of money to buy my medical records from him before Doc Rose came on the case. Doc Rose was told that they had been destroyed in a fire."

"All right, now that I know so much of your past," Night Hawk persisted, "what is it you want me to do? Surely it has to do with your secret past."

"Very much so," Ralph said, staring at the ceiling. "Ah, yes, very much so." He shifted his gaze back to Night Hawk. "Son, for many weeks after the disappearance of my wife, the cavalry searched for her. They found no signs of her or the outlaw who took her from me. When I became strong enough to travel, I had one of my men take me in my buggy to Louisiana to see if my wife's family had heard anything about her whereabouts." He swallowed hard. Tears filled his eyes. "I . . . was . . . told that she and the child were dead."

He placed a hand over his eyes. "God, my whole world stopped then, to know that my beautiful Penelope was dead, and also our . . . our child," he gulped out, the torture evident in his voice.

"The outlaw killed your wife?" Night Hawk asked, feeling his father's pain deep inside his own heart. "He killed your child?"

"I didn't know," Ralph said, his voice breaking. "No one knew. I . . . didn't . . . even get to see her grave. All I knew was that she was dead."

Ralph's eyes narrowed and his jaw tightened. "But it was all a lie," he said, almost choking on the words. "Penelope wasn't dead. My child wasn't dead. They lived all these years with the outlaw! The outlaw raised my daughter as *his*. My wife lived with him, not because she was forced to, but because she wanted to! She lived with the son of a bitch as though she was his wife!"

Night Hawk gasped. He was taken aback by this newest revelation! "How do you know this?" he said, his voice faint with surprise.

"Not long ago, Penelope's brother came to the ranch and met with me," Ralph said thickly. "Beauford is his name." He laughed sarcastically. "Sounds like a damn Louisiana aristocrat name, doesn't it?"

Ralph grew somber again. "Well, thank God, Beauford has a conscience after all," he said. "He came and told me the truth about everything. When he heard about a shooting in Beaumont and that it was an outlaw and his wife who had died, he thought it might be his sister. He went to the morgue and sure enough, it was Penelope. Penelope and her outlaw lover died together during a gunfight on the outskirts of Beaumont."

"So Beauford knew all along that his sister was alive?" Night Hawk said, slowly piecing things together.

"Yes, her whole damn family knew," Ralph replied somberly. "Seems she went and revealed herself to them shortly after she began living with the outlaw. She wanted them to know that she was alive, and that the child she was carrying would be taken care of. She begged them not to tell me where she was. She knew I would go to the ends of the earth to find my child. And she had told the outlaw that the baby was his."

"The baby lived?" Night Hawk asked softly.

"Yes," Ralph said. "My *daughter*. I now know that I have a daughter. After Penelope's death, Beauford got to worrying about his niece. He knew that my . . . daughter . . . was left alone to fend for herself in the 'Big Thicket.' He thought that I might have the means to influence her to come out of the Thicket and live like a true human being for a change. He was too afraid to go into the Thicket himself. And he is too embarrassed over being kin to someone who was raised with outlaws to send anyone in there to look for her. So he came to me, knowing I'd die trying, if it meant having my daughter with me at long last."

"And that is where I come in, isn't it, Father?" Night Hawk asked. "You want me to go for her? You want me to bring her home to you?"

"Will you do that for me?" Ralph implored, grabbing Night Hawk by the arm, his desperation evident in the tight, trembling grip of his fingers. "Please . . . go for her? I know you are skilled at tracking. Go into the Thicket, son. Find her. Even if you have to hog-tie her, bring her to me. I expect she's something wild and untamed after living in hiding for so long. Rope her if you must and bring her home to me. Like the wild mustangs I used to tame during my days of riding and roping steers, I'll tame my daughter into something meek and gentle."

"Yes, I'll go and see if I can find her," Night Hawk said, easing his father's fingers from his arm. "I'll do what I can to persuade her to come here and face her true father."

He looked over his shoulder at the door. "When are you going to tell Mother?" he asked softly.

"While you're away, I'll tell her," Ralph said, sighing. "She might not take the truth as well as you have. She's always thought she was my first and only wife."

"Yes, I can see why she might not like the knowing." Yet, Father, I would not wait too long to tell her."

Remembering the promise he had made his mother, about telling her what he found out from his father, Night Hawk clenched his jaw. "Would you rather I told Mother for you?" he asked guardedly.

"No, son. It's best I tell her in my own way. You concentrate only on one thing now—finding my daughter. She's vulnerable all alone in that dreadful Thicket. Go and find her. Take her away from the danger."

He swallowed hard. "Before I die, I want to know my child," Ralph said. "I want to hold my daughter in my arms. It's wrong that she's been kept from me. Why, she doesn't even know that I exist. So that's something else you've got to do for me, son. You've got to convince her who her true father is. It's a shame that she had to believe all of these years that her father was an outlaw. The shame she must feel. The utter shame of it all!"

"Father, if she doesn't believe me, and she refuses to come with me, I can't see myself forcing her," Night Hawk said, his gaze wavering.

"Son, you have a way with people." Ralph laughed softly. "I've seen you in action. You can charm the stripes off a snake! And most of all, I've heard about how you have a way with women that most men don't."

Night Hawk looked incredulously down at his father. "How did you know about me . . . and women?" he asked, his cheeks heating up.

"The men talk about it," Ralph said, chuckling. "They tell me how the women in Abilene swoon at the very sight of you, and that all you have to do is crook a finger at them and they will follow you wherever you lead them." He laughed between his wheezes. "And most times that's to a bed upstairs over the Big Red Saloon."

"I've got to have a talk with those gossipmonger cowboys." Night Hawk was now also chuckling, glad at least to see that this kind of talk brought some life back into his father's pale cheeks.

"So you see, Night Hawk, it's up to you and your charm to get my daughter to come home with you."

"I'll leave now for the Thicket," Night Hawk said, rising from the chair. He turned to leave, then stopped and wheeled around to gaze at his father. "I'd like to take Crying Wolf with me. He's also good at tracking."

"Yes, take him," Ralph said, nodding. "It's best you

have someone with you in case you are outnumbered by outlaws."

"What is her name, Father?" Night Hawk asked softly. "What is your daughter's name?"

"Jae," Ralph said, then chuckled. "That's a helluva name for a girl isn't it?"

"*Huh*, yes, a strange name . . . more like a man's than a lady's." Night Hawk tried to envision a woman who lived wild and free in the Thicket.

"We'll make her into a lady, Night Hawk." Ralph gazed at the door, then turned pleading eyes up to his son. "Please go, son. Time is wasting."

Night Hawk nodded and then left the room.

When he came face to face with Lois just outside the door, he stopped, then eased the door closed behind him.

"Well?" Lois asked, her eyes wide. "What did you find out?"

"Father has much to tell you," he said tightly. "I cannot. He asked me not to. Be patient a while longer. He will tell you soon."

"I don't understand," Lois said, taking a shaky step away from him. "Why all of this secrecy? Why should I be forced to wait for answers?"

"I am sorry, but it is not my place to tell you. And, Mom, I will be leaving for a few days. Father will tell you where I am going . . . and why."

"Night Hawk, I insist that *you* tell me," Lois said, lifting her chin angrily.

"Father will tell you soon." Running Hawk reached a gentle hand to her cheek. "Just please be understanding when he tells you. He needs us both to be understanding."

Lois sucked in a wild, nervous breath, her eyes filled with a sudden fear.

Night Hawk swallowed hard, then grabbed her into his arms. He hugged her to him. "I love you, Mother," he said, his voice drawn.

He released Lois and walked away from her. Night Hawk felt her hurt, and hurt for her, yet he had other things on his mind. As he went outside and hurried toward the bunkhouse to tell Crying Wolf about the journey ahead, he could not help thinking of this daughter named Jae. He was curious to see how a woman who lived in the wilds of the Big Thicket would behave.

Crying Wolf had told Running Hawk a lot about the Thicket. Who didn't know of the legends of that evil place? It was also called the "Big Woods." A wedge of Texas jungle, it was said to be a sanctuary for specters and visions and things that glowed in the night. The ghosts of bears and wolves, and panthers that screamed like women, traveled there. It was a place inhabited by men long dead who still haunted the dark.

"Jae," he whispered to himself. "I wonder if she is a wild thing like the panthers that roam the dark recesses of the Thicket? I wonder if she *is* tameable."

Chapter Five

At dusk on the second day of travel, Night Hawk and Crying Wolf arrived at the outskirts of the Big Thicket.

Without hesitation, Night Hawk rode on into the dark, dank region, Crying Wolf quiet and tense beside him. They made their way through the trees where lacy Spanish moss grew beardlike from the branches, and where resurrection ferns grew like pale green fur along the limbs of the huge cypress trees.

Night Hawk soon realized that what had been said about East Texas's Big Thicket was true. It certainly didn't resemble the familiar Texas he knew of the big sky and far-off horizons. It was a region of enormous trees and scattered swamps and blackwater sloughs, laced with dense tangles of yaupon and interspersed with open savannas.

A shiver crawled up and down Night Hawk's spine as he and Crying Wolf rode down a small, narrow path that had been made by someone's frequent travels. Recalling how Crying Wolf had described the

Thicket, Night Hawk looked slowly around him, thinking that it *did* seem dark and mysterious, as though ghostly visions might suddenly appear floating through the air. It most definitely was a place of wild creatures!

The farther he traveled into the Thicket, the more Night Hawk was astonished at the idea of a young lady living there, away from the real world, where there was sunlight, laughter, and blue sky!

Surely she *was* like the wild animals she lived among. How could she be anything but untamed, living in hiding, as if she, herself, were wanted by the law.

Night Hawk traveled relentlessly onward, glad at least for the moment to be able to enjoy the jasmine-scented air of the glade they were now passing through, where native orchids, like lady's tresses, flourished in clustered seclusion.

Night began to fall all around them, and Night Hawk peered through the gray shadows. He felt a foreboding sense of mystery and madness as he rode beneath huge, scaly-barked pines, hundred-foot-tall magnolias, and monstrous, gray-barked beeches. A lizard had fallen into a voracious pitcher plant; the plant's enzymes had devoured it down to the skeleton.

"We should have waited until morning to enter the Big Woods," Crying Wolf suddenly blurted out. He gave Night Hawk a wary glance. "I feel danger all around us. And I have a sensation that I have felt before while in the Thicket. It is a mysterious, supernatural feeling."

He looked over his shoulder at the path they had just traveled, then gave Night Hawk a steady stare. "*Kee-mah*, come. Let us backtrack and camp outside the Big Woods," he said, his voice drawn. "Let us go. Let us enter again tomorrow when we have more time to search for the woman while it is daylight. Tonight, who is to say what might jump out at us? Demons live in the Big Woods . . . dark, hairy demons who howl like wolves!"

"*Hait-sma*, I have never seen you like this," Night Hawk said, drawing a tight rein and stopping. He reached a gentle hand to Crying Wolf's arm. "And if you remember so much about coming here before, does that mean that your memory has been restored?"

"Enough to remember that this is a dangerous place with a *che-kas-koi*, a bad heart." Crying Wolf looked guardedly from side to side, then glanced over his shoulder again. "Let us go and camp where we are not camping with ghosts!"

"Crying Wolf, you know how eager I am to find my adopted father's daughter," Night Hawk said, dropping his hand to his side. "And not altogether for *him*. I am intrigued by such a woman. She lives as no other person I have ever known. Are you not as eager as I to meet her?"

"She will be someone you will not wish to know for long," Crying Wolf predicted. "Anyone who has lived among the mysteries of this dark place cannot be normal in any respect. She is probably as wild as the animals that lurk in the shadows even now as we speak! Who is to say she is not here, watching us? We are interlopers on her land. She might kill us before you have a chance to say that you have brought news of her true father."

"I am not afraid of her, but of her reaction to the knowledge that she has lived a lie." Night Hawk gazed around again, hearing all sorts of night sounds as the night finally claimed the forest in total darkness.

He was glad that there were enough breaks in the trees overhead to see the sky. It was full of stars and the moon was full, sprinkling its silver light over the treetops and on the floor of the forest.

Farther up the trail, on both sides, the trees pressed in, dark against the sky. In the swamps beyond, frogs chirped and croaked.

Night Hawk winced when he heard the scream of a panther. It sounded like a woman crying in despair. Then he heard the far-off, long, and melancholy howling of a wolf. He turned his gaze back to Crying Wolf. "I must go on," he said, ignoring the frown that his declaration caused. "At least for awhile longer. Then we can make camp."

"I will not make camp in this place of ghosts and mystery," Crying Wolf said flatly. "We will soon be deep in the devil's pocket. If I must, I will turn back now, alone."

Night Hawk was stunned, never having seen this side of his friend before. Crying Wolf had always been so strong, had always shown such courage in the face of danger. It seemed odd now that he would let a few dancing shadows and sounds disturb him so deeply.

It did not seem right, but it was something that Night Hawk had to accept, for nothing Crying Wolf said or did would cause him to delay his search. He had come too far now to let his friend's foolishness dissuade him.

"I shall go on alone," Night Hawk declared, not surprised at all to see dismay enter his friend's dark eyes. "Make camp where I can find you when I leave the Thicket."

"You do not heed my warnings?" Crying Wolf asked tightly. "Never before have you ignored this old Indian. Why do you now?"

"Because I promised my father I would find his daughter," Night Hawk said softly. "I hope to find her *tonight*."

"I fear you will find more tonight than you bargain for." Crying Wolf wheeled his horse around, leaving Night Hawk to stare after him.

After Crying Wolf had disappeared from view, Night Hawk sighed deeply. Then he continued his journey through the deep black of the night, soon entering the area where the moon was no longer his guide.

His heartbeats skipped when he suddenly heard strange noises on all sides of him. For a moment he thought he saw movement in the brush at his right side, then he thought he saw it at his left.

His spine stiffened when he thought he heard someone moving through the brush. He could hear twigs breaking. He could hear the crunch of leaves.

And then the night grew quiet again. Night Hawk sighed with relief and rode onward, thinking that whoever had been there had retreated.

He reached for his rifle, which was nestled in its gunboot at the right side of his pinto. As his eyes moved in all directions, searching for any sort of disturbance, he rested his hand on the butt of his firearm. He was experienced enough with his rifle that he could jerk it from its gunboot in a matter of seconds. He could fire it in the blink of an eye!

But he knew that he had to be careful who or what he might recklessly shoot. Jae could be there even now, following his each and every movement. She was a creature of the Thicket. Surely she roamed as freely and quietly as the wolf and the panther. While Night Hawk was in her domain, she was the predator—*he* was the *prey*.

Not allowing himself to be unnerved by such thoughts, Night Hawk rode on at a soft lope through the trees.

Suddenly, gasping, he drew a tight rein. He was scarcely breathing as he squinted his eyes and gazed ahead of him. What had he seen among the trees? Had it been a light? Or had his eyes played tricks on him? If Crying Wolf were with him, he would surely call this the Thicket's fabled "Ghost Light."

Night Hawk shrugged and sighed heavily. Whatever he had seen was gone now. He slapped his reins and rode onward, then stopped again. His spine stiffened when he saw the same thing up ahead in a break in the trees.

It *was* a light . . . a dim, tiny point.

But suddenly it grew brighter. It moved, grew brighter still, then abruptly dimmed and went out.

Night Hawk's pulse raced. He slid his rifle from its gunboot and placed his finger on the trigger. When nothing else appeared to him, he sent his horse onward, his rifle resting on his knee.

He could not help thinking back to Crying Wolf's warnings and his tales of ghosts and demons. Night Hawk had scoffed at them then, thinking they were a figment of the old Indian's imagination. But now he knew that what he had seen was real. The only question was where it had originated.

There was just one way to find out, he thought to himself, and that was to travel onward toward the mysterious, dancing light. Perhaps that was where he would find Jae!

He hated the noise his horse's hooves made in the

forest, knowing that surely it echoed all around him, warning whoever was there exactly where Night Hawk was traveling.

He was glad when he reached a thick layer of dead leaves beneath a scattering of huge cypress trees. They would cushion the sound of his horse's hooves. He could ride soundlessly now without worrying about anyone hearing his approach.

Yet as he continued on through the Thicket, he could not help being apprehensive of all things around him. He sat quietly in his saddle, his body tight and strained, his heartbeats echoing through him like loud claps of thunder.

Eyes wide, he drew a tight rein when he again saw the light. First it was faint, and then it appeared as a dull glow, the color of pumpkin.

Then it was gone again.

Suddenly, a spattering of gunfire filled the dark night. Night Hawk recoiled when he heard several other shots, followed again by a strange, foreboding silence.

He now felt truly threatened, and he edged his horse into the darker shadows of night.

After waiting for only a moment, he once again saw the light up ahead, only this time it was no longer moving. It was a steady glow, like a beacon to Night Hawk as he sank his heels into the flanks of his horse and rode toward it.

Night Hawk winced when he heard a great swishing sound overhead, made from what sounded like a thousand wings flapping in excitement. He peered through the dark when he heard the frantic sound of frightened birds chirping overhead as they settled into the trees above him.

Smiling, Night Hawk relaxed his shoulders. "Passenger pigeons," he whispered. He had heard about passenger pigeons that were so numerous during migration that at night, people could hear the tree branches cracking under the weight of the flock.

Finally the birds became quiet.

Everything was quiet.

But Night Hawk could still see the glow of light up ahead. He rode toward it. And as he drew closer to it, he realized that it was a lantern. It had been wavering before because someone had been carrying it. Whomever had been carrying it had now placed it on the ground.

His pulse raced at the possibility that perhaps he was about to find Jae. He drew a tight rein and quickly dismounted, securing his reins to a tree limb. Then with his hand clutching the rifle, he made his way toward the light.

When he got close enough to make out the lantern, he stopped and stared at the woman who was standing in its light. She was picking up dead pigeons and placing them in a leather bag. He now knew why the gun had been fired.

But the dead birds strewn along the ground didn't keep his attention for long. He turned his gaze to the woman. In the dim light of the lantern, Night Hawk could just make out her features and the way she was dressed.

"Jae?" he whispered as he studied her.

He smiled, confident that he had found his adopted father's daughter! How many other women would be wandering in the Big Thicket alone? How many other women, except someone raised with outlaws, would be brave enough to go out at night on a hunt for tomorrow's dinner?

He was taken by the woman's uniqueness, her

earthy loveliness. She wore the clothes of a man, but her breeches were cut off short, leaving her shapely legs exposed from her knees downward. She wore leather boots and a blue denim shirt that was buttoned only halfway up the front, revealing the fullness of her breasts and their deep cleavage.

His gaze shifted upward. He arched his eyebrows as he stared at her hair. It was cut off so short that it did not even reach her shoulders!

But even that did not keep his attention for long. It was her loveliness that made him gaze at length at her face. Despite her strange way of wearing her coal-black hair, which was shorter than most men's, especially Night Hawk's own waist-length golden hair, he still found her beautiful. And he saw nothing wild about her. Her oval face revealed soft features and large, alluring dark eyes. Her lips were perfectly shaped. Her nose was slightly upturned and pretty.

Night Hawk could not help being drawn by her mysterious loveliness. It was as though fate had led him to her. He had known and bedded many women. But never had he found that perfect woman with whom he wished to share his every thought and desire.

Strange how looking at this woman, who he knew must be as wild as the forest panther, stirred feelings unknown by him before. He now knew without a doubt that he would not leave the Thicket without her!

Not realizing that she was being observed, Jae smiled as she counted the pigeons that she had managed to kill tonight. With the spray of pellets from her shotgun, she had killed several at once. Tonight and tomorrow, she and her pets would feast on the birds, glad that this time every year, during the birds' migration, she could depend on the delicacy of baked pigeon on her dinner table.

With only one more bird to place in her bag, she bent to grab it, but then stopped and sucked in a wild breath of fear when she heard the sound of a horse from somewhere close by.

Night Hawk paled when his pinto whinnied behind him. He watched the woman drop the bag to the ground. Before Night Hawk could even take another breath, she had her rifle aimed in his direction, her eyes squinted warily.

"You there! Step out into the open," Jae shouted, her heart thumping wildly. "Do it now, or by damn, I'll fire! And don't let me see no gun anywhere near your hands, do you hear? I've got an itchy trigger finger. I won't hesitate to kill you!"

Feeling foolish for having been caught spying on her, Night Hawk saw no choice but to do as he was told, and *quickly*. If she was feeling threatened, she wouldn't wait long for him to show himself to her.

He dropped his rifle and with large, steady steps, he stepped out into the open. Their eyes met and locked; both scarcely breathed. Neither moved.

"Who the hell are you?" Jae finally blurted out. The light of the lantern revealed a tall, slim, and handsome man to her . . . a half-breed.

In all her days of avoiding men, she had never met anyone like him. She could not help staring at him.

Everything about him was beautiful: his flaxen hair, his copper face, his dark eyes, his muscles!

She hoped that he had a good explanation for his presence. She would truly hate to shoot him!

Chapter Six

"Cat got your tongue?" Jae said when Night Hawk didn't respond quickly enough to her question. "I asked you who you are. What are you doing here in the Thicket?" She narrowed her eyes angrily at him. "Are you a lawman?"

"And what if I am?" Night Hawk asked, wondering if she *might* be wanted by the law. Had she ridden with the outlaw who she thought was her father, committing crimes alongside him, as if it was a natural thing to do?

"If you are, I'd say you'd best make a fast retreat," Jae said, her pulse suddenly racing at the possibility that he had come looking for her. Her father and mother had not been dead for long, gunned down by a rival outlaw.

Although she was innocent of the crimes committed by her father, this lawman might think the money and valuables he had stolen were still in her possession.

Hating the way her father had lived, Jae had already taken the valuables and money to a bank in

Beaumont, to see if everything could be returned to the rightful owners.

If this was a lawman coming for the valuables, that had to mean that the bank president with whom she had transacted the business had been untrustworthy. He might have kept it all for himself. If so, he was now one of the wealthiest bankers in Texas!

"Is your name Jae?" Night Hawk blurted out, unable to hold back his curiosity any longer.

Jae paled when she realized that he knew her name. That had to mean that she had assumed correctly—he *was* a lawman. And he had come to tear apart what was left of her world!

She took an unsteady step away from him, and her finger trembled as she placed it on the trigger. "Leave now, or by damn, I'll shoot you," she hissed. "And don't come back, do you hear? I've got nothing you want. I . . . I took everything into Beaumont. The gold . . . the stacks of bills . . . the bags of coins . . . the jewels! Everything my father stole is now in the hands of Delbert Dowling in Beaumont. He's the president of the State National Bank. I trusted him to get in touch with the law. The law was to help find those robbery victims who might still be alive. I tried to make things right. Seems I was duped. I can't be held accountable for *that*. Now *git!* I'm tired of fussing with you!"

"You *are* Jae," Night Hawk said, standing his ground. He realized from the way she spoke of her father that he *had* been an outlaw! And the fact that she had taken his stolen property to a banker, trying to make restitution for her dead father's wrongs proved who she was and that she had had no part in the outlaw life herself. It proved that she was an honest, law-abiding citizen, or was making an attempt at it!

"Yes, my name is Jae, and you could only know that if you had come to find me," she said, looking at him with resentment.

With a tilt-nosed exhalation of disdain, she glared at him. "Well, 'breed,' you found me. Now just turn around and find your way back out of the Thicket, and don't come back again or I won't bother warning you, I'll shoot you at first sight," she said icily. She motioned with her rifle toward him. "I won't say it again."

When Night Hawk stood his ground, Jae's knees weakened. Was he actually going to force her hand? What was she to do? She had never shot a man before. She now wondered if she *could*, even if forced into it. Or would it be easier than she thought it might be? Because of her outlaw father, did she have a killer's instincts without even knowing it?

Except for one time, she had not been tested, and then she had managed to get out of the scrape without shooting someone—or being shot.

That day, when she had been accused of cheating during a game of poker in Beaumont, she had scarcely made it out of the saloon alive. It was her mother who held the outlaw off with a firearm as Jae ran for their horses.

When she and her mother had ridden from Beaumont, laughing about the look on the man's face, they had not known that they had humiliated one of the most ornery outlaws in Texas. Even the law never made an honest attempt at touching him. That was how he had managed to get in the card game without being arrested and thrown into the hoosegow.

How were Jae and her mother to know that they

had faced down the notorious Jonas Adams, one of Jae's father's worst enemies?

It was this very outlaw who had gunned down not only Jae's precious mother, but also her father, as they rode together on their way to a trading post to get supplies just outside of Beaumont.

Jae had buried them only a few days ago.

Since then, she had known that she was vulnerable. She had humiliated Jonas Adams. She expected for him to search for her and finish what he had started when he gunned down her parents. He surely would not rest until he saw *her* dead! She realized now that she had been foolish to have fired off her shotgun tonight. Yet she'd had no choice. Her food supply was low. She knew that she would have to chance going to the trading post soon to collect the supplies that her parents had gone for.

Her father's outlaw gang had disbanded after his death. Except for her slew of pets, she was now all alone in the world.

"Jae, am I dressed like a lawman?" Night Hawk asked, holding his arms away from his sides as she slowly raked her eyes over him. "Do I truly look like a lawman?"

"I guess you have to know that I haven't come face to face with many lawmen," Jae said sarcastically. "So how am I to know what to look for in them? All I know is that you have entered my territory and you know my name. Why else would you be here?"

"I want nothing from you except to make a request that you leave the Thicket with me and go and meet the man who is your true father," Night Hawk replied, his eyes searching her face as she gasped and took a shaky step away from him. "Yes, your true father needs you. He's dying. He wants to know you before he dies."

"What . . . are . . . you . . . saying?" Jae stammered. "Why would you say such a thing as that? Why would you want me to believe that the man who raised me isn't my father? What do you hope to gain from such an out and out lie?"

"It's no lie," Night Hawk said thickly. "The outlaw *wasn't* your father. Your mother was married to another man before she was abducted by Clifton Coldsmith. She was pregnant with you when he abducted her and brought her here, to live with him in hiding. Seems she fell in love with him. She willingly stayed with him. When you were born, the outlaw thought you were *his*. Your mother lived a lie. She allowed him to think you *were* his daughter. She even forced this lie on you by allowing you to believe he was your father."

Jae's head was spinning. She felt dizzy from the confusion of trying to follow what this man was saying, to make sense of it. She didn't see how any of this could be true! Her mother couldn't have lied to her! Her mother knew how Jae hated the fact that her father was a criminal!

Yet Jae had loved her outlaw father. When he was with her, he was tender, loving, and caring. Except for when he taught her how to shoot a firearm, and how to ride a horse, he had treated her like a delicate princess.

"No," she cried, her voice trembling. "It can't be true. I won't let you do this to me! I won't believe your lies!"

Jae brought the shotgun up, leveled the firearm at Night Hawk's chest, took careful aim, then slid her finger onto the trigger. "I'll give you to the count of five to get back on your horse and leave me in peace. One . . . two . . ."

Night Hawk saw that she meant business this time. He turned and started to walk away, then stopped when he heard a gun blast behind him. Expecting to feel the sting of the pellets enter his back, he gritted his teeth and closed his eyes.

But he felt nothing. She had missed!

Then he heard a commotion behind him. He turned on one heel.

Wide-eyed, he saw Crying Wolf holding Jae in his powerful arms as she struggled to get free.

His gaze shifted. Her shotgun lay at her feet. It had apparently gone off when Crying Wolf had jumped out at her to grab her. He felt lucky that Jae's aim had been ruined when she was startled.

He stared disbelievingly at Crying Wolf. "I thought you stayed behind," he said, his eyes locking with his friend's. "I thought you didn't want to spend the night in the Thicket."

"*Na*, it was not something I wished to do, but I got concerned over you being alone," Crying Wolf said. "I followed you."

"I heard a noise several times," Night Hawk said, nodding. "So that was *you?*"

Crying Wolf didn't get a chance to answer him. Instead, he winced as Jae bent her head and bit him on the arm. He saw her gaze up at him with defiance and smugness in her eyes.

Not wanting her to know that she had inflicted pain or disturbed him in any way, Crying Wolf lifted his eyes away from her and looked at Night Hawk again.

"*Huh*, I followed you. I stayed hidden, to be there in case someone or something suddenly became a threat to you. Hidden, I could defend you better than traveling with you."

Night Hawk watched Jae, stunned that she had actually bitten Crying Wolf! He was amazed at the intensity of her struggles to get free of Crying Wolf's ironlike hold on her. She fought like a wildcat.

"Let me go, you son of a bitch!" Jae screamed, kicking and grabbing at Crying Wolf's arm, which was like a solid piece of steel around her waist. "I'll bite you again if you don't!"

"Bite me again and I will bite you back," Crying Wolf said matter-of-factly.

Jae turned her head to stare up at Crying Wolf. "You would bite me back?" she said, her voice calming somewhat.

"Bite me, *mah-tao-yo*, little one, and see." Crying Wolf's gaze locked with hers.

"Jae, give up the struggle," Night Hawk said, bending to retrieve his rifle. He reached over and grabbed Jae's firearm from the ground as well. "No one is here to hurt you. We have come to take you to your rightful home. Your father awaits your arrival with an anxious, yet very weak heart. It has been unfair that you have been kept from him. He only recently discovered that you even existed."

Jae turned and gazed at Night Hawk. "Who told him such a tall tale as that?" she said, laughing sarcastically. "Who has anything to gain from such a lie? Oh, yes, now I know. Everyone thinks I'm wealthy because of all that my father stole. The one who told this man who claims to be my father hopes to get his hands on the money." She smirked. "Well, he *and* the man who claims to be my father have a surprise coming. They will continue to be poor after they discover I have nothing to give them . . . that I gave it all away."

Running Hawk shook his head as he took a step closer to her. "Your true father is one of the wealthiest landowners in Texas. The man who told your father about you is your very own *uncle*. You surely know how wealthy he is."

He nodded to Crying Wolf. "Release her. If she tries to run, she won't get far."

"And so Uncle Beauford spilled the beans to this man who says he's my father, huh?" Jae said, jerking herself free when Crying Wolf dropped his arms from around her. She stepped away and placed her hands on her hips. "Why didn't *he* come to me with this so-called truth?"

"He didn't want to enter the Thicket," Night Hawk replied. "And he was sworn to silence until your mother died. She told him never to let you know that you had a different father. When he discovered that she was dead, he thought it only fair to finally reveal to your *true* father that you were alive. Your uncle didn't like to think of you being alone in the Thicket. And he didn't want you living with *him*. He sees you as an embarrassment. That was why he was so eager to tell your *father* about you."

"I have a question I'd like to ask about my so-called father," Jae said stiffly. "Why did he allow the outlaw to take my mother? Why didn't he go after her?"

"During the robbery, one of the outlaws shot him in the back," Night Hawk said thickly. "He's been partially paralyzed since."

"Paralyzed?" Jae said, her eyes widening. "One of the outlaws shot him in the back?" She placed a hand to her throat. "No, please don't tell me that my . . . my outlaw father did something so despicable!"

"He didn't, but I hold him responsible anyway. He was the head of the outlaw gang who took so much from your true father that day."

Night Hawk took a slow step toward her. "Jae, your true father is dying," he said, his voice drawn. "Give him the chance to see you, to know his daughter. Do you not think that he has been cheated of knowing you long enough?"

Jae felt torn. This disarmingly handsome man seemed to be telling the truth. But his revelations made her feel a bitterness toward her mother that she never thought possible. If what this "breed" said was true, everything about her life had been a lie! Living in hiding in the Thicket, living the life of an outlaw's daughter, disgusted by what her father did to innocent people, yet loving him, too, for his generosity—all this had been forced on her by a mother who had never been truthful to Jae her entire life!

Tears she did not want to shed spilled from her eyes. Humiliated over being so weak, she turned her back to the strangers.

Then, sobbing, she broke into a run and ran blindly through the dark, savage shadows of the Thicket. She was aware of the usual night sounds—the owls, who came out in the deepest night, were hooting from somewhere overhead; she heard the cry of the panther she had named Jezebel; she heard the howl of the white wolf that she had named Snow; she heard the peaceful sound of the crickets and frogs in the creek that bisected the land behind her cabin.

Always before, those sounds had comforted her. They had made her feel as one with the creatures of the Thicket, which had been her home since she was born. Although forced to live in hiding, she had grown to love this dark place. The animals had become her companions, as had the beautiful flowers, the lovely vines, and the Spanish moss that hung from tree to tree like fancy lace.

It was all so beautiful. How could she regret living here?

This place, this place with which she had developed an emotional connection, had been her refuge and the centerpiece of her solitude!

And now she must think of leaving it behind. Must think of never seeing the animals again.

Now she found that she resented both her mother and her "pretend" father so much that she wished she had never even known them. Yes, suddenly everything in her life had changed, and she was not sure if she could live with this change. She was not sure if she even wanted to try!

As she stumbled onward, realizing that she was being followed, she saw the shine of lamplight in the windows of her cabin a short distance away.

That, too, she would miss if she were to leave. Although plain and not filled with luxuries, it was her home.

So often, while standing in the outdoor shower rigged up by her father at the back of the cabin, lathering her body with some sweet-smelling soap, she had looked up through the lacy leaves of a centenarian pepper tree, pondering the stars and wishing upon them.

She could not deny wishing that some time in her future she might have the opportunity to wear silks and satins . . . to have frothy lace running down the front of her dress, and to wear satin slippers.

She had closed her eyes and envisioned the strong arms of a man holding her, whirling her around a dance floor, whispering sweet words of love to her.

Yes, so often, while alone, she had become someone else in her imagination, then had retreated to the real world of animals and shadowy swamp, content in the simpler things of life, which she knew were better than that world out there where outlaws murdered and maimed. While living in the Thicket, she could never become a victim.

But recently she had begun to feel threatened even in the Thicket, knowing that the very same outlaw who had killed her parents might be having sleepless nights while scheming how he might kill her.

For now, she had only one concern—to gain more time to ponder the stranger's words. She had to decide whether or not she would go and see for herself if it were true. To leave the Thicket meant to leave behind so many things that were precious to her!

Jae rushed on inside the cabin and closed the door. Breathless, she rested her back against the door. Her breasts heaving, she looked around the cabin, the only home that she had ever known.

Her mother had seen to it that this mere log cabin had the appearance of something better. A small bedroom lay to the left of the front door under a shed roof shaded by beautiful magnolia trees. This was Jae's bedroom.

The only other bedroom stood at the other side of the house. It had been her mother's and . . .

She found it hard to use the word "father" at this moment when thinking about Clifton Coldsmith. If he wasn't her father . . .

She continued looking around her, knowing that even if she left this house, it would never die inside her heart. The dining area seated three; four was a crowd. The kitchen hung out the back, like an architectural caboose.

The furniture in the parlor was comfortable enough, consisting of a thickly cushioned sofa, a matching chair, and a rocker, all of which were positioned before a stone fireplace that took up one end wall.

She gazed at length at a rag rug that covered a good portion of the floor, under which lay the trapdoor that led to a cavernous cellar, where all of the booty from the robberies had been stored.

Since she had taken it all to the bank, the only thing that remained in the cellar was a stray swamp snake or two, several nests of mice, and cobwebs in the corners, sporting the most ungodly large spiders that she had ever seen and could not get rid of. After one was done away with, there seemed to be ten to take its place.

Jae's gaze shifted. Tears welled up in her eyes as she watched five tiny baby opossums nursing from the teats of their mother, who lay cuddled in a soft box of blankets that Jae had prepared for her before the birth of her babies.

The father opossum noticed Jae standing there and waddled toward her, so fat from her generous feedings that he found it hard to walk.

Before she had taken "Sam" and his "bride" into her home, he had been an ill-mannered, long-toothed oaf who hissed at her every time she got near him. She had won him over quickly by feeding him scraps.

She glanced over at her favorite pet, Snoopy. She had chosen that name for her raccoon because of his skills at snooping, not only in the kitchen, but throughout the house. He lay close to the fireplace on a pillow made just for him. Warmed by the fire, Snoopy snoozed peacefully most of the day.

She smiled to herself as she recalled their first acquaintance. After he was fed his first meal outside the door of the cabin, Snoopy began inviting himself into the cabin through the unlocked front door. One day she walked in on the twenty-pounder raiding the shelves in the kitchen. He stood his ground when he saw her, wringing his hands and hissing.

The little bandit, with his bright eyes and rather humanlike hands, never stopped with just snooping around and eating what he could of the food supply. He ate anything and everything—even the soap in the trays of the outdoor shower.

She gazed past Snoopy and sighed when she saw her two pet squirrels. They were cuddled so close together, wrapped around one another, it was as though she was looking at one squirrel instead of two.

The sound of feet outside the cabin, moving toward the door, made Jae's smile and her melancholy thoughts slip quickly away. Her heart pounding, she turned and stared at the door.

When Night Hawk spoke up from behind it, she stiffened and hurriedly slid the bolt lock into place.

"Go away!" she cried. "I can't leave my home. I *won't*."

How could she leave her pets behind? she asked herself. They had been her only true friends, her only companions! She could not find it in her heart to abandon them! They had never abandoned *her*. They had given her their devotion, their love.

To her, they were more human than some people she had known in her lifetime!

"Open the door, Jae," Night Hawk said, his voice

drawn. "I haven't come all this way to be turned down flat. Do you know the opportunities that await you back at your true father's house? You won't have to live in hiding any longer. You will have anything you want. Clothes . . . a beautiful home . . . horses. . . ."

Jae could not help envisioning the silk dresses of her midnight dreams that she might have if she chose the new life being offered her. She could not help closing her eyes and envisioning a grand mansion, with a wide, sweeping staircase. She envisioned sparkling jewels and oh, so much more.

But then she returned to the real world, hating this man who was trying to lure her away from it!

"I don't want any of that," Jae cried, turning to gaze at her animals again. She stifled a sob behind her hand to think of leaving them. Yes, she knew that there could be much more in life for her away from the Thicket. But having lived in such isolation for so long, and not being skilled at conversation as educated people were, she doubted that she would fit in anywhere but here.

She hung her head, realizing more and more what she had missed out on during her twenty years of life. Her mother had taught her to read and write and to work mathematical problems, but that had not been the same as attending school with children of her own age, learning how to socialize with them.

"It's too late," she murmured. "I'm too old now to learn any of the basics of being . . . of being anything akin to someone normal."

"Jae, please?" Night Hawk slowly shook his head back and forth as he glanced over at Crying Wolf, who had come up next to him, carrying the bag of pigeons.

"She has locked the door?" Crying Wolf asked, looking from Night Hawk to the cabin.

Night Hawk had not yet attempted to open the door. He gazed at it for a moment longer, giving Jae a last chance to reply.

When she still did not open the door, he cautiously placed his hand on the latch and soon discovered that she had the door bolted.

He frowned. "Jae, I'm going to ask you just this one more time," he said, taking a step away from the door. "Are you going to open the door or not?"

When she didn't respond, he lifted his foot and kicked the door open, the bolt springing free and flying halfway across the room.

What Night Hawk discovered inside the door made him take a shaky step backward. He found himself staring into the barrel of a rifle.

"You don't hear so good, do you?" Jae said, smiling mischievously up at Night Hawk.

Chapter Seven

The sudden noise of gunfire outside of the cabin and the splintering sound of glass made Jae momentarily freeze in alarm.

She was jolted out of her frozen state when Night Hawk lunged for her and knocked her to the floor, disarming her.

Thinking that the old Indian had shot at her through the window, and that Night Hawk had knocked her to the floor in an effort to keep her from shooting him, Jae struggled to get free.

"Get off me, you 'breed,' " she shouted, shoving at Night Hawk's chest. "Let me up!"

Her words halted abruptly when more gunfire rang out. She knew that the old Indian had seen her being tackled, so why would he continue firing his gun? That had to mean someone else was outside shooting at the house and that Night Hawk had shoved her to the floor to get her out of the line of gunfire. He was protecting her from harm!

Night Hawk looked anxiously over his shoulder just as Crying Wolf rolled through the door, blood seeping through the left sleeve of his buckskin shirt.

"It is only one man," Crying Wolf cried. Ignoring his wound, he moved to the window that had been broken and placed his rifle on the sill. "After he shot me I got off one last shot. I heard him cry out with pain. I know I wounded him!"

Night Hawk moved away from Jae. He grabbed her rifle, rushed across the room, and kicked the door closed with a foot. Then he went and stood on the opposite side of the window from Crying Wolf.

"Crying Wolf, you are alright?" Night Hawk asked, though he did not look toward him. He kept his eyes searching through the darkness outside, seeing no movement, hearing nothing.

"Nothing herbs cannot heal," Crying Wolf said stiffly, his eyes still watching for movement outside the cabin.

Jae went to the window on the other side of the door. She slid a pistol from a holster that hung from a peg on the wall. She watched outside for any more movements, only occasionally glancing over at Night Hawk. He had actually saved her life by shoving her to the floor and blanketing her with his body. If he hadn't, one of the bullets might have hit her.

Something inside her melted as she thought of how Night Hawk's body had felt against hers. For a moment, their eyes had met and held, stirring feelings inside her that she had never experienced before.

"Are you certain it was only one man?" Night Hawk asked, neither seeing nor hearing anything outside. Even the night sounds had been silenced by the gunfire.

"I saw him just as he fired off the first round at the house," Crying Wolf said, glancing down at his arm.

He winced when he saw the pool of blood on the floor, where it had dripped between his fingers. "He did not see me at first standing in the shadows. When I made my move, lifting my rifle to shoot at him, the barrel must have picked up the light from the lantern in the window. The man was an accurate shot. He got me with his first bullet." He cast Night Hawk a sly smile. "But I am also accurate with a firearm. I got *him* with *my* first shot."

The sound of a horse approaching the cabin in a hard gallop quickly silenced them. They peered more intently out of the window, then jerked away from it when they saw the horseman and the pistol he held in his uninjured hand.

He fired at the house one more time, then rode away.

"It was *him!*" Jae cried, paling. "I saw his face! It was Jonas Adams! It was that same son of a bitch outlaw that attacked me when I got the best of him in the card game in Beaumont. It was that same son of a bitch who gunned down mother and . . ."

She felt awkward now when she started to refer to the man whom she had thought was her father. What should she call him? She again recalled the wonderful times she'd known with him, when he had showed her such love, such gentleness!

It had been easy to forget the ugly side of his nature. She never allowed herself to hate or resent him.

Now it was her mother she could not help resenting with every fiber of her being!

"You saw him close enough to know that it was Jonas Adams?" Night Hawk asked, being familiar with the notorious outlaw. He had seen wanted posters on him in more than one Texas town. Jonas was dreaded by all settlers, especially those who were new in the area and unaccustomed to violence.

Night Hawk edged himself closer to the window and peered outside. He expected Jonas to make one more pass outside the cabin. He rested the rifle on the windowsill, his aim steady. Yes, he would gladly gun down the hated, heartless outlaw!

"The moon!" Jae said. "That is how I saw him. The moon revealed his face to me." She was afraid to leave the window, afraid of Jonas returning. And she did not trust that Jonas was alone . . . unless the law had found him and broken up his gang. He might even now be on the lam, a hunted man!

Crying Wolf suddenly slid to the floor, groaning. Jae gasped when she saw how pale he was and how his wounded arm hung limply at his side, the blood still seeping from it. He hung his head and dropped his firearm, and she feared that he might have lost consciousness.

She glanced at Night Hawk as he dropped his rifle and quickly knelt at his friend's side. Touched by the devotion between the two men, Jae watched for a moment longer, then slid her pistol back inside its holster and rushed into the kitchen.

Her fingers trembled as she poured water from a pitcher into a wooden basin. She grabbed fresh towels from a shelf, then went back inside the parlor and knelt down next to Crying Wolf.

"Go back to the window and keep watch," she said, easing Crying Wolf down onto his back on the floor. "I'll see to your friend's wound."

Night Hawk stared disbelievingly at her, then gazed down at Crying Wolf. Sweat pearled his old friend's brow. His eyes were scarcely open as he sucked in heaving breaths.

"Go on," Crying Wolf said thickly. He placed a gentle hand on Night Hawk's shoulder. "Night Hawk, you keep watch now. I will take my turn later."

"I don't think you are going anywhere for a while," Jae said, ripping Crying Wolf's shirt sleeve away from his wound. She cringed when she saw the injury. The bullet was still lodged inside.

She looked quickly up at Night Hawk as he stood tall and silent by the window, his right hand clutching a rifle. "The bullet must be removed," she said, her heart skipping a beat when Night Hawk gave her a slow, uneasy stare. "I'm not sure I can do . . . the . . . surgery required to remove it."

"Then you stand guard and I will do it for my friend," Night Hawk said, his eyes locking with hers. He knew that this was not the time to feel anything for this woman, yet how could he not? She was fascinating and beautiful!

And she was proving to be a person who felt compassion for others. It was evident in the way she had gone to Crying Wolf's aid, and in the way she now looked so innocently up at Night Hawk.

He saw a true concern in the depths of her dark eyes that told him she was a good person, someone who would be easy to love.

"I think we will both be needed for the bullet's removal," Jae murmured. "It won't be an easy task. I . . . I've seen it done often after . . . after my father, I mean Clifton, returned home from one of his raids. My mother performed the surgery. I never offered my help. I only watched. I never approved of the injured outlaws being brought into our home, nor did I approve of the loot from the raids being brought here. I wanted the thieving outlaws gone from my home!"

Night Hawk could hear the utter contempt in Jae's

voice when she spoke of the deeds of the man who had served as her father. He felt a deep empathy for her when he thought how she had been forced to live.

Yet he saw that it had not turned her into someone who despised humanity.

He was determined now, more than ever, to take her away from this environment and introduce her to a world she probably could not even envision. He would show her the good side of life; the sort of people who fit into it . . . namely her true father and Night Hawk's sweet adopted mother!

And he knew now that he would do everything to draw this woman into loving him. He would make her life so peaceful and alluring that she would never wish to return to this place where memories lay dark and sordid all around her.

"It's been too long now. Surely Jonas won't be back," Jae said, glancing up at the window and then guardedly at the door. "If he was wounded, he might not be any better off than your friend. He will have to concentrate more on seeing to his wound than seeing to my demise."

Night Hawk stood the rifle against the wall, then went and pushed several pieces of furniture against the door. Then he shoved a tall chest in front of the broken window.

He then knelt down beside Crying Wolf. Panic filled him when he saw that his old friend was now unconscious, his breathing raspy and uneven.

"Point me to a bedroom," Night Hawk said, gently lifting Crying Wolf into his arms. "I want to get him off this floor before I cut into his flesh."

"Follow me," Jae said, lifting the water basin in her hands.

Then she paled and suddenly stopped. Water

splashed from the basin as she stared frantically around the room. "My animals!" she cried, giving Night Hawk an anxious, frightened look. "Except for Snoopy, they are all gone! The gunfire must have frightened them away! They must have scampered out of the door before we closed it. I . . . I didn't notice them leave!"

Snoopy hunkered against a far wall, visibly shaking, his beady, dark eyes filled with fear.

"Oh, Snoopy, poor baby," Jae said. She started to put the basin down to go to him, but Night Hawk's stern voice broke through her despair.

"We must see to Crying Wolf now," he said flatly. "You can see to your animals later. Lead me to a bedroom, Jae. *Now.*"

Jae looked over at Night Hawk. She had a notion to tell him what she thought of being ordered around, but stopped when Crying Wolf let out a low moan of pain that went clean into her heart. She knew that his age could go against his healing; perhaps he would not even recover.

She swallowed hard, gave Snoopy another quick glance, and gave the room a quick once over to see if she might see her other pets cowering behind the furniture. Then, knowing that they were gone, she hurried out of the parlor, down a narrow hallway, and led Night Hawk into her mother's bedroom.

She flinched and felt a renewed despair inside her heart when she smelled her mother's familiar perfume, which still clung to the fabric of the curtains and to the blankets on the bed. She had not entered this room since her mother's death, nor had she yet sorted through her belongings.

Now she knew that she wouldn't ever look through her mother's things. Jae was certain now that she

83

would be leaving with Night Hawk. She knew that after tonight, the Thicket could never be the same for her. She was not safe alone. She would not be truly safe until she knew that Jonas Adams was dead! Nor did she care to stay where the bad memories outweighed the good.

Tears came to her eyes when she thought of her devoted pets. What was to become of them? She hoped that they had not forgotten how to forage for themselves!

"Is there any whiskey in your house?" Night Hawk asked, tenderly slipping off Crying Wolf's shirt.

"Yes, there's plenty," Jae said, moving to the other side of the bed, opposite from where Night Hawk stood. She set the water basin on the bed and reached around for the kerosene lamp. Once she had found it and some matches, she soon had the room filled with the soft glow of lamp light.

"Go and get two bottles of whiskey," Night Hawk said. The light of the room revealed to him the concern in Jae's eyes. She could have run away now, while he was occupied helping his friend, yet she was here, instead, offering her help. The longer he was with her, the more he realized that she was a woman of heart, someone who had somehow managed to come through her questionable upbringing without being too harmed by it.

Yet he now recalled the story of how she knew Jonas Adams and what had caused the rift between them. He realized that she knew how to gamble, that she even took her skills into the gambling halls and saloons of Beaumont!

He could not help smiling to himself as he imagined her sitting in a smoke-filled room at a table of hardened gamblers, getting the best of them! Although she seemed an angel in comparison with most of the women he had seen in the gambling halls and saloons, there *was* that side of her that had sent her where no decent woman would go, to mingle with men as though she was one of them.

He glanced up at her short-cropped hair, wondering if that was why she wore it short. Was it so she could act like one of the men while she sat with them, shoving coins to the center of the table or shuffling her cards as the men watched and waited?

He wondered if she also smoked cigars or cigarettes to blend in with the men. Did she wear a complete outfit of men's clothes instead of the cut-off breeches? Had she hidden her facial features beneath the shadows of a wide-brimmed hat?

Or had she gone to the saloons openly defying the looks of the townsfolk by showing them that she was a woman and not ashamed to do as she pleased, regardless of the stares and gasps of those who thought she might be the daughter of the devil!

Had she worn her cut-off breeches, flaunting her shapely legs for everyone to see? For the women to hiss out the words "shameful hussy" to her, enjoying it?

He watched her leave the room. The way she walked was most definitely the walk of a woman! It was a walk of confidence, of a nameless grace and dignity.

His gaze lowered to the shapely curve of her bare legs, realizing that she did not feel at all shameful by revealing them to whomever might want to look at them.

Except for in the whorehouses and saloons, never had he seen a woman who so willingly showed her legs. He was somewhat *glad* that she did not follow protocol and wear what she was supposed to wear because she was a lady. He enjoyed looking at her legs. They were legs to be proud of, so smooth, so shapely and sun-bronzed!

His gaze shifted again. He watched the slow sway of her hips until she left the room.

He was very aware of how having seen all of these alluring things about her had affected him. His pulse was racing. His loins were on fire as they were wont to do when he saw a lady he wished to have in his bed! He *did* desire Jae! He *did* wish to hold her, to protect her!

Crying Wolf emitted a low, long groan.

Feeling guilty for having thought of someone else besides his friend, when his full concentration should be on getting the bullet removed from Crying Wolf's arm, Night Hawk turned his eyes back down to Crying Wolf and finished undressing him.

As he drew a blanket up to lay just above Crying Wolf's waist, Jae came back into the room, a bottle of whiskey in each of her hands.

Still bothered inside by his recent feelings about her, Night Hawk slid her a slow gaze.

When their eyes met and held, he knew that she felt the same about him. No matter how she might ever try to deny it, he knew that she had feelings for him other than to despise him for having come to take her from her home.

Surely, deep down inside, she knew that had he not been there tonight, she would have not lived through the outlaw attack.

Had Jonas not seen the horses outside and known that she was not alone, he would have surely sneaked up on her in the night.

Night Hawk did not want to think of what might have happened to her then.

Almost shyly, feeling so unnerved by Night Hawk staring at her and knowing what his thoughts were by the way he looked at her, Jae went over to him and shoved the whiskey bottles in his hands.

Shaken by her feelings for him, not feeling so sure of herself anymore while being around this man—a stranger, yet someone who stirred her insides so deliciously—she turned to leave the room.

"I need your help," Night Hawk said, placing the bottles on the floor beside the bed. "Speed is of the essence. Come and help. I can get done in half the time if you assist me."

Her heart pounding, her knees weak, Jae turned slowly around.

When Night Hawk reached a hand out for her, she felt torn. It would be so easy to flee into the Thicket and hide while he was occupied with his friend. By the time he was able to look for her, she could even be long gone into Beaumont, where she had friends who would look after her welfare.

Yet by the silent pleading in Night Hawk's eyes, and by Crying Wolf's painful groans, she knew that this was where she belonged for now; escape would come later. She just could not allow herself to give into her feelings for this man, or she would lose her total identity. She knew of women whose whole personalities changed by the overpowering presence of a man.

Had it not happened to her own mother? Had she not left a home filled with love and luxuries to live with a man who was despised by all humanity?

No, she did not want anyone to dictate to her. She loved being free, being what some called wild.

Well, maybe she was, she thought to herself as she went to stand over the bed. And no one was going to tame her, not even this handsome "breed" who stole her breath away almost every time he looked at her.

"Now do as I say," Night Hawk said as he opened a bottle of whiskey and set it aside.

When she didn't respond, Night Hawk looked up at her with arched eyebrows. "Well?" he said thickly. "Will you? Will you do as I say so that we can work jointly at getting this surgery behind us?"

Jae swallowed hard and nodded.

"When I say pour the whiskey onto the wound, do it, then set the bottle aside and hold down Crying Wolf's arms as best you can while I dig into the flesh with the knife," Night Hawk said, his heart pounding as he stared down at the wound. He had done this before, but never for such a dear friend as Crying Wolf. If he should make an error in judgment with the knife, he knew that his friend could die.

"Pour it now, Jae." Running Hawk felt the blood throbbing through his veins as his fear mounted at what he had to do.

Jae winced as she tipped the bottle and poured the whiskey in a steady stream onto the wound. She shivered when Crying Wolf cried out in his unconscious state; surely the pain was so severe that it cut through to the very core of his being.

"That is enough," Night Hawk said. "Now, Jae, hold down his arms. And turn your eyes away. I don't want you fainting on me."

"I'll have you know I have never fainted in my life," she said, her spine stiffening.

"Jae, this is no time for trivial arguments."

Jae gazed at him and saw the uneasiness in his eyes, now understanding what he must be going through. "I'm sorry," she said, something she rarely said to anyone. She had learned to stand behind her decisions and actions without apologizing to anyone. She never wanted to look weak in anyone's eyes, and apologies made one appear weak!

Jae bent low over Crying Wolf as she held his arms down. She knew the instant that Night Hawk had entered the old Indian's flesh with the knife. Although Crying Wolf was unconscious, he again cried out in pain and struggled to get his wrists free.

"Hold him!" Night Hawk shouted. "Jae! Hold him! I have to do some more digging!"

Crying Wolf's eyes flew open wildly. He looked from his friend to Jae, then down at his arm.

Night Hawk's eyes wavered when he discovered that Crying Wolf was awake, but he went on with what had to be done. "Jae!" he cried, blood dripping from his knife and hands. "The whiskey! Give him some whiskey to drink!"

Trembling, Jae grabbed a bottle of whiskey. She could see the pain in Crying Wolf's eyes. She could almost feel it!

"Here," she murmured as she sat down on the bed beside him. "Drink some whiskey. It might help dull the pain.

She placed a gentle hand beneath his head and eased it only a little ways from the pillow. As she held his head up far enough to make it possible for him to swallow, she fed him the whiskey.

After Crying Wolf had drunk several deep gulps and closed his eyes, Jae eased his head back down onto the pillow.

"I think things are going to be all right now," Night Hawk said, sighing heavily. "Now to proceed. I see the bullet. I have only a little ways to go and . . ." He laughed with relief as he reached his fingers into the wound and plucked the bullet out. "There it is," he said, showing it to Jae.

Then he frowned at her. "I need a needle and thread," he said, dropping the bullet into the basin of water. "I had to make more of an incision than I had planned to. Jae, do you have a needle and thread?"

Her gaze shifted and she found her mother's sewing basket sitting on the floor in the corner. Although her mother loved the wild side of life as much as Jae, she had also loved to embroider. On the long, cold nights of winter, she had taught her daughter how to sew.

Tears came to Jae's eyes as she went to the basket and opened it. Her mother's thimble lay like a miniature tomb at the bottom, surrounded by many beautiful strands of embroidery thread and a pincushion filled with needles.

"Jae, I need thin thread, as thin as you can find," Night Hawk said, taking a cloth from the basin of water and bathing Crying Wolf's wound.

Jae got a spool of regular white sewing thread and a thin, long needle. She went and stood beside Night Hawk. "Let me," she said. "I know how." She had stitched up many of her beloved forest animals after they had gotten into one scrape or another with their enemies.

Night Hawk stepped aside. He was touched even more deeply by how Jae again showed compassion toward Crying Wolf. And it was not done for any ulterior motive. She offered because she, in her own way, cared.

Delicately and carefully she sewed up the small wound.

"I think that should do it," she said after cutting the thread with her tiny sewing scissors.

"I thank you for Crying Wolf," Night Hawk said, gazing from his friend to her, smiling.

Feeling awkward and at a loss of words in Night Hawk's presence, Jae placed the scissors on the table and started to leave the room.

A warm hand on her wrist stopped her.

Eyes wide, and scarcely breathing, she turned and found herself being drawn into Night Hawk's arms. Her insides went mushy with a strange sort of warmth as his lips claimed hers with a soft and gentle kiss.

When she found her body responding to the kiss in ways she never experienced before, a quick panic filled her.

Breathless and wild-eyed, she yanked herself free. Still feeling his kiss, the wonders of it, in how it shot passionate thrills through her, Jae covered her lips with a hand.

Her pulse racing, she gazed at Night Hawk for a moment, then turned and fled from the room.

Panic seized Night Hawk. What if she ran farther than the parlor? What if she ran away and lost herself in the Thicket? Only *she* would know the haunts that could give her the cover she needed to keep him from finding her.

Knowing that Crying Wolf was sleeping soundly and was going to be all right, Night Hawk ran from the room. When he reached the parlor and discovered that she wasn't there, and that she had managed to shove all of the furniture away from the door and flee outside into the dark of night, perhaps even *weaponless*, he broke into a mad run and left the cabin himself.

But once he got outside, he realized that it was too dark to track her. He had only one thing to do. He had to make a wild guess as to which avenue she would take while running from too many truths: the truth that she had a true father awaiting her arrival, the truth that she had feelings for Night Hawk, and that he felt so much for *her!*

"Jae!" he shouted, his voice echoing back at him from all directions. He grew cold inside. If Jonas Adams was still lurking about in the Thicket, shouting Jae's name in an obvious panic would let the outlaw realize that she was out there somewhere alone and vulnerable.

Night Hawk chose a route to take and took off running.

Chapter Eight

Scarcely breathing, huddled behind a thick stand of magnolia trees, Jae's eyes were wide as she watched for Night Hawk. Although she had thus far succeeded at eluding him, she realized that he knew the Indian way to track people.

She wondered, what tribe he was from.

She also wondered why he had chosen to live the life of a white man over that of an Indian, yet had a full-blooded Indian as his companion?

She was wrenched back to the present when a sound at her left side made her stiffen. Remembering that Jonas Adams might still be nearby, just waiting for a chance to grab her, her heart began to race.

Scooting back farther into the shadows, wishing now that she had taken just that one more minute to grab her rifle, Jae looked guardedly from side to side.

She flinched when she heard the rustling of dried leaves not that far from where she was hiding. Someone was drawing closer . . . and closer!

Desperate now with a building fear that it truly *might* be Jonas, even though she was keenly aware that Night Hawk was searching for her, Jae raked her eyes over the ground on both sides of her for something with which to defend herself.

Smiling, she picked up a large rock. She clutched it to her bosom as she waited for whomever was there to make an appearance.

Then she let out a squeal of happiness and dropped the rock when she saw what had been rustling through the leaves—her family of opossums! They had surely caught her scent from wherever they had been hiding. Sam waddled on toward her, Mama Opossum lagging behind with her five babies clutching to the fur on her back.

"Oh, Sam," Jae said. She swept the obese opossum up into her arms and hugged him to her bosom.

When he let out his low, familiar hiss, which would scare anyone who didn't understand that he was harmless, Jae giggled. "You sweet thing," she murmured. "Are you glad to see me?"

She watched Mama Opossum amble on toward her. Tears of joy spilled from Jae's eyes as she gazed at the babies and noted how cute they were as they rode their mother's back. It wouldn't be long now before they would walk on their own.

Jae had wanted to be there to see the babies as they left their mother's side for that first time. Now she was not sure what her *own* future was going to be. Night Hawk seemed to be a determined sort of man who would not give up on her all that easily.

She felt a sense of melancholy swim through her at the thought of her working with Night Hawk to perform the surgery on Crying Wolf. It had seemed so natural to be with him, for the moment having pushed aside her animosity toward him for having invaded her territory . . . her private life.

Yes, she was sorely attracted to the man in ways unfamiliar to her. Never had she seen anyone as handsome: his flaxen hair; his smooth, copper skin; his midnight-black eyes. And his classic facial features, which made him look as though someone had taken him directly from a painting.

When she was around him, she found it harder and harder not to be civil to him. For the first time in her life, she wished to be friends with a man, as a lady is friends with a man in that special way when she wishes to be held by him; when she wishes to be kissed by him; and when she wishes to be caressed by him.

The more she thought of Night Hawk, the more dangerous her thoughts became. Recalling his kiss and how it had affected her brought a strange sort of tingling to between her thighs even now. It was a different sort of heat that she had never felt before.

Her jaw tightened and anger flashed in her eyes at how easily she had responded to his kiss. She must get rid of him, or her life as she had always known it was doomed. She must continue to elude him!

"Jae?"

Night Hawk's voice, his nearness, made Jae jump. She had been so lost in thoughts of him that she had not even realized that he had come upon her in the dark and was now standing over her.

Holding tightly to Sam as he emitted several low hisses while gazing up at Night Hawk, Jae swallowed hard. She knew that there was no escaping. Running Hawk was too determined to take her to her father.

"How did you find me?" she said, moving slowly to her feet. She still clutched Sam in her arms, very aware of Mama Opossum settling down at her feet, actually *on* them, as she had done countless times

95

before while Jae had sat by the fire, or had stood outside, breathing in the fresh air early in the morning.

"I will admit that it was not all that easy," Night Hawk said, chuckling. "You slipped up or I would still be searching for you."

"I . . . slipped up?" she asked, forking an eyebrow. "How? What did I do? I've been hiding in this same place for some time now."

"Apparently finding your animals made you forget you were in hiding," Night Hawk said, glancing first at the opossum in her arms, and then at those at her feet. "Your squeal led me right to you."

Jae sucked in an annoyed, frustrated breath. She lifted her chin defiantly. "And so you have found me. What now?"

"You know the answer to that," Night Hawk answered, his eyes locking with hers. "Jae, I've come to the Big Thicket for only one reason: To get you and take you back to your true *father*. And that is exactly what I plan to do."

"Over my dead body," Jae hissed out, her eyes narrowing angrily. "This is my home. I don't belong anywhere else. I'd be like some freak in a circus. I wouldn't fit into any sort of other life."

Jae clutched Sam more tightly. With softness in her eyes, she gazed down at Mama Opossum and the babies. "These critters are my family," she said. "They are all I need."

"Would they want you to stay here and be stalked by Jonas Adams? You do know that once the outlaw's wounds are healed, he will come back for you. He will kill you."

Eyes wide, Jae looked up quickly at Running Hawk.

"So you see, Jae, it's impossible for you to stay here any longer," Running Hawk said. "Yes, this is your home, and I do see your camaraderie with the animals. But you know as well as I that it all changed tonight. Don't be so stubborn. Admit that you must go forward now with your new life. You can't even want to live where danger lurks all around you in the savage shadows of the Thicket. I won't allow you to stay alone another night."

"Allow?" she shouted, taken aback by how he suddenly placed himself in charge of her life. "How dare you assume that you can allow or not allow me to do anything! I have always been my own person. So shall I be until the day I die!"

"And if you stay here, that might be way sooner than you can imagine," Night Hawk ground out. "If you truly wish to die, then perhaps I should just go on my way and let Jonas Adams grant you that favor."

Knowing that what he said was true, that her life was no longer worth spit if she stayed behind alone in the Thicket, Jae swallowed hard.

Yet she could not find the words to tell him that. She did not like to back down to anyone, especially a man! Most men she had become acquainted with were worthless, no good sons of bitches.

And although she had always known that her very own father—oh, well, the man she thought was her father—was as worthless and ruthless as those men who rode with him in his gang, she had found it in her heart to set him aside from the others.

But never had she let down her guard around his gunmen and ruthless friends. When any of them would make eyes at her, if she wasn't fast enough to put him in his place, her father would.

This man standing before her, ah, ever so hand-some, was not a worthless, filthy gunman. He seemed clean-spirited through and through . . . as pure as the stars that twinkled overhead in the heavens. And she had never met a man who did not look at her and at the same time undress her with his eyes.

Yes, she had seen this stranger look at her with a genuine admiration. But there had been *respect* in his eyes. His only slip-up was to kiss her, and that had seemed oh, so natural. It had most definitely not been an ugly thing to do.

Deep down inside herself, where her desires were formed, Jae ached to be kissed by him again. She hungered for his arms.

Sensing that she was battling decisions inside her mind, Night Hawk patiently waited for her to come up with the right answer. While he waited, he gazed at her and how the moon spilled through the trees, illuminating her beautiful face. There was no denying how her loveliness affected him.

And although she knew how to handle firearms as well as any man, and even though she could out-argue him in a minute, he could not help but be drawn to her like a man who is drawn to a woman he has fallen in love with. Outwardly, she was so del-icate in appearance, and knowing how alone she was, he could not help but feel the need to protect her.

"Jae," Night Hawk blurted out, feeling that she had been given enough time to decide which life offered her the most, "your father—your *true* father—is dy-ing. Each day brings him closer to the end. If we delay much longer, you will lose the opportunity of getting to know him, if even for only an hour, or a few days. He is a man worthy of knowing. He has been like a father to me. I can just imagine how he would have treated you, a *daughter*. He would have treasured every moment with you. Do not deny him at least the time he has left."

"Why should I care about him when Mother left him so easily . . . and took up with an outlaw?" Jae said, her voice breaking. "There had to be something about my father that she despised. Otherwise she would have found her way back to him, especially after *I* was born. If she had loved him, if he had deserved to *be* loved, after I was born she would have found a way to take me to him. She wouldn't have allowed another man to claim me as his."

"You don't know the whole story," Night Hawk said, gently clasping her shoulders. "Jae, their marriage was arranged. There was no physical desire between them. There was mutual respect. But when the outlaw came along and swept your mother off her feet, she chose *that* . . . she chose *passion* . . . over a man she could never love."

"If that was true, she would at least have found a way to let him know that she was alive," Jae argued softly.

"She would have placed the man she truly loved in danger," Night Hawk said, dropping his hands to his sides when she stepped away from him. "Had she sent word to your father that she was alive, and told him with whom she was living, he would have sent out the cavalry until he found her and brought her back, killing the man she loved in the process. No. She would not chance that. She chose the other side of the coin instead. She let everyone believe that she was dead, except . . ."

"Except?" Jae said, arching an eyebrow.

"She eventually went to your grandparents and

told them that she was alive, but begged them not to tell your true father. They agreed. Even when your true father went there and questioned your grandparents, they told him that she was dead."

"How cruel of my grandparents," Jae gasped out. "How cruel of my mother."

"*Huh*, very cruel, indeed," Night Hawk said, reaching a hand to touch her cheek, drawing it quickly away when she flinched and stepped even farther away from him.

"That word you spoke, it's Indian," she said, their eyes locking. "Which Indian tribe are you a part of?"

"Comanche," Night Hawk said, understanding why she gasped, for he, too, knew of the rumors of atrocities being done by some bands of Comanche.

"What I know of the Comanche is that they are worse than the outlaws that rode with my father," Jae said guardedly. "They kill, mutilate, scalp . . ."

"I cannot speak for those who are kin to me in the Comanche tribe, whether or not they are a part of the atrocities spoken of in circles of white men and women. I can only vouch for myself and my friend Crying Wolf. We are men of peace."

"Do you often visit your Comanche people?" Jae saw something enter his eyes as he hesitated at answering her.

"Well? Do you?" she prodded.

"That is something I do not wish to talk about," Night Hawk replied, his voice drawn as he recalled the way his father had abandoned him on the fateful day of his sweet mother's death.

He found the words hard to speak, as hard as it still was for him to understand how or why a father with whom he had been so close in feelings would leave him at the mercy of the white pony soldier cavalry.

He felt blessed that his life had been spared. And because it had been, he had felt that it was for a purpose. But he was not sure just yet what that true purpose was. He had been content to live with his adopted parents: they had given him a reason for living after watching his mother shot down by one of his father's very own Comanche warriors.

Night Hawk had often wondered if his Comanche father had ordered the killing. He would not allow himself to think that he had, or his hate for his true father would be twofold! He did not want to be driven by a need for vengeance. There was more to life than being bitter toward those who had betrayed him.

"Then your life has not been all that perfect, has it?" Jae said, smiling slyly up at him. "And you wish for me to enter that world that you are not even all that happy with yourself?"

"My life has been what I have made it, and I am perfectly content with the road that I have chosen to travel." He glanced over his shoulder, in the direction of the cabin. Then he frowned at Jae. "I must get back and check on Crying Wolf. I've already been gone too long."

"Go ahead, I'm not stopping you," Jae said, laughing sarcastically.

"You sure have a tendency to try my temper," Night Hawk said, grabbing her by an arm and causing the opossum to fall to the ground.

"Now see what you did?" she said, yanking her arm free. She fell to her knees and hugged Sam, then stroked Mama Opossum's fur as the babies snuggled at her teats.

"You have been wrong to treat them like humans," Night Hawk said, seeing the animals' devotion to her. "They must stay behind. It might be hard for them, since you have so obviously pampered them as though they were your children. But they will learn to fend for themselves. When needed, their instinct to survive will kick in."

Jae frowned at Running Hawk. "I never said I was going to leave them. Nor did I say I was going anywhere myself."

"You *are* going to leave them, and you *are* going somewhere," Night Hawk said, leaning to grab her arm again. "*Mea-oro,* come. Let us go. Right now we are going to see to Crying Wolf's welfare. As soon as he is fit to travel, there will be three horses leaving this devil's pocket, not two." He forked an eyebrow as she rose to her feet and glared up at him. "I doubt I have to ask whether or not you know how to ride a horse. You seem to know how to do everything else a man knows to do."

"If you are trying to insult me, you are not succeeding," Jae spat out. "I'm proud of my abilities to take care of myself, *all* of them."

"You do know how to walk, then, don't you?" Night Hawk jested, his eyes dancing into hers.

"What?" she said, taken aback by such a ludicrous question. "What do you mean?"

Night Hawk laughed softly when he saw her frustration building. "I will ask you again. Do you know how to walk?"

"What a stupid question," she said, stamping on away from him, toward the cabin.

"Well at least it got you to do what asking nicely wouldn't," Night Hawk said, taking large, quick steps that took him to her side. "I could not get you to go

102

back to the cabin with me any other way, now could I?"

"You'd best shut up or I'll freeze in my steps so hard nothing you say or do will ever budge me." Jae flashed him a warning glance.

"Well, now, I can't have that, can I?" Night Hawk said, chuckling beneath his breath.

He turned to her and swept her up into his arms and carried her toward the cabin, ignoring her ranting and raving and how she kicked and pummeled his chest with her fists.

His eyebrows raised when she included in her vocabulary a few choice curse words, the likes of which he had only heard in brawls in saloons!

He laughed to himself for thinking only a little while ago that she was so vulnerable, that he wanted to protect her. It seemed that this little hellcat had long ago learned the art of defending herself.

He smiled when her struggles waned. Night Hawk could hardly believe it when she gently lay her cheek against his chest. He had to wonder if she was trying to dupe him by pretending to give up and be sweet like the magnolia blossoms that bloomed overhead in the trees.

He was not sure if he liked this game. She did seem to have lots of tricks up her sleeve, which she surely had learned from the outlaw she had grown up with!

He now knew that she was more of a challenge than he had perhaps bargained for when he had agreed to come and find her.

Having always enjoyed challenges, he smiled. She seemed the best of challenges!

Chapter Nine

Night Hawk gently carried Jae into the cabin. He was stunned that she still lay so quietly in his arms, her cheek still pressed against his chest, because she was asleep, and not because of some ulterior motive.

Now in the soft lamplight he gazed down at her and saw how sweet she looked. Her long, thick lashes were like beautiful black velvet veils against the pink flesh of her face. Her lips, so full and inviting, were slightly parted as she slumbered so peacefully, as though she belonged in his arms . . . as though she belonged to *him*.

His pulse raced as his gaze roamed lower. Where her half-buttoned shirt lay open, he could see the generous swells of her breasts. He had not touched them, yet he knew they would be soft, as soft as the petals of a rose.

His eyes ventured lower and he again took the liberty to look at her shapely legs. He had to wonder if she did not realize how legs affected a man. Did she not even realize how improper it was to display them so boldly?

He smiled. This difference in her, as well as everything else about her that was way different than anything he had ever seen in a woman before, made her so intriguing. His passion for her built into something he knew might be foolish, even *useless*, for she seemed hell-bent on ignoring the fact that he existed.

He knew that when she awakened, she would become that same defensive rebel who would escape his clutches at her first opportunity.

The fact that she had fallen asleep in his arms had had nothing to do with her feeling anything for him. It only proved that today's activities had taken their toll. She had become exhausted, perhaps mentally as well as physically, by the battle she had to fight to keep her life as it had been from the beginning.

He thought back to when *his* life had changed. At first it had been hard for him to accept the changes, to adapt to a life and a family that were totally strange to him.

Surely if *he* could do it, after having lived the life of a Comanche for the first ten years of his life, she could adapt to the changes that were needed.

But first he must get her away from the Thicket. Only then could her life begin anew. He felt that once she arrived at the "Wide Chaparral," she would be so impressed by it that she would find it easier to accept her new life and her true father.

A movement behind Night Hawk made him stiffen. His deep thoughts had distracted him from the need for caution. It had been foolish to forget that Jonas Adams could still be near. He was more of a threat to getting Jae from the Big Thicket than her stubborn refusal to leave. Now that Jonas had found her, surely he would not rest until he finished his last act of vengeance against her family by killing her.

"Night Hawk?"

Crying Wolf's voice made Night Hawk breathe a heavy sigh of relief.

He turned on a heel and stared blankly at Crying Wolf, who stood before him with something smeared all over the wound on his arm. He had even put on his breeches and moccasins.

To Night Hawk's surprise, Crying Wolf's moccasins were wet with mud. That had to mean that he had left the cabin while Night Hawk had been in pursuit of Jae.

"Is she injured?" Crying Wolf asked, walking stiffly toward Night Hawk, his eyes on Jae.

"She is all right," Running Hawk said, still stunned to see his old friend up and about, and confused about where he might have gone in his weakened state. "She is asleep. But you, Crying Wolf. How are you? What is that on your wound? And I see mud on your moccasins. Where have you been? Why?"

"I was wrong to talk badly of the Thicket," Crying Wolf said, gazing down at his arm. "It was generous to me tonight. It offered me many herbs for medicine for my wound. I searched and found what I needed. I am already healing."

"But Crying Wolf, I dug a bullet out of you," Night Hawk said, his voice low so that he would not awaken Jae. "Surely you were not strong enough to walk through the Thicket, let alone leave the bed."

"We will speak of it later," Crying Wolf said, placing a gentle hand on Jae's arm. "The woman will sleep much more comfortably in a bed. While you take her there, I shall sit by the door and keep watch for movement outside. We must not let down our guard until we leave the devil's pocket."

"After I get Jae to bed, I will keep watch through the rest of the night while you return to your bed and rest. We need to ride out of here tomorrow. And I will not take no for an answer. You have already pushed your luck by getting out of bed to search for herbs. If you had passed out from weakness, I would have not known where to look for you."

"*Huh*, I should have waited," Crying Wolf agreed, nodding. "But as it is, I am here safe. You are here safe. The woman is safe. Let us not dwell on what might have been. We must look forward to what should and *will* be. Tomorrow, after you get a turn to rest, and before darkness descends, we will ride from this place with the woman."

"Let us hope so."

"*Mea*, go," Crying Wolf said. "Get the woman to bed. She has a long day ahead of her."

Night Hawk nodded and carried Jae into the room that he concluded was her bedroom, since it was the only other bedroom in the cabin. The moon shone through the window, giving him enough light to see her bed.

A rag rug cushioned his feet and muffled his footsteps as he carried her to the bed. Slowly, gently, Night Hawk laid her on the bed.

His heart hammered inside his chest as he stood over her and gazed at her at length. Lying there so quiet and pretty in the moonlight, she was like a delicate flower he might have plucked from the forest floor. He longed to run his hands over her cheeks, to feel the softness of her flesh. He wished to fill his hands with her breasts. He hungered for her lips again, his remembrance of their one kiss causing his knees to become weak with desire.

107

Knowing that where his mind was taking him was dangerous, Night Hawk went to the foot of the bed and lifted a blanket to spread over Jae.

But he stopped and dropped the blanket back on the bed as he stared at her boots. They looked so stiff and uncomfortable. Surely she would sleep more soundly and comfortably if he removed them.

He decided to remove her boots and then leave the room to relieve Crying Wolf at the door. He knew, though, now that he had studied Jae while she slept, now that he had seen her alluring sweetness, that it would be hard to get her off his mind. While he watched the savage shadows of night, she would be there in his mind's eye. Her lips. Her beguiling eyes.

Jae stirred and sighed in her sleep, causing Night Hawk to flinch and return to his senses.

He watched her for a moment longer, to see if she was waking up. When he realized that she wasn't, he bent low over her and slipped off first one boot, then the other.

As he set the boots on the floor beside the bed, he gazed at her tiny feet and delicate, slender toes. He could not resist touching them.

Slowly, he reached his trembling fingers toward one of her feet. When he finally touched the flesh, he gasped at her milky-white softness. Slowly he ran his fingers over her feet and toes, and then let his fingers travel higher, to her ankle.

He had the strongest urge to kiss her ankles. He brushed a kiss across one of them, and then across the arch of one of her feet, this boldness causing flames to ignite anew in his loins.

Feeling too reckless, knowing that he wanted more than this and could not take it, he started to move away from her, but stopped when she let out another soft sigh in her sleep and then rolled slowly to her right side.

Seeing her total innocence, her vulnerability, and feeling ashamed for having taken advantage of her in her sleep, Night Hawk covered her with the blanket, tucking it beneath her chin. He left the room and closed the door behind him.

Then a thought sprang to his mind. The window. What if she was feigning sleep and escaped through the window at her first opportunity?

He slowly opened the door again to take another quick look at her, to see if she had left the bed and was preparing to leave. When he found her soundly asleep, lying curled up in a ball, Night Hawk sucked in a breath of relief, then closed the door again. But this time he went back into the parlor where Crying Wolf stood guard, his eyes peering through the broken window.

Crying Wolf heard Night Hawk's approach. He turned toward him. "She still sleeps?"

"*Huh*, yes, and I hope she does not awaken until morning," Night Hawk said. He lifted a rifle into his large hand. "If she still has escaping on her mind, there is a window in her room that would make it easy."

"Position yourself outside between the window and door. Then you will not have to worry about it," Crying Wolf said, laying his rifle aside. Weary-eyed, he ambled toward the door that led to the narrow hallway. "I am often not one to need rest as much others who are my age. But my body has never before had scars made by a white man's bullet. *Huh*, I must rest. I must feel strong enough for the long travel ahead."

Night Hawk waited for Crying Wolf to leave the

room, then he grabbed up a chair and left the cabin. He did as his friend had cleverly suggested: He sat down between the window and the door. There would be no way that Jae could escape without his seeing her.

He stared at Jae's bedroom window at length, envisioning her just inside it, lying sweetly on the bed, for the moment at peace with herself.

He watched the window, and then the door, and then found himself drifting off, his eyes burning with the need to sleep. His head bobbed. The grip of his fingers loosened on the rifle. And then a sudden night sound, a loon's eerie cry, brought him quickly awake again.

Repositioning himself in the chair, straightening his back, and forcing his eyes to stay open, he gazed ahead into the shadows of the Thicket. Things were now so still, so peaceful, so sweet smelling, there seemed no way that only a while ago there had been a gun battle raging here.

Thinking about the outlaw's sudden attack made Night Hawk grip the rifle more determinedly and his jaw tightened. He kept a steady watch, then he started when he heard the telltale squeak of a window being raised. He turned his head with a jerk and watched, his lips parted in dismay, as Jae crawled through the window.

The moon was too low now for Jae to see Running Hawk sitting there. She crawled out of the window, a small derringer in her right hand. Her back against the cabin, she started inching her way along its side.

"Going somewhere?" Night Hawk suddenly said, startling Jae so much that she raised her gun and fired it, the bullet just barely missing Night Hawk's head.

Angry, frustrated, and downright tired of Jae's foolish tactics and her inability to realize what was best for her, Night Hawk stamped over to her, glaring.

Pale, realizing now her mistake, Jae took an unsteady step away from him.

"You foolish, ungrateful, stubborn *tosi-mah-ocuak!*" Night Hawk said from between clenched teeth as he grabbed the derringer from her. "White woman, you almost killed me. Is that what you want? You do know, do you not, that is the only way to rid your life of me? Are you so devoted to this hellhole of a life that you would kill me to assure yourself of staying, so you can again be the target of that madman Jonas Adams?"

"I didn't know you were there," Jae stammered. "And, no, I don't want you dead. Lord, you are . . ." Afraid of revealing too much of her feelings to him, she let her voice trail off.

"I thought you were in bed for the night," Night Hawk said, glaring down at her. "You *do* have a long journey ahead of you. You will be riding with me, Jae, no matter how many times you try to escape. If you did manage to elude me, do you not know that I would search until I found you again? And not only because your father wishes to know you. But also because of my . . ."

Having come that close to telling her that he had deep feelings for her, Night Hawk stopped.

"Because of your what?" Jae asked, searching his eyes, her heart racing. She could not erase the memory of how it felt to be kissed by him from her mind! He had kissed her with such feeling, with such *passion*. He did care for her . . . as she cared for him.

Yet she still could not help fearing such feelings,

for she had vowed long ago never to love a man. The men she had known before were a sordid lot, and she'd feared they were a fair representation of the sex.

But Night Hawk was so kind and gentle, he banished her fears! She was afraid to let down her guard, afraid that his behavior was just a ploy to get his way with her.

Surely once he delivered her to her father, he would go his merry way and return to the arms of whatever woman he had been with before Jae came into his life!

"Get back inside the house," Night Hawk mumbled, ignoring her question. He took her by the wrist and led her to the door. "Your escape plan was foiled tonight. And I have learned by your sneaky, devious ways not to take my eyes off you. I will make you a pallet in the parlor and keep watch on you while I also keep a lookout for that damn outlaw."

"I wasn't attempting to escape again," Jae said softly. "I was just going to get my opossums and bring them into the house. I don't have much more time left with them. I . . . I know they can't make the journey with me to my father's house. I know that I will soon have to say a final farewell to them."

She gave Night Hawk a soft, pleading look as he gazed down at her.

He was touched by her genuine sweetness. Should he trust her?

"Please?" she murmured. "Let me go and find Sam and Mama Opossum. I do love them so. I am going to miss them so terribly much."

Everything she said seemed to support her claim that she had decided not to fight leaving the Thicket. Night Hawk sighed deeply, hoping that she was not playing a trick on him. He did not see how she could suddenly do an about-face and be so cooperative with him.

He gazed at her a moment longer, then nodded. "*Kee-mah*, come on. I will help you find the opossums. Then, young lady, I insist that you go back to bed and stay this time. Dawn is fast approaching, and with it comes the beginning of our two-day trip back to your father's ranch."

"He lives only two days from the Big Thicket?" she asked, her eyes wide. "He has lived this close to his first wife and daughter, and he was not even aware of it?"

"And so you do finally see the cruelty of it all?" Night Hawk said, touched by her remark.

"Perhaps so," she murmured, lowering her eyes.

"Jae, Jae." Night Hawk swept an arm around her waist, drawing her against him. "You can be so sweet."

Jae gazed up at him. Her pulse raced as he brought his lips down on hers in a deep kiss. This time she did not struggle to get free. Inside herself she knew that she was already his.

Chapter Ten

Riding astride a strawberry roan on the leather saddle that had been a birthday gift from the man she had always thought was her father, Jae was trying to put on an air of confidence. In truth, her insides were quivering like jelly. She had given in and had agreed to leave the Thicket.

She could not deny the excitement she felt. No longer would she have to live in hiding. Perhaps soon she would have the comforts and wear the sort of clothes she had only been able to dream about before.

She also wanted to include Night Hawk in her life somehow, without making herself look foolish. Having such feelings for a man was new to her. Until Night Hawk, she had thought all men revolting and disgusting.

But she could not help feeling that Night Hawk and Crying Wolf still did not trust her. They rode on each side of her, as if to curtail any attempt to escape.

The three of them were making their way through

the Big Thicket, to the wide open spaces and a new life that was more than a little frightening to Jae. But her curiosity was building. The closer they came to leaving the Thicket, the more her heart pounded.

The trail they were following cut through several species of oaks, among them the massive, gnarl-limbed live oaks whose branches spread out luxuriously overhead. Spanish moss draped from limb to limb, filtering the light, yet allowing the breeze to pass through the foliage.

Jae could hear the familiar loud staccato hammering of a pileated woodpecker echoing through the forest. The fiery wattles of wild turkey gobblers in their springtime finery drew her attention, reminding her of the pets that she had left behind.

She would never forget the tug of her heart as she had hugged her opossums for the last time. She had searched and searched for Snoopy, to give *him* a farewell hug. But Snoopy and her precious pet squirrels seemed to have disappeared from the face of the earth since those moments of gunfire and mayhem.

After packing her horse with the few belongings that meant something to her, Jae had left the cabin, making sure the door was propped open so that her animals could come and go as they pleased. Until now, they had shared it with her.

Now it was altogether theirs. They would have a place to go when storms hit. They could still cuddle in their blankets and boxes. They would take delight, she was sure, in going through the kitchen shelves, whereas before she had scolded them if they got anywhere near them.

She smiled when she envisioned them getting in her mother's flour bin, their noses turned white from the flour.

She had purposely left them some turtle dove eggs that she had found only this morning while taking one last stroll to her mother's grave, to say her final goodbye. She had left the eggs on the floor in the kitchen just before leaving the cabin. She knew that her pets would sniff them out before she had gotten out of eyesight of her home.

Flicking tears from the corners of her eyes, Jae rode over a rich carpet of grass, liriope, moss, and myrtle. She rode past walls of shrubbery and vines that twined and twisted around the trunks of the trees, rising to the lacy canopy overhead.

"Do you see it?" Crying Wolf said, suddenly breaking the strained silence. "There is a bloody kerchief."

Night Hawk looked down at the path. He drew his rein tight, slowing his steed. He dismounted, stooping to examine the blood-soaked bandanna. "I am almost certain that is the blood of Jonas Adams," he said. "Your aim *was* good, Crying Wolf. I wonder how far he got with a wound that seeped so much blood?"

"I do not see how he got this far," Crying Wolf grumbled. He smiled smugly. "But the fact that he came this far without stopping to tend to the wound proves that he was afraid to stay in the Thicket. He surely did not know that he shot me. He expected us to follow him."

Night Hawk turned a slow gaze to Jae. "Jae, at least Jonas Adams is finally out of your life. He will have no idea that you have plans to live elsewhere. If he ever returns to the Thicket, all he will find occupying your cabin will be animals."

Jae paled. "I never thought of that possibility. If Jonas goes there and sees that I no longer live there, he might kill my animals."

"By the looks of the amount of blood he lost, I truly doubt he will be going anywhere except to his grave," Night Hawk said, chuckling. He reached a gentle hand to Jae's cheek, not so surprised now that she allowed it. Slowly she was letting down her guard in his presence. Their last embrace and kiss seemed to have been the true turning point for her. Since then, she had been totally cooperative.

Night Hawk would not allow himself to wonder why she was acting so sweetly. She did seem sincere now, even anxious to get to her new home and to meet her true father.

"Men like Jonas Adams don't die easy," Jae said flatly. "I've seen it many times. The wounded outlaws were brought to my mother for doctoring. I thought many of them were on death's doorstep, yet most were out wrecking havoc again in only a matter of days."

She looked over at Crying Wolf. "I am absolutely amazed at your recovery, Crying Wolf," she said softly. "You lost a lot of blood also. For a short while you were even unconscious."

"My body might be old, but my spirit and will-power are still as young as a brave's before he has been on his vision quest," Crying Wolf said, proudly lifting his chin. "And I have much faith in The Wise One Above, as well as the herbs I collected from the deep woods of the Thicket." He chuckled. "*Na*, you cannot keep this old man down for long. I have an eagerness to live life much longer than I have already lived."

The undergrowth alongside the trail had been disturbed here, as if someone had left the path. Tense and frowning, Night Hawk wheeled his horse to a stop and dismounted.

117

He handed his reins to Crying Wolf, who remained in his saddle. He slowly followed the trampled trail into the deeper shadows.

Jae slid from her saddle. She also handed her reins to Crying Wolf, then ran and caught up with Night Hawk.

He slid his pistol from its holster. Jae slid her derringer from its holster. Side by side, walking stealthily, they followed the signs that someone had passed that way before them.

Then they found where the person had stopped . . . at a river that bisected the Thicket.

"He came here for water," Night Hawk said, looking slowly around him.

Jae looked guardedly from side to side. "He must have traveled here on foot. He couldn't have gotten his horse through this thick brush."

"He probably left his horse back there, close to the path."

"This is such a peaceful place," Jae murmured, gazing at the bright green lily pads floating on the water's surface. "I visited it often. I shall miss it." At her right side, dogwood blooms laced the forest with white and pink petals.

A blue heron glided low over the water, then landed on a gnarled, yet beautiful limb that hung out over the river.

"I love rivers," Night Hawk said. "Rivers have a pulse. They are alive, almost spiritual."

"I have often thought the same about them." Jae was filled with wonder that their thoughts were sometimes almost the same, as though they were of one mind.

Night Hawk gave her a quick, surprised look. As each moment passed, he was becoming more intrigued by her. Now that she was behaving like a lady instead of a stubborn wildcat, he was drawn more and more to her.

She was a complex person. Despite the fact that she had never attended school, she was very intelligent. One of the personal possessions that she had brought from her cabin was a book of poetry that she had received from her mother on her sixteenth birthday. She even had a journal in which she made nightly entries!

Huh, he was intrigued by her. He only hoped that she could adapt to a new life that was so different from that which she had always known. He did not want her to be embarrassed by not knowing the proper way to do things. If so, she might flee right back to the Thicket.

He would make her want to stay; He would teach her patience.

"We had better get back to the horses," Night Hawk said, knowing that if they stayed there much longer, alone and with so much awakening between them, they would forget why they were there in the first place. He would kiss her, and she would allow it. He might even lower her to the ground and show her the many other ways a man could make her feel wonderful.

Jae only nodded. She knew that if she spoke out loud at this moment, her voice might betray her. She had felt something awakening between them earlier, but now it seemed stronger. She was almost afraid to delve into the mystery of their feelings. She knew so little of life! Surely the women he had always known understood how to please a man! She knew nothing.

Running Hawk reached out a hand for her. "Come

on, Jae. I think it's safe to assume that Jonas Adams isn't anywhere near here now. We will travel until dusk, then stop and make camp. By then we should be far from the Thicket."

Jae slid her derringer back into its holster, then smiled shyly at Night Hawk and took his hand. "I've so much to get used to," she said uncertainly. "Do you think I will be able to?"

"I do not doubt that you can do anything you set your heart and mind to," Night Hawk said, his eyes locking onto hers.

She gazed into his midnight-dark eyes a moment longer, then looked quickly away from him and lost herself in her thoughts again.

When they reached their horses, Night Hawk took another slow look around him, then looked up at Crying Wolf. "I have no idea where he went," he said thickly. "The trail stopped at the river."

"No, I found signs of his passing on the path ahead," Crying Wolf said. "I searched until I found them. I still believe he was alive when he left the Thicket. I fear we have to be on our guard for that man."

"And so we shall," Night Hawk said, swinging himself into his saddle. He decided not to help Jae into hers. She was too independent to allow a man such courtesies.

He hoped that in time she could see the good in allowing such courtesies—they would make her seem more feminine in the eyes of others. He did not want the cowhands at his father's ranch to ridicule her for her unique qualities; he knew that not everyone would find her differentness intriguing. There would be those who would enjoy making jokes about a woman whose hair was shorter than most men's and who wore cut off men's breeches, displaying a good bit of leg as though it was perfectly correct behavior.

Yes, he had his job cut out for him, but he would succeed at helping her learn the proper way to do things.

They rode on, and sure enough, only a short distance away they found signs that Jonas had passed that way ahead of them. Only when they left the Thicket and entered the tall swaying grasses did they lose his trail.

They rode onward, stopping often to water their horses and to give them time to rest. They stopped more than once to eat hurried meals that Jae had prepared from the small amount of provisions that she had been able to find on her kitchen shelves. Having had no time to prepare the pigeons she'd shot for eating, they had left them behind.

They rode until the sun touched the horizon and shadows began to lengthen all around them.

They made camp for the night beside a stream, where small fish splashed and sliced the water's glassy surface. Red-winged blackbirds nested near cattails. Roseate spoonbills, great blue herons, and cattle egrets waded in the shallow waters.

The embankment was decorated with morning glory vines, goatsfoot, and sensitive briars. A tiny tree frog hopped into the tall grass and disappeared.

Jae could not help being nervous as she lifted her travel bags from her saddle. Although she had already spent one full night with Night Hawk at the cabin, there had been too many things happening to keep them from actually being together.

Tonight was different. They felt free of the threat of Jonas Adams. Life seemed already to be changing for Jae. She could feel it the farther she got away from the Thicket. The silent thrill of what might lie ahead reverberated through her entire being. She had never thought that she would be so glad to be away from her only home.

She no longer even worried about her pets. They belonged there. They would learn to forage for food again; they would survive.

Tonight Jae would sleep beneath the stars. There would be no thick trees overhead blocking her view. And the moon! How beautiful it would be as she gazed at it without the interference of the large magnolias and live oaks!

She shivered at the excitement of it all, at the freedom she felt now that she had left that place of hiding and secrets.

"You see the beauty of the evening, also, do you not?" Night Hawk said as he stepped up beside her.

Jae hugged the one travel bag she still held to her chest, having placed the other one on the ground. She gazed up at the loveliness of the sky, where a few stars were already visible. They were so bright, so like diamonds, as they twinkled against the darkening heavens.

"I have never seen it quite like this before," Jae murmured. "I feel as though I am a part of the night."

"That is because you are finally free," Night Hawk said softly. He placed his hands on her shoulders and turned her to face him. "From now on, you will discover many things that were deliberately kept from you. It is like being let out of prison."

"Yes, that is one way to describe my feelings," Jae said, laughing softly.

"Here, let me take your bag." Night Hawk felt her

stiffen at the suggestion and then slowly relax as she handed it over to him.

"Thank you," she murmured.

Night Hawk placed this bag with her other one and stared up at the sky again. "I have learned to enjoy a night like this to the fullest," he said, chuckling. "For in Texas, you never know when the weather will change abruptly."

She looked up at the sky, then jumped back and squealed with surprise when something crawled out of one of her bags.

"Snoopy!" she cried, kneeling and sweeping the raccoon up into her arms. "Oh, Snoopy, I thought I had lost you forever."

She hugged him to her and smiled sweetly up at Night Hawk. "He must have sneaked into my bag when I set it outside before placing it on the horse. Oh, Night Hawk, although I know you think it is best to put my past behind me, I can't. I must keep Snoopy."

"I would never ask you to leave him behind." Night Hawk bent to pet the raccoon.

When Snoopy snapped at him and hissed, Night Hawk drew his hand quickly away.

"Shame on you, Snoopy," Jae said. She giggled when he cuddled next to her and burrowed his nose into the crook of her arm, his eyes hidden from Night Hawk.

"I have caught our supper," Crying Wolf said as he came to them with a largemouth bass on the end of a long, pointed stick.

As Jae cuddled Snoopy in her arms, a fire was built and the fish was placed over the coals.

After they had eaten their fill, and had watched Snoopy eat his, Crying Wolf and Jae fell asleep almost immediately in their bedrolls. But Night Hawk found it hard to sleep. He had watched Jae write in her journal, and he stared at it now as it lay beside her travel bag. He could not help inching his hand over to get it, to read her entries.

But he yanked his hand away quickly when Snoopy appeared suddenly, spitting at him, and swinging at him with one of his little hands.

"All right," Night Hawk mumbled as he went to his own bedroll and slipped into it.

He still could not sleep. He could not help staring at Jae. He had learned a lot about her tonight as they talked during their evening meal. He had discovered that she was educated, sensual, and sweet.

He had discovered something else about her when she had admitted to him that she had always envied the ladies in Beaumont their fancy gowns and hats. She had said that she wanted to be like those ladies. She hungered to wear beautiful clothes and to have her hair long and flowing.

She had also spoken to him openly about her fear that she might look stupid and awkward since she had never been around proper ladies before. Her mother had grown rough from living the life of an outlaw's woman. There had been no reason for her to teach Jae proper etiquette.

Night Hawk had convinced Jae that things would be just fine, that she was an intelligent person who would learn quickly. She had grown excited, saying that she was ready to live life to the fullest, that she had been poor for too long!

That remark had bothered Night Hawk. He did not want the money and the fancy dresses and jewelry to change her too much, or else she would turn into the same sort of woman that had always left him cold. He wanted her to remain sweet and innocent.

He longed to go to her bedroll and hold her. He wanted to ask her not to change, to stay the same, to be the woman he had fallen in love with.

"Only time will tell." He sighed.

He closed his eyes, then flinched when he felt something crawl up next to his bedroll. He could not believe his eyes when he saw Snoopy lying there, ready to be his sleeping companion.

Night Hawk smiled. He had won points tonight, not only with this lovely, challenging woman, but also with her beloved pet.

"Want to come inside the bedroll with me?" Night Hawk whispered, rolling back one edge of his blanket so that the raccoon could crawl in beside him.

He was not aware of warm, loving eyes on him as Jae watched a bond beginning between him and her pet. Content, she closed her eyes and again fell into a soft slumber.

Chapter Eleven

Gunfire awakened Jae. Instinct drew her hand quickly to her rifle, which she had placed beneath her blankets. Looking guardedly around her, into the predawn darkness, Jae scrambled to her feet.

When she found Night Hawk crouched over her raccoon down by the stream, she went pale with alarm. Snoopy was lying on his side, his little hands curled up beneath him, his eyes closed. Had Night Hawk shot her pet?

But no! That didn't make sense! The last thing she remembered before closing her eyes was Night Hawk welcoming Snoopy beneath his blankets. She had thought they were becoming friends. She couldn't think of anything that Snoopy could have done to rile Night Hawk into shooting him.

Anger swept her puzzled thoughts aside. Her jaw set, she crept up behind Night Hawk. She placed the barrel of her rifle between his shoulder blades. "You no good, lying polecat," she hissed out. "I trusted you. Now I know how stupid I was to turn my back on you. How'd I ever trust you with Snoopy? Why'd you have to kill him? Why?"

Night Hawk stiffened when he felt the barrel of the rifle at his back. He couldn't believe that Jae was so angry with him. But when she spoke of her pet, it all made sense to him. It *did* look like he had shot the raccoon. He had fired his rifle, but apparently she had not been awake to see what he was aiming at.

He felt lucky that he had awakened when he did, or Snoopy *would* be dead, instead of only stunned by the coyote that had come sneaking into camp. He had seen the coyote stalking Snoopy as the raccoon went down to the stream for a drink of water.

"You have it all wrong," he retorted. "I did not shoot your raccoon. I rescued it. A coyote had it cornered. Seems your raccoon fainted from fear, not only from the coyote's presence, but from the gunfire."

Jae slowly lowered her rifle. "Snoopy . . . fainted?" she said, then smiled when she recalled the other times her raccoon had fainted when it had been cornered by various animals.

She dropped her rifle and knelt down beside Snoopy. She lifted her raccoon into her arms and hugged him close. Her eyes wavered as she gazed at Night Hawk. "I'm sorry," she gulped out. "I guess I have a ways to go before I can learn the art of totally trusting someone. I am truly sorry that I . . . I thought that you would harm my raccoon."

Night Hawk was torn between being angry at how quickly Jae had turned on him, and feeling sympathetic toward this woman whose life had been filled with reasons not to trust. Probably she had been forced to be on guard at all times against the men who frequented her home. Outlaws were the lowest form of animal on the earth, and she had been forced to live among them.

He understood how she had been hardened, through and through, and that it would take some time for her to change. He would help her see, and believe in, the goodness of others.

"Snoopy must have been awakened by Crying Wolf when he rode off a while ago," Night Hawk said, reaching a hand to pet the raccoon. "I thought Snoopy was still asleep in my bedroll when I bid my friend farewell."

Jae looked over her shoulder at the campsite, then turned questioning eyes back at Night Hawk. "Where did Crying Wolf go?" she asked warily. "Why did he leave?"

"I urged him to go on to the ranch and tell your father that you are on your way there," Night Hawk said softly. "Also, I wanted him to see to his wound. Doc Rose doesn't live far from our ranch. I advised Crying Wolf to go there and let him take a look at his arm."

"But I thought that it was healing quite well," Jae said, smiling when Snoopy's eyes fluttered open. She placed her hands on each side of his face and kissed his shiny black nose. "Hi, sweetie. Sorry you got a fright."

"I sometimes worry that Crying Wolf puts too much faith in his herbs," Night Hawk said, rising slowly to his feet. "I have seen too many arms amputated from gangrenous wounds. I don't want to see that happen to my old Comanche friend."

"You are very close to him, aren't you?" Jae asked, rising to her feet beside Night Hawk.

"*Huh*, we are bonded as brothers might be," Night Hawk replied. He eyed her rifle, then her, then bent low and picked up her firearm for her. She took it as he handed it to her.

They walked back to the campfire, where last night's embers were still glowing orange, and where flames were just awakening around the fresh wood that Crying Wolf had placed in the circle of rocks. Crying Wolf had even taken the time to set a fresh pot of coffee in the coals before he left. The smell of fish baking over the flames filled the morning air.

"Your friend thinks of everything," Jae said as she sat down on a blanket beside the fire. "I'm suddenly starved."

Night Hawk slid two wooden plates out of one of his travel bags, and then two tin cups. "A little excitement always arouses my appetite," he said, chuckling. He scooped some of the fish onto the two platters, poured two cups of coffee, then settled in beside Jae to eat.

Wild turkeys roosted in the giant pecans along the stream; the water gurgled peacefully in the river. Content, Night Hawk watched Jae feed bits and pieces of the fish to her raccoon, touched by how the animal ate the food with its hands like it was part human.

Then he watched Jae herself, taken anew by her loveliness. When she was relaxed and smiling, she was nothing less than ravishing. He could envision her in a lovely, long dress, the skirt billowing out from her tiny waist. He could hear her laughter as she swirled and twirled in delicate slippers, for the first time in her life feeling like a true lady!

He gazed at her hair and saw how it might look when it grew and fell in soft swirls around her milky-white shoulders. He imagined himself running his fingers through her hair, and then drawing her into his arms and kissing her.

"Do you realize that you are staring at me?" Jae said, interrupting his train of thought.

Night Hawk stiffened, then gave her a slow smile. "Yes, I guess I was. You are something to look at, you know."

Jae felt a blush rising to her cheeks. She turned her eyes away. She wasn't used to such compliments. Growing up surrounded by outlaws, she had been treated like one of them. Never had she felt pretty. Even when she left her girlish figure behind her and her breasts filled out, and the men looked at her more than what was decent, none of them ever said anything. The outlaws were too vile to compliment a lady. Their thoughts were only on their salacious hungers and how they might be quenched by such a body as hers.

She was thankful that none of those men ever ventured to touch her, and that they took their hungers to women who were paid to raise their skirts for them!

"Jae," Night Hawk said, leaning to place a finger beneath her chin, "I just paid you a compliment. How do you feel about that?"

Jae turned slowly to him. "How *should* I feel?" she murmured. "I have never been paid such compliments before."

"Well, Jae, I would hope that you believe me. I think you are beautiful."

He placed a hand on the nape of her neck and drew her close to him. "I want to kiss you, Jae," he whispered, brushing her lips with a soft kiss. "Jae?"

Jae's heart was pounding so hard that she could hear the thunder of its beating in her ears. She had never felt desired until now. She had never felt this rush of passion that being with Night Hawk caused.

"I . . . want . . . to be kissed," she stammered out, closing her eyes as his lips crushed down upon hers. Breathless, she twined her arms around his neck and returned his kiss with abandon.

Night Hawk slid his hands down to her waist and slowly lowered her to the ground. While still kissing her, he knelt over her and slipped a hand beneath her shirt. He heard her intake of breath and felt her tremble as he slid his fingers on up, across her belly, and then filled his hand with the soft sweetness of one of her breasts.

Jae was stunned by how it felt to have her breast touched by a man. It was so delicious that she felt faint from the pleasure. Never had she thought that being with a man could be so wonderful.

She was afraid of her feelings, yet she could not resist giving in to them. She wanted to experience it all with Night Hawk. He was so gentle, so caring.

And she did not think that he was taking advantage of her. The way he touched her and kissed her made her feel as though he genuinely cared for her!

Night Hawk gently kneaded her breast, his thumb tweaking the nipple. He loved the way she responded to his caresses. He could feel her hunger in the way she returned his kiss.

He could tell that she had been neglected for too long. The woman in her had been locked away—until now.

He smiled to realize that it was he; no one else, who was awakening the desire in her, who was teaching her that a man could be gentle.

He found himself lost, heart and soul, to this woman. In a sense, she was teaching him things that *he* had never known. He now knew how it truly felt to love a woman, a woman he knew that he could never live without! If his adoptive father had never sent for Jae, it would have been a terrible loss to Night Hawk, for he would never have known her.

Jae ran her hands down Night Hawk's muscled back, then moved her hands around to the front and slid them up inside his shirt. She ran her hands slowly over his muscled chest, and then slid them downward.

Boldly she undid his breeches and then slipped one hand down into them.

Night Hawk scarcely breathed as Jae's fingers found his manhood. He knew that she was inexperienced, yet it seemed that curiosity was guiding her.

And he would not argue with that. He loved the feel of her fingers on him. He sighed and closed his eyes when she ran them up and down the full length of his sex.

Moaning, hardly able to stand the pleasure her hands were invoking in him, he leaned away from her. His eyes locked with hers as he drew her hand from inside his breeches.

As they gazed at one another, he slid his breeches down. He tossed them aside, then brought her hand to him again.

"Feel my heat," he said huskily, flinching with pleasure when again she circled him with her fingers. "This is *your* heat. Claim it."

Jae's pulse raced as she turned her gaze down to what her hand encircled. She slowly moved her fingers on him, soon realizing just how much pleasure this gave him.

Night Hawk leaned back, closed his eyes, and enjoyed her caresses a moment longer. But knowing that this was not the way he wished her first sexual experience to be, he shoved her hand aside and rose to his knees beside her.

"Now let me touch you," he said, slowly removing her shirt. "Let me teach you how it feels to be pleasured."

Jae scarcely breathed as he removed the rest of her clothes, then urged her down onto the blanket on her back, his eyes slowly raking over her.

"I feel so . . . so . . ." she stammered, but did not get the chance to say any more. His lips were on hers, hot and frenzied. His hands were all over her, gently caressing.

And when his fingers touched that throbbing place between her legs, she felt as though she were going to melt from the pleasure it gave her.

And then he blanketed her with his body. She could feel the heat of his manhood pressing into the flesh of her belly. Just the feel of it there, hot, heavy, and long, made her head reel with ecstasy. She reached for him and moved her hand on him again, loving the way he moaned against her lips, proof that she was again giving him pleasure.

"Jae, Jae," Night Hawk whispered, his heart pounding. He shifted his body and placed his heat against her own pulsing heat. He softly probed. "Jae, tell me you want me. Tell me you won't regret it later. This that we are about to do is something that should be equally wanted, equally shared. Tell me you want me, Jae. Tell me that you love me."

Having never been with a man in this way, nor having had the need to confess her feelings to him as she wished to now, Jae felt a sudden clumsiness.

She *did* want him.

She had never wanted anything as badly as this!

133

Cassie Edwards

Yet she was afraid that she would not measure up to the other women Night Hawk had had in his lifetime. He was a masculine, virile man! Surely he had bedded many beautiful, skilled women. They would know how to please him. She knew nothing about pleasing.

Then another thought came to her that sent chills up and down her spine. Oh, Lord, she had never even asked him if he was married! Or if he had a woman waiting for him! Was he taking advantage of her because he knew she was so ignorant of these things? How *could* he want someone like her, when surely there were many lovelier women at his beck and call?

With the strength of a man, Jae shoved Night Hawk away from her. Sobbing, she rose to her feet and ran away from him. She fell to her knees beside the river and held her face in her hands.

She flinched when a hand fell on her shoulder. She tried to ignore Night Hawk. She tried to close her ears to his words as he began talking softly and pleadingly with her.

"Jae, I'm sorry," Night Hawk said, his voice breaking. "I wanted you so badly, I did not use common sense about it. Jae, I've brought you your clothes. Get dressed. We'll break up camp and go on to your father's ranch. Forget my stupidity, Jae. I never should have thought you were ready for someone to love you . . . for someone to love you as *I* love you. It will take a while for you to get adjusted to a man loving you."

"Surely there are other women," Jae blurted out, turning to face him. "Surely you have a wife. You are such a handsome, wonderful man. Surely you don't want me. I'm someone who has never known men in this way before. I'm so inexperienced."

He dropped her clothes and placed his hands at her waist. He drew her to him. "There *have* been many women in my life," he said softly. "But none I have wanted to take as a wife. When I saw you, my heart was lost to you. I love you, Jae. I have never loved anyone else."

"But how could you?" Jae said softly. "I am so plain. I am so simple."

"You only think those things about yourself because no one has ever told you otherwise," Night Hawk said thickly. "Jae, you are more woman than any I have ever known before. I want you. I need you. But I won't rush things. I want you to get used to having a man to love you. We will make love, but not now. I want you to be comfortable with the love-making. I want you to want it as badly as I want you."

"You make me feel things I have never felt before," Jae murmured. "Such wonderful, glorious feelings. Love me now, Night Hawk. Please love me now."

"I truly think it is best to wait until later," Night Hawk said, brushing a soft kiss across her lips. "Let us go now, Jae. Your father is waiting."

Jae smiled softly at him, gave him a hug, then hurried into her clothes.

As they rode away from the campsite, Jae was filled with a peace she had never felt before. She had a man who truly loved her!

And he was noble and wonderful. He could have had her sexually and he had denied his need. Any other man would have taken advantage of the situation. But Night Hawk had chosen to wait until she was truly ready for the experience.

It was wonderful to be respected and loved by such a man as he. She hoped that she would never disappoint him.

Chapter Twelve

Night Hawk gave Jae a quick glance as they approached the outer pastures of Ralph Hampton's huge ranch. After he had told her that they were near her father's ranch, she had become quiet. He knew she was apprehensive about coming face to face with Ralph Hampton, her true father. And she had to be thinking about the new life her father would offer her. It would be the total opposite of what she was used to.

Yes, he could understand her wariness. He remembered when he had had the same reservations, on that day, as a child of ten, when he had been brought to this new world. He had been frightened of how it would be to live away from his people.

But it had not taken long for him to realize that he had been wrong to be afraid of the family who had taken him in. They had not only offered him love and understanding, but also everything a young boy could want.

Since that day, Night Hawk had walked with head high and never looked back to how it had been. He always reminded himself that his Comanche father had forsaken him. He had abandoned him as though he were no more than a dog found useless by its master.

"Jae," he quickly said, "tell me more about yourself. Tell me about your mother."

He urged her to do this to take her mind off her worries. He knew that it would be useless to try to convince her with mere words that this life she would be entering would be something she should accept with a glad heart. This was something only she could discover, by doing.

"My mother?" Jae said, staring at the widespread, two-storied ranch house that suddenly appeared on the horizon. Knowing whose house it was, she swallowed hard.

She turned a quick glance at Night Hawk. Her mother had only been dead a short time, and it was still hard to talk about her. The hurt was too fresh in her heart.

Yet she felt the need to talk. It might alleviate her fears. After Night Hawk had told her about her true father, and the circumstances surrounding his paralysis, she worried that Ralph Hampton might have an ulterior motive for sending for her. If he still carried hatred in his heart for his first wife, might he not also hate his wife's daughter? Just seeing Jae might make him see his wife, for it was true that Jae was the spitting image of her mother.

"Tell me how you came to be called Jae," Night Hawk said. "That is more a man's name than a woman's. Did your mother choose the name? Why do you wear men's clothes?" He glanced at her cut-off breeches, then gazed up at her again. "Why do you wear your breeches cut off?"

"That's an awful lot to answer at once," Jae said, laughing softly. "But I will try."

She paused. "Because my outlaw father had men at his house so often, my mother and I were forced to live differently from other women," she explained. "Actually, Night Hawk, I hate the way I've been forced to dress. But it was necessary. Mother and I wore men's clothes to keep the outlaws from looking at us as female, since most went weeks without bedding a woman. And my name, Jae, sounds like a man's, but in truth, it isn't. A man's name is spelled J-A-Y. Mine is spelled J-A-E. It was just another part of the disguise that was forced upon me and my mother. My father named me, not my mother, but she chose the spelling. My father never knew the difference since he could not read even the first line of a book."

"And the cut-off breeches?" Night Hawk persisted.

"That was my personal way of rebelling over being forced to wear these ugly clothes," Jae said, laughing sarcastically. "The first time my father saw them, he lost all his color. When he told me to sew the bottom halves back on, I absolutely refused." She smiled smugly. "He got used to it," she said softly.

Then she grimaced as she touched her hair. "But the short hair was something that I hated most of all," she said, her voice drawn. "The first time my father held onto me while one of the outlaws cut my hair, I struggled hard to get free. I didn't want my hair cut. I . . . I have always loved long and flowing hair on women! But he made me wear my hair like this because I refused to wear the longer breeches."

"It does not make much sense," Night Hawk replied.

"Not much about my life as a recluse does." Jae swallowed hard.

"Yet you said that you loved the man who raised you," Night Hawk said, arching an eyebrow.

"In many ways I loved him. In many ways I hated him."

"Jae, you mentioned having played poker at a saloon. Did you do that often?"

Jae laughed softly. Her eyes brightened with memories. "Yes, as often as mother and I could sneak away from the Thicket. When father was gone on one of his outlaw raids, we took advantage of his absence and went into Beaumont and had some fun of our own."

"Playing cards?" Night Hawk asked, catching sight of the wide gate that led into his father's estate grounds. He kept Jae busy talking so that she would not realize that she was this close to her father's house. "Is that all you did?"

"No, not entirely," Jae said, in her mind's eye recalling how she and her mother would stroll down the boardwalks of the town, mingling with the other women, drawing their shocked stares. "We mixed with the crowds and had as much fun as the next person. With our wide-brimmed hats pulled low over our brows, and our hair hidden beneath the crowns of our hats to hide our true identity, mother and I played many a game of poker in the gambling halls. And when we weren't playing cards, we strolled along the broadwalks gazing into the windows, dreaming of a time when we could wear frilly dresses and fancy hats."

She became suddenly, sullenly somber. She lowered her eyes. "My mother never got the opportunity to dress as a lady," she said. "She never dared bring a dress into my father's house. Not especially a fancy hat!"

She gave Night Hawk a pensive stare. "Mother would have been so beautiful dressed up like a lady," she said, her voice breaking.

"The same as you, once you are given beautiful dresses at your true father's house," Night Hawk said, feeling her hurt clean inside his heart, for she was now everything to him. "Jae, turn. Look. Your father's house is only a few feet away."

Jae turned her head slowly. Her eyes wide, she gazed at the huge, two-storied, widespread adobe house. She gazed at the beautiful flowers in the garden that ran across the entire front and side lawns of the house. She looked past the house and saw all of the outbuildings, and farther still, she saw the hundreds of longhorns and mustangs grazing in the pasture.

She turned wide eyes to Night Hawk. "He is truly a rich man," she gulped out. "And . . . he . . . truly wants me to be a part of this? It's no trick? He genuinely wishes to have me here because he wants me?"

"How could you think otherwise?" Night Hawk said, frowning over at her. "Do you think he would send me for you for other reasons?"

Jae turned her eyes away from him. She did not want him to realize just how fragile she was. In truth, her knees were shaking, her throat was dry, and her whole insides were trembling.

"I have always wanted something other than . . . than what I had," Jae murmured. "But I never allowed myself to hope for it." Her eyes suddenly danced with new thoughts. "Do you truly believe my father has pretty dresses for me? Do you believe I might even have pretty hats like those women I saw in Beaumont? Will I wear sparkling jewelry? Will I have a bedroom that is pretty? Do you think I might even ask to have lacy curtains at my windows? My life has been so drab, Night Hawk."

"*Huh*, yes, you will have anything and everything your heart desires." Night Hawk once again felt somewhat uneasy over this quick change he was seeing in her. If having possessions was so important to her, would it not truly change that innocence he loved about her?

No, he would not think that anything could change that sweet side of her that he had grown to love. Once her vulnerability was shed, surely she would still remain as sweet and lovable as only moments ago, when she feared the very ground she now rode upon.

Jae glanced down at Snoopy, who slept soundly in a buckskin travel bag at the side of her horse. "What of my raccoon?" she suddenly blurted out—another reason to be afraid swimming through her insides. "He is used to sleeping near me. He is used to having the run of the house. If my father possesses riches and expensive furniture, surely he won't allow me to have my raccoon in the house with me."

Night Hawk reached over and touched her gently on the cheek. "Jae, your father will be so glad to have you with him, he will agree to anything you ask of him," he said softly. "Even your pet." He chuckled. "You might have to train Snoopy. I doubt Maxine, our cook, would approve of Snoopy running around in her kitchen. If she caught him climbing on the table, or on her work counter, she might want to take after him with the butcher knife."

Jae paled. "No, she wouldn't," she gasped out.

Night Hawk realized that he had jested about the

wrong thing. "Jae, I did not mean it," he said. "No one is going to do harm to your raccoon."

"But I know that I will have to train him to stay out of the kitchen," Jae said, patting Snoopy as he awakened and gazed up at her through his sleepy, dark eyes. "My raccoon can wreak havoc in a kitchen. I shall see to it that he stays in my room— at least until he becomes familiar with the entire house and what he can and cannot do in it."

The sudden tolling of a bell drew Jae's head quickly around. Her lips parted in surprise as she gazed at a woman sounding a bell just outside the door of the house.

"Who . . . is . . . that?" she asked, her voice drawn. "Why is she ringing the bell?"

"That's Rita, my father's personal maid, who will also be yours," Night Hawk said, waving at the woman. "Sometimes when I have been gone for a long spell, and Rita just happens to spy me riding toward the house, she rings the bell as a welcome to me, and also as a way to reveal to my father that I am finally home."

"I hope that father will love me as much, so that when I come home from my daily shopping sprees in Abilene, Rita will also ring the bell for me," Jae said, her eyes wide with excitement.

Night Hawk gave her a quick, questioning look. He couldn't believe that she was already envisioning herself on shopping sprees in Abilene, when she had not even yet met her father and been offered such opportunities of the rich. Slowly he was seeing more of the side of her that worried him. If she wished more for possessions than anything else, where did that leave him?

"Night Hawk!" Rita shouted as he drew his mount

up close to the porch and dismounted. "We're so glad that you're home." She gave Jae a questioning gaze. "And . . . is this Jae?

Jae slid out of her saddle before Night Hawk could come and help her. She smiled at Rita and rushed onto the porch. She extended a hand of friendship. "Yes, ma'am, I'm Jae," she said, surprising herself at how easy it was to make the acquaintance of this stranger.

"My, oh, my," Rita said, easing her hand into Jae's. She stared at Jae through her thick-lensed glasses. "You are somethin' else, young lady. Somethin' else."

Jae's smile faded; she quickly became self-conscious about her apparel and her short hair. She eased her hand away, took an unsteady step away from Rita, then ran from the porch and stood beside her horse.

Night Hawk saw Jae's sudden uneasiness. He went to her and took her hand. "Jae, come on, Father awaits your arrival," he said softly.

Jae gave Night Hawk a weak smile, then slipped her hand from his and went and got her raccoon.

Cuddling Snoopy in the crook of her left arm, she reached her right hand out for Night Hawk. "I'm ready," she said, her voice unsteady.

Night Hawk gazed at the raccoon, then looked into Jae's eyes. He realized that she was using her pet as some sort of security blanket. He walked with her up the stairs.

Rita opened the door wide for them, her face pale as she stared at the raccoon.

Jae stepped on past her into a wide corridor that took her breath away. She saw a long corridor of beautifully shined hardwood floors. The walls were covered in lovely wallpaper, and she saw row after row of portraits in gilt-edged frames. Several doors led to different rooms along the full length of the corridor. And at the far right side, a huge staircase led to the second floor.

"Is Father up there?" she asked, gazing up the spacious staircase. "Is his bedroom up there?"

Night Hawk took her gently by the arm and led her toward a room at his left side. "No, he has not used those stairs since he became paralyzed. His room is on this lower floor so that he can be a part of everything that happens in his house. And until recently, he was able to use a wheelchair to travel from room to room on this lower floor."

"A wheelchair?" Jae asked, swallowing hard.

"*Huh,* yes, a wheelchair," Night Hawk murmured. "His health has recently worsened. He is now totally bedfast."

"I'm sorry," Jae said softly.

She paused just as they reached the door that would take her to her true father.

Chapter Thirteen

Panic in her eyes, Jae turned quickly to Night Hawk. "I can't!" she gasped. She turned her eyes down at herself, then looked pleadingly up at Night Hawk. "Look at me. How can I go and meet . . . meet my true father looking like this?"

"Darling, you don't have to," a woman's voice said from behind them.

They both turned at once.

Night Hawk smiled at his adopted mother and went to her with a big hug.

"I'm sorry, son, that I wasn't here when you first arrived," Lois said, caressing his back. "I was in Jae's room, seeing to her clothes and making sure her room was ready for her."

Wide-eyed, her hands clasped tightly behind her, Jae stared at the heavy-set woman who she now knew to be her father's wife. Her heart pounded as Lois's eyes turned to her, then she relaxed when Lois gave her a smile that proved she just might be a good woman, one with whom Jae would be comfortable.

Night Hawk stepped away from Lois. "Then you

know all about everything?" he asked, searching her eyes for answers.

"Yes, I know," Lois murmured. "And I welcome my husband's daughter into our lives."

"I knew that you would," Night Hawk said, then smiled over at Jae. "Jae, this is my mother."

Still somewhat afraid of these sudden changes in her life, Jae gave Lois a weak smile.

"My dear, it is so good to finally meet you," Lois said, taking Jae's hands as the girl took an unsteady step toward her.

Lois drew Jae closer and hugged her. "I have your room ready for you," she said softly. "You have a chifferobe full of new clothes. The room that is to be yours has been newly decorated. And when I heard you and Night Hawk ride up, I ordered a tub full of warm water. I, myself, poured the bubble bath in it. It awaits you, Jae. We will go and see that you are made more comfortable in fresh new clothes after a bubble bath. *Then* you can go to your father and be proud to show yourself off to him."

"Thank you," Jae said softly. "I didn't expect such kindness."

"You are home, Jae," Lois replied. She eased Jae from her arms and gazed at her hair. She ran her fingers slowly through it. "It was wrong of your mother to keep you from your father. It was a *sin*. And your hair. Shame, shame."

"It will soon grow out. And I never plan to wear it short again." She gave Night Hawk a weak smile. "I want to be beautiful," Jae said.

Night Hawk returned his smile of reassurance, telling Jae in his silent way that she was already beautiful.

"Son, go and tell your father that Jae will be in to

see him soon," Lois said, whisking Jae away toward the wide, oak staircase. "Tell him that Jae and I are going to primp for a while, then come and say our hellos."

Night Hawk watched Jae and Lois until they reached the upstairs landing and disappeared down the long corridor. He then turned and looked at the closed door that led into the room where his father lay, waiting. Anxious to see him, and to set the record straight as to why Jae's presence at his side was delayed, he went into the room.

"Father?" he said, stepping up beside the bed. "How are you, Father?"

"Better," Ralph said, his voice stronger than when Night Hawk had last been with him. And he only barely wheezed when he talked. "*Much* better now that my Jae is where she belongs."

He leaned up somewhat from the pillow. "I saw her, son," he said, tears streaming from his eyes. "I had Lois fit more pillows beneath my head so that I could see better from the window. I saw Jae, son, as she rode up with you." He swallowed hard. "She's beautiful. Oh, Lord, I saw her face close enough to see just how much she looks like her mother. It's like looking at Penelope all over again, son. It's like she's come back to me, as though those years have not even been there to separate us."

Night Hawk was stunned to see his father's reaction. In truth, Ralph should hate his first wife with a vengeance, and here he was comparing Jae with her, talking about his first wife as though he still had feelings for her.

Throughout the years, Ralph had always spoken angrily of Penelope.

But now?

Seeing Jae there, her spitting image, it seemed that in that instant he had forgiven his wife for having abandoned him.

That's how Night Hawk hoped it was for his father. He was afraid that he might change his mood again and be that man who hated Penelope, and in turn, possibly hate Jae instead of wanting her for his daughter.

If Ralph decided that he had made a wrong decision in bringing Jae home, and he ordered her to leave, Night Hawk knew how devastated Jae would be. She had already seen the promise of a new tomorrow after living in hiding as though she were a criminal.

"She might look like her mother, but I am certain she is nothing like her," Night Hawk was quick to blurt out. He scooted a chair over next to his father's bed and sat down. "Father, Jae knows how to be loyal, for she was loyal to a fault to her mother and . . . the man who raised her. Father, she is sweet through and through."

Night Hawk heard something scratching at the closed door. He suddenly remembered Jae's raccoon, which she had absentmindedly placed on the floor just as she had entered the house.

"What might that be at the door?" Ralph said, his eyebrows arching.

Night Hawk chuckled beneath his breath. His father loved all sorts of animals. His many pets roamed the ranch: cats, dogs, rabbits . . . anything that had arrived, homeless, onto his property.

"I've got someone I'd like for you to meet," Night Hawk said, leaving the chair. He went to the door and slowly opened it. As though he belonged, Snoopy sauntered in, his dark and beady eyes assessing everything around him.

"A raccoon," Ralph said, his eyes dancing. "You said you had someone. Son, this here's a raccoon."

"Snoopy is so human, one tends to see him that way." Night Hawk swept Snoopy up into his arms and carried him over to the bed.

"Bring him to me," Ralph said, nodding his head. "Since my hands and arms have become stubborn of late, and won't cooperate when I want to move them, I can't pet him." He looked longingly at the raccoon. "Son, is he tame enough to place up close to my face? I'd like for you to rub his fur againt my cheek."

"He's never been known to bite unless threatened by something or someone," Night Hawk said, choking up with emotion when he held Snoopy's face against Ralph's cheek. Snoopy, in turn, reached his humanlike hand to Ralph's nose and touched it.

Ralph laughed throatily. "I think we're instant friends," he said as Night Hawk placed Snoopy on the floor. "Just let him roam where he pleases. As far as I'm concerned, he can own the whole damn place."

Night Hawk laughed softly, then turned somber eyes down at his father. "Father, I've so much to tell you about Jae. Should I now, before she comes to meet you? Or later?"

"If I know your mother, it will take a full hour for her to get Jae through her bath and to choose the right dress for her first meeting with me," Ralph said. "So, son, tell me how you found her, what sort of house she lived in, and how you encouraged her to return with you . . . to leave the Big Thicket."

His eyes filled with memories of these past days, Night Hawk leaned back in his chair and began telling it all to his father as Ralph listened, his eyes wide, his breathing anxious.

"The first time I saw her, I could hardly believe my eyes," Night Hawk said, chuckling low.

Chapter Fourteen

Jae could hardly believe her eyes as she stepped into a room bathed in sunlight. The room that had been readied for her was beautiful with its flower-designed wallpaper, sheer and lacy curtains at the two windows, and a white iron bed that was so big it took up half the one outside wall. And the bed was frilly from its skirt to the spread that covered it.

Flowers were in vases on tables on each side of the bed, filling the room with their heady fragrance. A soft, beige-colored carpet covered the floor.

Jae stepped farther into the room, gasping when she found a dressing table and many bottles of perfume mirrored in the huge, gilt-trimmed mirror above it.

Then she took a step away from a chifferobe that was open, revealing beautiful dresses and gowns hanging on wooden hangers inside it.

"Those are all yours," Lois murmured. "I had hoped that I had bought the right size." She sighed heavily. "And as you see, I did. You are now what I once was at the age of twenty. As I bought the clothes, I thought of myself and how I would have adored them when I was your age."

Jae dared to go to them. Her fingers trembled as she ran them over the silken fabrics. "They are so cool to the touch," she said, her eyes gleaming as she turned a soft smile to Lois. "Will I truly be wearing these?"

"Whenever you wish," Lois said, laughing softly. She took Jae by an elbow. "But first we must see to your bath."

She led Jae to a wicker screen, behind which stood a lavish copper tub, bubbles lapping at its sides.

"Lordy, I have never seen anything like *this*," Jae said, clasping her hands before her. "Back home, in the Thicket, I only had a shower that was rigged up just outside our cabin. It had no top to it." She giggled. "When I bathed, all of the stars in the heavens were my audience."

Lois paled. "How crude."

Jae grew somber. "Yes, the way I lived was quite crude," she murmured. "But it was all I knew. I dreamed of one day bettering myself. What young girl doesn't want better things when she has . . . has hardly anything."

She gasped and turned quickly toward the door. "Snoopy!" she cried. "I absolutely forgot about my raccoon!" She gave Lois a fearful glance. "What if he finds your kitchen? Will . . . will your cook kill him if he makes himself home in her kitchen?"

"A raccoon?" Lois said, placing a hand to her throat. "In my house?"

Then she brought her hand down and laughed softly. "Well, I must say, Jae, that's quite a surprise, but I think I can adjust." She began unbuttoning

Jae's shirt. "And don't worry about your pet," she murmured. "Maxine wouldn't dare take a butcher knife after it."

"Butcher knife?" Jae said, paling.

"Your raccoon is quite safe," Lois said, slipping Jae's shirt off.

Jae quickly grabbed the shirt back and hid her breasts behind it. "Ma'am, if you don't mind, I'd rather take my bath in private," she said. "I've never had an audience before. Not even my mama." She giggled. "As I said before, my only audience was the stars, sun, and moon." She laughed again. "And just perhaps a small forest animal or two over my head in the trees."

"Sweetie," Lois said, placing a gentle hand on Jae's cheek, "you can have all the privacy you want." She winced when she again looked at Jae's clothes. "Just get yourself clean and leave the clothes for me to burn."

Jae's eyes widened. "You will burn my clothes?" she murmured.

"Can you tell me that you truly want them after seeing the clothes that are in your chifferobe?" Lois said, her eyes twinkling as Jae suddenly shoved the shirt back into her hands. "I thought not, honey. I thought not."

Lois turned and walked toward the door. "Don't take too long, Jae," she said over her shoulder. "Your father is quite anxious to see you. He's waited a lifetime for this."

Jae waited until the door was closed and she was all alone. Laughing, her heart pounding, her eyes were anxious as she gazed at the sudsy water and all but ripped off the rest of her clothes.

When she sank into the warm, soft water, the suds clinging to her breasts, she held her head back and closed her eyes. "Thank you, Lord," she whispered, sighing heavily. "I do believe I am in Heaven."

Chapter Fifteen

The sound of footsteps behind him, entering his father's bedroom, made Night Hawk's heart skip a beat, for he knew whose they were. He had waited in anticipation of Jae's transformation into a lady, and he knew that it had been achieved. He could smell the perfume she was wearing wafting across the room toward him.

And he did not have to turn and look at Jae to know how beautiful she was. It was in Ralph's eyes as he stared at her, his lips parted in a gasp of wonder.

Night Hawk could also see tears swell in his father's eyes and knew that the transformation had not only enhanced Jae's loveliness, but also revealed to him just how truly she resembled her mother.

He knew this because he saw his father silently mouth his first wife's name as he continued to stare at Jae.

Knowing that it was dangerous for Ralph to think too much about the wife who had abandoned him, Night Hawk rose from his chair and turned to Jae. He had planned to go right to her and lead her on

155

into the room, but one look at Jae caused Night Hawk's thoughts to scramble. He forgot about his intention to help his father forget the past. All that he could think about was how beautiful Jae was.

Before, she had stolen his heart. But now she stole his breath as well.

His heart raced at the sight of her. The dress enhanced her loveliness, with its gathered waist, its white embroidered designs of flowers on a backdrop of blue silk, and its frills and lace at the low-swept bodice.

Her face was flushed pink with excitement. Her eyes were bright, her lips were red and slightly parted, and even her short hair was pretty, with the tiny sprigs of roses pinned into it above each of her ears.

Night Hawk could tell that Jae was nervous by the way she kept fidgeting with the folds of her dress. He knew that he must do something to make her feel more comfortable. For now, he had to place his enchantment with her aside. Later he would take her in his arms and tell her how beautiful she was.

He wanted her now with a fierce hunger that he had long denied himself. When he had chosen not to make love to her before, he had known that he would not be able to wait much longer.

And he knew she wanted the same. She would have completed their lovemaking had he not told her it was best to wait until later.

Later would be tonight, he vowed to himself.

He could not wait any longer to show her just how much he *did* love her!

Before Night Hawk had the chance to go to Jae, Lois led her into the room. She took Jae to the side of the bed opposite where Night Hawk stood.

"Ralph, this is your daughter Jae," Lois said. She clasped her hands before her as she looked Jae slowly up and down. She was proud of how she had transformed this wild thing into a thing of radiant beauty. "Jae, this is your father."

Night Hawk stood silently by, watching, then gasped when Ralph slowly lifted his arm, extending his fingers, which had recently lost their ability to move, toward Jae.

"And so you have come home to your father," Ralph said, wheezing from the excitement of the moment.

Jae felt too awkward to respond. She gave Night Hawk a pleading look. But he was still too shocked over having seen how Jae had caused her father to regain some of his ability to move.

Then Night Hawk slowly turned his eyes up at Jae. When he saw her uneasiness, and how she wasn't able to respond to her father just yet, he hurried around to that side of the bed and slipped an arm around her waist.

"You must excuse Jae, Father, for not responding." Night Hawk said. "This is all so new to her. It will take time."

"I understand. Jae, please take my hand. I have waited an eternity to see and touch you. I . . . only . . . wish I could be more presentable for you. I wish I could stand on my two feet like a gentleman and hug you."

Jae's hand trembled as she inched it toward his. Her heart went out to this man and how helpless he was, and all because of . . .

No! She would not think about the man who was to blame for all of this! He was no longer a part of her life. This man was her *true* father! And she did not want to show pity toward him. She could see the shame he felt at being an invalid.

"Father, it is so good to finally be with you," Jae forced herself to say, wishing she would truly feel something for him one day. He was a total stranger, yet, in truth, he wasn't. It was his blood that ran through her veins. He had fathered her, whether or not he had been there, physically, throughout her life. None of it was his fault. She could not cast blame anywhere but to . . .

Again she forced Clifton Coldsmith from her mind, even her mother, who had wronged this man perhaps more than anyone else.

She took her father's hand, then recalling what he had said about hugging her, she slipped her hand free and bent low over him and swept her arms around his neck. "Father, oh, Father, I'm so sorry about everything," she murmured, her voice breaking. "Had I known about you, I would have been here for you much sooner."

Night Hawk was relieved to see Jae finally open up and spill out her feelings to her father. Knowing they needed privacy, he slipped away from them. He turned and nodded to Lois.

She understood and left the room beside Night Hawk, closing the door behind them.

"I believe she has him totally mesmerized," Lois said, turning to Night Hawk. "She is quite beautiful, isn't she?"

"More beautiful than any woman I have ever known," Night Hawk said, glancing at the closed door.

"You are quite taken with her, aren't you, son?" Lois said, placing a gentle hand to his cheek. "You are in love, aren't you?"

"So it shows?" Night Hawk chuckled.

"When you look at Jae, your eyes say it all," Lois said. She grabbed him gently by an arm. "Come, son. Let's sit outside on the porch. Tell me all about it, how you found her, how you talked her into leaving the Big Thicket. Was it hard to do, since it has always been her home?"

Night Hawk glanced at the door of Ralph's room once again, then went outside on the porch and sat down on a rocker next to Lois, who was already slowly rocking back and forth, the breeze softly lifting her graying hair from her shoulders.

"The first time I saw Jae, I could hardly believe my eyes," Night Hawk said, waving at Crying Wolf as he stepped from the corral, leading a horse behind him.

He watched his friend mount the horse and ride away, his wounded arm causing one shoulder to hang somewhat lower than the other.

But it was obvious that Crying Wolf was past any danger of infection. His old friend was stronger than most men his age. It was just his memory that was sluggish.

Night Hawk hoped that one day Crying Wolf would share with him what he had recalled from his past. It was hard for the younger man to envision what it might be like to forget one's past. Yet perhaps it might be a blessing for someone like Night Hawk, whose past had so many bitter memories. He fought against them so often, he became weary of it all!

But now everything seemed right for him, since he'd met Jae. She was that one piece of the puzzle that had been missing in his life.

"Do you think Jae is going to be happy here, living such a different life?" Lois asked, drawing Night Hawk from his deep thoughts.

He gave her a slow smile. "From what I saw in there, Jae is going to make it here just fine," he said, chuckling. "And I do believe she is going to spoil father rotten."

His smile faded. "I can hardly believe how he lifted his arm and hand to her," he said. "I had expected quite a reaction from him when he set his eyes on his daughter for the first time, but never would I have thought she would have this sort of effect on him."

"It's God's blessing that has brought her here," Lois said, lifting her eyes heavenward. "I say praise the Lord for such miracles that I have seen today."

Night Hawk nodded, yet he could not help but feel some apprehension about his father's over-exuberance over Jae. If she ever chose to leave again because she missed her other life, it would devastate not only Night Hawk, but also his adoptive father.

"We'll have us a special dinner tonight to celebrate Jae's homecoming," Lois said, reaching over to pat Night Hawk's arm. "We'll have your father's favorites." She raised an eyebrow. "I wonder if Jae will enjoy the sort of food we eat. Living in the Thicket, I'm almost certain she never knew the likes of *arroz con pollo*, or *paella*. I am almost certain she has never had *vino de coyol*."

Night Hawk frowned over at his mother. "Let's not overwhelm Jae, Mother," he cautioned. "Give her time to get adjusted. Do it slowly. I would serve something simpler, like crab soup and roast capon and a La Rosa wine."

"Darling, you know that you are wasting words arguing with me, don't you?" Lois said, laughing softly. "And I say you are wrong to want to ease Jae into her new life in small measures. I think it will impress instead of frighten her. I see something in that child that I don't think you see."

Night Hawk arched an eyebrow.

Chapter Sixteen

The setting sun was casting a pink glow on the walls of the dining room. The lavish, long oak table was covered with a snowy white linen cloth. Tapers burned at each end. Food was piled high on expensive dishes brought over from China.

Night Hawk gazed around the table at everyone who was present, stunned that his father had managed to be there. He had asked to be moved from his bed and brought in his wheelchair, to have his first meal with his daughter.

Although it was obvious to Night Hawk that the chair was uncomfortable for his father, he continued to sit there, his face flushed red from his excitement that his daughter was there, so beautiful, so sweet, so caring.

Jae stared down at the sparkling silverware, at the beautiful china, and at the tall-stemmed crystal glass that sat before her. She had eaten at inns in Beaumont, but none had served food on such delicately beautiful dinnerware as this. Nor had she ever drunk wine in such expensive, beautiful glasses!

She glanced at the candles, the piles of food, and then gave Night Hawk a weak smile. He could see her uneasiness.

She turned slow eyes to her father. He was too blinded with happiness over her being there to see that she was not comfortable in this lavish setting. Yet there was a part of her that she could not deny enjoyed it . . . that part of her that wanted to be everything now that she never had been!

And she would be! As each new thing was introduced to her, she would learn from it. She would become her true father's daughter. She knew how important she was to him. While they had been alone, talking, she had discovered so much about him, and he about her.

The one thing that worried her was just how important she seemed to be to him. She never wanted to interfere in Night Hawk's closeness to his father. She wanted her father to recognize the importance of having a son, even though Night Hawk was not blood kin.

Nevertheless, he *was* a *son*.

Night Hawk had given his life to his father, running his business, keeping the ranch alive. If her father forgot all of this, in favor of her, she would not be able to bear it.

She gave Night Hawk another slow gaze, recalling something her father had said just before they had come to the dining table. He had said that his attorney was going to arrive tomorrow. Things needed to be changed in his will.

She prayed that the changes had nothing to do with Night Hawk!

As Maxine, the cook, made her way around the table, serving the food, Jae became anxious for the meal to be over, so that she could finally be alone with Night Hawk. It had been a long day. She needed his arms. She needed his lips, for he was truly all that was important to her. She had only pretended her feelings for her father. In truth, she saw him as little more than a stranger.

Night Hawk was all that was truly dear to her.

He caught Jae staring at him. He was not sure what he read in her eyes as she smiled at him, but he could not help but believe she was having needs that matched his own.

Tonight. The promise of tonight with Jae made his heart pound.

He returned the smile, then thanked Maxine as his plate was filled with the delicacies of his mother's choice. He saw Jae grimace as she stared at the food on her plate. He chuckled.

Chapter Seventeen

Feeling dejected, forlorn, and alone, Night Hawk gazed from his bedroom window as he lay naked on his back. Dinner in the dining room had come and gone. Jae had wheeled Ralph back to his bedroom, and she was still there when Night Hawk had retired to his room.

His plans for the evening had unraveled. He had not had the time alone with Jae that he had hoped for, that he had thought *she* wanted. Invitation was in her every look as she had gazed at him through the dinner.

No one had been any more surprised than he when she had jumped up from her chair and offered to wheel her father back to his room.

Ralph had given her a look of utter adoration when she had gone to him and kissed his brow before taking him away from the dining room. It was as though there had been no one else in the room. Suddenly it seemed that the world had become only two people . . . father and daughter, with no one else mattering.

After Night Hawk had gone to his room, he had

hoped Jae would follow shortly thereafter. But he had given up on that possibility long ago. It seemed that she had completely forgotten him, and he could not help feeling jealous.

He turned with a start when his door slowly opened. Standing there, outlined by the candlelight from the wall sconces in the corridor, was Jae.

"Night Hawk?" Jae whispered, taking another slow step farther into the room. "Are you asleep? I need to talk with you about something."

Unable to forget his anger at having been ignored by Jae ever since their arrival at the ranch, Night Hawk stiffened. He did not like being jealous. It was a new emotion for him, and he knew that he should not be jealous of his own father!

But he could not help having these feelings, for he feared that if Ralph took all Jae's time tonight, he might continue to do so. Night Hawk knew his father well; he knew how demanding Ralph could be. And as innocent as Jae was, she might feel it was her duty to cater to his needs until her father died.

If this happened, she would not have bettered herself by coming here. She would lead the same sort of isolated existence as she had in the Thicket. The only difference would be that this father was affluent and had wealth and power.

Yes, Night Hawk was jealous, and for all of the right reasons. He feared losing her.

As Jae came farther into the room, he glared at her. Despite his anger, he could not help the way his eyes roamed slowly over her, noting how delicate and pretty she looked standing there in the moonlight.

Jae wore a sheer, lacy nightgown, and the candle's glow behind her in the corridor filtered through the flimsy material, outlining her body as though she wore nothing at all.

He could see the gentle curve of her hips, her long, shapely legs, and then her breasts as she turned side-wise to close the door slowly.

When he saw the swell of her breasts, and could even make out the nipples through the thin fabric, he felt the heat stirring in his loins. He needed her. He wanted her.

The longer she stood there, the more he felt his anger waning. It was not hard to convince himself that he was wrong to be jealous. It was only right for Jae to show such devotion to her father. Night Hawk should not have wanted it any other way.

But he had not expected her to leave him out in the process. Night Hawk would have enjoyed being in the same bedroom as Jae and Ralph. He would have enjoyed seeing them becoming closer and shar-ing a love that had been denied them.

But Jae had not invited him in. Nor had his father. And a closed door meant something quite obvious to Night Hawk—that there was privacy desired on the other side!

"Night Hawk, I can see that you are awake," Jae whispered as she tiptoed toward him. "I see you in the moonlight."

She swallowed hard when she saw his nakedness. His muscles rippling beneath the moonlight caused her heart to flutter with need of him.

Her glance strayed down his body. She gulped hard and looked quickly into his eyes, feeling that was the safest way to keep her sanity. Her need for him was causing her knees to grow weak.

But at this moment, she had other concerns on her mind besides her need to be with Night Hawk!

"Night Hawk, why . . . why . . . are you treating me so coldly?" she blurted out. "Why don't you answer me?"

He leaned up on an elbow and glared at her. "Jae, why have you come now, when only a short while ago it was so obvious you did not wish to spend any time with me tonight? Do you know that I waited for hours for you to come to me? And why did you not at least ask me to join you in my father's room?"

"All of those questions are too much for me now," Jae said, now standing in the full moon's glow, which revealed her lips curved in a pout. "Night Hawk, I've come to ask if you've seen Snoopy. I haven't seen him since before dinner. Do you think he's got loose? If so, he is surely lost out there on grounds unfamiliar to him! I might never see him again!"

Night Hawk's eyes widened. She had come to his room not because of him, but because of her pet!

"Jae, just get out of here," Night Hawk grumbled, turning his back to her. He drew a blanket up to cover himself.

"What?" Jae gasped, paling. "I don't understand, Night Hawk. What have I done to make you so angry?"

"Jae, I would like to go to sleep now, if you do not mind," he said between clenched teeth. "Leave and close the door behind you."

"But have you or have you not seen Snoopy?" Jae persisted, slowly climbing on the bed with him. She placed a hand on his shoulder and felt him flinch at her mere touch. "You are so angry at me. I'm sorry. Please, Night Hawk, don't be mad at me."

"Get out of here, Jae," Night Hawk said, finding his reserves weakening as her hand began caressing his shoulders and then move down over his back.

"I love you, Night Hawk," Jae murmured. "Please say that you love me."

"Jae . . ." he said, sucking in a wild breath when her hand traveled beneath the blanket and circled around and touched his aching manhood.

"Do you really want me to leave?" Jae whispered, her worries about Snoopy slowly slipping away. Being with Night Hawk—alone—feeling his sex growing large between her trembling fingers, was changing her mood from anxious to euphoric.

Night Hawk closed his eyes and groaned as Jae slowly moved her hand on his sex, then cuddled down close behind him. She slipped the blanket away from him and tossed it on the floor, then slid her body against his, her breasts pressed into his back, her throbbing center arching against his hard buttocks.

"Night Hawk, we didn't make love before," Jae whispered, brushing soft kisses across his shoulder. "But I'm truly ready this time. I want you, Night Hawk. I want you now."

"I . . . thought . . . you were more concerned with the raccoon," he said, his heart pounding hard as passion built within him. "Surely you would rather leave my bed and go on looking for Snoopy. Go on, if you wish. I'll try not to hate you for it."

"Hate me?" Jae said, her eyes widening.

She giggled and slid one of her long, lean legs over his thigh, pressing her woman's center more directly into his flesh, allowing him to feel the soft feathering of hair at the juncture of her thighs. She slowly ground herself against him.

"Tell me you hate me, Night Hawk," she whispered, her hand still working him, her body, her utter sweetness, claiming his every sense. "Tell me you don't want to make love to me. Send me away, Night Hawk. Send . . . me . . . away."

"You little wench," Night Hawk said, reaching down to remove her hand from his hot, throbbing sex.

He turned toward her, his hands already at the hem of her nightgown, lifting it slowly up over her body, then over her head.

He tossed it aside, then leaned down and slid his tongue over first one breast, then the other. His hands roamed slowly over her, awakening her every nerve ending, causing her to desire him more than ever before.

She slid her hands around him and splayed them on his buttocks, guiding him closer so that his manhood lay at the very entrance of her throbbing center. "Fill me, Night Hawk," she softly begged. "Teach me how it feels to be with a man. I want all of you. Kiss me. Hold me. Caress me. I need you, Night Hawk. Oh, how I need you."

He wove his fingers through her hair and drew her lips to his. He gently probed at her woman's center with his aching manhood, taking his time, knowing that she would soon experience the pain that came with the first time.

He wanted to lead her mind elsewhere, so that she would not even know that pain existed. It would be over with quickly.

She would then feel pure bliss, as would he, while thrusting within her, her walls warm and sucking at him as he filled her to the hilt with his heat.

She drew her mouth from his. She traced his lips with a forefinger. "I'm sorry if I gave you cause to be angry at me," she whispered.

Her pulse raced as she felt the probing where she ached unmercifully and throbbed with need of him. "I never meant to neglect you. It's just that each time I started to leave, Father urged me to stay. How could I say no? He's such a pitiful, lonely man."

"He isn't lonely," Night Hawk said, slowly inching himself inside her. "He has his wife."

"She doesn't seem to be enough for him," Jae murmured, sweat pearling her brow as she felt Night Hawk shoving himself slowly inside her. She was becoming very keenly aware of the pain that such an entrance caused.

"When a man is paralyzed, a wife *does* seem less important," Night Hawk whispered.

He brushed soft kisses across her brow, her cheeks, and then her lips. He cupped her breasts within his hands, swearing to himself that surely he had never felt anything as soft. No woman compared to Jae. She was everything to him. And more.

"Am I important to you, Night Hawk?" Jae whispered, her head spinning now from his touches, his kisses, his very nearness.

She sucked in a wild breath and then bit her lower lip in an effort not to cry out from the pain when, with one insistent thrust, he broke through her virgin barrier.

"You are the world to me," Night Hawk said, then placed his hands on her waist and slid her beneath him.

She clung to him as he began his slow strokes within her. She sighed as he kissed her gently, his hands moving over her, making her skin tingle each place he touched.

He reached his hands beneath her legs and lifted them over his waist, so that she was more open to him, enabling him to delve more deeply into her warm softness.

"I love you so," Jae whispered, then kissed him again.

Their lips parted.

Their tongues touched.

Their bodies rocked.

Their groans filled the air.

Their sighs of gratification rocked the stillness of the room when their bodies quaked as the ultimate of pleasure was reached.

When it was over, Jae cuddled close to Night Hawk. "Can I stay the night with you?" she whispered, brushing kisses along the corded muscles of his shoulders. "I love my room, but it is so strange in comparison to what I am used to."

"If you do not mind shocking everyone in this household by sleeping with me, yes, stay," Night Hawk said, his hands roaming over her. He felt as if he could not get enough of her silken flesh.

"They need not know," Jae said, leaning up on an elbow. Her eyes were innocently wide as she gazed at Night Hawk. "Early in the morning, I can hurry to my bed before anyone has risen."

"Aren't you going to search anymore tonight for Snoopy?" he asked.

Jae saw a quiet amusement in the depths of his eyes. "Night Hawk, is there something you aren't telling me?" she murmured. She already knew his moods and personality so well, even though she had only been with him these past few days.

"I asked you if you are not going to search anymore for your raccoon?" Night Hawk said. He smiled at Jae and reached beneath his bed, touching Snoopy's soft fur as he lay asleep on a pallet.

Jae moved to her knees. She placed her hands on her hips as she looked at Night Hawk with glinting eyes. "Why are you looking at me like that?" she asked. She gazed at his one arm as it hung low over the bed. "What's beneath the bed?"

"See for yourself," Night Hawk said, gently shoving the pallet and the raccoon from under the bed.

Jae leaned over the side of the bed. Her eyes grew wide. "Snoopy?" she said, then gave Night Hawk a wide-eyed stare. "Why, you knew all along that he was safe, and you let me rant and rave on about him!"

"*Huh*, I let you rant and rave," Night Hawk said, grabbing her wrists when she looked as though she might pummel them against his chest.

He drew her down over him. His lips met hers in a frenzy of kisses. He felt the heat grow in his loins again. He felt the urgency of her hands as she moved them over his body, then circled his manhood and guided it inside her again.

"I just might *not* make it to my bed tonight," she whispered against his lips. "Do you truly care, Night Hawk, what anyone says if I don't?"

"Not at all," he said huskily.

She emitted a soft moan against his lips. "Nor . . . do . . . I," she managed to say between their fevered kisses.

They made love again.

And when they were hot and weak from the intensity of their lovemaking, they lay quietly in one another's arms. Jae broke the silence by telling him how she felt about her new bedroom, her clothes, and the things promised her.

She giggled. "Night Hawk, you must see my room."

"Even though I do not feel comfortable sleeping

there tonight, I do love everything about it."

She turned to him. He gazed into her eyes as she continued to rattle on.

"And, darling, there is so much that will be brought into our marriage," she said softly. "Lois told me that it is customary for a young woman to have a trousseau that includes a cache of linens and other bedding. She told me that a large collection of monogrammed linens and satin bedspreads are required for a status-conscious family."

"Status-conscious family?" Night Hawk said, arching his eyebrows over what he was hearing. It seemed unreal that these words were coming from Jae's mouth. As before, he was concerned that her changed circumstances might make her different from before. The more she talked, the more concerned he became.

"I shall also be given embroidered sheets and pillow shams, which Lois says are a timeless treasure for a new bride," Jae tumbled out breathlessly. "She explained to me what my bedroom should be once you and I are married. Though I love what is mine now, the one you and I will share together will be even more beautiful."

She sighed, then framed his face between her hands. She kissed him, then spoke on and on. "Lois said that we will have our own bed once we are married," she murmured. "She said that she will order an Italian four-poster silver-leaf bed."

Stunned by the way Jae had become absorbed in the worldly possessions that Lois had always showered her*self* with, Night Hawk placed his hands on her waist, lifted her aside, and then rolled off the bed.

Stiff, confused, and frustrated, he went to the window and stared out at the stars in the heavens.

"Night Hawk, did I say something wrong?" Jae murmured as she stepped to his side, peering innocently up at him. "Why are you so suddenly quiet?"

He turned slowly to her. He slid his arms around her waist and drew her close. "Jae, you do not truly want all those things you just talked about, do you?" he asked, his voice drawn. "Jae, do you realize that you sound more like Lois than yourself?"

"I *do?*" she said, eyes wide. "I don't understand. How can I sound like someone else?"

"If you had listened to yourself, you would not need to ask," Night Hawk said, then drew her into his embrace. He caressed her back. "Jae, I fell in love with your innocence, your sweetness, your wholesomeness. Let nothing take that away from you . . . from *me.*"

Confused, she clung to him.

Chapter Eighteen

Sweaty from a hard day of rounding up and branding horses, Night Hawk walked into the house and found a strange, awkward silence.

He stopped and looked up the long corridor, but he saw no one.

His heart skipped a beat when he stared at his father's closed door. When Night Hawk had left earlier in the day, his father had been all right.

As Night Hawk had worked diligently branding the mustangs, he had not seen a doctor arrive; there had been nothing to suggest that his father's health might have worsened.

Instead, Night Hawk had seen Charles Swainford, his father's personal attorney, ride up to the house in his fancy horse and carriage.

Only a short while ago, Night Hawk had seen Charles leave. He now recalled having found it strange that the attorney had ducked his head when he had seen him. It had been obvious that Charles had purposely avoided looking at him, whereas he was usually an even-tempered, cordial man, who always spoke to everyone.

That, and the silence in the house, truly puzzled Night Hawk.

But because his father's attorney, not his physician, had been there most of the day, Night Hawk did not think that the silence was because of his father's worsened health.

He untied the bandanna from around his neck and slowly wiped the perspiration from his brow.

He glanced up the stairs again, smiling as he thought of his long night of lovemaking with Jae.

"Jae," he whispered, taking long strides on up the stairs. "I shall question her. She has been here all day. She might know something."

When he reached Jae's room and knocked on the door, he got no response. "Jae?" he said, leaning his ear close to the door. "Are you in there?"

He frowned when again there was no reply.

He slid his sweaty bandanna inside his back breeches pocket and slowly turned the doorknob.

When the door was open just a crack, he was able to ascertain that Jae was not there.

Disgruntled, Night Hawk closed the door and sauntered to his room. When he entered, he raised his eyebrows quizzically. Although there seemed to be no one around, *someone* had taken the time to fill a tub of hot water for him for his evening bath.

"At least that is as it usually is," he grumbled to himself.

Yet where was Rita? She was the one who saw that this was done. Where was *she*, as well as everyone else? Why was everyone avoiding him like he had the plague?

He plopped down on a chair and yanked first one boot off, and then the other. He almost tore off his clothes in his anger at feeling as though he was the only one left out of whatever might be happening in the house.

Night Hawk sank into the water and ran the soap over his dust-covered, sweaty flesh. He sank his face into the water, and then his hair.

Feeling refreshed and ready to investigate the continued silence in the house, he rose from the tub and wrapped a towel around himself.

Hearing a horse riding up outside, Night Hawk went to a window and gazed downward. He arched an eyebrow when he saw that it was Jae. He was puzzled that he had not seen her leave, and he had had a good view of the house from where he branded the horses.

Then he remembered the short time that he had spent in the barn, sweeping out the loft. Sounds were muffled in there. If Jae had left on horseback then, he would not have known it.

He hurried into his clothes and stepped out into the corridor just as Jae came toward him in her new riding clothes. She stopped short when she saw him.

Night Hawk puzzled over how her face seemed to drain of color when their eyes met. He could not understand why she seemed so suddenly ill at ease with him, after they had spent all night together, loving, talking, and laughing.

"Jae?" Night Hawk took one of her hands.

He gazed down at her trembling hand then looked again into her eyes. "Are you going to tell me what the hell is going on here?" he asked, his voice drawn. "Do you not know that I feel the strain in the house? That I see your uneasiness? That I actually feel your hand trembling in mine, as though you are afraid of me?"

Knowing the answer to his question, yet not wanting to be the one to tell him, Jae swallowed hard and lowered her eyes.

Night Hawk dropped her hand, took an unsteady step away from her, then stepped toward her again and placed his hands on her upper arms. He tightened his fingers as she looked silently and pleadingly up at him.

"Jae, is it our father?" he asked thickly. "Has something happened to him?"

"No, not *to* him," Jae finally said.

"Then *what?*" Night Hawk insisted, his voice rising in pitch. "I knew something was wrong the instant I stepped into the house. It was as quiet as a tomb. It still *is*. Where is Lois? Where is Rita?" He stopped and recalled something else. "And where is Maxine? I now remember not having smelled anything cooking in the kitchen."

"That is because father has told Maxine to take the day off," Jae murmured. "He did not expect anyone to want much at dinnertime."

"And why is that?" Night Hawk asked, placing his fists on his hips.

Jae placed a gentle hand on his cheek. "Night Hawk, I love you so," she said, her voice breaking. "But I can say no more."

She turned toward the staircase, then looked slowly again up at Night Hawk. "Father is waiting for you," she said softly. "Go to him, Night Hawk, and try not to hate him too much."

"Hate?" Night Hawk said, taken aback by her warning. "Why would I ever hate him? How could I? I love him as though he were my true father."

Knowing that he would change his feelings soon, Jae swallowed hard.

"It's not my place to explain things," she then said.

She took him gently by an elbow and led him to the head of the staircase. "Go to Father. He is alone, waiting. Lois and Rita are in their bedrooms. I shall be in mine."

Jae flung herself into his arms. She hugged him fiercely. "After the talk, come to me, darling," she cried. "I shall be here for you. I shall be here for you, always."

So confused by everything, by the way Jae was acting, by what she said, Night Hawk placed his hands on Jae's waist and gently shoved her away from him.

He stared at her; then he turned and walked down the stairs.

He could not help feeling a strange sort of queasiness in the pit of his stomach. His knees were unsteady as he took the final step onto the oak flooring, for he felt that the world as he had known it since he was ten was soon to be over. Jae had behaved too strangely, was too apologetic and sad, for him not to think that something was terribly wrong.

A thought came to him that made his insides grow cold. The attorney! Charles Swainford *had* been at his father's bedside. And then there was the way Charles had eluded Night Hawk, whereas he had always before taken the time to stop and talk. Charles Swainford had treated Night Hawk like a distant stranger!

Charles's attitude could mean only one thing— that he had discussed Night Hawk with Ralph Hampton! That perhaps Night Hawk . . .

He stopped and flinched as though someone had hit him. His father's will. Night Hawk had seen Ralph poring over it just the other day, before he had left to search for Jae. Night Hawk had not questioned him as to why; he never interfered in that sort of private business of his father's.

But if he was right, that this was all about his father's will . . . Night Hawk almost knew before entering the bedroom what had happened. His jaw set, and wanting to get this behind him, he went to his father's door and lightly tapped it with his knuckles.

"Is that you, Night Hawk?" his father said from behind the closed door. "I've been expecting you."

Night Hawk didn't say anything. He just went inside the bedroom.

And when he saw the will strewn across the blankets before him on his father's bed, and then saw another will that had been ripped in half resting in a wastebasket beside the bed, Night Hawk's insides grew cold. His eyes narrowed, and he circled his hands into tight fists at his sides.

He dreaded the next moments, when he might be forced to relive another betrayal . . . when his Comanche father had abandoned not only him, but also his beloved mother.

Night Hawk had thought the bad times were behind him. But now? He could feel the rejection even before his father spoke the words. It was in his adoptive father's eyes as he gazed up at him. There was a silent apology. Even perhaps hurt.

Night Hawk waited for the words that would confirm what he already knew.

"Son, sit down," Ralph said, nodding toward the chair beside the bed. "I've much to say. I only hope you will understand, and that you won't leave this room hating me."

"I prefer to stand," Night Hawk said stiffly, his eyes on the will. From this vantage point, he could read some of the larger, bolder print. He had been given the best of education by private tutors brought to the ranch. He could read. He had great mathematical skills. He could . . .

"Have it your way," Ralph said, interrupting Night Hawk's thoughts. "What I have to say won't take long." He wheezed as he spoke, and his face was suddenly flushed.

He folded the will and handed it to Night Hawk with the hand that had been lifeless these past weeks until he met his daughter. "Read the will," he said tightly. "Charles was here a good portion of the day making changes in it. It's something that I had to do, Night Hawk. My daughter, my true flesh-and-blood kin, has come home. She had to be considered above everyone else. Even my wife comes second now, son. I've much to make up to my daughter. The will is the only way I can see to make the wrongs of the past finally altogether right for her. She should never have been denied the life I could have given her. She shall have it now—*all* of it."

It didn't take long for Night Hawk to run his gaze over the pages. And as he read, he felt strangely lifeless inside, as though he had no heart, no feelings, no soul . . . nothing.

In the amount of time that it had taken his father's hand to sign the will, Night Hawk's past and future ran together inside his mind, as though it were all a blank—as though his very life, had been, and would be, worthless.

With two fathers having turned against him, how could Night Hawk feel that he was worth anything?

There had to be something in him, he thought to himself, to make no man want him as a son!

Even after all that Night Hawk had done for his adoptive father, he had been cast aside as though he was nothing, a person without feelings . . . a person who was forced again to try to accept those who turned their backs on him.

He read again the words that pierced his heart: "Being of sound mind, I, Ralph Hampton, do bequeath the sum total of my possessions to my daughter Jae. . . ."

Always a man in control of himself, able to hide his feelings at will, Night Hawk folded the pages and handed them back to his father.

Their eyes locked.

Night Hawk forced himself not to show any shock or remorse as his father stared up at him. But he was glad to see the uneasiness in Ralph Hampton's eyes as they began to waver, then lowered.

"It had to be done, Night Hawk," Ralph said, wheezing. "She had to have it all, for up till now, she has had nothing."

Ralph looked up at Night Hawk again. "This doesn't mean that you will have nothing," he said. "You will stay on here at the ranch. You will still have everything you need. Jae will be generous to you. All you need do is ask her and whatever you want will be yours."

"I will not be here to ask anyone for anything ever again," Night Hawk said evenly. "And as for Jae, I am sure she will wallow in her newfound wealth. She has let me know often enough that she wants this sort of life, where she can have the worldly possessions of the rich."

Night Hawk laughed sarcastically. "Well, *Father*, I need none of this to make *me* happy," he said. "What is important to me is *loyalty* . . . is *love*. Seems I was wrong to believe I had both while living with you."

"But, Night Hawk . . ." Ralph said, looking at him with pleading eyes. "I didn't mean . . ."

"I am not certain what you meant, or how you truly feel about me," Night Hawk said, his voice void of feeling. "And do not mistake my reaction to this piece of paper. I am not angry because I receive nothing when you die. It is *why* it has been done—because of your lack of feeling for me, someone who has devoted his life to you. No. Worldly possessions mean nothing to me. It is the soul, the heart, the love between two people, that matter. Today you have proven to me that you are a man with a *che-kas-koi*, a bad heart . . . a man with no feelings. I pity you."

Night Hawk turned on his heel and with much dignity left the room.

But once he was out of his father's sight, he hung his head in his hands and wept. How could he be betrayed twice in such a way? he despaired to himself.

No, it was not the money! Never was it the money!

Night Hawk had enjoyed playing the role of "son" to the man he had grown to love and admire. He had willingly—lovingly—devoted his life since the age of ten to this ranch, to this *man*. Night Hawk had made the ranch what it was today. Disabled, Ralph would have lost everything had it not been for him.

And none of it was Night Hawk's, now, or ever. It would all belong to Ralph Hampton's only living heir, his daughter.

"Night Hawk?"

Jae's voice drew his head up with a jerk. He quickly wiped the tears from his eyes with the back of a hand when he saw Jae coming down the stairs toward him. She had changed clothes: She now wore an expensive silk dress. A diamond necklace sparkled around her neck and diamond earrings glittered in her earlobes. A diamond bracelet flashed its many colors into Night Hawk's eyes as it picked up the light from the candles burning in the wall sconces.

The sight of the wealth she flaunted sent bitterness into Night Hawk's heart. He knew that she understood the will, and that he had been left out. Knowing how he felt about worldly possessions, how could she dress this way?

He stared at her, feeling that he had never really known her. He recalled the many times she had spoken of wanting pretty dresses and jewelry and other riches, and Night Hawk could not help believing that she had had a part in Ralph's decision to turn his own life upside down.

Surely she had been playing a game with him by acting as though she loved him, when all along she hoped to coerce her father into changing the will in her favor. Perhaps that was why she had spent so much time with her father yesterday while Night Hawk had been waiting for her to come to him.

All the while she had used her charm—her outlaw cunning—to get all that she wanted from her father.

"It will all be yours, Jae," Night Hawk said as she stepped up close to him, her eyes imploring him. "That is what you wanted, is it not? To have it all? Well, you can have it. I am leaving. I want no more part of this life that was not mine to begin with." He leaned down into her face and laughed. "You sure did have me fooled. But why am I surprised? Your father is the master when it comes to fooling someone into believing he loves someone."

Jae paled. Her heart skipped a beat. She gazed disbelievingly at Night Hawk. "No," she said, her voice breaking. "You can't believe that I . . ."

Night Hawk placed a hand to her cheek. "Baby, at this moment, you don't want to know exactly what

I think of you," he said bitterly.

"Night Hawk, I love you," Jae cried. "I truly love you. And don't you see? I can hardly bear the humiliation and devastation you are feeling. Night Hawk, don't leave. Please? Everything can be yours. I will give it up willingly to keep you here."

"And I am to believe you?" he said, laughing sarcastically. He yanked his hand away and glared down at her. "I want no part of this ranch, or you. Everything will soon be rightfully yours. You have proven time and again how you feel about things . . . about wanting possessions. I warned you about being greedy. It changes a person into something ugly. That has been proven as far as you are concerned. Have you not beguiled your father into changing the will in your favor?"

Jae felt faint, his words like a hard slap to her face. "I would never do that," she gasped out. "And . . . and I truly want none of this. I was wrong to think it was so important. Night Hawk, I want to be with *you*. *Please* stay! I want to marry you!"

"I would not trust you any more than a rattlesnake coiled in the grass," Night Hawk hissed out.

He turned and stamped from the house, toward the corral, his head was spinning. He had no idea where to go, or what to do with the rest of his life. Was it truly only last night when everything seemed so perfect? As Jae lay in his arms, he had felt so blessed. He had felt as though he had everything . . . the *world!*

And now, he had absolutely nothing!

Crying Wolf met him at the corral. "I saw you leave the house, your head low, your walk without spirit," he said, placing a gentle hand on Night Hawk's shoulder. "What has happened, my friend, to cause

186

you to look so forlorn, as though you might have lost your best friend? Has your father died?"

"He is still alive in his bed, but inside my heart, he is dead forever," Night Hawk mumbled.

He then told Crying Wolf everything, how the woman he adored had duped him.

"Where can I go?" Night Hawk asked once the story was all told. "I feel like a man without a country, without a family—without anything."

"You have your Comanche people," Crying Wolf said, seeing the puzzlement enter Night Hawk's eyes as he looked quickly at him. "Your true father has waited a long time to see you. Now is the time to go to him."

"My true father?" Night Hawk stammered out. "Why would you say that? I told you how my Comanche father abandoned me."

"It was not like that at all," Crying Wolf said, his voice slow and measured. "Let me tell you about it, Night Hawk, how your father sent a friend out many winters ago to look for you . . . to find you and bring you back to him."

"How would you know?" Running Hawk studied his old friend's eyes, seeing a gleam in their depths.

"Because I am that friend," Crying Wolf said, smiling. "A friend whose memory was taken from him so that he could not complete his mission . . . a friend who now remembers everything. It is time to go home, Night Hawk. It is good that this has happened between you and Ralph Hampton. It gives me the opportunity to tell you everything. It is time to tell you about a Comanche father who did not leave his son because it was his wish to."

"Then how?" Night Hawk mumbled. "Why?"

"When the *to-ho-ba-ila*, whites, attacked our Comanche village," Crying Wolf said. "*Huh*, yes, *our* village, Night Hawk. Yours and mine. I was one of your father's closest friends, one of his most valiant warriors. I remember you when you were but a pup, nursing from your mother's breast. I was there when the whites attacked. I was among those taken captive by your father's own Comanche warriors, at the same time your father was taken captive. It was I who heard those who took over your father's band order the shooting of your mother. My hands were tied, as were your father's. When he heard the order given, he felt as though a part of him was dying."

"I find this all so hard to accept," Night Hawk said, kneading his brow as his head began to ache. "Are you saying that my father's own people went against him?"

"*Huh*, because they wrongly blamed him for lack of leadership, for so many of our people being taken captive by raiders, or murdered," Crying Wolf softly explained. "But your father had many who were still loyal. In time, their numbers swelled, enough for your father to again become the chief of our *Iteotao* band of Comanche, known as the Burnt Meat People."

"And so my father did not abandon me because it was his wish to?" Night Hawk asked, his heart throbbing anxiously. "He did not take my mother's life because he no longer wanted her? All these years I have hated him for naught?"

"*Huh*, for naught," Crying Wolf said softly. "And now it is time for us to go to your father. If the Wise One Above is willing, your father will still be alive and well. Had I not lost my memory for so long, I would have taken you to him long ago."

"Crying Wolf, you should have told me everything

as soon as your memory returned," Night Hawk said, yet he was not angry over the delay. He was feeling too exhilarated from knowing that he had a father who still truly wanted him.

Night Hawk's insides were filled with a wonderful warmth—a wonderful sensation of relief. He could hardly wait to go and be with his Comanche father again. He wanted to make up for all of the years he had silently hated him!

"I did not tell you because you had been accepted into the white community, and you were *happy*," Crying Wolf said. "Until now, I believed that your happiness, your well-being, was more important than telling you that your true father is alive. But now? Now that things have changed for you, I feel that I was wrong not to have been completely truthful the instant I recalled everything. I apologize for being wrong."

"No apologies are needed from you, my dear friend." Running Hawk gently embraced Crying Wolf. "Let us now and make things right in my father's world."

"It has been many years," Crying Wolf murmured. "Your father may not be alive for you or me to embrace. We may discover that we will have only his memory to embrace."

"My memories have been my enemy," Night Hawk said somberly, stepping away from Crying Wolf. "Every time I thought of my Comanche father, it was with much malice and hate. I hope I do have the opportunity to see him with love in my heart, instead of the festering sore that hatred leaves within one's soul."

"Let us leave tonight," Crying Wolf encouraged.

"*Huh*, tonight," Night Hawk agreed. He would

erase the white world from his life . . . from his heart
. . . as though he had never known it!

A thought came quickly to Night Hawk. "Crying
Wolf, it has been many years since you saw where
my father reestablished his village," he said. "How
can we find it?"

Crying Wolf chuckled. "With my regained memory
came my regained psychic powers," he said, his eyes
twinkling. "My powers are what led me to you many
years ago. Do not fear. They will lead you home to
your father."

Jae was running toward him. "Night Hawk!
Change your mind! Don't leave!"

He turned and glared at Jae as she stepped up to
him, breathless. Although he was angry at her, he
could not help noticing a change in her since he had
seen her only moments before. She no longer wore
her diamonds, and she had changed clothes. She had
managed to find a pair of men's breeches that fit her,
and she wore them with their legs cut off up to just
past her knee. She also wore a blue denim shirt.

He gazed down at her feet. She had managed to
keep Lois from burning her boots. She wore them
now.

"All right, if you are too stubborn to stay, I will go
with you," Jae said. She placed her hands on her
hips. "As you see, Night Hawk, I am ready for traveling. I've left all my worldly possessions behind me."

Snoopy came running after her. She picked him
up and hugged him to her. "Night Hawk, both
Snoopy and I will be so lonesome if you don't let us
go with you," she murmured, her lips quivering as
she fought back the urge to cry.

Night Hawk was suddenly uncertain what to do,
what to say. He believed she was sincere now, and

he felt ashamed for having doubted her love for him.

He felt even more ashamed for having asked her to give up so much when she had had so little all her life!

Then he grew angry again when another thought came to him. "You are a woman who does not know the meaning of loyalty," he hissed out. "A man lies paralyzed, a father who has waited his lifetime to see you, and you are ready to turn your back on him?"

He could not believe that he was defending the very man who had just moments ago broken his heart! But the word "loyalty" meant so much to him, and he saw that what Jae was planning to do was wrong.

"Loyalty?" Jae asked, eyes wide. "To whom do you truly believe I owe it? Surely you see that I owe it to you. I love you. I want to be with you forever. Surely I can explain this to my father so that he will understand."

Again Night Hawk was torn over what to do. He did want Jae, yet he was afraid of his desire. He feared that if she went with him now, she might change her mind again, especially if she went with him to the Comanche village and saw how she would be forced to live as his wife. This was a woman tired of living a life of drudgery. Surely she would not accept a tepee as her home!

"Go back to your father, Jae," he said. "Go back to a home that soon will be totally yours. That is where you belong. Not with me."

Hurt through and through, totally confused by Night Hawk's attitude, Jae stared disbelievingly up at him, then turned and ran from him, sobbing.

Seeing her hurt, almost feeling her dejection inside his heart, Night Hawk started to go after her.

But Crying Wolf placed a hand on his arm and stopped him. "Let her go," he said softly. "She does not belong in our world. Our world is the Comanche! Not whites! It is time to live Comanche!"

Night Hawk found it hard not to go after Jae.

"Let her go," Crying Wolf counseled. "Let us leave now. We have *our* life. She has *hers*."

Night Hawk sighed. "*Huh*, my friend, use your psychic powers and lead me to my real father."

Taking only his big pinto and his saddle, his large Bowie knife, rifle, and pistol, all of which he had bought with money earned from his hard labor at the ranch, and enough personal possessions to survive until he found his father's village, Night Hawk rode away from his father's ranch with Crying Wolf beside him on his mustang.

He looked one last time over his shoulder at the ranch. Images of "The Wide Chapparal" were imbedded in his childhood memories like a fossilized leaf in stone.

When he saw lamplight in his adoptive father's bedroom, he swallowed hard, then turned his head and lifted his chin proudly.

His true people, the *Ner-mer-nuh*, awaited him. He was proud and anxious to go to them! His true people, his true *father*, had been too long denied him!

"*Huh*, it is right that I am going home," he said, casting Crying Wolf a wide grin.

Tears of happiness filling his eyes, Crying Wolf nodded. Then, in a melancholy tone, Crying Wolf began to talk about his people. Night Hawk listened, knowing that he would learn things that he should have known all along, had his heritage not been taken from him.

"Our *Iteotao* band of Comanche gets their name

'Burnt Meat People' because we are known to put up more pemmican than we can eat in a winter. We throw out the surplus in the spring. The dumps of dried, black meat are found along the trail. That is how we received our name. . . ."

Chapter Nineteen

Chapter Nineteen

The sun was lowering in the sky, casting shadowy
images on the ground as Jae rode in a steady lope
along the dusty trail. She had waited in the barn until
Night Hawk and Crying Wolf had left the ranch.
Then she had saddled her horse and rode off after
them. She was keeping back just far enough to stay
out of sight.

She had not taken the time to go into the house to
explain to anyone that she was leaving, or why. If
she had done that, she would not have seen the direction in which Night Hawk's travel was taking him.
If she allowed him to get away from her, she might
never see him again.

And he was the only important person on this
earth to her. He was her true reason for living.

Yet Jae could not help being sad about leaving be-
hind the life that she had been so generously offered.
Still, she was willing to give up anything to be with
Night Hawk.

Although he had been bitter and had turned his
back on her, Jae knew that he still loved her and

would forgive whatever transgressions he thought her guilty of. She knew, without a doubt, that he would welcome her into his arms again, and his life.

She thought back to what Night Hawk had said about loyalty. He had accused her of having none as far as her true father was concerned. A sadness swept through her heart as she realized what she had done by leaving him without even saying good-bye. He would think her the same sort of person that her mother had been—a woman who knew not the meaning of the word "loyalty."

But Jae *was* being loyal—to the man she loved! She had seen, even felt, Night Hawk's hurt after he discovered the terms of the will that took from him everything that he had known since he was ten.

It angered Jae that Ralph Hampton had so callously done this to Night Hawk. Speaking of loyalty, *Ralph* was the one who knew not the true meaning of the word.

Ralph's loyalty had most definitely been misplaced when he left everything to a daughter whom he had never known. He had even turned his back on his wife! Lois had catered to his every desire, every whim.

Jae pitied Ralph Hampton, but she felt he was heartless in his dealings with the people who loved him.

No, she wanted no part of his life, even if it meant turning her back on everything she had always thought was important to a woman.

She laughed to herself when she recalled her image in the mirror after she'd put the diamonds around her neck, in her earlobes, and around her wrist. She had actually looked laughable! She had not felt truly herself while wearing those tokens of wealth, nor had she felt comfortable in silk and satin. She had felt odd in the clinging fabrics and the fancy lacy underclothes and crinolines.

Her father had looked at her as though she were a living doll. But she had felt like someone in the side-show in a circus!

She now felt wonderful and free in the cut-off jeans and the denim shirt. She loved not wearing lacy underthings that irritated her tender flesh.

She laughed into the wind at how she had dreamed of having those things that now held so little importance.

"Mother, you were wrong to miss such a life as that," she said aloud, staring heavenward. "It is all pure poppycock!"

Still smelling the expensive French perfume that she had splashed on her wrists and behind her ears after her bath, Jae did have to admit to enjoying the scent.

She reached inside her travel bag, smiling when her fingers touched the bottle of perfume that she had grabbed right before leaving her room. That was all that she had taken of the life she could have had. At times, she just might like smelling good for Night Hawk.

Jae frowned as she strained her neck to see him and Crying Wolf riding ahead of her. She still measured her distance carefully so that Night Hawk would not know just yet that she was following him. She did not want to give him an opportunity to send her back. After they got far enough down the road, she would reveal herself to him. He would have no choice then but to allow her to stay with him.

Jae gazed at the horizon where the sun was still creeping down. Her plans were to ride up and show herself just as Night Hawk got his campfire going.

She was certain that he would not send her away in the dark. He would welcome her beside him. He would offer her a hot cup of coffee. They would share the evening meal.

A thought came to her as quickly as a thunderclap. When Night Hawk had left, he had not taken the time to gather provisions. He had left without taking any worldly possessions belonging to his adoptive father, except for a horse, saddle, his firearms, and the very clothes that he wore.

It was certain that he was bitter. He would not want anything that might remind him of the man who had betrayed him.

"I'm sure he—we—won't starve," Jae murmured, knowing that rabbits and all sorts of wild things were out there for the shooting.

She shifted her gaze to the travel bag on her left side, where Snoopy slept so soundly and trustingly. She smoothed her fingers over her raccoon's soft fur. When it came to devotion, her pet was perhaps the most devoted of all. He had hardly left her side since they had found one another in the Thicket. He was the best of pals to her. She could never ask for a better friend.

As darkness crept lower over the land, Jae did not only feel the chill of the night, but also how vulnerable and alone she was in these wide open spaces. When she rode past a tombstone that seemed out of place at the side of the road, obviously having been placed there in haste by a lonesome traveler, she shuddered.

Drawing a tight rein, she bent low, and with the light that remained in the sky, she read aloud the epitaph on the stone. "Shed not for me the bitter tear, nor give the heart to vain regret. 'Tis but the basket that lies here. The gem that filled it sparkles yet."

The howling of a wolf drew Jae's attention away from the tombstone and the words written across it. She hugged herself as she looked slowly around her. Then her heart leapt into her throat when she saw the glimmer of the beginning of a campfire a short distance away.

Smiling and anxious, and thinking she was far enough from her father's ranch to make her presence known, Jae flicked her reins, sank her heels into the flanks of her horse, and rode off.

When she heard a lone gunshot, she believed it was either Crying Wolf or Night Hawk claiming what would be their evening meal. Her stomach growled; she was so hungry she could eat a bear.

She giggled. "Perhaps *two*," she whispered.

She rode onward, then tensed when she heard a sound behind her. She looked quickly over her shoulder and peered through the falling dusk. She could swear she had heard the muffled sound of hoofbeats behind her.

Her eyes squinting, she again looked slowly around her.

Seeing nothing, and no longer hearing anything, she shrugged and continued onward, this time at a harder lope. She was not the sort to frighten easily. While she had lived in the Big Thicket, she had gone out every night, alone. She had never felt threatened; she had never felt vulnerable.

But now it was different. She was no longer on territory familiar to her. She knew nothing about what lay ahead of her. She was trustingly following Night Hawk and Crying Wolf. She felt safe enough as long as they were this close to her. Should anyone or anything jump out at her, her screams would carry far enough to bring them to her rescue.

She felt foolish being skittish about riding alone. Always before, she had needed no one. Suddenly life had turned on her and she needed someone . . . but only one person: Night Hawk! She would not allow him to turn his back on her again. She knew that he loved and needed her—especially now, when he was surely feeling betrayed and at odds with himself and life.

She couldn't get Ralph Hampton off her mind. She felt much bitterness toward him for having caused Night Hawk's pain. He had been wrong to turn his back on Night Hawk, who had given of himself, a son in every true sense of the word, since the age of ten.

She set her jaw angrily. Her eyes narrowed, thinking that she had never been Ralph's daughter and saw no desire to be.

Yes, she felt a need to be loyal, but to only one man: the man she loved and wanted to live with the rest of her life.

Suddenly Jae's heart lurched and her throat went too dry to scream when a loop of rope came quickly over her head as someone lassoed her from behind.

She had no time to think or act. The rope quickly pulled her from her horse. She landed hard on the ground, the impact knocking the wind from her lungs.

Stunned, dazed, and puzzled, Jae lay there for a moment. Then she became aware of someone standing over her. She first looked at the dusty boots, and she cringed when she recognized them. She had seen them before, more than once. She had seen them as she had watched Jonas Adams enter the town of

Cassie Edwards

Beaumont on his white steed and saunter into the saloons and gambling parlors.

So he had managed to find her. She knew not to expect any mercy from him.

"You sneaky bitch," Jonas Adams snarled, yanking on the rope that was now positioned tightly across her breasts.

Jae cried out as the rope dug through her shirt, into her tender breasts. She gasped with pain when Jonas kicked her over, forcing her to lay on her stomach. She tasted the dust as it bled into her lips while it swirled around her face. She coughed and spit it from her mouth.

"You never thought you'd see me again, did you, bitch?" Jonas said. He knelt down beside her and twined his fingers through her hair.

He gave it a hard yank, turning Jae's face sidewise so that it would be closer to his as he spoke into it. "I've got you now. I'm going to have some fun with you, then adios, señorita." He chuckled. "I'll enjoy drawing my knife across your slender, pretty neck."

"You son of a bitch," Jae hissed.

She started to scream. Jonas slapped her across her face, stopping her. He leered at her as he wrapped a foul-tasting, sweaty bandanna around her mouth, silencing her.

He then wrapped a rope around her, from her arms, down to her legs, until she was rendered totally helpless. "I know your boyfriend ain't far away," Jonas said, glancing toward the fire in the distance. "So I'd best get you hid before I have my fun with you."

Jae winced when he took hold of the end of the rope and dragged her into the thick brush. She swallowed hard when he finally stopped beside a small

200

stream. Her eyes were wide over the bandanna as she watched him slowly begin to undress, a sneer lifting his lips into a crooked smile.

After his shirt was thrown aside, she saw the pucker of skin around the wound that had been inflicted during the most recent gunfire at her house, when Crying Wolf had laughed about having wounded Jonas.

He saw her gazing at the wound. "You thought I'd be dead by now, didn't you?" Laughing sarcastically, he sneered down at her. "Thinkin' of you and what I was gonna do to you kept me alive."

Fear grabbing her at the pit of her stomach; she knew that she was soon to be raped, then murdered. Jae looked away from Jonas as he slowly unbuckled the gun belt from around his waist. When she heard the thud of his pistols dropping to the ground, she flinched, knowing that his belt buckle would be next.

Jae prayed that someone might come along and save her. She prayed for it to be Night Hawk!

Yet she knew rescue was unlikely. Night Hawk had no idea she was here. He thought that she was back at the ranch, safe.

She moved her face sidewise, over to her right shoulder, and tried to nudge the bandanna away from her mouth. If she didn't get it off, she would be at this madman's mercy!

Chapter Twenty

Night Hawk stretched his long, lean legs out beside the campfire and watched Crying Wolf slowly turn a spit with a skinned rabbit skewered to it. The aroma was already sending its tantalizing smells into the early evening's open air. The juices made the fire sizzle.

Night Hawk could not get Jae off his mind. He felt guilty for having turned his back on her. Yet, for so many reasons, he felt no other choice. If he knew for certain that she truly loved him enough to live with him in an Indian village, that would be a different matter.

If she had not spoken so often of wanting so much, and then having it handed to her on a silver platter upon her arrival at her true father's house, he would have considered her accepting the way of life that he could offer her.

But she had given him too many reasons to doubt her.

And she had shown her inability to be loyal by having left her true father so soon after becoming acquainted with him!

Yes, he worried to himself, there *were* too many things that could go wrong if had he allowed her to stay with him.

And he had enough on his mind. The hurt still lay deeply inside his heart. He was not sure if he could ever get over the knowledge that he had meant so little to his adoptive father throughout the years. Surely Ralph had always seen him as just a "breed," something to use . . . to take advantage of.

Yes, it was best to put everything of his past behind him, a past that had anything to do with Ralph Hampton.

And, Lord help him, that included Jae!

A sound in the bushes behind him caused Night Hawk to reach quickly for the pistol that he had lain at his side after making camp.

Crying Wolf had also heard. He reached for his rifle.

They both stared in disbelief as a raccoon sauntered into view.

Night Hawk gasped with surprise when the raccoon came to him, its dark, beady eyes wide and imploring as it stared up at him, then scratched at him with its humanlike hand, as though trying to tell Night Hawk something.

Night Hawk paled and went cold inside when he realized that this raccoon was Snoopy. It was Jae's pet! And for it to be there, pleading with Night Hawk, meant that Jae had to be somewhere close by.

"Surely Jae followed us!" Night Hawk said, giving Crying Wolf a quick, frightened stare. "It's Snoopy. Jae has to be near. Perhaps she is in trouble."

A sudden shrill scream filled the night air.

Night Hawk died a slow death inside to think that it must be Jae!

203

He scrambled to his feet, and with a pounding heart, he followed the direction of the scream, Crying Wolf huffing at his side.

They soon found two tethered horses.

Night Hawk recognized one: it was the horse that he had seen Jae riding earlier in the day.

They went a short distance farther, then stopped suddenly when the moon revealed the naked body of a man kneeling over Jae, holding her against him, a rifle in his hand, leveled at Night Hawk and Crying Wolf.

Jonas glared first at Night Hawk and then at Crying Wolf.

"Drop your firearms," he said in a low, snarling hiss.

Stubbornly, they both held their guns steady on the outlaw.

Night Hawk gazed at Jae, whose eyes pleaded at him, then he again stared at Jonas's rifle. At least Jae was safe while the madman was focusing his attention—his hate—on Night Hawk and Crying Wolf.

"I should've slit her throat first, then raped her," Jonas grumbled. "I thought I had her gagged good enough. I should've known she was too tricky to trust that anything could keep her mouth shut while she still had breath left in her lungs."

He leered at Crying Wolf and Night Hawk. "The stupid bitch. Now not only does she have to die, but also you."

Snoopy suddenly came out of the bushes at Jonas's right side, the movement startling him so much that he dropped his firearm.

His eyes filled with a sudden fright, Jonas released Jae, then scrambled out of sight, into the bushes.

Night Hawk ran to Jae. He took her in his arms

and uncoiled the rope from around her.

Crying Wolf went off after Jonas, but soon lost sight of him in the shadows of night.

He then was taken aback when Jonas suddenly appeared only a short distance away, riding off on his horse, his bare skin flashing in the moonlight.

Crying Wolf steadied himself, aimed, fired, then fell back and dropped his rifle to his side when he realized that he had missed the outlaw. He started to go for his horse, to make chase, but Night Hawk calling his name made him decide not to.

He ran back to Night Hawk and Jae. Crying Wolf saw blood seeping through the denim material of her shirt. There were raw rope wounds on her bare legs.

"Get me some water!" Night Hawk cried, giving Crying Wolf a look of panic. "Damn him! He had the rope wrapped so tightly around Jae, it's cut into her flesh!"

Crying Wolf ran to his horse and got his canteen. He went to the stream and filled it with fresh water.

When he got back to Jae and Night Hawk, he stopped and stared as Night Hawk held Jae in his arms, slowly rocking her in them.

"My woman," Night Hawk whispered, Jae's soft sobs tearing his heart in shreds. Never had he heard her cry before. Never had he seen her so helpless.

"I'm so sorry about everything," she whispered, gazing up at him through her tear-soaked lashes. "Please forgive me?"

"Forgive you for what?" Night Hawk asked, brushing some locks of hair back from her cheeks. He had this quickly forgotten anything bad that he had felt for her.

She needed him.

He was there, for her, for always.

Chapter Twenty-one

The fire had burned down to glimmering ashes. The aroma of a pot of coffee enriched the clean, astringent air.

Night Hawk held Jae in his arms. He was stiff from having held her this way the entire night. As she lay on his lap, snuggled close to him, and still so peacefully asleep, he thought back to the previous evening. After having rescued her, he had removed her clothes and had bathed the blood from the wounds made by the rope. He had then medicated her wounds with herbs that Crying Wolf had collected from the embankment of the stream.

He had lovingly wrapped her within the softness of a blanket. He had held her, as though she were a child, until she had fallen asleep. Over and over again as he had watched her sleep, guilt splashed through him for having thought her capable of anything but sweetness. If he had not been so blinded by his hurt, inflicted by his thoughtless adoptive father, he never would have treated Jae so callously!

He would make it up to her now, twofold.

He cringed, and anger caused a bitterness to rise into his throat when he thought of the outlaw having come so close to raping, then killing, Jae.

Night Hawk could not help but blame himself. She would not have been vulnerable to such a vile man as Jonas Adams had he allowed her to travel with him in his search for his true people, his true father.

Jae would not be allowed to travel alone again, anywhere, Night Hawk vowed to himself. He would protect her, even though he expected her to swear up and down on all that was holy that she needed no protection.

Yet, perhaps that side of her that had been born of living a life with outlaws was long past. He would never forget how she had clung to him last night, sobbing. Jae had actually allowed herself to break down and show the part of herself that she had always kept hidden to the world.

Night Hawk had no need to pretend now. He was there for her. She could now be what she pleased to be, not what was expected of her when she lived the life of an outlaw's daughter.

Sighing, Night Hawk gazed around him, thinking that anywhere in Texas, the best time was dawn. The sun was now flaring above the prairies and sere hills, caressing the dew-kissed grass with its profusion of gentle colors. As morning suffused the sky, the mesquites and cottonwoods that hugged the banks of the stream were taking shape in the dim pewter light. A creamy fog clung to the stream like a fallen cloud.

Dawn in Texas was a protracted moment. Night Hawk had so often enjoyed watching the world emerge from the little death of night. But today it seemed even more surreal, so breathtaking, for he knew now what the future held for him—a life with the woman he loved, whether or not he ever found his Comanche people. Jae would be his world, his life. The children born of their love would be their *people*.

And then there was Crying Wolf. Night Hawk smiled as he thought of the loyalty of the old Indian. Even this morning, before the moon drifted out of sight, Crying Wolf had built this morning fire and had placed the pot of coffee in the coals. He had then ridden off. . . .

Night Hawk's heart lurched when he felt Jae stirring. He gazed down at her and watched her move again in his arms, her lips parting in a slow yawn, her eyes fluttering slowly open.

When she was fully awake and she found Night Hawk gazing down at her, she could not believe that she was still in his arms.

"Did you hold me like this all night?" she murmured, adoring how he looked in the morning light, his handsomeness enhanced by the way the sun splashed its hues of soft pinkish-orange colors on his face.

"*Huh*, and it is good to see that you rested so well," he said, his heart thumping by how she looked at him, her eyes filled with loving. He swallowed hard. "And how are your wounds? Do they still hurt?"

Jae looked down at herself, seeing the blanket that lay loosely around her shoulders, yet folded together in the front so that none of her nakedness was showing. "I feel nothing at all." She drew back a corner of the blanket to look at her arms, where she knew the rope had cut painfully into her flesh.

When she saw the powdery substance on the wound, she recalled Crying Wolf explaining to her that this medicine had been made from herbs. She had not even considered being bashful as she had lain there, her clothes removed, as the old Indian had doctored her wounds. He had treated her with much respect by not having allowed his eyes to wander to the parts of her that he was not medicating.

Afterward, Night Hawk had gently placed the blanket around her and had carried her to their campsite. She had forgotten her pain and had enjoyed a meal of rabbit and coffee with them.

She had crawled onto Night Hawk's lap and had soon after gone fast asleep, feeling so protected in the arms of the man she loved. She had felt so blessed that he no longer forbid her to be with him. Together now, along with Crying Wolf, they were looking for a new world, a new life, placing all sorrows and bitter feelings of the past behind them.

They had only discussed Ralph Hampton once, agreeing to send him a message that they were all right as soon as they could. Night Hawk felt that he owed at least that much loyalty and respect to the man who had taken him in and given him a home when he otherwise might have grown up homeless.

And as for his adoptive mother, she deserved far more than a mere message. But it was her fate to be married to a callous man.

Jae agreed because she felt guilty for letting her true father down, yet she had known almost the moment she was with him that she could never feel anything deeply for him. To her, Ralph was just another man . . . one to be pitied. And she doubted he would have wanted her to stay only out of pity.

"Where is Crying Wolf?" Jae asked, drawing the blanket more closely around her shoulders, the morning air still filled with a quiet chill. She looked all around her, stopping when she saw only two horses. She turned a quick look Night Hawk's way. "He's gone. Where? Why?"

"He left before sunup to go and scout ahead of us," Night Hawk said, scooting two tin cups over by the fire. "After your ambush last night, and Jonas having escaped, who is to say when he might show up again? Crying Wolf is riding ahead to make sure things are clear for our travel. If all is well, he will stop and build a fire. We will catch up with him. I am almost certain it is now safe to say that he is already preparing our morning meal."

Jae shivered as she recalled the quickness with which Jonas had thrown the rope over her head. She still ached where she had fallen to the ground.

"I truly thought that we'd never see Jonas Adams again," she murmured, snaking a hand from beneath the blanket to accept a cup of coffee from Night Hawk. "I guess he will haunt me until he's downed by a bullet."

"He had best not show his face to me again. I shall never forget him holding you captive, naked. Had it not been for Snoopy, I may not have arrived on time to save you."

Jae's eyes crinkled into a happy smile. "Where is that little rascal?" she asked, searching around her.

"He went with Crying Wolf," Night Hawk said, setting his empty cup aside. "Those two have made a fast friendship."

Jae giggled. "That sweet raccoon. I love him so."

"Hey, now, I might get jealous." Night Hawk chuckled, then caught himself the very instant the word "jealous" slipped across his lips. His jealousy of Jae, and how Ralph Hampton had kept her from him way too long that first night of their arrival at the ranch, had been wrong. Jealousy was something that ate at one's insides. And as far as Jae was concerned, it was a wasted emotion. He knew now the intensity of her love for him, for she had given up so much to be with him!

Jae clung to the blanket with one hand and crawled on her knees to Night Hawk. She knelt before him, and placed her hands to his cheeks, framing his face between her hands, the blanket sliding slowly away from her.

"I love you so," she whispered, drawing his lips to hers. "Only you, Night Hawk. Only . . . you . . ."

He wanted to draw her next to him, but the wounds on her body were still so fresh that he was afraid of hurting her. Instead, he gently took her wrists and slid her arms around his neck. He held her slightly away from him as he gave her a soft kiss.

Night Hawk was aware of how her lips trembled against his. He was not sure if it was from passion . . . or . . .

He held his lips close to hers and gazed into her eyes. "Are you cold?" he asked, his voice husky with a building passion. They were together, alone. They had come through so much, and had come out of it loving one another even more intensely!

He needed her. His body ached for her!

Yet he still held back from this need. Jae would have to be the one to say that it was all right. It was her body that was freshly scarred, not his. He knew that she still must be suffering some pain.

But so was he: The pain, the heat in his loins was almost unbearable!

"No, I've never been hotter," Jae whispered, her eyelids passion-heavy. "You do this to me, Night Hawk. You awaken a fire in me that sends flashes of heat throughout me. I never knew loving a man could be like this. Always while near you, I feel as though my insides are melting."

"You also arouse the heat in me," Night Hawk replied, sliding a hand down, drawing a deep, sighing gasp from within Jae when he lifted the weight of one of her breasts within his hand. His thumb moved in a slow circle around the nipple, then he bent his head low and flicked his tongue across her other breast, his lips stopping to suck gently on her nipple.

"It is pure heaven," she whispered, closing her eyes, enjoying the pleasure that was spreading through her in great leaps of fire.

She wove her fingers through his hair and drew him closer. "More. Please . . . more . . ."

He lifted his eyes and placed a gentle hand to her cheek. "Jae, we had best stop now," Night Hawk said, his voice drawn from the passion he was trying to hold at bay. "Surely you are not able to . . ."

She placed a finger to his lips, silencing his words, pleading at him with her eyes. "Shh. Don't say anything else. Just love me, Night Hawk. Your love will heal all my wounds, inside and out. I thought I had lost you. Oh, Lord, now that I know that I haven't, I want you. *All* of you. The only true pain that I feel right now is the pain of needing you to quench the fires burning within me."

Night Hawk heard her need. He felt it deeply inside his heart, for it matched his own.

He lay her down gently on the blanket that had fallen from around her. As she lay waiting, her eyes devouring each new piece of flesh revealed to her, he yanked off his clothes.

When he was finally naked, she reached her hands out for him. "Night Hawk, my beautiful Comanche

Night Hawk, come to me," she said, hardly able to recognize her own voice.

"Comanche," Night Hawk said, smiling as he knelt down over her. His eyes flared with hungry intent, yet he held himself away, careful not to press himself hard against her rope wounds. "*Huh*, it is good to hear myself called Comanche. For too long I answered to that white side of my heritage. From now on, it will be my Comanche side!"

"More than once these past two days you have used the word '*huh*,'" she murmured. "I believe I have asked you before, but, Night Hawk, when you say *huh* in Comanche, what are you saying?"

"I am saying yes," he whispered. "Listen now to what I say to you in Comanche, then ask me the meaning. *Nei-com-mar-pe-ein*."

"Darling, tell me what is the meaning of that Comanche word?" She sucked in a wild breath when he placed his throbbing heat against her own, at the juncture of her thighs. As he softly probed with the velvet tip of his sex, she opened her legs wide to him.

"Not one word, but *three*," he said, his pulse racing as he gently shoved himself inside her, her warm walls sucking at the tight flesh of his manhood. "I said to you in Comanche that I love you."

"I want to learn those Comanche words." Jae closed her eyes in ecstasy when he kissed her long and hard, his rhythmic strokes within her claiming her senses, sending her into a whirlpool of ecstatic euphoria.

There was no more talking except for their body language, which they now knew so well while together. He kissed her hungrily, and his hands touched her where she was not injured in soft, wonderful caresses. Night Hawk had brought a splendid

Cassie Edwards

joy to her life—and she had almost lost both the joy *and* him!

At that thought, she clung even harder to his neck. As he thrust more deeply into her, she responded by lifting her hips to meet him. Her woman's center swelled beneath the sweet, warm press of his moving body. She moaned throatily as his hands kneaded her breasts. She parted her lips and welcomed his tongue as he thrust it inside her mouth.

Delicious shivers of desire rode her spine as he slid his mouth from her lips and kissed his way along the slim column of her throat, to her breasts. She slowly swung her head back and forth as he continued to love her in his mind-spinning fashion.

Night Hawk was lost in a wild, exuberant, drugged passion that overwhelmed him, heart and soul. The very nearness of her, her body pressed against his, her breasts so soft and wonderful in his hands, made silver flames of desire leap high within him.

His heart throbbing, his body turned to liquid fire as the pleasure mounted. He kissed her savagely, groaning against her lips as he felt the explosion begin, rocking his very soul as he found that place where the ultimate pleasure overcame him. He held her gently in his arms as he plunged over and over again inside her, feeling her own release as her body quivered and her moans filled the air.

Afterward, they lay together, the fire warming their perspiration-soaked flesh.

"I'm so thirsty," Jae said, breaking the silence. She giggled. "Aren't you? And I am suddenly so *hungry*."

"Can you wait until we reach Crying Wolf's campfire to eat?" he asked, leaning up on one elbow, gazing at her and how she seemed to glow after lovemaking.

"*Huh,*" Jae said, sitting up, drawing the corners of the blanket around her. Her eyes twinkled as she watched his reaction to her using the Indian word.

He smiled at her, then laughed softly.

Then he was touched deeply when she used the other three words that he had taught her, telling him in Comanche that she loved him.

Night Hawk sat up and drew Jae against him. He gave her a gentle kiss, then stood up and yanked on his breeches. "I will get something for you that will be even better than water to quench your thirst," he said. He gazed around him as the morning became brighter with light and things became more definable.

Jae scooted closer to the fire as she waited for him to return. And when he did, her eyes were wide. "Cactus?" she asked as he sat down beside her. "I thought the milky sap of the cactus was poisonous to man."

This cactus was a round one. Night Hawk inserted his knife into the side, near the top, and made a horizontal cut around it. "The sap is poisonous, but the rest is safe to eat," he said, lifting the top off. He cut off a chunk of the center and offered it to Jae.

"Here. Chew it. The juice will quench your thirst and has some food value. But only chew, don't swallow."

Remembering the times she had eaten the fruit of the prickly pear cactus, having known that it was safe, she sucked and chewed on this different sort of cactus. As its cool liquid ran down her throat, she found it not only thirst-quenching, but also very tasty.

She spat out the remains. "I do like it," she said, smiling over at Night Hawk. "Very much."

"There will be many things like this that I will introduce you to as we live off the land as Comanche," he said, slipping his knife back inside its sheath.

Night Hawk glanced at the sun. "I am certain Crying Wolf is wondering about us," he said. He offered Jae a hand. "Come. We must break up camp and travel onward."

Jae took his hand and rose to her feet, then paled as she glanced down at the blanket. "My clothes! I can't travel like this. Where are my clothes?"

Night Hawk nodded toward a tree behind a tall cluster of bushes. "Crying Wolf washed the blood from your clothes. They have dried in the tree through the night. They are wearable now."

Jae's eyebrows raised. "Is there anything Crying Wolf does not think of?" she said, laughing softly.

"Hardly," Running Hawk said, folding the blanket. "Would you not say that he is a valuable friend?"

"Very." Jae hurried to the tree and dressed quickly. She knelt down by the stream and sank her hands into the water, then splashed some on her face. When she heard the crackling of a twig behind her, she jumped.

Jae rose quickly to her feet, pale. Then she laughed nervously when she saw that it was only Night Hawk standing there with the coffee pot to be washed out. "I guess I'm still full of jitters over what happened yesterday," she said, running a hand nervously through her hair.

"Always remember, Jae, that while I am around, you have nothing to fear. I will be there, always, to protect you."

Jae was taken aback over how she accepted his words. For so long she had bragged that she needed no one but herself.

It was good . . . it was *heaven* . . . needing someone, especially Night Hawk.

Smiling, she took the coffee pot and sank to her knees again beside the stream. "Let me wash that for you." She gave Night Hawk a soft smile across her shoulder. "I am the woman of the house, aren't I? You protect; I do dishes."

He knelt down beside her. "We are quite a pair, you and I."

When he swept an arm around her waist and yanked her to him, she dropped the coffee pot to the ground. "Quite," she whispered.

She ground her body into his, thinking that washing dishes would come later.

So would their arrival at Crying Wolf's camp.

Their bodies, their hearts, again beckoned!

Neither would be denied!

Chapter Twenty-two

They traveled for several more days. Night Hawk did not question Crying Wolf about why they had not arrived at the Comanche village yet. He believed in his friend's ability to use his psychic powers to find the village. Had Crying Wolf not found Night Hawk many years ago by following those special powers?

The day was hot, the sun scorching. Night Hawk frowned as he gazed over at Jae. For the past hour or so, she had begun to look bedraggled, even somewhat *limp*, in her saddle. When he had asked her if she needed to stop, to rest, she had said that she felt like going on until they made camp for the night.

But Night Hawk was doubting that, especially now that he just noticed how she appeared to be feverish. Her face was flushed red more than it had been these past days after the initial slight burn she had received from having been in the sun for too many days in a row. No, there was something more than a sunburn to worry about.

She suddenly hung her head and closed her eyes, and her body began to sway slowly back and forth in the saddle. When she dropped the reins from her hands, Night Hawk's heart skipped a beat. He hurriedly edged his horse closer to hers just in time to catch her as she slumped sideways.

"Jae!" he cried, lifting her over onto his lap. When she gazed up at him with hazed-over, feverish eyes, he was filled with a sudden panic.

"I feel so ill," Jae murmured, her body suddenly seized with shakes. "I'm hot, and then . . . I . . . am so cold."

Crying Wolf sidled his horse close to Night Hawk's. He reached a hand to Jae's brow. "We must find water. While I gather the necessary items to make medicines for your woman, you must keep bathing her. We must get that fever down."

Crying Wolf took the reins to Jae's horse and tied them with his own. "Come," he said. "I see the shine of water ahead. And the Wise One Above, the Creator, is with us, for I see sumac trees only a short distance from the water. It is the sumac leaves that are required for my medicine for Jae."

He rode on ahead, as Night Hawk maintained a slow lope, his eyes never leaving Jae. Her eyes were closed again, and her breathing was shallow. "Crying Wolf and I will make you well," he said, his voice breaking. "I have not waited a lifetime for you, to then lose you again so soon after having found you."

"*Nei-com-mar-pe-ein*," Jae whispered, cuddling closer to Night Hawk's powerful chest.

Her saying that she loved him in Comanche made Night Hawk swallow hard. He battled the tears that were burning at the corner of his eyes. "My woman . . ." he said, then lifted his eyes and made his way through a thick stand of cottonwoods. He yanked on his horse's reins to guide him around first

219

one tree, and then the next, sighing with relief when he finally reached the deep, blue pool of water.

Holding Jae firmly in his arms, he slid easily from the saddle. She was so limp in his arms. Night Hawk was afraid that she might pass out from the raging fever. He carried her close to the water and laid her down on the cool, crisp grass. He secured his horse's reins, took a blanket from the horse, then rushed back to Jae.

Feeling so much for Jae, his heart reaching out to her, Night Hawk spread the blanket, and then placed her gently on it.

Remembering another time, only recently, when he had to unclothe her and medicate the wounds inflicted on her lovely skin by the rope, he felt choked up. His fingers trembled as he took off her shirt and her cut-off breeches. He recalled how only this morning she had removed them and washed them in a river, the sun quickly drying them so that she could put them back on after her bath.

"Soon you will wear the soft buckskin clothes of my people," he whispered, laying the last of her garments aside.

He quickly undressed, then carried her into the pond. What better way to bathe away her fever than to immerse her all at once in the water, Night Hawk thought to himself.

He carried her more deeply into the water until he was standing in it waist deep. As he held her, he gently splashed water over her body. Every once in a while, her eyes would creep open and she would gaze up weakly. Then she would close her eyes again and cuddle closer to him as he continued to bathe her.

His thoughts were scrambled as to what might have caused this illness. They had been careful of what they eaten, making sure the roasted meat was cooked well enough, and ensuring that if they stopped to enjoy the juice from a cactus plant, that was all they took from it.

It puzzled him as to why she was ill, yet neither he nor Crying Wolf had grown sick. They had eaten and drunk the same things. Their experiences were the same.

"Except for her bath this morning . . ." he said aloud, a thought then coming to him that made his insides grow cold.

Water splashing everywhere, Night Hawk hurried out of the pond. His heart pounding, he placed Jae on the blanket again. He searched her body for signs of a snake bite. Perhaps she had been bitten while bathing this morning. The snake could have bitten her under water. It could have felt no worse than a fish nipping at her flesh. If it had been a snake, he prayed that it had not been a water moccasin: their bite was deadly.

But if it had been a water moccasin, she would not have lived this long. She would have grown instantly ill, and she would have died within the hour.

"What are you searching for?" Crying Wolf asked as he came and knelt down beside Night Hawk. He had built a fire over which he had placed a small kettle. Then he had gathered the items needed to make the medicine for Jae. He had taken reed roots, cleaned them, and mashed them into a pulp. He carried the pulp now in a small leather bag.

He had gathered many sumac leaves and the root of the palloganghy plant. Taken in equal parts, they were crushed separately until they were almost like a powder. Mixed together, he had placed them in the kettle, along with two times the amount of sumac berries. The whole mixture now simmered in water over the flames of the fire. Soon he would see that Jae drank it.

And when the fever began to wane, he would gather another root called *ouissousatcki*. He would prepare it, then give it to Jae to help her regain her strength. A little bit at a time would be placed in warm water for her to drink.

"There it is," Night Hawk said, paling. "See the two small puncture wounds, Crying Wolf? Here on the back of her ankle? She is ill from a snake bite. It surely bit her while she was bathing in the river this morning."

Night Hawk looked up, his eyebrows raised, when Crying Wolf hurried away. He was soon hidden from Night Hawk's sight as he entered the deep shadows of a stand of trees.

Night Hawk understood his old friend well enough to know that he was now searching for the right medicine for snake bites. His heart swelled with love for Crying Wolf. Never had he met anyone as caring, or as generous. Today Crying Wolf's thoughts were centered only on Jae. It was in the seriousness etched across his face as he had gazed down at her that he had grown fond of her.

"Night Hawk . . ." Jae murmured, slowly opening her eyes. She saw only shadowed images of him as she peered through a strange sort of haze that seemed to have covered her eyes. She squinted. She reached a trembling hand out, trying to find his face. "Night Hawk, I . . . can . . . barely see you."

"It is because of the fever," he said, sinking his hands into the pond. He lifted them out again, filled with water, and slowly drizzled it along her feverish face. "Soon you will be better. Crying Wolf is preparing medicines for you. Soon he will bring them to you. You must stay awake long enough to drink the potions prepared by him."

"It . . . is . . . hard," Jae said. Her limbs felt so limp, it was as though all of the life had been drained from inside her. "What's happening to me? Why . . . am . . . I . . . I like this?"

"A snake bite." Night Hawk gently caressed her brow with a wet hand. "While you were bathing."

Panic seized Jae. Her eyes flew open. "I am filled with poison?" she gasped out.

"It is not lethal," Night Hawk said. "Or you would have been dead long ago."

She circled her fingers around his arm. "Hold me," she said, her voice even weaker than before. "Darling, hold . . . me."

His eyes wavering, Night Hawk drew her onto his lap. He held her to him, one hand slowly caressing her back. "You will be all right," he whispered, placing his cheek on her fevered head. "Soon you will be laughing again. You will enjoy gazing at the stars with me and discussing them."

"Snoopy," Jae whispered, feeling dizzy from the soaring fever.

"He is resting beneath a tree. He does not understand that you are sick."

"If anything happens to me, please keep him with you." Jae's breath was hot on her lips. "He knows nothing now but the ways of a human. He . . . is . . . part human, himself."

"*Huh*, I know," Night Hawk said, glancing over at the raccoon and how it had its head tucked down, its face almost hidden beneath one of its humanlike arms.

Night Hawk's eyes brightened when he saw Crying

Wolf coming toward him, not only with the pan of medicine that he had prepared over the fire, but also with several tiny bags tied to the waistband of his breeches.

"I have it all," Crying Wolf said as he knelt down beside Night Hawk. "Lay her on the blanket. Her recovery shall soon begin."

Night Hawk gently placed Jae on the blanket. He scarcely breathed as he watched Crying Wolf first put a poultice made from crushed red elm leaves on the snake bite.

Then Night Hawk held Jae's head up from the ground as Crying Wolf fed her the different medicinal drinks. When Jae choked and gagged, Crying Wolf drew his medicines away from her mouth.

Once she was breathing easily again, he would again feed her the liquids.

"She has had enough," Crying Wolf said, setting his pan and several small bags aside. "Continue bathing her with water for a while longer. I shall go and pray to The Wise One Above. Prayer and my medicine will make her well enough to travel, even as soon as tomorrow."

"You seem so sure," Night Hawk said. Again he lifted water from the pond into his hands and drizzled it slowly back and forth across Jae's body, stopping sometimes to rub her flesh gently.

"The leaves of the trees are for the healing of all people," Crying Wolf said. "Also, it is my deep belief, my *faith*, that makes me assured of this woman's recovery. Believe as deeply, Night Hawk. She will become well twice as quickly."

"I believe in everything you say and do." Night Hawk lifted a hand to Crying Wolf's shoulder.

"Thank you, old friend. Thank you for caring for my woman as much as I."

Crying Wolf laughed softly. "I care as much, but not in exactly the same way," he said, his eyes twinkling into Night Hawk's.

"And I should be glad, should I not?" Night Hawk was glad to have something to be lighthearted about, if only for the moment. "Someone like you, whose heart is so big, could very easily steal a woman from any man."

"My heart might be big, but it is old, perhaps too old for a woman to share it," Crying Wolf said, chuckling. He rose slowly, bent to gather his paraphernalia, then walked away.

Night Hawk kept bathing Jae until he noticed that some of the scarlet color of her cheeks and breasts was lessening. And when she opened her eyes and smiled up at him, he knew that her fever was breaking, and that she realized it, too.

"I'm sorry I have caused a delay in our travels," Jae murmured. "I know how anxious you are now to get to your Comanche village. Crying Wolf said that it was not far. If I hadn't become ill, perhaps we would have arrived by tonight."

"Tomorrow is soon enough," Night Hawk reassured her. "Tonight is yours and for healing."

She reached a trembling hand to his cheek. "How was I lucky enough to find you?" Her voice was breaking with emotion. "My darling . . . my darling . . ."

Exhausted from the effort of having said so much, Jae closed her eyes. "I must sleep awhile now," she whispered.

Now that her temperature was lessening, Night Hawk began to worry about her becoming chilled from being unclothed and wet.

He wrapped the blanket around her and once again placed her on his lap and held her. Slowly he rocked her, quietly humming the way he recalled his true mother having hummed to him those many years ago when he had been ill. He had always thought that her songs were what had made him get well.

"I shall sing for you always," he whispered to Jae, brushing a soft kiss across her brow.

He looked up as Crying Wolf came and knelt down on his haunches beside him. "I have prayed, and the prayers were heard. The Wise One Above showed himself to me in the form of a great eagle. It came and hovered over me, its eyes locked with mine. *Huh*, the eagle *was* the Wise One Above bringing me the message that the prayers had been heard and will be answered."

"She is already better," Night Hawk said, smiling over at Crying Wolf. "Again I thank you."

"You need never thank me for anything." Crying Wolf placed a gentle hand on Running Hawk's shoulder. "Do you not know that I do everything willingly because of my deep love for you? And now also for her."

He glanced down at Jae. "While she rests, I shall ride onward and find our village," Crying Wolf said, slowly rising to his feet. "But I will not enter. I shall come back for you. We will enter together."

"You truly believe it is so close?" Night Hawk asked, his heart pounding at the thought. He had prayed over and over again to himself, that his father would be alive now that Night Hawk knew his father had not abandoned him. How wonderful it would be to walk up to his father and tell him that he was his

226

son! He could hardly wait to feel the arms of his true father around him again, as he had felt them so often as a child!

"Our people are so close that I can almost hear the drums of our village," Crying Wolf said, nodding. He laughed softly. "Yet I know that it is only in my memory that I hear them. But soon I will hear them for real again!"

"Never forget that you must watch for those who might ambush us along the trail," Night Hawk softly urged.

"My psychic powers will keep me safe," Crying Wolf said, ambling away. "And also the Wise One Above."

Night Hawk watched him ride away. Then he gazed down at Jae again. "My heart is so anxious for my true father," he whispered, his eyes misting to know just how long his father had been denied him, and all because of a misunderstanding. Had Night Hawk known that his father had been forced to leave a son behind, instead of having purposely abandoned him, he would have done everything within his power to make things right for his father!

His jaw tightened. "But I must always remember that I was a mere child then. Now I am a man. If I am fortunate enough to find my father on this earth, just let someone try and take advantage of him again! This son who is now a man will kill those who might try!"

Jae stirred. She cuddled more endearingly into Night Hawk's arms.

He looked down at her. "And pity the man who ever touches you wrongly again!" he growled out.

Chapter Twenty-three

It was another hot day. The sun was like a great ball of fire in the sky. The air smelled of scorched grass and horse flesh.

Jae rode slowly to the creak of saddle leather. She was somewhat weak, but upon arising early this morning, she had determinedly told Night Hawk that she was well enough to travel. She knew how anxious he was to get to his village, finally to be among his true people after having lived apart from them for so many years.

She was more concerned about Crying Wolf than herself this morning. He had not returned since he had left yesterday to search for the Comanche village.

Night Hawk had not been able to wait any longer at the campsite for Crying Wolf's return. He feared for his old friend's safety and had to go search for him, to see if he was all right.

As they rode onward in a slow lope, they followed the fresh hoofprints in the dust, more than likely made by Crying Wolf's mustang.

Stiff in his saddle, Night Hawk kept his eyes on the hoofprints, which went steadily forward. They showed that Crying Wolf had not stopped to rest or to eat.

But one thing that made Night Hawk have some hope that his old friend was all right was that all along the trail, no other horse's hoofprints ever joined those of Crying Wolf's. That meant that he was still traveling alone, that thus far, no one had accosted him.

"I see someone coming," Jae said, using her hand to shield her eyes from the rays of the sun. "Do you see the horseman, Night Hawk?" She gazed more intensely at the man approaching them, who was only now a slight speck on the horizon. "Do you think it's Crying Wolf?"

Night Hawk peered hard into the distance, then smiled when it was obvious that he and Jae had also been spotted as the horseman raised a hand and waved a greeting to them. "It *is* Crying Wolf," Night Hawk said, relief surging through him.

"Ride on ahead and meet him," Jae said, giving Night Hawk a soft smile as he looked over at her. "I shall soon follow."

He gazed at her a moment longer, then looked around them carefully.

"There is no one following us," Jae reassured him. "I will be safe enough while you go and meet Crying Wolf. I know how anxious you are to see if the news he brings to you is good."

She paused and reached a gentle hand to his cheek. "I am not quite well enough to ride this horse faster than a lope. Please go on, Night Hawk. See what Crying Wolf has to say."

He took her hand, kissed its palm, then nodded

and rode off in a hard gallop.

When he caught up with Crying Wolf and wheeled his horse to a stop, Night Hawk could tell by the happiness in the depths of his old friend's eyes that he had good news to share with him.

"You found it," Night Hawk said, anxious to hear the words. "You found our village."

"It is past that valley, only a short distance." Tears flooded Crying Wolf's eyes, knowing at this moment just how much he had missed his Comanche brethren. But soon he would be among them. It would be a moment to rejoice!

"It must have been hard not to ride on in and let them know that you are alive, but it is good that you did not," Night Hawk said, suddenly solemn at the thought of just how they might be received. His father might not be in charge of the village. If those in opposition to his father had taken over again, would not both he and Crying Wolf be riding into a trap? Would not Jae be as vulnerable as they, for she, too, would be looked at as an enemy! Especially Jae, for her skin was white!

And Night Hawk must never allow himself to forget the color of his own hair, and that he was a "breed" who might be shunned by the full-blooded Comanche.

Crying Wolf looked past Night Hawk. "When Jae catches up with us, we shall all travel together to our village," he said, his trembling voice proving his excitement.

"No, that is not the way it should be," Night Hawk said, lifting a heavy hand to his old friend's shoulder. "Not yet, anyhow."

Crying Wolf stared at his friend. "Why would we not go on ahead to our village? I *know* that it belongs to our people. I was there, looking from a butte early this morning. I watched long enough. I saw some that I remember. They will also know me."

"Are you sure they will welcome you?" Night Hawk asked. "You have been gone a long time."

"*Huh*, that is so. But why should that matter?"

"They may feel you were negligent in your duty to your chief. Unless you saw my father, the chief, while you were observing our village?" Night Hawk's pulse raced. He leaned closer to Crying Wolf. "Did you see my father?"

Crying Wolf frowned. He lowered his eyes. "No, and although I saw the large tepee that I knew once was your father's, I did not see him. And I could not venture closer. Had I been caught observing, instead of riding on into the village, I might have been considered a spy. And I promised you we would enter together. It is now time for us both to go and get the answers we seek."

"I still say to you, Crying Wolf, that it is best that only *I* enter the village this first time," Night Hawk persisted, his voice growing stern. "I am both anxious and apprehensive about our arrival. I do not want to place you or Jae in danger. In case we are *not* received well, I must go on without you. I will check out the village, the people's feelings about me, and whether or not my father is alive, and then I will return to you and Jae."

"I still say I should be the one to go," Crying Wolf replied. "And had I known that you would be stubborn about this, I would have gone ahead myself. I would have placed myself in jeopardy if necessary. It is better that someone as old as I be put in danger. Not you, who will soon rule as a powerful Comanche leader, yourself."

231

"I forbid you to go," Night Hawk stated flatly.

Jae rode up and drew tight rein beside the men. She felt the tension between the two friends, as though the air around them was about to explode. She was stunned by this, for never had she seen them exchange even one sour word.

"What's wrong?" she asked, looking from one to the other.

"We are having a disagreement, that is all." Running Hawk's eyes were still locked in silent battle with Crying Wolf's. "I will leave you now. Jae, Crying Wolf will explain why I am riding on ahead without you. He will explain the wisdom of it to you, won't you, Crying Wolf?"

Crying Wolf set his jaw and gave Night Hawk a solemn stare, then turned toward Jae. "*Huh*, I will explain," he said, his voice drawn. He looked at Night Hawk again. "Ride on, my friend. Jae and I will wait for your return over by the creek in the shade of the cottonwoods. Do not make us wait long. I cannot tell how long I can keep my promise not to follow."

"Night Hawk, why . . ." Jae began, but she could not finish her question, for Night Hawk rode off in a hard gallop.

She turned toward Crying Wolf. "Shouldn't we go after him?" she asked, concern for Night Hawk building within her heart. She knew there must be some danger in what he was doing, or else Crying Wolf would not have shown such anger over it.

"In time, if he does not return." Crying Wolf nodded toward the creek. "Come. Let us rest in the shade. I will explain to you the foolishness of what your man is about to do."

Jae paled. She looked quickly toward Night Hawk.

"Do not go after him," Crying Wolf said, grabbing

her reins. "Your place is here. Not there."

He led her horse alongside his to the grove of cottonwoods. Jae dismounted and watched from the shade until she could no longer see Night Hawk in the distance.

"Will he be all right?"

"If it is meant to be, *huh*," was all that Crying Wolf would say. He folded his arms across his chest.

"He did not even say good-bye," Jae whispered, feeling a chill of fear race up and down her spine.

233

Chapter Twenty-four

Following Crying Wolf's directions, Night Hawk traveled onward, looking every so often from side to side, and over his shoulder, to make sure he was not being followed or stalked.

He followed a well-beaten trail that led in a north-westerly direction. Upon reaching the head of the valley, he turned to the left and began ascending a wide, low range of mountains, winding in and out of narrow passes and defiles, but still gradually ascending, traveling in this manner for another mile before reaching the summit.

Night Hawk soon guessed that it must have been from this vantage point that Crying Wolf had observed his village. He edged his horse closer to the edge of the cliff and gazed down at a village nestled in the valley, where ravines were overgrown with stunted trees. The adjacent mountain was rocky, but occasionally, between the ridges that rose in succession one above the other, were small, level meadows covered with heavy growth and grass, upon which buffalo, deer, and antelope were feeding.

Along one of the ravines were row after row of stately tepees. People were busy with their daily chores. Young children played, dogs barked, and horses neighed in their corrals at the back of the lodges.

Night Hawk's gaze sorted through the tepees and his heart beat like thunder when he found two larger lodges. He remembered enough of his past to know that one of these would be the Civil Chief's, and the other the War Chief's. He also remembered the designs that his father had painted on his lodge—those of animals and forest scenes. His heart throbbed as he gazed at one of the lodges, knowing that it must be his father's! As he watched, an aged man left the lodge. The chief's face had not changed, except for a few wrinkles.

"Father . . ." Night Hawk gasped. Memories of his childhood raced through his mind—he remembered being held, being taught how to ride a pinto pony, being taught how to shoot a tiny bow and arrow at small creatures.

But his smile faded when he saw his father stumble, almost falling to the ground but for a young brave who came and quickly offered assistance.

He watched his father being led slowly back inside his lodge.

"He is not well," Night Hawk said, his voice breaking.

A noise behind Night Hawk made him turn suddenly. He'd been so absorbed in watching his father, and so happy that he had finally found him, that he had not heard the horses approach. Their hooves were covered with buckskin to muffle any sound they made on the ground.

Night Hawk stiffened when he discovered several

warriors in an aggressive position, some with their lances upraised, some with their bows notched with arrows, and some with rifles aimed at him.

They were all dressed in breechclouts and moc-casins, their hair tied back from their brows with a band.

"Who are you?" one of the warriors, who rode a white mustang, said flatly. "Why are you, whose hair is the color of wheat, and whose skin color matches my own, watching my Comanche village?"

Night Hawk looked from warrior to warrior, knowing that surely among them were those with whom he had played as a child, who had escaped the wrath of the white pony soldiers all those years ago when their village had been raided.

Yet, as he had grown up to look so different, so had they all, for he recognized none of them.

Night Hawk squared his shoulders and lifted his chin proudly. "I am Night Hawk," he said, his eyes watching for some reaction from those who might remember him, yet seeing none. "My father is Brown Bull, your War Chief."

The warrior in charge stared icily at Night Hawk. "Night Hawk, you say? *Huh,* I do know you." His gaze roamed slowly over Night Hawk, then he looked over his shoulder at the others. "My warrior friends, do you not also remember this 'breed'? I should have recognized him by his golden locks of a woman!"

The warrior turned back around and glared at Night Hawk, his eyes narrowed. "It is *Yo-oh-habt-popi,* Yellow Hair," he hissed. "It is the one I called Yellow Hair when we were young braves."

"Only one brave called me Yellow Hair," Night Hawk said, his voice tight. "His name was Black Crow."

"And it is *still* Black Crow who calls you Yellow Hair." Black Crow threw his head back in a fit of mocking laughter.

For certain now that he was not among friends, for the warriors all jeered and taunted him along with Black Crow, Night Hawk said nothing more. He waited to see what their next move might be. In truth, he felt as though he might have entered a hornet's nest.

Black Crow leaned closer to Night Hawk. He frowned a most ugly frown. "I, Black Crow, am now War Chief of our band of Comanche," he boasted in a low hiss. "Brown Bull is now only Civil Chief, and he is *powerless*."

Night Hawk paled. He edged his horse back from Black Crow's. "Powerless?"

"His age and his health have weakened his importance to our people," Black Crow said in a mocking tone. "They look to me for security, for leadership. Not your father."

Black Crow lifted his chin haughtily. "And you do not deserve to live among us," he said stiffly. "You wear the clothes of white people. You have lived among them these past years, have you not? Why have you come now to call yourself Comanche? Is it because you tire of being called 'breed' in the white community? Or have you come to us to pretend to care for us in order for you to try and take a place of leadership among us? If you cannot become a leader in the white community, you think you can come here among our people and get what you could not get among the whites?"

"Listen well, Black Crow. I remember you from my past as one who knew well the art of stirring up hatred," Night Hawk said, his eyes flashing angrily.

"Listen well to why I am here, and to why I was not here these past years. And listen well, Black Crow, when I tell you that I *have* come to challenge you, especially now that I know that my father might be in danger under such a leadership as yours."

"I listen with only half a heart and mind to someone I see who has, in truth, come to the Comanche village in pretense, to infiltrate the tribe, to spy on our Comanche people, to take back news to the white pony soldiers," Black Crow said, his voice low and measured. "I will listen to what you say, and *then* decide what must be done with you."

Seeing the cleverness of Black Crow, Night Hawk now knew just how much danger he was in. He had to choose his words wisely. Most of all, he must get to his father before Black Crow succeeded at coercing those other warriors into believing him.

"I am here for only one purpose, to see my father. So I see no more need for talk. What I say would be mocked, anyhow. I go now to my father. I will tell him everything. He is the only one who deserves to know."

"You, who are a traitor to your people, deserve nothing," Black Crow hissed. He raised a fist in the air. "Seize this man!"

Before Night Hawk could defend himself, he was surrounded and thrown from his horse, and his wrists and ankles were bound.

Then he was thrown over the back of his horse and tied to it.

Black Crow's laughter filled the air, causing birds to fly from the trees and rabbits to hop with desperation away from their hiding places in the thick brush.

"Take him to our village," Black Crow shouted as

one of the warriors took the reins to Night Hawk's horse and slowly led him down the side of the bluff.

Night Hawk scarcely breathed as he looked over at Black Crow. He now understood that this War Chief was not only *his* enemy, but also his father's. Black Crow had shown his bitterness when he had spoken of Brown Bull.

And Night Hawk knew that if Black Crow was brazen enough to take the son of the Civil Chief into the village tied on the back of a horse, then he had far more power among the Comanche people than his father ever could have.

If not, Black Crow would not dare humiliate Brown Bull's son in such a way! In the days of Brown Bull's reign as War Chief, had anyone gone against him in such a way, the warrior would have been seized and would have died quickly for his sin!

Night Hawk felt suddenly doomed.

Then another thought came to him that made his heart sink even lower. If Black Crow and his warriors had found *him*, would they not also find Jae and Crying Wolf? If so, what would *their* fate be?

Surely death!

Chapter Twenty-five

As Night Hawk was brought into the village, he could see people standing shyly inside their tepees, the entrance flaps held aside only far enough for them to see this stranger tied to a horse.

Everything had changed from the time he had seen so much activity in the village. At the first sight of the bound stranger, the chores had been left for another time. The children had been ushered into the lodges. Even the dogs had been taken inside.

Night Hawk strained his neck to see his father's large lodge, wondering if *he* would be standing at the entranceway, watching. He recalled how his father had been led inside the lodge by a young brave. Perhaps he was now too weak to see the wrong that was being done to his very own flesh and blood—his son!

When Night Hawk reached the point where he could see his father's lodge, his heart sank, for no one was there, watching. That had to mean that his father was quite ill, and that Black Crow had been right when he had said that his father was now powerless. If not, surely his father would go to the door to see what was causing the sudden silence in his village.

Sadness and helplessness crept into Night Hawk's heart. It was not for only himself that he felt these things: He mourned for his father, who might not be able to speak up in behalf of his son once he realized it *was* Night Hawk who was being humiliated before his very own people.

Night Hawk mourned for Jae and Crying Wolf, who might soon meet this same fate. He felt as though he had let everyone down.

He swallowed hard, and his muscles tightened when his horse stopped. Out of the corner of his eye he watched Black Crow dismount from his steed. Night Hawk's jaw tightened and his eyes narrowed angrily as Black Crow came and stood over him, his thin lips lifted in a smug sneer.

"*Now* where is that great man you call your father?" Black Crow taunted. "Do you see him here, speaking in your behalf? You were wrong to come here. You should have stayed with the whites."

"You, who know nothing but hate and greed, will one day pay for what you have done to my Comanche father and those who followed him as though they were his shadow," Night Hawk said from between clenched teeth. "If ever I am released from these ropes, I will see that you die a slow death, staked to the ground beneath the hot rays of the sun."

Black Crow held his head back in a loud, roaring laugh, then grew somber again. He thrust his face near Night Hawk's. "You are foolish to speak such words to a man who holds you prisoner. And it is *you* who will be staked to the ground, not I. Let us see then, 'breed,' who will die slowly beneath the rays of the sun. It certainly will not be *this* Comanche."

241

Black Crow straightened his back and glared as his eyes roamed slowly from tepee to tepee, then gazed down at Night Hawk again. "Do you see how everyone cowers inside their lodges?" he said, laughing sarcastically. "That is because my power over them makes them shudder like frightened puppies at the very sight of me, their War Chief."

"That is something to brag about?" Night Hawk asked, raising an eyebrow. "You are more foolish than I thought. One who rules with force, who is feared, is no true leader at all."

Running Hawk laughed. "I am not certain how long you have been allowed to rule my father's people, *my* people, with an iron fist. But I will say this to you—whoever rules with hate falls the hardest when finally the people tire of him."

"Again you speak so openly and foolishly while you are my prisoner?" Black Crow's voice was rising as his anger grew within him. He yanked a knife from its sheath at the side of his waist and sliced the ropes that held Night Hawk to the horse.

When Night Hawk's body hit the packed-down earth, the impact momentarily knocked his breath from him. But soon he recovered and grew cold inside as he watched stakes being driven into the ground.

He felt as though he were living an ugly dream as he was taken to those stakes. The ropes that bound his hands and ankles were released. While several warriors held rifles on him, others stripped him of his clothes. He was then tied to the stakes, his arms and legs so widely spread that they pained him.

But he made no sound. He would not humiliate himself by showing any emotion, nor would he give

Black Crow the satisfaction of hearing him utter any sound.

Night Hawk forced himself to block out everything, how Black Crow twisted his flaxen hair into mock braids, then placed cockleburs among them like miniature, mock crowns. He stared blankly ahead when the women and children of the village were ordered to march past him.

"See what happens to enemies of the Comanche!" Black Crow shouted to the people. "See this man? He is a 'breed.' Yes, he is part Comanche, but he has chosen to live with whites!"

Black Crow placed his fists on his hips, his eyes gleaming. "And why is he here?" he shouted. "He is here to spy on us, to find out our secrets, to take them back to the white pony soldiers! If he was allowed to do this and then leave, some night under the cover of dark, the pony soldiers would come and take our lives from us."

It was hard for Night Hawk to listen and not fight back with his own words of explanation. But he knew that if he spoke up, one of Black Crow's warriors would quickly silence him with the butt of a rifle.

So he lay there, the sun beating on his bare flesh, while biting ants crawled over him.

His eyes did stray, though, and stopped at the lodge that was his father's. It was evident now to Night Hawk that his father must be gravely ill. He must also be terribly frightened of Black Crow and the power he held over the Comanche people.

Night Hawk then gazed from lodge to lodge, wondering if there might be any warrior there who might still love his father, who might align himself with his father's son, if he could just find a way to get free.

243

He recalled Crying Wolf telling him how his father had lost his leadership once before. If he had regained it then, perhaps he could do it a second time.

No, Night Hawk thought to himself, it was almost impossible for an ailing, aged man to regain his standing in the village, especially if his son was not there to help him.

Night Hawk's eyebrows arched when another thought came to him. *Had* he been the only son born to his father? Had he been the only child?

If not, where were the other children? How had they allowed this to happen to their father?

The worries mingled with his fear, draining his strength. And still the sun beat down onto his flesh. His throat was dry. His lips were parched. His nostrils flared, the moisture gone from inside his nose.

He strained against his bonds, succeeding at only rubbing his flesh raw as the rope dug into his skin.

He tried to think of things that did not drain him of energy. He focused his eyes on his father's lodge. Then he looked past the lodges, at the far pastures, awed by what he saw. Never had he seen so many horses in one place, not even back at his adoptive father's ranch!

But, of course, he reminded himself, the Comanche were always adding to their herd, either by catching horses wild on the range, or stealing them from their enemies.

To the Comanche, horses constituted wealth!

Again Night Hawk turned his attention to his father's lodge, sliding his gaze to those smaller tepees that sat in a small cluster around the outside of his lodge. There were four such smaller lodges, and from time to time, Night Hawk had seen women staring from the entrance flaps at him.

He could remember a custom of the Comanche that he recalled from his childhood. The wives of a Comanche man lived in the smaller dwellings away from the husband's big lodge. In the smaller tepees, they raised their husband's children.

Night Hawk had been raised in such a lodge away from his father. And from what he could observe today, he guessed that his father had four wives. Since they lived apart from him, surely there *were* children!

Black Crow kicked him in the side as he was thinking that if his father was still virile enough to have so many wives, perhaps his health had only recently worsened.

"You will be left alone now," Black Crow said, glaring down at Night Hawk. "I have more important duties than watching a 'breed' die. I have many horses to see to. I will let the sun, ants, and flies have their way with you."

Night Hawk returned his glare, yet he said nothing. He knew that words would be wasted on Black Crow, and Night Hawk knew he had to save whatever strength he might have until later. Surely there would be one among those who had been his father's friends who might have mercy on him. For his father's friends were warriors whose hearts were big. They would not enjoy seeing any man tied there, especially one who had not come to the Comanche people with threats.

The activity in the village resumed all around Night Hawk, except for a few children who came from time to time to stare down at him. He was glad that they did not laugh and point at him. This proved that they did not approve of how he was being treated.

His body grew weaker by the minute as the sun

Cassie Edwards

drained him of his energy. Night Hawk slowly closed his eyes.

He fell asleep, and when he awakened he stared up at the sky, relieved that the sun was no longer a threat. He noticed that it was still some time before darkness would fall around him.

His thoughts went to Crying Wolf and Jae. He hoped that they did not grow restless and come ahead, to see what might have happened to him. He prayed to himself that Crying Wolf would keep Jae safe. Yet he knew his old friend well enough to know that if he had not returned to them by nightfall, Crying Wolf would come searching for him.

Night Hawk's breath caught in his throat when he saw a beautiful maiden moving toward him. She came and stood over him, staring. When he saw sadness in her eyes, surely over how he was being treated, again he found a reason to hope.

"What is your name?" Night Hawk managed to say through his parched lips; his tongue was so dry it felt heavy. He was aware that his nudity caused her some embarrassment. He saw how she avoided looking lower than his eyes.

"I am called Touch the Sky," she murmured, nervously clasping and unclasping her hands before her. "And your name is?"

"I am called Night Hawk," he replied, swallowing hard as his dry tongue caught on the roof of his mouth. "Untie me, Touch the Sky. I have come to see my father, Chief Brown Bull!"

When he saw the surprise that leapt into her eyes, and how she took an unsteady step away from him, panic rose within him. "Do not go," he cried. "Listen to what I have to say. When I was ten, white soldiers attacked our Comanche village. I was taken away.

My mother, who was white, was killed during the skirmish."

While she stood there—stunned, speechless—Night Hawk's gaze swept slowly over her. She was nothing less than ravishing. Her eyes were dark and slightly slanted like his. Her copper face had perfect features. She was tiny and slender.

Her coal-black hair hung down to her waist. Her ears had been reddened and her cheeks were orange with rouge in the shape of a triangle.

The part of her hair had been painted with vermilion. Her eyes were accentuated with yellow lines above and below her lids, crossing at the corners.

She was dressed in a fringed gown that reached from her chin down to the ankles. It was made of elkskin, with long fringes of elk's teeth worn around her neck. Colored beads were sewn on the gown in pretty designs, and she wore bands of wire around both wrists.

And she wore no moccasins. She was barefoot.

When she turned and began to run away from him, Night Hawk tried to cry out to her, but his voice failed him.

Then his heart raced when he saw whose lodge she entered: his father's! Surely she was kin to his father, or at least, a very good friend. Surely she was going to tell his father what he had said . . . that he was Chief Brown Bull's son!

Then another thought came to him that caused his heart to soar. This beautiful woman might even be Brown Bull's daughter! She might be Night Hawk's sister!

He gazed again at the other smaller tepees clustered close to his father's. His eyes widened when he saw several children playing around the outside of

Cassie Edwards

the entrances. Their ages ranged from three years to perhaps eight.

But there was one boy who stood away from them, whose eyes were now on Night Hawk, staring at him. To Night Hawk, he appeared to be about twelve winters old.

Suddenly he recalled when he had seen this young brave before. He was the one who had helped Brown Bull to his lodge earlier.

Night Hawk smiled at the boy. His heart filled with gladness when the young brave returned the smile. He might be a friend who would help Night Hawk when the sky became dark. Many things could be achieved under the cover of darkness that could not be done during the daylight hours.

Night Hawk hoped that the ropes would soon be gone from his aching wrists and ankles.

Chapter Twenty-six

Touch the Sky knelt down beside her father's bed of blankets and placed a gentle hand on his ashen brow. "Father, the one who has been brought to our village, and who is now staked to the ground as though he is a worthless being, an enemy, calls himself by the name of the son you have spoken to me of so often," she murmured. "Father, he calls himself Night Hawk. He says that you are his father! He tells about the attack on our people those many years ago by the whites. Father, he even has the flaxen hair of the son you have mourned for so long! Could he truly be your son? If so, why does Black Crow treat him so inhumanely? Why did he not bring him to you?"

Brown Bull tried to get up, but he fell back down on the bed, his limbs too weak to hold him up. "My son," he gasped. "My son, Night Hawk. He has heard my silent pleas! He has come home to me. He has come to help me in my time of trouble!"

"But, Father, Night Hawk can help *no* one," Touch the Sky cried. "He is helpless! Why, oh, why, Father, would Black Crow do this to him? I do not understand the logic of it, except that Black Crow *did* say that Night Hawk has come with evil on his mind, to spy on our people for the whites. Do you believe that is so, Father?"

"I believe nothing Black Crow says. He is a man with a *che-kas-koi,* a bad heart. Everything that he does is evil! And why does he imprison my son? Why does he humiliate him? Do you not know, my daughter? My son's sudden arrival is a threat to everything Black Crow plans. This man puts our people in jeopardy each time he raids and kills; this man wants war over everything else; this man is greedy for power—he will not want my son here to take over for me."

He reached a trembling hand to Touch the Sky's arm and clutched it hard. "Daughter, be careful," he warned, his eyes wild. "But try to find a way to set my son free. Go to Eagle Wing, the one who *should* be War Chief. Get him to help you, but do nothing to stir up the anger of the other factions of our people who align themselves with Black Crow. Their number is greater than those who will follow Eagle Wing's leadership."

"Father, I shall do what I can," Touch the Sky said, leaning to give him a soft hug. "Father, oh, Father, is there truly some hope for our future after all? Do you think this newcomer is the messenger of such hope?"

"If he is the true son of your father, *huh,* I believe the Wise One Above has truly sent him to help our people rise out of the despair brought to their lives by the conniving, evil ways of Black Crow!" Chief Brown Bull said, his old heart eager to know if this were truly so.

Chapter Twenty-seven

Jae could not relax. She paced nervously back and forth. As she watched the sun lowering in the sky, she peered in the direction in which Night Hawk had headed. "Where is he?" she whispered, clenching and unclenching her hands at her sides.

A gentle hand on her shoulder made her stop and turn toward Crying Wolf. "He's been gone for so long," she said, her voice breaking. "I don't think we should wait much longer. It will soon be dark."

"That is my own thought." Crying Wolf glanced up at the sky. The sun was all but gone from sight. He turned his eyes back to Jae. "We will leave now. Night Hawk *should* have returned."

"You think we should go on ahead, even though Night Hawk told us to wait?" Jae asked, recalling the firmness with which Night Hawk had told Crying Wolf to stay there until he returned.

"If Night Hawk has not run into danger, then we, too, will be safe when we reach him, and he will have no true cause to be angry over our having come to him. If he *is* in danger, and we *rescue* him, he will have even less cause to be angry."

Crying Wolf dropped his hand to his side. His lips tugged into a smile. "And he knows me well. He knows that this old man does not listen well to orders from someone much younger than he, especially when this old man knows what is best."

"But he seemed so serious when he told you not to follow him," Jae said, arching an eyebrow.

"*Huh*, he was serious in that he was concerned over our welfare," Crying Wolf said. He took Jae gently by an elbow and walked her toward their tethered horses. "Otherwise, he would not have used such a stern tone with either of us."

He stopped and turned Jae to face him. He clasped his hands to her shoulders. He searched her face with his eyes. "Are you truly well enough to travel onward? You are strong enough? The fever drained you of much of your energy. You used much of it to get this far. Have you enough left to travel tonight?"

"My thoughts are not on myself and how much energy I have to get me here or there," Jae said. "My concern is only for Night Hawk. Please, let's go now. Let's see if he is all right."

"There might be those from my village who would want to see Night Hawk harmed if they realize who he is," Crying Wolf said, his thoughts taking him back to the time Chief Brown Bull had been betrayed by those in his camp who were his enemy.

Even after Brown Bull had regained his powers as chief, Crying Wolf knew there were those of the younger generation who were already becoming dissatisfied with his leadership.

He recalled one such young warrior—Black Crow! Even when Black Crow was a young brave, his views were radical. If *he* was still alive, and had the power of persuasion he had only just begun to have as a young warrior, he, alone, could cause trouble for Night Hawk.

"*Kee-mah namiso*, come, hurry. Let us go," Crying Wolf said, moving away from Jae with a wide, quick stride. "We will not arrive at the village until long past dark. I hope we will meet Night Hawk halfway there. If he decided to go on into the village, he may have found it a most unwise choice."

Jae caught up to Crying Wolf and took hold of his arm, stopping him. She stepped around and faced him. "Do you think he might have done that?" she asked, a strange sort of dread entering her heart.

"Let us hope that if he *is* in the village, it is because he went there of his own volition." Crying Wolf saw the instant fear that entered Jae's eyes and wished now that he had not spoken so openly of his fears to her. But he had, and there was no way to take them back.

Jae gulped hard. She watched Crying Wolf go to his horse and pull himself into his saddle.

She then ran to her own steed and swung herself into her saddle. Suddenly she felt no tiredness, only a restless energy that was caused by the need to see that Night Hawk was all right.

As she rode off with Crying Wolf, Jae glanced at the darkening sky. She wondered where Night Hawk might be as the shadows deepened.

Chapter Twenty-eight

Touch the Sky ran to the usual meeting place where she and her beloved Eagle Wing had their evening trysts. But tonight she had something quite different on her mind than being held in her lover's arms. She could not forget the man who was staked to the ground, who professed to being her father's son . . . her *brother*.

If everything the captive said was true, Eagle Wing must help him. Her father was too weak even to walk now. She had watched his energy being slowly drained away. These past two days, he had worsened so much that he could rarely even rise from his bed.

"I must also find a way to help him," she whispered to herself. She feared Black Crow's hunger for power. If her father became so ill that he was no longer able to function as Civil Chief, Black Crow would have the power to coerce his people into choosing her father's successor.

She could not help being suspicious about her father's strange malady. Both she and her father suspected his debility was caused by something other than old age. They both believed that someone was causing his illness.

They both had suspicions as to who this person might be, and they were planning to trap him. But for now, Touch the Sky focused her attention on helping the stranger.

The sun was gone from the sky, the shadows were deepening at the foot of the cliff where Eagle Wing would be waiting for her. Touch the Sky broke into a fast run. When she finally reached their trysting place, she flung herself into Eagle Wing's arms, breathless.

"My woman, your flight to me tonight seems frenzied," Eagle Wing said. "I even feel a desperation in the way you cling to me."

"Hold me," she cried. "I need you, Eagle Wing. Please hold me."

Eagle Wing wrapped his arms around her, always relishing her closeness.

Then he held her at arm's length. "What is wrong?" he asked, frowning when he saw so much in her eyes that was unfamiliar to him. Usually he found strength. He found joy. He found love. Tonight there was fear and puzzlement.

"My father needs your help," Touch the Sky blurted out. "The man who is staked on the ground in our village says that he is my father's son, Night Hawk. If so, he is my *brother*. I never knew him, Eagle Wing. I was not yet born when my father was forced to leave his firstborn behind on the day of the white pony soldier attack on our village. No one ever knew what became of my brother. My father sent a friend to search for him long ago, a man whose name I cannot remember. I do know, though, that he never returned. He was probably killed while searching for my brother. There are those, you know, who would not want my brother to be alive."

"*Huh*, I know," Eagle Wing said, again drawing her into his embrace. "I have listened when your father talked of Night Hawk, also your father's white wife. He was told that she had been killed by the white pony soldiers, yet discovered later that she was, in truth, killed by a Comanche."

"My father has confided all this to me," Touch the Sky said. "And also you, my love. Thank you for listening to him."

"What does your father wish for me to do about this imprisoned man?" Eagle Wing asked, his jaw tightening. "Does he wish that I set him free?"

"*Huh*, but how can it be done without Black Crow finding out?" Touch the Sky asked, her voice breaking. "There will be guards who watch the captive. Black Crow might even spend the night with his warriors, watching Night Hawk, gloating over his capture."

Eagle Wing chuckled. "I know Black Crow well. He is a most virile man who will let nothing stand in the way of being with his women, not even tonight. I have watched him. He takes one into his lodge, uses her, then takes another one who usually stays the night with him. *Huh*, I am sure he will be gloating over having brought a captive into our village. But he will be gloating to his women friends, not to his warriors."

Touch the Sky shivered. "He looks at me often as though he might want to take me into his lodge to be used and degraded. And it *would* be for the purpose of degrading, for there is much bad feeling between us."

"You are beautiful," Eagle Wing said, framing her face between his hands, looking adoringly at her. "That is why he wants you. Who would not?"

Touch the Sky smiled weakly. "I so want you tonight," she murmured. "My body aches with need of you."

"Soon we will marry and we will have each other for always. When your body cries out for me, mine will be there for you."

She eased into his arms again. "My love," she murmured. "At least touch me. Caress me. Then we shall go and find a way to release the man who may be my brother."

He moved his hand down her back, then slid it up inside her dress and found her warm woman's center. Slowly, he caressed her. Their tongues met in a frenzied kiss. She leaned closer to him, lost in a world of ecstasy as he brought her to that wonderful brink of euphoria. She trembled in his embrace and sighed.

Then, her face flushed hot with embarrassment, she stepped away from him. "I feel so ashamed," she whispered, lowering her eyes. "I cannot seem to control the hungers of my body."

"And that is good, as long as it is always this warrior who feeds them," Eagle Wing said. He placed a finger under her chin and lifted it, so that their eyes could meet and hold. "I love the sensual side of you. Most women are afraid of it. They shy away from it. Never be ashamed of allowing yourself to enjoy it."

"You are so understanding." She placed a gentle hand on his cheek. "It is no wonder that I love you so strongly."

He took her hand, kissed its palm, then led her toward their village. "Let us go now and watch for

257

an opportunity to release the prisoner," he said. "We *will* find a way, even if we have to render those who guard him unconscious."

Touch the Sky looked up at him with alarm in her eyes, then she smiled, thinking that this sort of daring might be as exciting as those moments in his arms.

And for her beloved father, she would willingly take chances!

Chapter Twenty-nine

Night Hawk's stomach ached. His throat was so dry it felt as though it was filled with cotton. He had tried not to think about it, or the fact that the sun had set and the air was growing colder.

His only salvation was the huge outdoor communal fire that flamed hot and high not far from where he lay on the ground. He cherished the warmth that reached out to him and caressed his body.

As night fell, the people of the village retired to their lodges, except for the two warriors standing guard close beside him.

As the black cloak of night enveloped Night Hawk, his hopes of getting free waned. He shivered as the breeze changed into a strange, howling wind, blowing the warmth of the fire away from him. He watched leaves tumbling over the ground all around him, blown in from the neighboring forest. He heard the eerie sound of an owl hooting in a distant tree.

Then his insides lurched and his eyes grew wide as he heard another sound. Someone was approaching.

The guards had also heard. They prepared their weapons, ready to stop whomever it might be.

When they saw that it was only the Civil Chief's young son, Little Horse, who came to amuse himself by gazing at the prisoner, they lowered their rifles to their sides. They laughed and turned their backs to Little Horse and Night Hawk.

When the moon crept from behind a cloud, Night Hawk recognized his visitor. It was the young lad whom he had seen standing outside one of the smaller lodges clustered close to his father's. It was the lad who had helped his father inside his lodge while Night Hawk had watched from up high!

He still wondered if this might be one of Brown Bull's sons . . . if the boy might be Night Hawk's very own brother.

"I am Little Horse," the lad said, falling to his knees beside Night Hawk. "I am son of Chief Brown Bull. I see the evil in torturing you." He leaned his face closer to Night Hawk's. "Tonight I will find a way to release you."

There was more movement in the dark. Night Hawk and Little Horse watched as the two guards were rendered unconscious by blows to their heads.

Night Hawk could not believe his eyes when he saw that one of the attackers was the beautiful maiden Touch the Sky. He gazed at the man who helped her as he knelt down beside him and cut his ropes with a knife.

"Hurry, Eagle Wing," Touch the Sky whispered, glancing all around them. "We must get to my father's lodge before Black Crow discovers Night Hawk is gone!"

Night Hawk's eyebrows arched when he heard her refer to him by his name. Perhaps she believed that he was who he professed to be.

When he saw that he was being taken to her father's lodge, he realized that Brown Bull had sent her to help release him.

He looked quickly over at Little Horse, touched deeply when the young brave gently took his arm and helped him up from the ground.

"You have been wronged by Black Crow," Little Horse said, a keen bitterness in his voice. "Someday he will pay for all of his wrong deeds." He gazed up at Night Hawk. "My father believes you are his son. That makes you my brother. My father also says you have come to help our cause. Is that so? Is that why Black Crow treated you as an enemy?"

"I have come first to see my father, second to help him in any way I can." Night Hawk stumbled as he tried to take his first step. He smiled at Touch the Sky when she came to his side and helped him.

"We must hurry," she whispered. "We must get you hidden. But first you must talk with Father. He believes you might be his son." She smiled up at him. "I hope that he is right, for there is much about you that speaks of kindness."

Night Hawk gave her a smile, then focused his attention on walking, each step a challenge. When he was finally inside his father's large lodge, Touch the Sky placed a blanket around his shoulders.

Choked up with emotion now that he was so close to his father and could see the same look of love in his father's eyes that he had seen as a child, Night Hawk approached Brown Bull's bed and knelt down beside it. He leaned over his father and hugged him.

"It *is* you," Brown Bull said. Tears flowed from his eyes as he reveled in the embrace of his son for the first time in fifteen years. His arms trembled as he placed them around Night Hawk. "My son. My son."

"I would have come sooner had I known the truth," Night Hawk said, still hugging his father. "Only recently did Crying Wolf remember why he had come for me . . . to tell me that you did not abandon me, to tell me that he had come to take me back to you!"

Brown Bull's breath caught for a moment. His old heart seemed to stop momentarily. "Crying . . . Wolf?" His voice was breaking.

He unclasped his arms from around Night Hawk. He gently shoved him away so that he could look into his eyes. "What of Crying Wolf?" he asked. "It was many years ago that I sent him for you."

"Father, Crying Wolf was robbed of his memory," Night Hawk said, his eyes devouring his father's face, seeing him unchanged except for wrinkles and signs of illness.

"And all along I thought he was dead," Brown Bull said, tears once again welling in his eyes. He wiped his tears away. "If he is not dead, where is he?"

Night Hawk explained everything to his father, about Jae and Crying Wolf, and why Night Hawk had urged Crying Wolf to stay behind with Jae until he made sure things were all right in the village.

"It is good to know that my old friend is alive," Brown Bull said. "And even better to see you, my firstborn son." He then reached a trembling hand to Night Hawk's hair. He slowly ran his fingers through it, releasing the mock braids and cockleburs. He swallowed hard. "You have the hair of your mother. I loved her so."

"As she loved you," Night Hawk said. Then he looked over at Touch the Sky and Little Horse. "But I see that you have married again."

"Many times," Brown Bull said, chuckling. "Four

wives are in their lodges next to mine. As did your mother so long ago, each wife has her separate and distinct apartment. A deerskin cord is attached to the corner of each of my wives' buffalo mattresses, the other end extending under the canvas into my tent. A slight twitch of the rope is all that is needed to bring a certain wife to me."

Brown Bull turned slow eyes to Touch the Sky, and then Little Horse. "Night Hawk, you have already met two of my children, Little Horse and Touch the Sky," he said, pride in his voice.

"It is good to know that I have brothers and sisters," Night Hawk said, reaching a hand to each. When their fingers twined around his, he felt an instant bonding. "I have never known the love of a brother or sister. I was raised alone by the family who adopted me."

"And now you are home," Brown Bull said softly.

"*Huh*, I am home, but my welcome was not what I hoped it would be." Fearing discovery at any moment, Night Hawk glanced toward the entrance flap.

Then he gazed down at his father again. "What can I do to help you, Father?" he asked, easing his hands away from Touch the Sky's and Little Horse's. He leaned over and again hugged his father. "I want to make life right for you again. But with so many opposing you, it might take longer than . . ."

He did not finish his thought, that his father might not live to regain his power. As he rose away from his father, their eyes locked.

"That is so," Brown Bull said, having suspected what his son was about to say. He glanced up and nodded toward Eagle Wing. "But fret not. There is still hope. Eagle Wing, who will soon be my son by marriage, leads a faction of Comanche who still support me, yet there are not enough to go against Black Crow."

Eagle Wing stepped up to Night Hawk. "It is good to meet you," he said, grasping his hand. "We will work together for the betterment of your father and our people as a whole. Although my group is secret, it is building by number each day as the warriors see the wrong in how Black Crow leads."

"Long ago I became more interested in horses than in killing," Brown Bull said, drawing Night Hawk's attention back to him. "I was once a chief who thought warring was the only way to battle the whites. I have since changed my views. I see peace as the only way to survive among whites. Black Crow wants to lead our people into warring against the white pony soldiers. Until recently, I have been able to stop him. But as you see, I am now an aging, ailing man. My leadership has been weakened."

Brown Bull paused, then his eyes seemed to look back in time as he talked of his younger days in a monotone. "When I was a young brave, just turned warrior, the acquisition of horses by plunder appealed to me, for it enhanced my prestige among our people. Taking horses from enemies under difficult conditions provided an opportunity for valor and cleverness. It was a distinguished mark of honor, and those who were the most successful in this enterprise were highly respected."

He chuckled and gazed up at Night Hawk. "My son, a Comanche who took a guarded horse was called a *ghost*," he said, his old eyes dancing with remembrance. "Stealing the hobbled, guarded mounts of soldiers was great fun. Often I have crawled into a bivouac, where a dozen soldiers were sleeping, each with a horse tied to his wrist by a lariat. I have cut the rope within six feet of the sleeper and got away with the horse without waking a soul."

He suddenly grew sober. "That was then," he said. "This is now."

He beckoned for Little Horse to come to him. The boy knelt down beside his father's bed.

"Night Hawk, you are gazing upon a young brave with a great future," Brown Bull said, patting his young son's shoulder. "He will never let anyone like Black Crow best him!"

His eyes implored Night Hawk, and then Eagle Wing. "It is up to you to see that my younger son *has* a future," he said, his voice breaking.

"Night Hawk must eat and have water, and then we will take him into hiding," Touch the Sky said, bringing a huge platter of food to her newfound brother. "Eagle Wing and Night Hawk can then put their heads together and begin making plans to oust Black Crow."

Night Hawk sat down beside his father's bed, and while he listened to his father talking about Black Crow's hold on the village, he feasted on broiled venison, dipping his meat into a salt brine as he ate it. He devoured a good portion of hard, parched corn, then finished the meal off with a dish he remembered from his childhood, a sweet dish of mush made from buffalo marrow mixed with crushed mesquite beans.

He washed all of this down with great gulps of honey water.

"Fate has led you home to save your father and your people," Brown Bull then said, placing a hand on Night Hawk's shoulder. He gazed up at Eagle Wing. "Eagle Wing, it is good not to see jealousy in your eyes when I speak so favorably of my son, Night

Hawk. You know there is no reason to be jealous."

Eagle Wing placed a hand on Night Hawk's shoulder. "Although we are not kin by blood ties, we are brothers all the same," he said. "Never will there be jealousy between us. We will work together as though we are each other's shadow, to the betterment of our people." He gazed over at Brown Bull. "I feel as you do, Chief Brown Bull, that fate has led this man home to his people."

"*Namasi kahtoo.* Quick, quick. We must leave for the mountains," Touch the Sky said, pleading with Night Hawk with her eyes.

He set the platter aside and rose to his feet. Then he took two quick steps backward when Black Crow burst into the lodge, flanked by armed guards.

"No!" Touch the Sky cried as Night Hawk was yanked away and thrown outside on the ground.

She rushed outside with Eagle Wing and Little Horse, watching helplessly as Night Hawk was dragged, naked, back to the stakes and imprisoned there once again, this time the ropes tied more tightly than before.

Black Crow turned dark, angry eyes to Touch the Sky, then looked slowly at Little Horse and Eagle Wing. "Do not interfere again or you will all join the prisoner!"

They stood their ground, glaring. Then Touch the Sky stubbornly walked past Black Crow. He glowered as she threw many logs onto the fire. Soon flames shot higher into the sky.

She turned and knelt down beside Night Hawk. "The fire will keep you warm while we find a way to release you again, this time forever," she whispered to him.

She screamed when Black Crow came and

Savage Shadows

grabbed her by the hair and yanked her back to her feet.

"If you disobey me just one more time, you will be sorry," he hissed into her face.

She wanted to spit on him, but knew that she must reserve revenge until later, when he was finally at the mercy of her father's faithful followers. Oh, what a day of rejoicing that would be!

She smiled smugly, causing him to raise his eyebrows with wonder.

"You smile?" he asked warily. "I threaten you and yet you smile? Why?"

She stubbornly refused him an answer.

Chapter Thirty

Jae was frightened at not having found Night Hawk along the trail. Now that they were nearing the valley of the Comanche village, her fears mounted. If Night Hawk had been taken into the village as a friend, he would have stayed only long enough to explain who he was, and to see if his father was alive.

Then he would have left to get Jae and Crying Wolf, to bring them back to the village, to let them be a part of the excitement of being with his people again. But Night Hawk had not returned for them. And there had been no signs of him on the trail, only the prints left in the dusty soil by his horse as he had made his way toward the village.

Even they had been lost from sight as night had deepened. Jae feared the worst—that Night Hawk had been taken captive. Crying Wolf had acted as though he had not heard her when she questioned him about it. She knew by his silence that he did not want to admit that possibility.

She rode in a slow lope beside Crying Wolf. Wary of every noise they heard, they rested their hands on the rifles in the gunboots at the sides of their horses.

When Crying Wolf suddenly held an arm out in front of Jae, she drew a tight rein and stopped. Scarcely breathing, she followed his gaze as he nodded toward a butte.

She stiffened when she saw the flash of a rifle's barrel as it picked up the rays of the moon.

"Sentries guard the village," Crying Wolf said softly. "Follow me."

They made a sharp turn to the right and rode close enough beneath that butte for the sentries not to see them.

After four other sentries had been spotted, they made another tight right and started a slow climb up a steep incline that led them to a butte that was not occupied. Before they reached the summit, they tethered their horses to a tree.

Then they moved stealthily to the edge of the bluff. Crying Wolf placed a gentle hand on Jae's back and urged her to stretch out on her stomach. From that vantage point, they were able to see the village down below.

"Finally I am home," Crying Wolf said, his voice breaking. "Yet I am not. Look at me! I am lying on my belly like a coward instead of entering my village with my head held high!"

"I'm sorry," Jae murmured, reaching a gentle hand to his arm. "I truly wish things were different . . . that you were able to go on to your village. I know how your heart must be aching to see your old friends and family."

"Do not be sad for me." Crying Wolf was watching the activity below. "I do what I do because of my love for Night Hawk. He is my first and only concern."

Jae eased her hand from his arm. She propped her

269

chin up with her hands, taking a more comfortable position from which to study the village. "If he is there, I wonder if he is safe," she said, swallowing hard. "I am so afraid for him."

"We will wait to enter my village tomorrow during the daylight hours," Crying Wolf said.

"But don't you think it was daylight when Night Hawk arrived at the village?" Jae asked, squinting her eyes as clouds slid over the moon, making the darkness even more ominous. "If he is being held captive, the daylight hours did not help *him*."

Crying Wolf frowned over at her. "Twice you have spoken that word 'captive' to me," he said flatly. "Do not speak it again. Do not think it. Those are my people. Those people are Night Hawk's!"

"But, Crying Wolf, you both have been gone for so long from your village," Jae said softly. "You are both strangers to your people."

In deep thought, Crying Wolf turned his eyes away. Then he gazed at her again. "What you say is true," he said, his voice drawn.

"Then you, I, and Running Hawk could be in mortal danger." Fear crept into her heart like icy, crawling fingers.

"That is so, but remember this, Jae. A time comes when one must place all fears aside and meet trouble head on," Crying Wolf said, shifting his position, bringing his rifle up closer beside him. "The wait tonight will be long for us, and much longer for Night Hawk. If I only knew which lodge he was in, the darkness would be the best cover to go to him. As it is, I know not where he is, or how to help him."

Jae slid her eyes slowly over the village, seeing the shadowy lodges, and then . . . and then . . .

Her eyes widened. She grabbed for Crying Wolf

and gripped his arm hard. "I see him!" she cried in a harsh whisper. "Oh, Lord, Crying Wolf, look at the large outdoor fire! Look just past it! Please tell me that isn't Night Hawk staked to the ground!"

Crying Wolf stared downward. "It . . . is . . . Night Hawk."

Jae choked back a bitterness in her throat. She looked quickly away and closed her eyes. "Lord, they had no mercy at all. They have him tied to the ground, naked."

Crying Wolf stared, anger rising within him in hot, jagged flashes. It took all of his willpower not to cry out to the heavens in his Comanche tongue, asking why the Wise One Above would allow such a thing to happen to such a man as Night Hawk! Crying Wolf could not believe that his very own people could be so unfeeling and heartless.

"They have wronged one of their own kind, the son of Chief Brown Bull!" he said, his voice trembling with rage. He rose quickly to his feet, held his rifle in the air, and shook it toward the heavens. "Whoever is responsible will pay!" he said, not in the shout he wished to release from his inner soul, but in a quiet, venomous way that made Jae shiver.

Crying Wolf glared down at her. "We no longer wait for morning," he said. "And we no longer lie on our bellies like cowards! We are going to the village. We are going to release Night Hawk!"

Jae stared at him for a moment, so afraid her knees were weak. But thoughts of her beloved lying on the ground, a captive, gave her a sudden spurt of energy—and courage.

She ran with Crying Wolf from the edge of the cliff. When they reached the horses, Crying Wolf stared at them, then turned to Jae. "They must stay here.

We must do everything on foot."

Jae nodded.

But when she recalled Night Hawk's nudity, she took the time to get a blanket from her saddlebag.

Clutching her rifle, and throwing the blanket across her left shoulder, she followed Crying Wolf down the side of the cliff.

When they reached the outskirts of the village, and the sentries still had not seen them, they moved noiselessly, with catlike stealth, behind one tepee and then another.

When they were close enough to see Night Hawk's face, they hunkered low, for close beside Night Hawk sat two sentries, their legs crossed, their rifles resting on their laps.

Crying Wolf and Jae exchanged smug smiles when they noticed that the sentries were fast asleep.

Gripping their rifles, Crying Wolf and Jae rushed forth and slammed the butt ends of their firearms against the heads of the guards.

Unconscious, the warriors both rolled over to their sides, their weapons falling to the ground beside them.

"I'll remove the warriors' rifles while you cut Night Hawk's bonds," Jae said as her eyes locked with Night Hawk's.

"Darling," she murmured. "We've come to free you."

Night Hawk was so filled with emotion that he found it hard to speak. Fearing not so much for himself as he did for Crying Wolf and Jae, he looked frantically from one to the other.

"*Namasi-kahtoo*, quick, quick," he said, as he watched Crying Wolf slice through the ropes at his ankles. "The sentries at the outskirts of the village might hear you. And the camp dogs might be awakened."

"From what we saw, most sentries are asleep," Crying Wolf said as he cut through the ropes at Night Hawk's wrists. Angrily, he threw the ropes aside.

Night Hawk rose to his feet, then fell to his knees again when he realized that hours of immobility had left him weak.

He felt blessed, though, for having had the opportunity to eat in his father's lodge before he was taken to the stakes a second time.

Jae's eyes wavered when she saw Night Hawk's weakness. She wanted to run to him and embrace him, but she knew that time did not allow it. Instead, she went to him and slung the blanket around his shoulders.

Crying Wolf knelt on one side of Night Hawk, Jae on the other, as they helped him up from the ground.

Crying Wolf stopped long enough to ask the question that ate away at his insides. "I need to know, is your father alive? Is he here?"

"*Huh*, he is alive," Night Hawk said solemnly. "He is here. But he is in trouble."

Crying Wolf's eyes wavered, but he knew this was not the time to ask any more questions.

Jae felt a rush of tears as she watched Night Hawk swing one of his muscled arms around Crying Wolf's shoulder, welcoming his help as they moved slowly into the shadows.

Her eyes constantly watching for any movement, Jae followed Night Hawk and Crying Wolf past the lodges. She ran up next to Night Hawk when Crying Wolf stopped to let the younger man catch his breath.

"How could this have happened to you?" she softly

cried. "Who did this to you?"

"Later," Night Hawk said somberly. "When we are safe, I will then tell you everything." He glared past her at the back of Black Crow's lodge. "One man is responsible. Only . . . one . . . man."

"We need another horse," Crying Wolf said, staring at the many horses grazing in the corral.

A thought came to Night Hawk that made his lips tug into a slow smile. "There *is* one horse that I would like to steal, since I do not know where mine is being kept," he said, chuckling. He looked from Crying Wolf to Jae. "Wait here. I shall return soon with a horse of my choosing."

The thought of stealing Black Crow's steed gave Night Hawk the strength required to go to the private corral just behind Black Crow's lodge. Night Hawk had a way with horses, and the beautiful white mustang made not a sound as he was led out of the corral.

Smiling, he led the horse up to Crying Wolf and Jae. "Black Crow's," he said, giving Crying Wolf a nod. "You do remember Black Crow, do you not?"

When Crying Wolf's eyes gleamed, it was answer enough for Night Hawk.

They managed to get past the sentries and began a slow climb up a slope of land where thick layers of pink gneiss formations paved the hillside, accented by a dense growth of prickly pear cactus.

After they reached the bluff where Crying Wolf and Jae's horses were tethered, Crying Wolf gave Night Hawk a buckskin outfit from his own pack.

Jae could wait no longer. She flung herself into Night Hawk's arms. "I'm so sorry for what you have been forced to endure." She sobbed, clinging to him. "We should have come sooner."

Night Hawk relished having her in his arms. He had begun to think he might never see her again. "My love," he murmured, "do not blame yourself for any of this. How were any of us to know what awaited me in my very own village? How were any of us to know that one man held such power over my father's people?"

Jae eased from his arms. "Who is this man? Tell me about him. Tell me and Crying Wolf everything that happened. Tell us about your father."

Night Hawk told them how he had been ambushed, why he had been staked to the ground, and all about his father and his family.

He spoke angrily when he talked of Black Crow's hold on the Comanche people. "He must be ousted from power. Crying Wolf, Black Crow is the ruination of our people. And I do not believe my father's weakness is from natural causes. I believe there is a conspiracy to kill him. I fear someone is slowly poisoning him." His eyes narrowed. "I believe Black Crow is the one behind this conspiracy."

Crying Wolf gasped and hung his head. He grabbed onto his horse and leaned against it.

"Do not fret so," Night Hawk said, placing a gentle hand on Crying Wolf's shoulder. "Now that you have freed me and I am able to help my father, things will change for our people, especially my father. He will soon be in charge again. Crying Wolf, you and I will assist him."

Crying Wolf turned slowly to face Night Hawk. "If Black Crow holds so many of our people under his spell, how do you think we can turn things around?" he asked, his voice breaking.

"I said that Black Crow has many followers, but there are also some who are still faithful to my father," Night Hawk said. "*Huh,* there are not many, but with the right plans, a few can sometimes do much more than many!"

"*Huh,* I see logic in that," Crying Wolf said, kneading his chin thoughtfully. "What is our next move, Night Hawk? How can we foil those who are in power?"

"While lying on the ground, a prisoner, I had much time to think." Night Hawk smiled mischievously. "And all I could think about was getting free and what I would then do for my father . . . for my people. I seek vengeance, and I know how it will be achieved. I have thought it through and through until it is as clear now inside my head as the morning skies of spring. Black Crow's time of power is nearing its end. He will rue the day he wronged my father—and Night Hawk!"

"What is your plan?" Crying Wolf asked, his heart pounding with the excitement of the moment. He now saw hope in the future. He knew Night Hawk well enough to know that if he was determined to achieve a certain end, it would be achieved!

"I must go now and make plans with my father. I must go before daybreak, and before my escape is discovered."

"*Nah,* you must not leave just yet." Crying Wolf clasped a hand on Night Hawk's shoulder. "We must establish a place of safety for ourselves. We must find a place to hide, for once your escape is discovered, there will be a search mounted for you."

"But where can we go?" Jae asked, gazing first at Crying Wolf, and then at Night Hawk. "Surely the Comanche know every inch of the land. Where could there be a place to hide?"

Crying Wolf closed his eyes. He bowed his head

and slowly kneaded his brow.

Then, smiling, he raised his head and opened his eyes. "It is good to have my psychic powers back," he said, laughing softly. "It is good to discover what those powers disclose to me. I see a cave. I see it well hidden. It is large. We can go deep into the cave and even be safe lighting a fire for warmth and food."

"Where is this cave?" Night Hawk asked, always in awe of his friend's powers. "Is it far?"

"It is so close that if you turn around, you will be looking where its opening begins," Crying Wolf said, chuckling.

Jae and Night Hawk turned together and stared, seeing nothing but boulders and brush.

Jae glanced back at Crying Wolf. "I see no cave," she said, having always doubted the existence of psychic abilities.

"*Kee-mah*, come," Crying Wolf said, leading his horse behind him. "I will take you inside. Just watch your step. We do not want to start a landslide that might seal us inside once we are there."

"A landslide?" Jae gasped, her eyes wide. "Surely then it is not safe."

"It is a risk, that is true," Crying Wolf said, glancing over at her. "But which risk is worse? Facing Black Crow and his warriors? Or . . ."

"Say no more," Jae said, laughing nervously. "I trust your judgment. I truly believe, anyhow, that I'd rather die behind a wall of rocks than staked on the ground, naked."

A rustling in the buckskin saddlebag at Jae's side reminded her about her raccoon. She was relieved that he had apparently slept through everything.

She lifted him from the bag. "Sweetie, have I neglected you?" she whispered, then felt warm through

277

and through when Night Hawk took the raccoon and
gave him a hug and a kiss on his black nose.

He cuddled Snoopy close in his arms as he followed Crying Wolf past the thick brush and around
the piles of rocks, through more thick brush, and
then into the coal black darkness of the cave.

"It's unbelievable," Jae said. She squinted as she
stared around her. "You are a true psychic, Crying
Wolf. I never thought anyone could do what you've
just done."

"I doubt anyone else knows of the cave," Crying
Wolf said, surrounded by the rank odor of mildewy
dampness. "None of the brush at the entrance has
been trampled. And the boulders make it look as
though it is a natural rock pile. *Huh*, I do believe we
will be safe here."

"I would feel better leaving you to go to my father
if we move farther into the cave," Night Hawk said.
He reached over and drew Jae closer to him as they
moved slowly through the shadows of the cave. After
they had gone some distance and found the perfect
camping place, they stopped and soon had a fire
built.

"It feels just like home," Jae said, laughing softly.
"My home back at the Thicket, that is. I remember
nights when I felt as though I was living in a cave."

"That is in your past," Night Hawk said, placing
gentle hands on Jae's shoulders. He gazed down at
her. "I must leave now to safeguard your future."

"Please be careful. I shall never forget seeing you
on the ground, so helpless, so . . ."

He grabbed her into his arms and held her close.
"That is also in the past," he said gruffly. "Have faith
in our future, Jae. I promise it will be far better than
both of our pasts."

She clung to him.

Then he stepped away from her.

Jae stifled a sob behind her hand when he embraced Crying Wolf and then walked away, tall and proud.

"He *will* make things right," Crying Wolf said, nodding as he gazed over at Jae. "I see it in my heart as well as in my mind."

Jae wiped tears from her eyes. "Yes, I know. I must have faith." She swallowed hard. "I . . . *do* have faith."

Chapter Thirty-one

As Night Hawk moved stealthily toward the Comanche village, his thoughts would not stop. Inside his mind he was making many plans. The cave was large enough for even a herd of horses, which meant that it was a good rendezvous place for those warriors who aligned themselves with his father and Eagle Wing.

A broad smile split Night Hawk's face. He now knew exactly what he would tell his father and what he would encourage him to do. *Huh*, in the end, things would work out for them all.

Night Hawk vowed to himself to make it so!

If not, he would die trying. He owed his ailing father much loyalty and devotion, both of which had been long denied him. Night Hawk felt proud that he would be the one who helped Chief Brown Bull regain his rightful position. But as he stepped into the shadows of the lodges, he could not help having some apprehension about his plans. In truth, there were many obstacles to success. He knew that the warriors who had been guarding him had not been discovered yet, or the people of his father's village would no longer be asleep—they would have been awakened by Black Crow's shouts of rage.

Stopping to catch his breath before stepping inside his father's lodge, Night Hawk gazed heavenward. Thus far, the night had been his ally; it had hidden his movements. But daylight would be a certain enemy! He prayed that he would have enough time to explain his plans to his father and to get his approval.

If it stayed dark long enough, and if no one stirred and found the unconscious guards, he believed he could achieve what needed to be done tonight before returning to the cave.

Then another thought came to him. He had worried earlier about the guards waking up before he finished his mission. He had brought ropes enough to bind their wrists and ankles. He had brought neckerchiefs to gag them.

Realizing that he had taken enough time to rest and to contemplate his plans, he hunkered low and crept on around his father's tall, round tepee. He wanted to hurry inside, but first he must totally disable the guards.

His steps as light and soundless as a panther's, he hurried to the guards, who still lay unconscious. Quickly, he secured the two warriors, then turned and ran silently on to his father's lodge.

Not wanting to alarm his father, Night Hawk stole quietly inside. He stopped just inside the entrance flap and looked slowly around the lodge. The fire had burned down to dying embers, yet the orange glow gave off enough light for him to see. He found Touch the Sky sleeping on a pallet of blankets beside her father's bed, proving her dutifulness as a daughter.

Then he gazed at his father, smiling when Brown

Cassie Edwards

Bull gave a long, lip-trembling snore.

"Like father, like son," he whispered to himself, for Night Hawk knew that he was guilty of snoring. The ladies he had bedded had all teased him about it after having nudged him in the ribs at night to awaken him.

Afraid that he might be taking too long with his mission, Night Hawk crept over to his father's bed.

He gazed down at Touch the Sky again. He reached a hand out to awaken her, yet paused long enough to take in her earthy loveliness. She was dressed in a long, sleeveless gown made of pale blue cotton. She looked so angelic and innocent as she lay there on her side, soundly sleeping. He doubted that she had ever done anything questionable in her life. He doubted that she had yet been bedded by a man.

He smiled as he pictured her as a young bride! He could see her now in his mind's eye, casting her eyes bashfully downward in the presence of her husband as he came to her nude for their first time.

Huh, so innocent, he thought to himself. So endearingly sweet!

Again realizing that he was taking too much time with trivial thoughts, he knelt down and placed a gentle hand on his sister's bare arm. "Touch the Sky," he whispered, watching her eyes begin to flutter. "Awaken, sister. It is I, Night Hawk."

Touch the Sky's eyes flew open. She gasped when she found Night Hawk there, gazing down at her. She moved quickly to a sitting position. "How did you get free?" she whispered, eyes wide. "How, Night Hawk? Who cut your bonds?"

"There is not enough time to explain everything just yet." Running Hawk shot a quick glance at his father. "You must know ways to awaken him gently.

Do it, Touch the Sky. It would be best if he saw your face first when he awakens. He is not yet that familiar with mine."

Touch the Sky nodded. She turned and faced her father. On her knees, she reached a gentle hand to her father's cheek. "Father, awaken," she murmured. "Someone is here for you."

Brown Bull's eyes opened slowly. He ran his tongue over his lips and he coughed, then wheezed.

Once he was fully awake and he saw Night Hawk standing over him, Brown Bull leaned slowly up on an elbow. "Son," he said, his voice filled with excitement. "You have been released? Did Black Crow change his mind? Has he thought better of keeping the son of his people's Civil Chief in bondage?"

"No, he is not smart enough to know that is the correct thing to do," Night Hawk said, his voice drawn. "Father, it was Crying Wolf and my woman who helped me escape."

"Crying Wolf?" Brown Bull looked anxiously past Night Hawk, then frowned. "He is not here." He implored Night Hawk with wavering eyes. "Where is my old friend?"

"He and Jae are both in hiding. Soon you will be with them. And, Father, I am so anxious for you to meet my woman. I plan to marry her as soon as the troubles here at our village are behind us and there is calm and brotherhood again among our warriors."

"You say that Black Crow did not release you. Then what of the guards who were assigned to watch you?" Brown Bull asked.

"They are rendered helpless," Night Hawk said.

He explained how he had dealt with the guards as his father and Touch the Sky listened.

"It is fate that has brought me back to be a part of

283

your life again," Night Hawk said, smiling at his father. "It is fate that has brought me here to remove Black Crow and his warriors from your life."

"You have a plan?" Brown Bull asked, his eyes anxious. He turned his face to the side and coughed. He wheezed.

Then he gazed over at Night Hawk again. "Tell me your plan quickly, then flee, my son, before Black Crow finds you no longer staked to the ground like an animal," he said, his old eyes locking with his son's.

"Father," Night Hawk said, overjoyed at being able to say the word to his true father, not the man who had adopted him for all of the wrong reasons. "Wait until two days and nights pass, to give Black Crow time to tire of searching for me, then send Eagle Wing and those warriors who align themselves with him to me."

He then explained about the cave and where to find it.

"But first, before sending Eagle Wing to the cave, tell him to go hunting with his warriors," Night Hawk said. "It is not so much for the purpose of bringing back game for his family as it is to make things look normal to anyone watching his movements. Tell Eagle Wing to hunt for one full day, to mislead Black Crow in case he becomes suspicious and sends his warriors out to spy on them. Tell Eagle Wing to come to the cave on that second day with his warriors, but only if he is certain he is not being followed. They will come with their travois loaded with meat. They will not take it to their lodges until after our meeting. While they are at the cave, plans will be made to oust Black Crow!"

"There are not enough men to do this successfully," Brown Bull said solemnly.

"Father, when the time comes, there *will* be enough men to oust Black Crow from power," Night Hawk said. "Father, where I lived after I was adopted by a white family, there are many men who are my friends. They are my adoptive father's cowhands. I know they will come if I ask for their help. Although it took many days to find your village, I believe the ranch is not more than a day's ride from here."

Night Hawk lowered his eyes, and he kneaded his brow. "It is only fair that I let my adoptive father know that both Jae and I are all right. She and I both left the ranch so suddenly, we told no one of our departure. I feel bad about having treated my adoptive mother in such a way. She deserved much more than that from me."

"More than once you have spoken of the woman you plan to marry," Brown Bull said. "You said that her name is Jae?"

"*Huh,* Jae," Night Hawk said. "You will become fast friends with her soon, Father. She is someone that no one can dislike."

Except for one man, Night Hawk thought to himself, wondering where the murderous outlaw was and if he was still a threat to Jae!

He brushed Jonas Adams from his mind as quickly as he thought about him, knowing that Black Crow was more of a threat now than Jonas could ever be.

"She will ride with you back to your adoptive father's home?" Touch the Sky asked, suddenly breaking her silence.

"No, and even I will not make that journey," Night Hawk said, turning to Touch the Sky. "Crying Wolf will go. I will stay behind and refine our plans."

Their eyes turned quickly toward the entrance flap

when they heard someone approaching outside the lodge.

Touch the Sky looked frantically toward Night Hawk. "It is Sun Eagle," she whispered harshly, "our village medicine man. He always rises before the sun. He comes and gives father medicine!"

His heart pounding, Night Hawk bolted to his feet. Feeling trapped, he looked quickly around him.

Touch the Sky rushed to her feet. She took Night Hawk by the hand. "Come with me," she whispered. She led him toward several thick skins that hung from the overhead rafters. "Hide behind these."

Night Hawk cast his father a worried glance, then went on to the skins.

He then grabbed Touch the Sky by the shoulders. "This man, this medicine man, surely he saw the bodies of the guards!" he said, his voice filled with sudden alarm.

"He is a man with failing eyesight," Touch the Sky said, standing on tiptoe to brush a kiss across Night Hawk's cheek. "He can barely see his hands before his eyes if he holds them out to look for them. He will see only what he must see to get to my father's lodge. He is a most determined medicine man. He does not miss a late-night or early-morning visit to feed my father his strange-smelling medicines."

"Strange medicines?" Night Hawk asked, raising an eyebrow. "Are you saying you do not know what he is giving your father?"

"No," she said. "But why do you question our village medicine man?"

"I just wonder," Night Hawk said, kneading his chin contemplatively.

Touch the Sky turned with a start when Sun Eagle spoke her father's name just before entering the lodge. She gave Night Hawk a shove that got him fully hidden behind the skins, then scurried back to her father's bedside and smiled weakly up at the older man whose thick, black hair dragged the ground behind him when he walked.

"It is good to see you again," Touch the Sky said, casting a quick glance toward the hiding place, then again forcing a smile as Sun Eagle came and knelt down beside her.

"Brown Bull, how does this early-morning hour treat you?" Sun Eagle asked as he peered almost sightlessly at the chief.

"Better," Brown Bull said. He cast a quick glance toward the pelts.

"Better?" Sun Eagle asked, a strange sort of alarm in his voice as he leaned closer to Brown Bull. "You are truly better?"

Brown Bull leaned away from the man he no longer trusted. "You seem to be alarmed that I am better," he said, frowning. "Is that not why you give me medicine? To make me better?"

Sun Eagle cleared his throat nervously as he laid several small buckskin pouches along the side of Brown Bull's feather mattress. "*Huh*, it is my endeavor to make you well again," he said. "But of late I had thought you were weakening." He gave Brown Bull a look of wariness. "How is the cough? How is the wheezing? How is your weakness?" He leaned closer again. "Are all of those better, or worse?"

Brown Bull paused, then sighed. "What would you wish for me to say?" he said, closing his eyes. "What would make you happy?"

"The truth," Sun Eagle said sternly.

Night Hawk listened to the conversation, his suspicion that his father was being fed something poisonous again aroused. The way the medicine man was acting did not seem natural.

Night Hawk planned to investigate this man's honesty. But he knew that he could not do this until he was free to roam as he pleased. He prayed that if this man was trying to harm his father, his father's own suspicions, which seemed obvious today, would cause the medicine man to stop feeding the poisonous herbs to him.

When Night Hawk heard the medicine man encourage his father to take the medicine, he wanted to jump out and stop him!

But he knew he must remain hidden. What he had planned would take only a few days. Surely his father would be all right until then! The Wise One Above would surely not allow him to die now that his future was bright again!

After Sun Eagle was gone, Night Hawk rushed back to his father's side. He placed a hand on his cheek and turned his father's eyes to him. "What did the medicine man give you to drink?" he asked guardedly.

"Why do you ask?" Brown Bull asked.

"I fear he is poisoning you," Night Hawk answered, his voice breaking.

"So do we," Touch the Sky quickly interjected. "We became suspicious a few days ago. My father takes no more medicine. Sun Eagle does not see that my father pretends to drink, then cleverly spills the liquid beside the bed before he hands the vial back to Sun Eagle."

"He sees so little he does not notice?" Night Hawk said, stunned and relieved.

"He sees a blur, that is all," Touch the Sky said,

giggling. "I sometimes think he sees even less than that."

Night Hawk sighed heavily. He leaned over his father and hugged him. "I felt so helpless standing among those pelts like a coward," he said softly. "I am glad to know that you understand what Sun Eagle is doing. He must be in cahoots with Black Crow."

"*Huh*, no doubt he is," Brown Bull said. "Unfortunately, the poison I consumed before becoming suspicious of Sun Eagle is still very much in my body. My legs are still too weak to hold me up. My body feels like a big, heavy rock when I try to walk."

"Soon you will be as good as new," Night Hawk said, rising.

"I *hope* to be better. But I fear that too much time has elapsed for this old man ever to feel new again."

Little Horse suddenly came into the lodge. "Father, I heard voices," he said softly. "I knew it was not only Sun Eagle's." He smiled up at Night Hawk. "It is good to see you again, my older brother."

Night Hawk knelt down before Little Horse and embraced him. "It is good to be with you again, also, but I must leave now," he said. He leaned away from him. "In my absence, you watch out for your sister and father for me, will you?"

"*Huh*, I will," Little Horse said. "How did you get free of the ropes?"

Night Hawk looked over at Touch the Sky, then at Little Horse again. "Your sister will tell you," he said as he walked toward the entranceway.

"Let me go with you," Little Horse said. He rushed to Night Hawk and grabbed one of his hands. "Please?"

Night Hawk again knelt before his brother. He

placed a gentle hand on his shoulder. "Your absence will arouse too many suspicions," he said softly. "Be patient. If everything works out, soon you and I can have all of the time we want . . . to hunt, fish, and to ride together across this spacious land of waving grasses."

"That sounds good." Little Horse flung himself into Night Hawk's arms. "I wish you a safe journey wherever your travels take you."

Night Hawk embraced Little Horse for a moment longer, then fled from the lodge. He cast his eyes heavenward. The sky was just now dividing itself between day and night. He did not have much time to get back to safety—most warriors rose with the sun!

Night Hawk got as far as the butte when he suddenly heard men shouting from down below. He knew that his escape had just been discovered. He smiled and hurried on inside the cave.

When he reached the campsite, he found Jae there alone. She ran to Night Hawk and embraced him. "Crying Wolf left shortly after you," she said softly. "He has gone to get help from your father's ranch hands. He was afraid that if he waited until daylight, he would be spotted by the sentries. By now he should be out of danger."

"He uses his psychic powers well," Night Hawk said, chuckling. "It was in my thoughts to send Crying Wolf to the ranch."

He smiled as he held Jae away from him and slowly began to undress her. "I have missed our moments alone together," he said huskily. "I need you, Jae. I need you now."

"Can we . . . ?" she asked softly, her pulse racing as he tossed her shirt aside.

"We will make the time," he said, now sliding her

290

cut-off breeches past her hips, then down her shapely legs.

Jae kicked her breeches aside, then stood back and watched him undress. When he'd finished, he led her down on a blanket beside the fire.

"For a while I doubted that we would ever be together again," Jae murmured, tracing his facial features with a forefinger. "Even now I fear this might be our last time."

"We will always be together," he said, brushing a soft kiss across her brow as he leaned down over her. "Because of your courage, we have a future together. Had you not come and released me, I would even still be Black Crow's prisoner."

"Because of Crying Wolf, you mean," she murmured. "I doubt I would have been brave enough to enter the village to help you escape without him."

"Knowing you and your strong will, *huh*, I believe you could have even done it without Crying Wolf," Night Hawk said.

He then wrapped his arms around her and brought her body hard up against his. "I no longer wish to talk of anything but you," he whispered against her cheek. "I no longer wish to think of anything but you. My love, I want your body. I want your lips. I want your everything. Give it all to me before I die from the need eating away at my insides."

With exquisite sensations spinning a web of rapture around her heart, Jae wove her fingers through Night Hawk's thick hair. "Yes, yes," she whispered against his lips. "All those things you say you want, I want twofold from you. I want your lips. I want your heat. I want . . . your everything."

He slid his hands down and around her. He placed them beneath her hips and lifted her higher, toward him, then thrust his aching heat inside her.

His mouth seized hers. With trembling lips, he kissed her. Surrounding her with his solid strength, he began his steady, rhythmic strokes within her.

Jae wrapped her legs around his thighs. Her breath quickened as his kiss deepened. She sighed when he reverently breathed her name against her lips as his hands slid around and cupped her breasts, sensually rolling them beneath the palms of his hands.

Jae rode with him, feeding his desires, taking from him that which fed hers as he filled her with an ecstasy so sweet it made her swoon. She closed her eyes and whispered soft cries against his lips as his hands moved slowly and teasingly over her slim, sensuous body.

Stroking the satiny flesh of her silken thighs, he flicked his fingers over her woman's center while his manhood moved past it in great, heaving thrusts.

He kissed the slender, curving length of her throat, and then licked his way down to her breasts. His whole insides quaked as his world melted away, and Jae's groans of pleasure fired his passions even more.

Searing, scorching flames shot through Night Hawk as he felt the brink of pleasure drawing near. Breathing hard, he paused for a moment.

Resting, he gazed into Jae's eyes. He ran his fingers gently over the gentle, sweet curves of her face. He ran them over her breasts, then lowered his mouth to her lips and kissed her again.

She clung to his neck, her senses reeling in drunken pleasure as he plunged deeply into her again, once again stroking her with his heat.

She kissed him with a wild desperation. She arched herself closer to him, clinging, flying, floating, then cried out against his lips when she reached that final pinnacle of release.

Night Hawk held Jae tightly as he also reached the peak of pleasure. He lunged over and over again inside the yielding silk of her. His fingers pressed urgently into her flesh as he swept his arms around her arms and drew her even closer to his hard body, her breasts crushing into his chest.

And then they lay quiet. The fire lapped at the logs beside them. Night Hawk nuzzled the softness of Jae's neck. "While I was cold on the ground, helpless, I closed my eyes and thought of you," he said huskily. "You brought me through those miserable, lonesome hours. Although you weren't there in the flesh, you *were* there in my heart. I could feel you. I could smell you. I could hear your laughter."

"I'm so sorry that you were a captive for so long," Jae murmured, cuddling closer.

"Let us think no more of it. Let us lie like this and feel blessed for this time we have together. There are always men like Black Crow and Jonas Adams who will try to steal it away from us."

"Black Crow?" Jae asked, leaning up on an elbow. "Tell me about him."

"I knew him well as a child," Night Hawk said, glaring into the fire. "I shall not want to know him much longer as an adult." He paused, then looked slowly over at Jae. "I *will* end his reign of terror in our village."

Jae had never heard Night Hawk sound so cold, so determined, so unlike himself. She hoped that his return to his Comanche people would not make him like those she had heard about who killed for the pleasure of killing. It *did* sound as though he looked forward to killing this man named Black Crow.

It made a chill ride her spine at the thought of him changing into someone she did not know. She swallowed hard, suddenly dreading the life she had dreamed of before.

Chapter Thirty-two

Crying Wolf stood stiffly over Ralph Hampton's bed, waiting for Ralph's response to the request for cowhands to go and give Night Hawk a helping hand.

Upon Crying Wolf's arrival at the ranch, he had been welcomed with many handshakes and hugs from the cowhands. He had not told them why he had returned, or why Night Hawk was not with him. He first had to get Ralph's permission.

"And so my son has sent you here to seek my help?" Ralph glared at Crying Wolf. "Crying Wolf, now wouldn't you say that took some nerve on his part? First he deserts me, leaving me short-handed, then he takes my daughter away after I had just met her for the first time in my life."

Lois stood at the far side of the room, scarcely breathing as she listened. Ralph had ordered her to leave the room, but she had gone only to the door.

She had then turned around and given him a stubborn stare. Of late she had begun to refuse to let him order her around. Especially now. Crying Wolf had news of her son, and Lois wanted to hear it all! She knew that if she waited and got it secondhand from her husband, she might never know whether Night Hawk was all right.

As for Jae, Lois could not help resenting her. Jae's arrival at the ranch had changed everything, and nothing for the better. Lois had discovered that the husband to whom she had dedicated these many years had placed her second to a daughter he scarcely knew!

This "daughter" had caused Night Hawk to leave, because of the new will, which left him nothing . . . not even his pride.

No, Lois felt nothing for Jae.

But, Lord, she felt everything for Night Hawk. And she sorely missed him.

"Night Hawk left to find his people because he felt that he was no longer truly wanted here," Crying Wolf said, trying hard not to sound as though he was chiding Ralph. "Moments ago when you spoke of Night Hawk leaving, you did not speak of him as though he was a son who had left a hole in your heart because of his absence. By saying that he had left you short-handed, you spoke of him as though he was only a hired hand. Think about how you treated him after the arrival of your daughter. Then you will understand his flight, a flight that took him back to his true people, where he should have been all of these years, instead of here, pretending to be white."

"Do not lecture me," Ralph said, suddenly wheezing. His face turned crimson from his building rage. "I loved my son. And yes, I was wrong to favor Jae over Night Hawk. If he would return, I would tell him so. I . . . would . . . change the terms of the will. I would make an equal split between my daughter and son."

Lois gasped softly from the far side of the room, finding it hard to believe that her husband was *still* forgetting her existence in his life!

She moved stiffly up to the bed and stood beside Crying Wolf. She inhaled a quivering breath, then turned toward the old Comanche. "Take however many men you need to help Night Hawk," she said, boldly lifting her chin. "Do what must be done to help my son. Then, Crying Wolf, tell Night Hawk that if at all possible, I would like for him to find a place for me in his newly established home. I feel as though I have wasted my years here, caring for a man who . . . who cares nothing for me."

Ralph gasped and paled. He tried to rise from his pillow, then groaned as his head fell back. He closed his eyes. "Why? Why?" he cried, shaking his head back and forth. "What have I done to deserve this?"

"What have you done?" Lois said, her throat almost constricting from her need to cry. "Lord, Ralph, if you don't know, I surely will not waste my time trying to explain it all to you."

Ralph's eyes opened and he glared up at her. "You have no right to tell this Indian that he can have my cowhands. You have no right to give any orders around here. You . . . are . . . just . . . my *wife*."

Lois laughed sarcastically. "Not even that, Ralph. All I have been to you is nothing more than Maxine or Rita. I have been a fool all these years waiting on you hand and foot. What were you doing behind my back—laughing at my stupidity?"

She doubled her fists at her sides. Again she looked at Crying Wolf. "I shall go with you out to the bunkhouse," she said softly. "I'll tell the cowhands they are to go with you."

"No!" Ralph shouted, his eyes bulging with anger.

He started wheezing almost uncontrollably. "You . . . can't . . . do . . . this!"

Crying Wolf felt caught in the middle. He looked at Ralph, then at Lois. He knew that she was now the one in control. It made Crying Wolf smile to see this new side of Lois. Throughout the years, he had seen Ralph Hampton treat her as though she were a piece of furniture.

Huh, Crying Wolf welcomed Lois's newfound independence and courage to speak her mind and to act on her convictions.

"Come with me, Crying Wolf," Lois said. She slipped an arm through his and led him away from the bed. "Let's get this show on the road. The sooner you get back to Night Hawk with the men, the sooner he can send for *me*. I hate this place. I hate . . ."

She stopped short of saying she hated Ralph. In truth, she pitied him.

Lois stopped and gazed up at Crying Wolf, her eyes wavering. "Night Hawk *will* send for me, won't he?" she gulped out.

"You do realize, do you not, that once Night Hawk gets his life in order again, he will be living in a lodge made of hide instead of this white man's mansion that you are used to living in?" Crying Wolf watched her eyes to read the reaction in their depths.

"Yes, I understand," Lois said, nodding. "And I would live anywhere, in anything, to get away from this ungrateful man, and . . . and to be near my son again. Of course, he is not my son by blood ties. But by the strings that bind our hearts, we are mother and son."

"He will welcome you," Crying Wolf said, drawing Lois into his arms and hugging her. "He will send for you."

They ignored Ralph's rantings and ravings behind them as they walked from the room and hurried out to the bunkhouse.

Before night fell again, Crying Wolf was riding from the ranch with forty cowhands, leaving only enough behind to care for the land and cattle.

Crying Wolf had made Night Hawk's decision for him where his mother was concerned. He had told Lois to leave now, not later. He wasn't comfortable leaving her at the mercy of Ralph Hampton. Crying Wolf had told Lois to pack whatever clothes she could get into a saddlebag. That would be all that she needed until she became a part of the Comanche people. Then she would dress as the Comanche women—in buckskin!

Although her hips were much wider than they had been many years ago when she had been younger and had enjoyed horseback riding, Lois rode beside Crying Wolf. She had learned how to ride beautiful racehorses long ago while her father had been alive. A gambler at heart, he had almost lived at the race-tracks, and she had frequently gone with him. Lois had even ridden in one of the races.

While married to Ralph, that side of her nature had been stifled. Now? Having finally broken her ties with her husband, she felt as though she had a new lease on life.

As the wind blew through her waist-length, graying hair, she held her head back and laughed throatily. "I feel alive again!" she cried into the wind.

Crying Wolf smiled over at her. Suddenly he felt alive too. He was seeing Lois in a much different light than ever before. He was seeing her as a woman . . . not as a white man's wife!

Chapter Thirty-three

Eagle Wing stood beside Brown Bull's bed. Touch the Sky was beside him, their hands intertwined.

"Do you understand, Eagle Wing, the details of my son's plans?" Brown Bull asked. He'd regained some strength and was sitting up in the bed today.

"*Huh*, we are to hunt for two days, and on that second day, we must be sure we are not being followed. Then we go to the cave where Night Hawk waits for me and my warriors," Eagle Wing said, excitement building in him. If Crying Wolf could bring back many cowhands, there would be enough men to overpower Black Crow and those warriors who were loyal to him!

"May the Wise One Above go with you," Brown Bull said. He lifted a hand and rested it on one of Eagle Wing's arms. "We have waited a long time for a miracle. I believe my son is this miracle."

"Father, soon it will all be over," Touch the Sky said, leaning down to embrace him. "And I am so glad to see you feeling better today. I feel so wonderful myself, Father." She pulled away from him, her eyes twinkling. "I find all of this so exciting."

Eagle Wing placed a hand on her shoulder, drawing her eyes up to him. "Exciting, but dangerous," he growled out. "You stay close to your father. Do not even leave his lodge except to get water required for bathing and drinking. You have enough food stored inside this lodge. Do not venture out to get anything else. Who is to say when Black Crow might decide to retaliate against your family for Night Hawk's escape? *Huh,* he had no proof we knew anything about it, so he could not lose face in front of our people by punishing you for it. But as time goes on, and as his anger deepens over Night Hawk's absence, who is to say what he might choose to do?"

"I will stay with Father," Touch the Sky said. She rushed to her feet and threw herself into Eagle Wing's embrace. "*You* be careful. Although you are going to look as though you are legitimately hunting, Black Crow is clever. He might see past that and guess the truth. You and all of your warriors are in grave danger until Black Crow is overthrown."

"*Huh,* I understand and I will watch my back carefully," Eagle Wing said.

Touch the Sky leaned quickly away from him when Little Horse came into the lodge.

"Have you talked it over yet?" Little Horse asked, his eyes anxiously wide. "Can I, or can I not go with you on the hunt, Eagle Wing?"

Eagle Wing turned slowly to Touch the Sky, and then Brown Bull. "It would look even more legitimate if we took a young brave with us on the hunt," he said. "And I would guarantee Little Horse's safety as much as I can guarantee my own."

"And I soon will be a man, a warrior myself," Little Horse said, proudly puffing out his chest. "Let me go, Father. Let me prove that I am worthy."

Touch the Sky gazed at her father but said nothing. She could not encourage her father to let Little Horse go, for in truth, she still saw him as a small child!

And she would not interfere by discouraging him. This was between father and son.

"My son, you can shoot and ride a horse like a man and will soon claim the status of a man," Brown Bull said, reaching a hand out for Little Horse. "Come to me, son. Give me a farewell hug. *Mea*. Go. Hunt. But follow all of Eagle Wing's commands. He understands, above all else, the importance of this particular hunt."

Little Horse ran to his father and sat down on the edge of the bed. "Thank you, Father," he said, hugging Brown Bull. "And do not worry about me. I also follow orders like a man!"

They all joined in soft laughter.

Then Little Horse and Eagle Wing joined the others outside the lodge, where the warriors waited on their horses.

Little Horse ran and got his pinto pony, then rode up beside Eagle Wing. "I am ready for the hunt," he said, smiling broadly.

Eagle Wing smiled at him, then looked at his warriors. Some had a travois tied at the back of the horses for the transportation of the game they would kill. Others had pack mules with supplies.

He grew cold inside when Black Crow rode up and drew a tight rein beside him.

"And so I see you are all going on a hunt," Black Crow said, looking warily from warrior to warrior. "So many? Are all of your families so low in supplies that you must hunt at the same time?"

"We will be gone for two days," Eagle Wing said sullenly. "And because of the length of the hunt, yes, we all go at once. What does it matter? Your warriors are still at the village to protect our people. Let us, those warriors who mean so much less to you, do the hunting. As always, I will bring home meat for your table, Black Crow."

Black Crow nodded. "That is good," he said, smiling smugly.

Black Crow glared at the others. "You all bring home double what is your normal number of game," he shouted. "Eagle Wing is right to suggest you feed my warrior's wives, children, mothers, and fathers. My warriors will enjoy smokes while you labor on the hunt."

He laughed sarcastically as that remark brought him many glares.

Eagle Wing stayed solemn and silent. He glanced at his men. One by one, their eyes locked with his, for they knew that this was not an ordinary hunt.

They rode from the village with dignity.

Touch the Sky stood outside behind her father's lodge and watched the warriors' departure. She then gazed at the heavens. "Wise One Above, please allow my brother's plan to work for my people," she begged. "They have gone for so long with so little!"

She bowed her head. "Thank you, big brother Night Hawk, for remembering your people and returning to them when they need you the most." Tears were streaming from her eyes.

Chapter Thirty-four

The moon in the east was two hours high when Night Hawk was awakened by a sound at the far end of the cave. The fire's glow had dimmed, giving off only enough light for him to see to get up and slip quickly into his breeches.

Jae stirred but didn't awaken.

Night Hawk bent to one knee and pulled her blanket up just beneath her chin.

He gazed at her for a moment longer. Then when he heard a noise again, he grabbed his rifle and slowly made his way into the total blackness of the cave. After he had walked for only a short distance, he saw the wavering light of a torch.

He slid behind a crevice and waited for the interloper, his finger anxious on the trigger of his firearm.

But when the light came closer and it illuminated the face of the torchbearer, relief swept through Night Hawk.

Night Hawk stepped out into the open, causing Crying Wolf to stop abruptly.

When Crying Wolf saw him, he smiled. "As you

wanted, the cowhands have come to lend a helping hand," he said, taking eager steps toward Night Hawk. "They are just outside the cave. They wait for you to come to them and instruct them."

Night Hawk gazed wide-eyed at Crying Wolf, stunned to think that his father had sent his cowhands to help. Ralph Hampton would be short-handed for several days without them.

Yet Night Hawk had hoped that his adoptive father would help him. If he had not, Night Hawk's plans could never come to fruition.

He had hoped that Crying Wolf would say the right things to his father to convince him of the good of this venture, and it was obvious that he had.

"You did it," Night Hawk said, his lips tugging into a smile as Crying Wolf stepped up to him. He clasped his friend's shoulder. "You actually did it. You talked Father into lending me his cowhands." He frowned as he slowly dropped his hand to his side. "How are he and mother?"

"Your father? I would say that at this moment he hates the world, especially his wife."

"Why would he hate Mother?" Night Hawk asked, arching an eyebrow.

"Because it was *she*, not your father, who gave permission for the cowhands to come and give a hand," Crying Wolf explained.

"My mother?" Night Hawk gasped. "How could she do that? Father would never allow it."

"And that is why he is lying in his bed even now hating her," Crying Wolf said. "She asked for volunteers. Forty of your father's best men are waiting outside the cave entrance for you. And not only are *they* there, waiting for you, but so is your beautiful, caring mother."

This truly took Night Hawk by surprise. "My mother is here?" he asked, eyes wide. "I don't understand."

"She found the courage to leave your father." Crying Wolf lowered the torch and looked over his shoulder toward the cave entrance, then gazed at Night Hawk again. "She has come to make her home with you, Night Hawk."

"I can hardly believe she has left him," Night Hawk said, laughing. "And to have ridden all of this way on horseback? I have never seen her on a horse, or *any*where but in the house in her dainty dresses and beautiful diamonds."

"She wears one of her dainty dresses now," Crying Wolf said, then chuckled. "But it has lost its luster during the trip. I promised her buckskins once we have things righted at our village."

"And I welcome her into my heart again," Night Hawk said. He looked over his shoulder as Jae came sleepily toward him, rubbing her eyes.

Jae gazed from Crying Wolf to Night Hawk, and back again to Crying Wolf. "You're back," she said, stepping up to Night Hawk's side. "How did it go, Crying Wolf?" She looked past Crying Wolf, into the darkness of the cave, then gazed at him with disappointment in her eyes. "You weren't allowed to bring any of the cowhands here to help Night Hawk, were you?"

"I have brought many. They wait just outside the cave." Crying Wolf smiled at Jae when he saw relief rush into her eyes.

Night Hawk turned to Jae and took her hands in his. "Someone else has come tonight," he said. "My adoptive mother. She has left my father and has come to be a part of our lives. Will you help make her welcome?"

Jae was stunned speechless for a moment.

"She . . . is . . . here?" she finally said, disbelief in her voice and eyes. "She has left your father's palatial mansion to live in a tepee?"

"When one's life is nothing but misery, one adapts quickly to another life," he said. "Will you help her?"

"Night Hawk, I don't think your mother cares much for me," Jae murmured. "Yes, upon my arrival at the ranch, she helped me with my bath and saw that I was given beautiful clothes. She was nice enough then, when she had no true cause to hate me. It was after the will was read that I saw the instant resentment—the hate for me—enter her eyes. I doubt she will ever get over blaming me for what I have done to her life by emerging from the Big Thicket to be with my true father."

"It is *she* who has come to *us* to live this new life," Night Hawk pointed out. "It was not forced on her. So I do not think that she would have come to us with bitterness in her heart."

"Not toward you, but yes, I believe she will feel bitter toward me," Jae said sullenly. "Perhaps she won't show it, but no doubt it will be there all the same."

"Will you help her?" Night Hawk said more forcefully. "She is still important to me. I wish only to make her happy."

"I will do the best I can," Jae said. "But don't blame me if things do not go as you wish between us."

"I would not cast blame on you or my mother. I am just happy to have you both in my life."

Crying Wolf walked with them down the long,

dark avenue of the cave until they came out into the moon-dappled night.

Jae stopped and stared at the many men who were there on their horses. She could hardly believe they had all made it undetected past the Comanche sentries.

When she felt eyes on her, she turned a slow gaze up at Lois, who still sat on her horse. Her eyes locked with the older woman's.

Jae waited to see if Lois would smile at her, and when she didn't, an icy coldness circled her heart.

Determined to show Night Hawk that *she* was not at fault for the silence, Jae marched right up to Lois. "It is good to see you again," she said, extending a hand of friendship.

Recalling just why she should resent Jae, Lois hesitated, then knowing that their lives would now be forever linked, she inched her hand out toward her. "Likewise," she said, her voice drawn.

Their handshake was quick. Soon they both eased their hands away from each other.

"Come on inside the cave and get warm by the fire," Jae said, offering to take Lois's reins.

Lois kept her reins and slid out of her saddle. "I don't believe I have ever been so tired," she remarked, finally breaking the ice between them. "I welcome the fire, Jae. Also a blanket, if you have one. This night air has put a chill into my bones."

"Yes, I have a spare blanket." Jae was relieved that Lois was not going to continue giving her that cold glare. She was beginning to see some promise in their relationship. "Come on with me. We can leave the men to their plans. I'm sure they wouldn't want two women offering their suggestions."

Lois gave Night Hawk a soft smile as she walked

past him. But knowing that their hugs could come later, when there was not so much of an audience, she went on inside the cave with Jae.

Just as Jae got Lois settled in beside the fire on a blanket, with another blanket wrapped around her shoulders, the men and their horses came into the cave.

Once the horses were tethered farther back in the cave, where there was a small stream snaking along the rocky floor, everyone settled in around the fire and began talking about their experiences traveling to the cave.

"I thought the Comanche sentries had us that one time," one of the men said, chuckling. "Had we not broken into small groups to slip past them, I imagine we'd all be captives of Black Crow."

"And so Crying Wolf has told you all about that black-hearted Comanche war chief, has he?" Night Hawk said, accepting some beef jerky from one of the men. He bit into it and began slowly chewing. "With all of your help, Black Crow will soon be running scared."

They talked awhile longer, then the men went to their separate bedrolls and were soon fast asleep.

Jae gazed at Lois, who was asleep by the fire, then at Crying Wolf, who had placed his blankets close by, his eyes hardly leaving her. Jae had to believe there was something brewing between them, and it surprised her that this Comanche would take any interest in women at his age.

She smiled at the possibility of a romance blossoming between them, although Lois was twenty years younger and had never lived anything but a life of affluence. It was hard to imagine her in a tepee cooking over a small cookfire, or tanning hides along with the Comanche women.

Jae had the same experiences ahead of her, but *she* had lived crudely in the Thicket. She understood all aspects of hardship.

Jae went to Night Hawk, who had left the cave and was standing outside, staring down at the village.

"Night Hawk, what are you thinking so deeply about?" she murmured, sidling up next to him.

"That tomorrow the warriors under Eagle Wing's leadership should come to the cave, if all has gone as planned." He slipped an arm around her waist and drew her closer to his side. "I am worried about my father, though. Yet surely if he, or any of my family, had been blamed for my escape, Eagle Wing would have come immediately to me and told me. Since he didn't, I have to believe that all is well and be thankful that my plan is finally set into motion." He clenched his left hand into a tight fist at his side. "That bastard Black Crow. He, and renegades like him, are the sort of Comanche that give *all* Comanche a bad name."

"There is only so much that you can do to correct that misconception," Jae said softly. "When this is all over and your father leads your people again, *please* allow yourself to feel good about having done that much for your tribe."

Night Hawk smiled down at her. "You are so good for me," he said. "You will be good for my people. It will be a lesson taught to them that not all whites are bad." He laughed softly. "It is not enough that I am part white. I am also Comanche. So, my woman, it will be up to you to show my people the goodness that can be found in the hearts of whites."

"Do you think Lois will also be a good representative of the white people in the eyes of your people?" Jae asked.

Night Hawk nodded. "*Huh*, she will also work to the betterment of my people," he said. "She loves me and will want what *I* want. She always has. I wish it could have been the same for my adoptive father."

Jae placed a gentle hand to his cheek. "Darling, when we were together the last time, we thought it might be the last opportunity to be together for a while," she murmured. "Darling, we were *wrong*." Her eyes twinkled as she smiled seductively up at him. "Do you think we can take these quiet moments to . . . to . . . ?"

"To make love?" he said, chuckling beneath his breath.

"*Huh*, to make love," Jae said, her heart already throbbing with the promise of what lay ahead.

Night Hawk smiled and inhaled as he listened and looked around him. The moon was full.

The air was warmer than most nights high on this butte where the wind whispered secrets.

A loon echoed its haunting refrain from somewhere in the distance.

A wolf howled at the moon.

It was a perfect night somewhere for a lone brave to seek guidance from his eagle spirit.

It was a night made for lovers.

"I see no better way to spend the rest of the night, my woman," he then said. "I doubt that I can get any sleep while waiting for Eagle Wing to arrive." He paused. "But won't you get a chill out here away from the fire?" he asked, running his hands up and down her arms.

"How can you ask that?" Jae gave him a flirtatious

311

gaze. "You know the heat that our lovemaking generates between us."

"*Huh,* my insides are already on fire," he said huskily. He swept his fingers up and twined them in her hair and drew her lips to his and kissed her.

Jae's insides trembled from the building ecstasy. She ran her hands up inside his shirt and stroked his powerful chest. She then slid her hands downward and unfastened his breeches. Her fingers crept lower to the front of his breeches.

And when she touched his manhood and found it already thick and long with need of her, she gasped softly against his lips.

As she ran her fingers up and down the full length of him, she could feel his body stiffening against hers, then relax, stiffen, and then relax again.

When a droplet of liquid pooled at the tip of his velvet tightness and she smoothed this liquid over the full head of his manhood, his guttural sighs of pleasure filled the night air.

Feeling too much too soon, Night Hawk clasped a gentle hand on her wrist and guided her fingers away from his throbbing sex. "Woman, you have learned too quickly the skills of how to please a man," he said huskily.

He led her away from the edge of the cliff. When he found where moss lay smooth and green along the rocky surface, he urged Jae down on it.

His eyes hazed over with need, he removed Jae's clothes. Then as she watched, he removed all of his garments.

Jae's heart thumped wildly as she swept her gaze slowly over his body, at how the moon sheened his smooth, copper chest, and at how just seeing the way his swollen sex jutted out from his body caused her head to spin with rapture.

Night Hawk leaned down and spread himself over her. His body protected her from the night air; his hands gripped her breasts and softly kneaded them. His mouth brushed her cheeks and ears. He lightly, tenderly kissed her eyelids closed.

Jae moaned when his mouth lowered and he moved it over one of her breasts, his tongue licking the nipple.

He swept a hand on down her body. She sucked in a wild breath of pleasure when he came to her pulsing center. It seemed fluid with fire as his fingers flicked, rubbed, and played across it.

Jae whimpered tiny cries against his lips when he kissed her again and plunged his thick heat into her pulsing cleft. She lifted her hips and gyrated them against him.

Night Hawk kissed her again, long and deep. He moved slowly within her, then more powerfully and determinedly, feeding her hungers; feeding his own.

The pleasure was building within Jae. Her breathing came in quick gasps. The sensations he was arousing in her were searing.

Then purposely postponing their explosion of ecstasy, Night Hawk withdrew from inside her and held her in his arms with an exquisite tenderness.

"*Nei-com-mar-pe-ein*, I love you so," Jae whispered. She ran her fingers through his hair and gazed into his eyes. "I wish tonight would last forever. I so fear tomorrow. What if you don't achieve what you have set out to do?" She drew his cheek down against hers. "What if you don't survive?" she whispered, her voice breaking.

"I have not come this far to be defeated by the likes

of Black Crow," Night Hawk whispered back.

"If anything happens to you, I would not want to live, either," she said, trembling inside at the thought of their parting in such a tragic way.

He placed a forefinger against her lips and gazed into her troubled eyes. "Now is not the time to show doubts about what I have planned for my Comanche people." He ran a hand up and down her spine, then slid his fingers around to fill them with a breast. "Now is not the time to think of anything but the joy of being together; of making *love.*"

He took her mouth by storm and kissed her again.

His lips drugged Jae, sending all thoughts but these precious moments with him from her mind.

He surrounded her with his powerful arms and lunged inside her again.

Her body absorbed the bold thrusts. She arched and met them; She wrapped her legs around his waist and rode him.

They made love in a wild, dizzying rhythm. His body hardened and tightened, and his blood quickened as he felt himself drawing close to the ultimate of pleasure.

Jae abandoned herself to the torrent of feelings that were swimming through her in crashing, hot waves. She felt the ecstasy growing . . . growing to the bursting point.

Then the sensual shock of release grabbed at her heart. Her gasps of pleasure became long, soft whimpers.

Night Hawk joined her. He threw his head back, and he closed his eyes as the great shuddering in his loins released his seed deeply inside Jae.

They both shimmered and swayed as the climax claimed them.

Then their bodies subsided exhaustedly together.

Night Hawk rolled away from Jae. Breathing hard, he lay on his back and gazed up at the stars.

Still on the cloud of ecstasy that she had just shared with Night Hawk, Jae lay there for a moment, her eyes closed.

Then she opened them and gazed over at him. Tonight she found it hard to get enough of him. No matter how hard she tried, she could not get her fears of tomorrow off her mind. She could not help wanting to touch him again now, to kiss him again, to make love with him again.

Smiling wickedly, she moved to her knees next to him, then bent low and slowly began kissing her way along his body.

Night Hawk's skin trembled with a renewed aliveness. He wove his fingers through her hair and led her lips where he again ached for her.

Jae smiled as she felt his sex grow again into something thick and long as her tongue flicked and teased along his shaft. His groans made her know that she was giving him the pleasure he sought.

She continued making love to him in this fashion, until suddenly he reached for her hand and eased it from his sex, then led her back down, onto her back.

He loved her with his lips, tongue, and mouth, until she was again mindless with pleasure. She sighed and tremored.

When he felt that she was close to that brink that would take her into that other world again, and wanting to follow her, he rose over her and thrust his heat inside her.

The stars flickered like diamonds overhead. The moon seemed to be smiling as over and over again Night Hawk and Jae rode the sensual waves of love.

There was no tomorrow.

There was only now.

Chapter Thirty-five

The next day, as the morning mist was rising with the sun, Jae stood with Lois and watched the Comanche warriors, under the leadership of Eagle Wing, file into the cave on their horses, their many travois piled high with meat and pelts.

Jae watched the cowhands as they stood back, waiting and watching. It was obvious that this was the first time they had been in the presence of Comanche.

Her eyes roamed from man to man, seeing only a few who wore guarded expressions on their faces. Night Hawk had talked with them before the arrival of the Comanche. Although they had known when they had left the ranch that they would be mingling with the Comanche, even perhaps fighting side by side *with* them, Night Hawk had taken the time to reassure them that this faction of Comanche fought for the right of peace among his people, which in turn, might help keep peace with the white settlers.

Jae turned her gaze to Night Hawk, who reached a hand out for a young brave who slid from his saddle to the ground. She wondered who the child might be, especially when Night Hawk bent low and gave him a big hug.

Her gaze shifted again to the Comanche warriors, and then to the cowhands. Crying Wolf brought them together. Introductions were made, and Jae was glad to see smiles and handshakes among them.

She turned again and looked at Night Hawk, who was now walking the young brave toward her and Lois.

When he reached them, he gazed proudly down at the child, then smiled from Jae to Lois. "This is my brother, Little Horse," he said, his pride in having a brother evident in the pleasant gleam in his eyes.

Night Hawk nodded toward Jae. "And, Little Horse, this is Jae, the woman I will soon marry and bring into our village." He nodded at Lois. "And, Little Horse, this is Lois, the woman who I call Mother. She, too, will be a part of our Comanche lives."

Little Horse had gone suddenly glum. He looked suspiciously from woman to woman, then turned wary eyes up at his older brother. "They are truly to be trusted?" he asked, taking Running Hawk aback by the question. "Although you are part white, you *are* Comanche. How can these women ever become as one with our people when their skin and thoughts are totally white?"

Night Hawk looked over his shoulder at the activity behind him. The warriors were all safely inside the cave and had dismounted. They were mingling with the cowhands.

And Crying Wolf had already placed some of the meat offered him over the fire on a tripod. The tantalizing smell of roasted venison filled the air.

He gazed at Eagle Wing, who was standing in the

cluster of warriors and cowhands, his face serious as he talked to them in perfect English.

Night Hawk knew that he must soon join them. Time was of the essence. Should Black Crow send warriors out now to look for these warriors, and they could not find them, his suspicions would be aroused. A search party would be sent out in earnest.

If someone saw the many hoofprints that led up the side of this cliff . . .

That thought made Night Hawk hurry onward with this smaller chore of trying to console a young brave who would one day be a great warrior. "My brother," he said, moving to his haunches before Little Horse, "trust is earned, is it not?"

Little Horse nodded. *"Huh."*

"I have known my adoptive mother for many moons, and her trust has been earned." Running Hawk clasped a gentle hand on his brother's shoulder.

Little Horse shifted his gaze toward Jae. His eyes slowly roamed over the way she was dressed, in her cut-off jeans and white shirt. The clothes alone made him distrust her. He was surprised that his brother would even be planning to marry her.

"What of *her?*" Little Horse mumbled, nodding toward Jae. His eyes narrowed as he caught her staring at him in wonder. "Have you known her long enough to truly trust her?"

Night Hawk looked over his shoulder at Jae. Their eyes met and held. He smiled.

Then he gazed into Little Horse's untrusting eyes. "My brother," he said softly, "I have not known her even one moon, yet I know that she is worthy of our trust. Would I have given her my heart had she not been trustworthy?"

"A man is sometimes hasty with trust when a woman flashes her eyes a certain way at him and hypnotizes him," Little Horse said, still not to be persuaded so easily.

Night Hawk's patience was running thin. "Little Horse, go and join the warriors," he said sternly. "I will be there momentarily to reveal my plans to everyone. You chose to come here today to be with the warriors as though you are one of them. Go. *Be* what you are expected to *be*."

Taken aback by his older brother speaking in a scolding fashion to him, Little Horse took a step away from Night Hawk, who saw how startled Little Horse was over the scolding. He reached a hand out and rested it on his brother's shoulder. "A sign of a true warrior is patience," he said. "Be patient with not only me, a brother who is new to you, but also these women. We are all here for the right reasons."

Little Horse thought for a moment, then nodded. He flung himself into his brother's arms. "I am sorry for bringing you trouble while your mind should only be on helping our people. And thank you again, my big brother, for allowing me to be here. My heart swells with pride to be allowed to be a part of this scheme against the evil War Chief!"

Night Hawk hugged Little Horse for a moment, then gently shoved him away. "*Mea*, go. I shall be there soon," he said, glad to see Little Horse's frown replaced by a wide smile.

Little Horse scurried away. He stood beside Eagle Wing, his eyes wide with admiration as he gazed up at him, listening.

Night Hawk embraced Jae and Lois, then went and joined the men. "I thank you all for coming," he said. He looked from warrior to warrior, wondering who among them might have played with him as a child.

But now was not the time for such trivialities. Later, after their lives were set back in proper order, he would discover old friends. He would cherish them. They would never part again!

All but Night Hawk and Eagle Wing sat down on blankets beside the fire. With Eagle Wing beside him, Night Hawk stood with squared shoulders and a set jaw. "Here is my plan," he said solemnly. "To keep all of our Comanche women, children, and elderly safe, they must all be temporarily removed from the village."

"And how could that be managed?" one of the warriors asked, and the others nodded in approval of the question.

"It will not be as simple as I would like for it to be," Night Hawk said. "It can only be achieved in Black Crow's absence. Does he not leave often, for full days and nights of raiding and plundering?"

"*Huh*, that is so," echoed many warriors.

"We will prepare ourselves for his next exit from the village," Night Hawk said, smiling smugly. "While he is gone, the women, children, and elderly can be brought to this cave for safekeeping. When Black Crow returns to the village, he and his men will ride into a surprise ambush led by Night Hawk and Eagle Wing!"

Eagle Wing turned to him. "My friend, I see that as an excellent plan. It can be arranged!"

"It is good you approve, my brother." Night Hawk smiled at Eagle Wing.

He again slowly roamed his eyes over the men. "Furthermore, to make the plan a true success, Crying Wolf and I will hide under blankets and pelts on two of your travois," he said. "We will travel secretly in that fashion to your village. We shall then hide in your lodges as we wait for Black Crow to leave. We will be there then to see that our people's exit from the village is swiftly done."

He looked from one cowhand to the other. "You will wait here, in the cave, until the Comanche people are safe. When they are, you will then come on to the village. You will wait along with us Comanche in the lodges and surprise Black Crow upon his return. When he sees that it is many warriors and cowhands with firearms in the lodges instead of the Comanche people, he will then know that should he fight to keep his hold on our people, he will die. My father will then again be the leader of our people, not Black Crow." Night Hawk allowed himself a smile.

With the plan agreed upon, Night Hawk felt confident that it would work. "We will take the time to eat, then we will set our plan in motion," he said.

He slid his knife from its sheath at his right side and sliced into the meat. He then handed the food to the men.

Jae and Lois joined them, and, laughing and joking, everyone had a feast.

But when the time came for everyone to leave, to return to the village, and Night Hawk and Crying Wolf were ready to hide beneath the pelts on the two travois, there were suddenly solemn, worried faces among those who had only moments ago felt carefree and confident.

Jae had kept quiet about Night Hawk's plan, until now. There had been one thing about it that she did not agree with—she had been left out of the most exciting part of it!

"I'm going with you," she said. She knelt down and began removing pelts from a third travois.

Jae stopped abruptly when Night Hawk grabbed her wrist and pulled her up to stand before him. "You cannot go," he said tightly. "We are taking chances entering the village in such a way. You will not be a part of that risk."

"I can't just stay behind and wonder what is happening to you," Jae said, her voice drawn. "And . . . and I want to be a part of it. You know that I am capable of fending for myself. I can shoot as straight as any man."

Lois went to Jae. "I truly think you'd be better off here," she said, gently taking her by a hand. "Come on, Jae. Let the men be on their way. It's obvious that time is wasting."

Jae gazed, wide-eyed, at Lois, then slipped her hand free. "I have never turned my back on a fight," she said, pride in her eyes. "I have never been a typical woman who sits by and twiddles her thumbs or bakes cookies in a kitchen. I love adventure." She turned to Night Hawk. "Even after I am a wife and mother, I will have to feed my hunger for adventure. Will you allow it, Night Hawk? Will you allow me to go with you?"

"The word 'allow' seems wrongly used here," Night Hawk grumbled, not wanting ever to look as though he was the sort of husband who gave strict orders to a wife. He had fallen in love with the strong, adventure-loving side of Jae. Never would he stifle it!

"Are you saying . . . ?" Jae began, but was stopped when Night Hawk slid a finger across her lips, sealing them.

"*Mea*, come," he said, taking her by the hand. "I

shall see that you are well covered by pelts and blankets on the travois."

Jae almost squealed with delight, she was so happy over his decision. She gave Lois a soft look over her shoulder, hoping she understood. They had come to an understanding. She even liked Lois, and she did not want to ruin their newfound bond. It was nice to have Lois's companionship; Jae even looked toward her as a mother figure.

"May God be with you, Jae," Lois said, smiling at her.

Jae sighed with relief. "Thank you." She scrambled onto the travois, scarcely breathing as Night Hawk covered her with pelts.

Jae's pulse raced as she left the cave on the travois. She grasped the poles tightly when it rolled and scraped and bounced as the horse dragged her down the side of the cliff.

She was relieved when flat land was finally reached.

The farther the warrior carried her on the travois, the more Jae's heart pounded, knowing that at any moment Black Crow could appear and perhaps scrutinize what was beneath the blankets and pelts.

Her fears mounted when she heard the sound of horses arriving, thinking that surely it *was* Black Crow!

But when she heard a voice that was now familiar to her, and heard what he said, she heaved a sigh of relief and relaxed. It had only been Eagle Wing. He had gone ahead and made some plans with Night Hawk's father.

Brown Bull now knew when to expect the entourage of hunters *and* their hidden "guests."

He had told Eagle Wing that his daughter, Touch

the Sky, would prepare a lodge in which Night Hawk and Crying Wolf, and now Jae, could hide. She would see to it that one of her father's wives would go and stay with another of his wives, while *her* lodge would be used for their hideaway.

From there, Night Hawk, Crying Wolf, and Jae could listen to all of the activity in the village.

For certain they could not hide in Brown Bull's lodge. Too many came and went from his tepee: not only Black Crow but also the medicine man Sun Eagle.

Night Hawk had confided in Jae about Sun Eagle, about how he didn't trust him, his suspicion that he was guilty of having fed his father poison. Soon Night Hawk hoped to prove that!

They traveled onward, and when they entered the village, there was much cheering and laughter as the people came and stared at the amount of meat that had been brought to them.

Before the people had a chance to marvel over the pelts, several of the warriors eased away from the others. As they came close to Brown Bull's lodge, they made a quick turn and went behind it.

Breathing hard, Jae scrambled from beneath the blankets and pelts.

Along with Night Hawk and Crying Wolf, she slid beneath a slight opening that had been rolled up at the bottom of the tepee, left that way purposely for them at the rear of the tiny lodge.

The warriors quickly went back in front of the lodges, circled around, and stopped in front of their own.

Just as they were carrying the pelts and blankets inside their lodges, Black Crow came and questioned them.

"Do you not wish to display your pelts to our people?" he said, glowering from warrior to warrior. "Are you selfish men?"

They rushed inside their lodges and grabbed an armfull of pelts, mingling those that they had gathered on their last hunt with those few brought today. When they took these out and laid them on the ground at Black Crow's feet, he seemed pleased enough.

He turned and went back and joined the celebration.

Little Horse was at the center of the laughter and singing. He had been successful on the hunt! Many young girls surrounded him and began to serenade him.

Jae heard the young voices lifting in song. She peeked from the tepee and saw that it was all for Little Horse.

"Night Hawk, your brother is being treated like someone very special," she whispered, making room for him at her side. She leaned back so that he could see better.

"It is his first successful hunt," he explained. "A young warrior who has great success on the hunt is serenaded on his return. This evening there will be a Victory Dance. Although Black Crow will not wish for my brother to be honored in such a way, he knows better than to interfere. It is a custom long used by my people when a young lad proves he is worthy of soon being called warrior."

He glanced over at Jae. "During the celebration, the young maidens of the camp will dress like warriors," he said softly. "They will dance and sing all around my brother. He will be pleased with such an honor."

"I would think so," Jae said, laughing softly.

They sat back down around the lodge fire with Crying Wolf. "I wonder how long we will have to wait for Black Crow to make his move," Jae said, drawing her legs up before her, hugging her knees. "Do you think he will leave soon on one of his missions of terror?"

"*Huh,* I believe he will leave soon," Crying Wolf offered. "He will be so unhappy over Brown Bull's son being honored in such a way, he will have to go out and release his rage."

Jae shivered at the thought of the sort of slaughter he might leave behind. While in Beaumont, she had read accounts of such raids in newspapers. Never had she thought anyone could be as evil as what was described in the articles.

But now, knowing the likes of Black Crow and Jonas Adams, whom she could not allow herself to forget, she knew that anything was possible.

The celebration went on into the night. Loads of wood were added to the huge communal fire in the center of the village. Buffalo tongues were roasted over the coals, and there was much dancing and singing.

When everything became quiet, Jae peeked outside again. It was evident that the tongues were finally ready to eat. The men sat down in a wide semicircle around the fire. The women took a position about twenty steps from the opening of the circle and then sat down.

"What they do now is called the Shakedown Dance, yet there is no actual dancing," Night Hawk whispered, recalling this ritual from when he was a child. "Watch. Listen. Learn."

Jae nodded. They watched the medicine man light

a pipe, then blow the first puff of smoke toward the darkening heavens.

He blew a second puff toward the earth, and one in each of the four directions.

The pipe was then passed to the other men, who smoked it likewise.

"Smoking the pipe in such a way is an oath in which the smokers bind themselves always to tell the truth," Night Hawk said.

When the pipe had finally made its rounds and was laid aside, the women were called upon to serve the tongue.

As pieces of meat were passed around, the women made shrill cries, saying, *"Li-li-li-li."*

Then the tongue was consumed.

"And that is the completion of the Shakedown Dance," Night Hawk said, smiling over at Jae.

She gave him a puzzled look.

"I understand your puzzlement over this custom," he said, taking her into his arms. "It is just the beginning of your lessons about the Comanche."

Crying Wolf placed a hand on each of their shoulders. He lifted his eyes skyward and prayed silently that Night Hawk and Jae would have the opportunity to live the life of the Comanche. He knew that so many things could go wrong with their plan; he had just not voiced his doubts aloud, for it was important that now that Night Hawk had returned to be among his people, he was given the opportunity to lead, not be questioned over everything he said or did.

He would make sure things were always right for his best friend in the world!

Chapter Thirty-six

Night Hawk continued to watch through the slight opening at the entrance flap. "Something else is about to happen," he said, his heart skipping a beat, his excitement rising.

"What?" Jae whispered. She edged closer to him and drew the flap back far enough for her also to see better.

"I can tell you without even looking," Crying Wolf offered, drawing both Night Hawk and Jae's eyes to him.

"I noticed today there were more to the songs than just celebrating a young brave and the warriors' return with food," Crying Wolf said. He placed another log on the fire in the fire pit. "They sang war songs. Did you not notice, Night Hawk?"

Night Hawk slowly shook his head back and forth. "No, I noticed nothing unusual."

"That is because you have been gone too long from your people to recognize war songs," Crying Wolf said. "Of course, I have been gone for many moons myself. But when I left, I was not a young pup of ten winters, as you were when you were forced to leave. I had lived many long years with my people before being sent out to find you. I was acquainted with everything our people did."

He smiled. "My heart throbs at the thought of the war dance and the parade of Black Crow and his warriors through our village on their proud steeds. They will soon be leaving. We then can show ourselves to our people. We shall lead them from the village to the cave."

"No, I did not recognize the war songs," Night Hawk said. "But I do know the meaning of warriors sitting around the fire, painting their faces with war paints! They are doing that now. They *are* going to be leaving soon. We *will* be able to go out of hiding." He frowned. "How many of Black Crow's warriors do you think will stay behind? How many will we will be forced to disable before we can remove our people to safety?"

"I doubt that any who are loyal to Black Crow and his devious ways will stay behind," Crying Wolf said flatly. "Just as I know that those who align themselves with Eagle Wing will not be asked to go with Black Crow. They are two separate factions of warriors; they do not mingle. One wars. One does not."

Holding the flap aside only far enough to see, Jae turned and watched from the entranceway again. "The warriors are now fully painted and are dressed in war clothes. Now they are tying some sort of tails to their *horse's* tails. I wonder what sort of animal they killed to get the tails?

"Skunk," Crying Wolf said, drawing Jae's quick attention back to him. "Skunk has great power. Warriors receive its power by placing its tail on their horses. Their horses also receive the power of the skunk. They are able to ride faster. As though they have wings, the horses can leave a scene of atrocities much faster than an ordinary horse that does not have the special skunk powers."

Thinking that she would never know, or perhaps not even understand, the customs of Night Hawk's people, Jae sighed heavily.

She slowly turned and once again watched the proceedings outside. She singled Little Horse out from the other youths. He was standing among the young braves, but he did not show the same excitement in his eyes as he watched the warriors preparing for warring. His father's son, who now saw warring as wrong, his eyes showed his resentment.

Night Hawk turned and also watched the ceremony. "Soon," he said, his eyes gleaming. "Soon they will be gone!"

The light of the moon illuminated the darkness. And the huge outdoor fire leapt like orange fingers heavenward, reflecting against the sky like a brilliant oil painting on black canvas.

"The Comanche prefer raiding during the period following the full moon," Crying Wolf said.

Jae and Night Hawk listened, yet continued watching the excitement building outside.

"The warriors never raid when the moon is a crescent with the horns pointing upward," Crying Wolf continued. "The moon is then 'full and running over' when there is likely to be rain and their horse's tracks could be traced. Tonight, those Comanche warriors, whose faces are painted and whose horses are hung with skunk tails, will strike swiftly, since the moon's glow is bright as though it might be daylight."

"Oh, Lord." Jae gasped as she watched the frenzied dancing that had just begun around the fire. The warriors who were going to leave a trail of blood behind them tonight were circling round and round the fire in a spasmodic trot, their tomahawks and scalping knives in their uplifted hands.

"Let them dance," Night Hawk said through clenched teeth. "Let them dream of killing and maiming! Tonight will be the last time they will wreck havoc upon the countryside!"

"I wish there was a way to stop them," Jae said, swallowing hard. "I feel so helpless. It is awful to think that those men might soon be killing innocent people."

"There is no way to stop what has already begun tonight, but we can make sure that it never happens again," Night Hawk grumbled out as he watched the painted warriors mount their horses and begin their slow parade through the village.

"They are now on their horses, parading, showing their war colors, and singing," Crying Wolf said solemnly without even having to look outside. He was familiar with it all—the frenzied dancing and the parading of the warriors four times through the village in single file while singing their war songs.

"What a surprise Black Crow will receive when he returns from his raiding," Night Hawk said bitterly. Then he laughed. "What a surprise he would have if he knew that we are here, so close, scheming to end his reign of terror."

He looked at the warriors who were *not* painted for warring and who stood together, glaring at those who were. He singled out Eagle Wing. Night Hawk smiled when he saw the smirk on Eagle Wing's lips, knowing that he was thinking perhaps the same thing that Night Hawk had just voiced aloud—that Black Crow would not be sitting so smugly on his horse if he knew who was hidden in a lodge close by, contemplating his doom!

"Soon," Night Hawk whispered. "See how they are now turning their horses? They are ready to leave!"

Jae's pulse raced as she watched the warriors wheeling their horses around away from the crowd and the huge outdoor fire. She listened to their loud war whoops as they rode away.

And then things seemed so strangely, forebodingly quiet as those who were left behind stood around, waiting for Black Crow to get far enough away before setting their plan in motion.

They watched the women begin dispersing, returning to their lodges, the children following along behind them.

They watched the elderly men move slowly behind the children.

Only a few knew what was about to transpire in the absence of their War Chief!

Then everything changed.

Night Hawk, Crying Wolf, and Jae stepped outside the lodge. Eagle Wing gave instructions for everyone to leave their lodges and explained the plan to them.

After everyone understood, and all agreed to it, except for the children, wives, and lovers of those who were out tonight raiding, they started their escape from the village under the protective wing of warriors.

Those who did not want to cooperate, among them Sun Eagle, were forced to leave. They were guarded as they marched from the village.

His legs still too weak to hold him up for long, Brown Bull left on a travois, Touch the Sky proudly riding the horse that took him away.

Once the village was emptied out, except for those

who stayed behind to launch the surprise attack on Black Crow when he returned, everyone waited for the arrival of the cowhands who would assist in the removal of the Comanche tyrant.

Little Horse, who had been given the honor of staying with his brother since he had already proved his bravery in many ways, stood at Night Hawk's side now as they watched the arrival of the cowhands.

After everyone was instructed about where to hide, and they had made their final plans for Black Crow's surprise, Crying Wolf brought a vial from Chief Brown Bull's lodge.

"Let us all rub the oil of the beaver on our bodies," he said, looking from man to man, even the white cowhands. "It will give us absolute protection from the rifle bullets of our enemy Black Crow if gunfire erupts tonight between us."

The cowhands took unsteady steps away from him, refusing to be anointed in such a way.

Jae stood back and watched Night Hawk and the others bathe their arms and faces with the beaver oil.

When Night Hawk turned to her with the vial of beaver oil, a silent pleading in his eyes, she gazed at him for a moment. She most certainly did not want to cover her face with the greasy, stinking stuff.

But she never wanted to disappoint Night Hawk, and seeing how he had already been stung with disappointment over the cowhands refusing the oil, she forced a smile and began rubbing the oil over her face. She did not stop until all of her bare flesh gleamed in the glow of the outdoor fire.

"Your beauty is enhanced by the oil," Night Hawk said, gently smoothing one of his hands over the sleekness of one of her cheeks.

Feeling anything but beautiful, Jae managed a soft smile.

After everyone was hidden in the lodges, Night Hawk looked slowly around him. He had chosen to wait in his father's lodge, along with his young brother Little Horse, Jae, and Crying Wolf.

"And so this is how my father lives," Night Hawk said, moving slowly around the lodge, looking at his father's possessions. "As a child, I was only but a few times in my father's lodge. I spent more of my time in my mother's. But I recall many of these things from my past."

He stopped and stared at a beautiful war shield. "I remember this." He ran his fingers slowly over the round buffalo-hide war shield that hung by the door on a rack. It was about two feet in diameter. He recalled his father telling him that the purpose of hanging the shield by the door was for it to absorb the powerful medicine from the sun. Brown Bull had also told him that the shield was round because it was made in the imitation of the sun.

"Next to his bow and arrow, the war shield is the most important possession of the Comanche warrior," Crying Wolf said, moving to Night Hawk's side. With admiration, he gazed at the shield. "The shields are made from the shoulder hide of the buffalo because it is the toughest part. Very few bullets go through such a shield."

"It's so beautiful," Jae said, also moving closer to admire it. "It has so many beautiful decorations on it."

"I remember my father explaining the decorations to me," Night Hawk said. He smiled at Jae, then gazed at the shield once again. "Do you see the bear teeth painted on the shield? That means that the

335

owner is a great hunter, that he is as tough as a *bear*."

"Are those horse or mule tails hanging around the inside of the shield?" Jae asked, so glad to have something to take her mind off her anxiousness for Black Crow's return. She had such mixed feelings: A part of her was afraid, yet a part of her looked forward to the challenge of the fight!

"Those are horse's tails," Crying Wolf interjected. "Night Hawk, I watched your father attach them. They represent a man who was at one time an accomplished raider."

Jae looked quickly over at Night Hawk, her eyes wide. "Your father raided? he killed . . . ?"

"*Huh*," Night Hawk said glumly. "But he raided only for *horses*. Horses are a sign of wealth to the Comanche. The more horses a warrior possesses, the more he is enhanced in the eyes of those who know him."

Jae sighed with relief.

"Do you see the feathers attached to the outside of the shield?" Night Hawk asked. "They always have to be in even numbers, usually four. For my father, it is six. The feathers are shaken to distract the enemy's aim."

"The war shield possesses mystical powers," Crying Wolf said. "It is also sacred."

"Jae, this shield has been passed down from generation to generation, from father to son," Night Hawk said, running his fingers across the various painted objects on the front. "Upon my father's death, it will be mine instead of Little Horse's, since I am the eldest son." He smiled at her. "Then one day it will be *our* son's."

A warmth spread through her at his mention of a son. "Our son," she murmured aloud, making what

Night Hawk said very real inside her heart. "I am so anxious to be a mother, Night Hawk. I will cherish a child born of our love."

He reached out with one arm and drew her closer to his side. "You will be a beautiful, caring mother," he said. "I will be a dutiful, doting father."

He gestured toward the shield. "Do you see these paintings?" he said, again running his fingers over them. "And how they differ?"

"Yes, I see scenes from nature, as well as animals," Jae said, watching his fingers touch first one drawing, and then another. "They are so beautiful."

"Each generation adds some design to it, to make it its own. I will one day make my design on the shield," he said, pausing to send Jae a half frown. "That is, if I live through the upcoming battle."

"Please don't even think about not surviving," Jae said, gasping at his seriousness. "You *will* be the victor, darling. It can't be any other way. Black Crow will be ousted. I am not Comanche, and still I can see the wrong he has done your people."

"He has even brought our people's medicine man into his evil," Crying Wolf said. He went to Brown Bull's bed and picked up a leather vial that had been left there right before Brown Bull had left to go with the others to the cave. Sun Eagle had just arrived with a vial of his medicine.

Night Hawk went and took the small leather vial from Crying Wolf. He gazed angrily at it. "Sun Eagle is still trying to hasten my father's death," he said, his jaw tight.

He loosened the drawstring, opening the vial. "We have proof here in my hand that what I fear is true," he said. "I will taste it, and I will identify the herb that is being wrongly used. One taste should be proof enough."

He dipped a finger into the herbal liquid medication.

"No!" Jae cried as Night Hawk placed a taste of the medication to the tip of his tongue.

Chapter Thirty-seven

With a start, Night Hawk spit out the bitter-tasting liquid, not because of Jae's outburst of alarm, but because he had heard the sudden firing of two rifles in the distance. He had seen to it that sentries were placed around the village. Those who first saw Black Crow and his warriors returning were to wait until they were just inside the perimeter of the village, then they were to fire off one round of bullets to warn those who were waiting in the lodges that it was time to launch their surprise on the enemy.

"It is too soon for warning shots," Crying Wolf said, tensing.

Night Hawk dropped the vial of herbal medicine. His lips parted in a gasp, he stared down at the liquid being absorbed into a mat, slowly disappearing, and with it the proof that Sun Eagle worked *against* his father, instead of for him.

But now was not the time to worry about it. His eyes wide, his heart pounding, Night Hawk grabbed his rifle and stepped to the entrance flap.

He swept the buckskin flap aside, gasping when he

saw that Black Crow and his warriors *had* returned.

And it was obvious that the warning shots had also warned Black Crow that something was wrong in the village. His warriors were dismounting, and as they proceeded to move farther into the village, they used their horses as shields.

"I do not know why he chose to return, but now is not the time to ponder over it," Night Hawk said. He looked over his shoulder at Jae; their eyes locked for a moment. She smiled weakly at him as she gripped her rifle in her right hand.

He shifted his gaze to Crying Wolf, their eyes speaking silently what words would not say. They had grown so close that if one died, the other would feel only half alive.

Night Hawk then glanced at Little Horse. Their time together had been short. It would not be fair if they were not given more time as brothers. Night Hawk depended on the Wise One Above to make it so!

"Little Horse, are you certain you wish to join the fight?" Night Hawk asked. "It will be deadly."

"I am certain," Little Horse said, proudly lifting his chin. "I am destined to be a great Comanche warrior. Today I fight at your side, proving that I will be worthy of the title!"

Night Hawk slid a slow gaze Jae's way. Again their eyes locked. "I wish you would stay where it is safe," he said. "But I know not to ask that of you."

Gunfire was going off like firecrackers outside the lodge.

War whoops filled the air.

Cries of pain echoed through the village like screeches of frightened birds.

Night Hawk rushed from the lodge. He steadied

himself, lifted his rifle, and began to fire at the enemy. Black Crow's men were in the middle of the village, surrounded, as the warriors who fought for the rights of those they loved stepped from the lodges, firing.

Some used bows and arrows. Some used rifles. Some used long, powerful, deadly lances.

Jae stood at Night Hawk's right side, Little Horse at his left. Crying Wolf stood apart from them all, his old eyes steady as he shot first one Comanche enemy, and then another.

As Night Hawk continued spraying bullets at the enemy, his eyes searched for Black Crow.

When he finally saw him, he could hardly believe his eyes. Black Crow was crawling away from the battle, attempting to keep himself hidden either behind the bodies of his fallen comrades, or the fallen, wounded horses.

Out of the corner of his eye, Night Hawk saw Little Horse take slow aim at Black Crow, draw back the trigger, and fire.

Black Crow cried out in pain and grabbed at his arm as blood poured from his wound. He then grabbed a horse and swung himself into the saddle with his other arm.

Black Crow ducked low and rode from the village, three of his Comanche friends with him on their frightened steeds.

And then suddenly the firing ceased. The smoke drifted heavenward, the stench of gunpowder filled the air.

All but those warriors who had escaped with Black Crow lay strewn along the ground, dead or wounded. Only a few who fought for the good of the village were wounded, and none of their wounds were life-threatening.

Little Horse stood and gaped, wide-eyed, at the bodies that lay strewn about and at the blood that seeped from their bodies. He was stunned for a moment, then remembered Black Crow. "I must go after him!" he cried, rushing toward a horse. "I shot him, but my aim was not accurate enough. I did not kill him. I must finish what I started. He is still a threat to our people!"

Seeing Little Horse's determination to go after Black Crow, Jae ran to him and grabbed him around his waist. She swung him around, then knelt and framed his face between her hands.

"Little Horse, you have been so brave today," she murmured. "Everyone will know that it was your bullet that wounded Black Crow. No one expects you to go after him and put that second bullet into his wretched heart. In time, Little Horse, it will be done. Stay here now. There is still much to be done here."

Little Horse swallowed hard and gazed past her at the dead warriors. "*Huh*, yes, there are many burials to be seen to," he said. "Although those who died today fought for the wrong cause and followed the wrong path with the wrong leader, those men were no less Comanche warriors. They must have proper burials. I will do what I can to help see that this is done."

"That is exactly what I believe your father would want to hear you say." Jae drew Little Horse into her arms and hugged him. "And he will be so proud of you for having fought like a grown-up warrior today."

Before she even got to her feet, those who had been taken to the cave for safekeeping were entering the village. The sentries had told them the fight was over.

Jae rose slowly to her feet and watched the families of the fallen warriors run to them. As the wailing began, the cries of despair made Jae shiver.

She looked slowly around for Night Hawk. He was kneeling beside one of the fallen enemy, holding his head up, talking to him. She went and knelt down on the other side, listening.

"Why did Black Crow return to the village after having been gone for only a short while?" Night Hawk questioned, glaring down at the injured warrior.

"He . . . got . . . suspicious . . . over the difference in behavior of Eagle Wing," the fallen warrior said, blood pouring from the corners of his mouth. "Black Crow noticed that Eagle Wing was suddenly too co-operative. Black Crow thought about it and . . . and felt that surely it might have to do with you, Night Hawk. He . . . was . . . right. But he was wrong to . . . lead us into . . . an ambush. I . . . warned . . . him to be more careful. He . . . did not listen."

Jae covered her mouth with a hand when the warrior's body trembled violently, then went limp, his eyes locked in a death stare.

Eagle Wing came and stood over Night Hawk, then placed a hand on his shoulder. "I did not play my role well enough," he said. "But, except for Black Crow's escape, the end is the same. Our people are rid of him and his vengeful ways. Our people's lives are filled with hope again."

"*Huh*, Black Crow escaped, and with him only three of his warriors," Night Hawk said, laying the dead warrior's head on the ground. "Black Crow cannot wreck much havoc with so few. His strength has been reduced to nothing today. I doubt we will have him to worry about ever again."

Night Hawk rose to his feet. He smiled as he watched Touch the Sky bring his father on the travois into the village. He walked square-shouldered to him.

When the horse stopped, Night Hawk knelt and embraced Brown Bull. "Father, the village is once again yours," he said. "There was much bloodshed, but is that not what warring brings to those who live *for* warring? None of our men died. Some are wounded, but not seriously."

He eased away from his father's arms and helped him up from the travois. As Brown Bull leaned his weight against him, Night Hawk helped him walk toward his lodge. "You need not worry yourself with anything now except to go to your bed and revel in the knowledge that Black Crow's reign is over."

Night Hawk then smiled over at Little Horse, who ran toward them. "And, Father, you have a son who is responsible for Black Crow being wounded," he said, his eyes gleaming with pride over the courage his young brother held within his heart.

"And so you, Night Hawk, wounded the evil-hearted man?" Brown Bull said, giving his son a wide grin.

"No, it was your younger son, Little Horse. He stood at my side during the fight. It was his aim that was accurate as he pointed his rifle at Black Crow."

Little Horse stood beside Brown Bull as he stopped and gave him a look of pride.

"And so, my young son who proves in so many ways he is a skilled warrior, it was *you* who maimed Black Crow," Brown Bull said. He placed a gentle hand on Little Horse's shoulder. "I am so very proud. So very proud."

Little Horse beamed with the recognition and wonderful words of his father, then lowered his eyes. "But, Father, Black Crow still lives," he said, his voice breaking. "My aim was wrong. I would have wished to brag about having killed Black Crow for you, not only wounded him."

"Did Black Crow ride away from the fight like a coward?" Brown Bull asked, placing a finger to Little Horse's chin, bringing his eyes up.

"*Huh*, that is so," Little Horse murmured, his eyes wide as he gazed into his father's.

"Then, my son, you have done enough for this father today," Brown Bull said, patting Little Horse's shoulder.

"Not enough just yet," Little Horse said softly. "Father, I shall now go and help with the burial preparations for the dead. Although they were not warriors whose hearts were pure, they should be allowed to enter the afterlife with some dignity."

"My son has the heart and mind of a man." Brown Bull pulled Little Horse into his arms and gave him a fierce hug, then released him. "Now go. Be proud of what you did for your people today. Be proud for always thinking of others, instead of only yourself. That is the mark of a great leader!"

Smiling, Little Horse ran away and mingled with those who were lifting the dead from the ground, taking them to their lodges.

Jae's heart skipped a beat when she saw someone sneaking into a lodge. "Sun Eagle," she whispered, knowing that this man was as much an enemy to Brown Bull as Black Crow. Perhaps worse. A medicine man who was suspected of trying to kill the village's Civil Chief was a man who worked for the sake of evil, not good.

Lois then came into view. She had tagged along behind everyone else. It was apparent that she had dreaded entering a place where so much blood had been spilled. She was pale as she gazed all around her, then fell in a dead faint from her horse.

"Oh, no," Jae mumbled, uncertain what to do first. She knew that Night Hawk should be told about Sun Eagle's suspicious behavior, yet Lois lay on the ground, as white as a ghost, unconscious. Jae felt that she should go to her and help her.

Yet someone had to be told about Sun Eagle!

She ran toward Lois and at the same time shouted at Night Hawk over her shoulder. "Night Hawk, Sun Eagle!" She winced when her voice carried as far as the medicine man. Jae grimaced when he stopped and glared at her, then darted on inside his lodge.

Night Hawk knew that Sun Eagle was as bad an enemy as Black Crow, but he had spilled the one vial that would have proven his guilt to Night Hawk's people. He now had to find another way to prove his theory. It was not every day a medicine man turned against a chief. *Huh*, proof was needed! And once the proof was at hand, Sun Eagle's fate would be decided in council.

Night Hawk doubted that anyone would vote to allow Sun Eagle to live if proof was shown that he had been slowly poisoning Brown Bull.

Even the wives of the fallen warriors, whose loyalty was to Black Crow, would surely see the wrong in what the medicine man had done. More than likely, a death sentence would be handed down.

"Eagle Wing!" Night Hawk shouted. "Come! Help my father to his lodge!"

Eagle Wing hurried to him. As Night Hawk released his father to him, Eagle Wing slid an arm around Brown Bull's waist and steadied him.

"Where are you going?" Eagle Wing asked as Night Hawk ran away from him.

"I have someone to see!" Night Hawk shouted over his shoulder.

He hurried to Sun Eagle's lodge. As he stepped inside, he found Sun Eagle emptying vials of dried herbs into the flames of his lodge fire.

"No!" Night Hawk shouted. "Stop!"

Sun Eagle smiled wickedly at him and continued dumping the medicines into the fire until Night Hawk reached him and grabbed him by an arm. They battled with their eyes, for Sun Eagle was too old to wrench himself free from Night Hawk's firm grip.

"You would only be destroying the herbs if they were to be used for evil instead of good," Night Hawk ground out, his eyes flashing. He looked past Sun Eagle, and his lips shifted into a slow, easy smile when he saw that there were many more such vials lined up against a far wall.

As Night Hawk held Sun Eagle steady, he dragged him over to the vials, then lifted them one by one and sniffed. He stopped when he found what he was searching for; the same, distinctive-smelling herbal medicine that had been taken to his father's lodge.

"Kneel," he said, his teeth clenched.

When Sun Eagle refused to do what he was told, Night Hawk gripped his wrist more tightly and forced him to his knees.

Night Hawk nodded toward the vial in question. "Drink from this vial," he said, his voice drawn. "Drink every drop."

Sun Eagle paled. His eyes wavered as he glanced from the vial of medicine to Running Hawk.

"Drink it," Night Hawk said, a slow smile tugging at the corner of his mouth.

"Why must I?" Sun Eagle said, cowering beneath Night Hawk's smugness.

"Is not that what you have prepared for my father?" Night Hawk bent low, grabbing up the small vial.

"Perhaps yes, perhaps no," Sun Eagle said weakly. Night Hawk squeezed the man's wrist more tightly, stopping the blood flow. "Is it, or is it not, what you have prepared for my father?" he shouted.

"*Huh*, yes," Sun Eagle said, lowering his eyes.

"Then come outside with me." Running Hawk yanked on Sun Eagle's wrist.

"Why . . . must . . . I?" Sun Eagle stammered, trying to keep from being led from the lodge, yet too old and weak to keep Night Hawk from leading him away. He took a shaky step outside, cowering behind Night Hawk, who shouted for everyone to come close.

"We have a demonstration for you to see," Night Hawk shouted to his people as they gathered around in a tight circle. He looked past them and saw Jae standing with Lois. Lois still looked dazed and pale, but at least she was standing and conscious.

"Sun Eagle is going to drink the medicine he has prepared for my father!" Night Hawk shouted, then smiled slyly over at Sun Eagle when the medicine man gasped and tried to yank his arm free.

Night Hawk held the vial to Sun Eagle's lips. He knew he could not allow the old man to hold it—he would take that opportunity to pour it out! "Drink, old man," he said tightly. "Drink . . . now!"

Sun Eagle pursed his lips tightly together. He glared at Night Hawk.

"Do I have to force you to drink?" Night Hawk snarled as his people drew closer. "Do I have to pour it down your throat?"

Still Sun Eagle would not open his lips.

Everyone gasped and took a step away when Night Hawk threw Sun Eagle to the ground.

Before Sun Eagle had the chance to get back up or concentrate on keeping his mouth closed, Night Hawk dropped to his knees and poured the liquid between his lips.

Sun Eagle's face looked like a chameleon as it changed color, from an ashen gray, to dull red, to bright crimson as he grabbed at his throat, gagging.

When he went suddenly unconscious, proving that Night Hawk had been right to accuse him of poisoning Chief Brown Bull, Night Hawk turned and gave his father a soft smile.

He then looked quickly up at a guard. "Seize this man," he said. He glared at Sun Eagle. "Remove his clothes! Stake him to the ground until a council is held to decide his final fate!"

Little Horse came and stood beside Night Hawk. He stared down at Sun Eagle, then looked up at his brother. "I do not believe a council is needed," he said softly. "I think Sun Eagle is dead."

Night Hawk's eyes widened and his heart skipped a beat when he gazed down at Sun Eagle and saw how he lay lifeless on the ground.

He knelt quickly at the medicine man's side and placed his fingertips to the vein in Sun Eagle's throat. When he found no pulsebeat, Night Hawk leaned a cheek next to the medicine man's mouth. When he felt no breath, he moved slowly back to his feet.

Doubling his hands into tight fists at his sides, Night Hawk glared at Sun Eagle for a moment longer, then turned to his people.

"There is proof enough that what he planned to take to my father next was the final dose of medicine that would have ended my father's life," he said, his voice drawn. "I came that close to losing my father."

There was total silence as everyone stared at the dead man in whom so many had placed their total trust when they had been ill.

Jae crept to Night Hawk's side and slipped a hand in his. When he looked down at her, she gave him a soft, knowing smile. "Darling, I now truly believe that some unseen force led you here for the purpose of saving your father."

"Had I not come . . ." Running Hawk said, almost choking on the words.

He swept Jae into his arms and held her tightly. Night Hawk closed his eyes and forced thoughts of how it might have been from his consciousness.

Huh, yes, he had arrived home just in time!

Chapter Thirty-eight

The village was in a clamor of excitement. Many days had passed since blood had been spilled on their land. The burials were behind them; the families of the fallen warriors had been given a choice to stay or leave.

Because they truly had nowhere else to go, they had stayed, promising to accept the changes, especially concerning who would now be their leaders. Brown Bull's strength was returning. Although he was still slow and sometimes needed assistance, he could now walk among his people, proud to be their Civil Chief again.

Night Hawk often walked proudly with him, father and son growing closer as each day passed.

One afternoon, Jae and Night Hawk were in their lodge, preparing for a long evening of excitement ahead of them.

"I'm so excited," Jae said, clasping her hands together before her as she gazed at Night Hawk. "Tonight your father will be naming a new War Chief. Night Hawk, surely it will be you."

She watched him dress in a breechclout and buckskin leggings decorated with beadwork of porcupine quills and glass baubles. His shirt was richly fringed around the neck and sleeves. He wore a headband that held his long and flaxen hair back from his brow. Except for his golden hair, today he looked, oh, so much a Comanche.

And never had Jae been as proud of him as now, or as in awe of his handsomeness. She could not believe, still, that she had been lucky enough to have met him, a man who would soon be her husband.

"If my father announces to everyone in our village that he wishes for me to be War Chief since Black Crow has been stripped of the title, I shall have to refuse," Night Hawk said, bending to slip on intricately beaded moccasins.

Jae paled and stared disbelievingly at him, then knelt quickly down before him. "Night Hawk, why would you do that?" she asked, her voice drawn. Their eyes locked, and she placed a gentle hand to his cheek. "Don't you want to be War Chief? It's such an honor. And, Night Hawk, after Black Crow abused the powers of War Chief, your father has to be assured that the one chosen today will respect it. He has to be certain that the one carrying the title of War Chief will not use it to raid white settlements. Your father is a man of peace. Surely he can only trust that you, his son, will ensure that peaceful measures will be used while dealing with whites."

Night Hawk's lips tugged into a smile. "Are you through?" he asked, chuckling beneath his breath.

Jae laughed awkwardly. Her eyes danced. "I guess I was going on and on, wasn't I?"

Then her expression went somber again. "But, Night Hawk, that is because I so badly want you to be sure to do what is best for not only your father, but also yourself," she said in a rush of words. "You are home among your people again. Your father is alive. Black Crow has been defeated. You can be such a wonderful leader in his place."

"You are doing it again," Night Hawk said, taking her hands, urging Jae to her feet.

"Talking too much?" Jae said, eyes wide.

"*Huh*," Night Hawk said, still smiling. "I see now that when you believe in something, it is with much conviction. Each day I discover something new about you. Each time I am not disappointed."

"Nor am I ever disappointed with you," Jae said softly.

"But I sense that you might be, if I refuse the title of War Chief." Night Hawk searched her eyes for hidden truths. "Is that so? Would you be disappointed?"

"No, not I," Jae said, sighing. "But I believe that your father would be."

"So it means nothing to you if I refuse the honor of being named War Chief?" Night Hawk asked, still studying her reaction.

"All that I want, my darling, is your happiness," she said, easing into his arms and hugging him. "If you wish not to be War Chief, that is fine with me. But please consider your father's feelings."

"I have, and he will understand," Night Hawk said, stroking her hair, which had grown these past weeks. Before long, the tips would just be touching her shoulders. In a full year's time, it would be past her shoulders. In two, it might even be at her waist. He would enjoy having longer hair to stroke and to admire, and to twine his fingers through while they were making love.

"I am so happy for everyone," Jae said. She stepped

away from him and tied a beaded headband around her brow to match the doeskin dress that Touch the Sky had made for her. "Hear the music outside our lodge? Hear the laughter? And smell the food cooking over the outdoor fire?"

"There will be much dancing, laughter, and feasting today before the choice for War Chief is announced," Night Hawk said. He reached out to run his fingers slowly down the front of Jae's dress. "You are so beautiful dressed as a Comanche. How do you feel in the dress? It fits you like a glove. All of the warrior's eyes will be on your curves."

"I had looked forward to wearing it today, but I don't know now," she said, blushing. Jae stepped away from him and gazed down at herself. "Is it too tight? I don't wish to make a spectacle of myself."

"I talked out of turn," Night Hawk said. He took her hand and drew her into his arms once again. "I did not mean to make you feel awkward by what I said. It was meant only as a compliment."

"And I thank you, Night Hawk," she said, again stepping away from him to look at herself. "But please tell me if it's too tight . . . too revealing."

"It is neither of those things." Night Hawk was again raking his eyes slowly over her. She was everything to him—beautiful, sensitive, caring, and generous. But most of all, she was *his*. He felt blessed today for so many things, but especially for having her love.

"Then I shall quit worrying about it," Jae said, laughing softly. "For you see, Night Hawk, I feel like a princess today, a princess who stepped right out of a story book. You are my white knight who rescued me on his white charger."

"No, I am your Comanche warrior who rescued

you on his big pinto," he said, chuckling. "And you? *Huh,* you *are* a princess. *Mine.*" He framed her face between his hands. "You are my Comanche princess."

"It is a dream that I am here with you," Jae murmured. She trembled when he drew her lips to his and kissed her, then sighed when he stepped away from her. "I know that we must go to the celebration, yet my heart is beating so fast, and my knees are so weak from the kiss, I'm not sure I can even leave this lodge," she said, laughing softly.

Jae turned and gazed at the tepee. It was brand new, smelling of fresh pine and cedar wood and buckskin. She had helped Night Hawk erect it. There they would live while raising their children.

It had been fun to help Night Hawk build the lodge. It had been made from twenty poles and seventeen buffalo hides. The tepee was fifteen feet in diameter across the floor.

The lodge was tilted slightly backward. The door faced east. A fire pit, fifteen inches across, was in the center of the floor. The smoke hole was above it, at the top of the lodge. A narrow ditch around the outside of the tepee kept the floor dry.

Their bed, elevated by means of poles and rawhide, was at the back of the tepee directly opposite the entrance. Robes were spread to form a support for the bedding. The bed was raised six inches off the ground. Food was stored in parfleche bags in the space below it. Other bags held ornaments, bowls, dishes, and personal belongings.

They slept with their heads to the west, on pillows made from the skins of small animals stuffed with grass.

Jae paled as a thought came to her. She turned

frightened eyes up at Night Hawk. "Your father has four wives, and each wife has her own lodge separate from his," she said warily. "Night Hawk, please don't tell me that you might eventually have more than one wife. Please don't tell me that I can't share your lodge once we are married. Night Hawk, I want to live with you. I want our children to be in our same lodge." She gripped his arm. "Night Hawk, please say that you will never take another wife! If you did, I would want to die!"

"You are doing it again," Night Hawk said, his eyes dancing. He took her hand and unclasped it from his arm. He held it affectionately.

"Rambling?" she said, wincing when she realized that she *had* been doing so again.

"*Huh*, you are so filled with questions, you rush through them before I can tell you that none of them are necessary," he said. "But let me answer them now, one by one. No, there will be no more wives. No, our children will *not* live apart from their father, nor will you from your husband. We shared in the building of this lodge. We shall share living in it."

Tears flashed in her eyes. She flung herself into his arms. "That makes me so happy," Jae whispered. She again became weak in the knees when he kissed her, his hands caressing her breasts through the sleek fabric of the doeskin dress.

Her ecstasy was so overwhelming that she drew quickly away from him. "We'd better stop or you might have to call your new medicine man to our lodge to check on my heart," she said, giggling. Jae reached for Night Hawk's hand and placed it over her heart. "Feel how it thuds so strongly? It is as though it is echoing the beats of those drums that are playing outside our lodge."

"I am the only one who has the cure for such a heartbeat as that," Night Hawk said teasingly, his eyes twinkling. "We should make love."

"That would make my heartbeats *worsen*," she teased back.

"The cure comes *after* the lovemaking," he said, enjoying their lighthearted banter after so many days of confusion. "After we are through making love, does your heart not beat normally again?"

"*Huh*, but we don't have time now for such a cure," she said, laughing softly. She took his hand. "Come, my darling. We'd best go and join the others before things *do* get out of hand inside our lodge."

He walked outside with her. They stopped and gazed around them. It was growing dark. The fire's glow filled the heavens. Songs were being sung while the men and women danced around the fire, their eyes filled with peace, their voices filled with gladness.

When Little Horse came into view, dancing with the other village children and looking so handsome in his new buckskin outfit, his breechclout flapping as he lifted his legs and feet with the rhythm of the drums, Jae's heart was stolen away. Except for his hair color, he was the spitting image of Night Hawk. She knew to expect him to be a lady killer when he left his youthful days behind him.

Jae smiled to herself when she saw that the young girls would not even wait *that* long to admire him. She watched as they came up to Little Horse and crowded around him, fighting amongst themselves as to who would dance beside him.

Then she recalled the other time, when the girls had greeted him upon his return from his first successful hunt. Their admiration was done with no

Cassie Edwards

more energy now than then, and he had done nothing more this early evening than be the handsome
young lad that he was.

Jae watched him smile his winning smile from girl
to girl, obviously enjoying the power he had over
them.

Then Jae looked around again. She found Lois
among the crowd of those who were not dancing,
standing with Crying Wolf. She had a possessive arm
locked through his. As she gazed up at him, there
was complete adoration in her eyes.

"I think we may have another wedding besides
ours in the near future," Jae said, smiling up at Night
Hawk.

"You are speaking of Touch the Sky and Eagle
Wing?" Night Hawk asked, looking at them and how
they seemed lost in one another's nearness.

And he recalled how he had earlier thought that
his sister might be bashful and shy in the presence
of men.

He was discovering as each day passed that wasn't
so.

In fact, he had oft times seen Touch the Sky and
Eagle Wing leave the village, a blanket tucked under
his arm. Night Hawk had even seen them climb the
cliff that led to the cave. He knew that they did not
go there just to talk: They were lovers.

"No," Jae said, yanking on his arm. "Not *them*.
Look at Lois and Crying Wolf. They are in love, Night
Hawk." Then she frowned. "But she can't marry *him*.
She is already married to my father."

"In a sense, she was never his wife," Night Hawk
said, his voice flat. "They never shared a bed. They
never made love. In the eyes of her Lord, she has the
right to an annulment."

"But there is no one here who can annul the marriage," Jae said softly.

"There *is* someone who can do this for her," Night Hawk said, shifting his gaze to White Fire, the newly appointed village medicine man.

"White Fire?" Jae said, her eyes focusing on the new medicine man, who was much younger than Sun Eagle, and in whose eyes one could see much trust, peace, and love.

"*Huh*, the man who will marry them and who will also bring *us* together as man and wife, can end the marriage of my adopted mother to her white husband," Night Hawk said, nodding.

He then looked down at Jae. "It is good that Sun Eagle is no longer among my people. He is no longer even a part of this earth. The ravens came down from the air, the wolf came up from the valley, devouring the evil medicine man's body. His bones were gathered up by the Evil Spirit and deposited in the land of terrors."

Jae shivered at this description of the final fate of Sun Eagle's body. "How horrible," she said, her voice drawn.

"The soul of the wicked, after death, never rests," Night Hawk said. "The Wise One Above drives him far off into a region that is barren and cold and desolate, there to wander forever through thorns and among rocks, forever thirsty, hungry, and in pain."

"Say no more," Jae said, shuddering. "Let's think of good things—of *happy* things. Tonight marks a new beginning for your people. Isn't it wonderful to see? To be a part of it?"

Night Hawk had no chance to respond. His father came from his lodge, proudly walking without assistance, his face all smiles as he gazed at his son.

Jae silently admired Chief Brown Bull. He was dressed in a sleek bear robe. His long, dark hair hung way past his waist, streamers of bear fur woven into it. His stride was proud. His eyes glistened as he walked toward his son.

The music and dancing stopped. Everyone stepped back as Chief Brown Bull went to a platform, sat down, and leaned against a backrest of painted buckskin stretched across a frame of woven wood.

Crying Wolf went and stood at Chief Brown Bull's right side. Little Horse hurried to stand to his father's left, his smile wide as he gazed at his brother, Night Hawk.

Jae stared at Crying Wolf. She saw something different about his hair. It was not so much that he wore it in braids; it was the length of the braids that puzzled her. They touched the ground.

She tugged at Night Hawk's shirt. "Look at Crying Wolf's hair," she whispered. "Look at how long it is. What did he use to make it grow so fast? Perhaps if I knew the secret, I wouldn't have to wait so long to have long hair, myself."

Night Hawk chuckled as he leaned low and whispered into her ear. "Crying Wolf wears false hair from a horse's mane. Shall I cut some horse's hair for you tomorrow?"

Jae paled. She gave him a shocked stare.

"I thought not," Night Hawk said, smiling.

Then he erased the smile and again gazed with a proud and uplifted chin at his father. He hoped that his father would accept and understand his decision, a decision that would favor someone else to be the new War Chief.

While Night Hawk and everyone else listened intently, Brown Bull spoke first of Night Hawk as he was as a child, and then of the years that Brown Bull had been without his older son, and of now, and how things had changed in the village because of Night Hawk.

"It is now time for a new War Chief," Brown Bull said, smiling at Night Hawk. "I wish to give the honor to my elder son, Night Hawk."

"Father, I am proud to stand here, a son to such a man as you," Night Hawk said. His voice was steady, although his emotions were running rampant inside him. He spoke for a long time about those emotions and feelings, then finally said what he hoped would be understood, for it was being said from the bottom of his heart.

"Father, thank you for offering me the title of War Chief." He dropped to his haunches directly before his father so that their eyes were level. "But I have not been with my people long. I have much to learn that one learns by living. There is someone else who deserves the honor more than I. He has dedicated his life to our people. That man is Eagle Wing. I truly wish that you would honor him with the title of War Chief."

There was silence among the Comanche people. Night Hawk saw the surprise leap into his father's eyes.

Then he saw something else: a slow smile tugging at his father's lips . . . a pride that ran even deeper now for Night Hawk.

"My son," Brown Bull said, clasping Night Hawk's shoulder. "You are a generous, giving man. You could never make me any more proud of you than now."

Night Hawk put his own hand on his father's shoulder, then stood back up, beside Jae. He took her by an elbow and guided her to one side, making room for Eagle Wing.

"Eagle Wing, step forth," Brown Bull said, smiling into his future son-in-law's eyes.

Touch the Sky ran up to Night Hawk. She took his hand and squeezed it, beaming as she looked up at her brother.

Then she watched her lover accept the title of War Chief. She had always wanted this for Eagle Wing. Always! And now it was his!

The words were said that finalized everything. The celebration truly began then. There was more dancing, feasting, and singing.

Jae was glad when it was all over and she was back in the lodge with Night Hawk. They lay nude on a thick cushion of pelts beside the fire.

"You truly do surprise me," Jae said, cuddling close to Night Hawk. "Do you realize you just gave away such power?"

"I have never been a man who hungered for power," he said huskily, turning her so that she was now beneath him. "My hungers are for more serious things . . . like making love with my woman."

"My love," Jae whispered, a sensual shock sweeping through her when he thrust his thick shaft within her pulsing heat.

He took her mouth by storm with a fiery kiss. His tongue surged between her lips, touching hers. His hands could not get enough of her. He kneaded her breasts, then ran his fingers slowly down across her belly, flicking his forefinger over her swollen nub.

Their bodies sucked at each other, flesh against flesh, as they made love.

Night Hawk kissed his way down to Jae's breasts. Jae held her head back and closed her eyes, nervously chewing on her lower lip as the ecstasy mounted inside her, Night Hawk's tongue hot and wet as he swept it around each of her nipples.

And then he rolled away from her, knelt down over her, and gently spread her legs.

Jae's breath caught and held when she felt his tongue dipping inside her, and then flicking across her woman's center, causing the fires to rage higher and higher within her. The tip of his tongue flicked. His mouth sucked. His hands spread her more openly to him.

Again his hands touched and turned her. He led her into a way of loving that was new to her. He urged her to move to her hands and knees, then he knelt on his knees behind her. As he reached under her and filled his hands with her breasts, he filled her warm woman's cocoon with his heat again. He thrust maddeningly into her, his hands caressing her breasts, his thumbs flicking the nipples.

He then clung to her hips and drew her closer against the warmth of his body. He held her in place as he filled her more deeply.

He shoved in.

He drew out.

He held his head back.

He groaned with pleasure.

He sighed.

Jae was unfamiliar with this way of making love, yet she found it to be no less stimulating and exciting. Each stroke he took within her brought her closer to the brink of bliss that she felt herself climbing toward, as though she were on a ladder, taking one rung at a time. Each rung seemed made of roses. They were soft. They were sweet.

And then she felt as though she had stepped away

Cassie Edwards

from the ladder onto a soft cushion of clouds, for she was floating, drifting, singing, soaring, tumbling over the edge into total ecstasy.

Night Hawk's movements sped up when he felt her familiar shudders of pleasure. He closed his eyes and made one last deep thrust, joining her cloud of euphoria.

Afterward, Night Hawk turned Jae so that she now lay on her back. He wrapped her within his arms and held her close to his hard body. "And did you find tonight exciting?" he whispered, stroking her back.

"Which part?" Jae giggled.

Then she moved quickly and sat astride him as he lay on his back looking up at her. "*Huh*," she said, her cheeks blushed hot from the lovemaking. "I found it all exciting." She ran her hands over his chest, then circled his manhood with eager fingers. "But it is not yet over, is it? It is still so early, my darling."

Chuckling, he placed his hands to her waist and lifted her only high enough so that he could shove his renewed manly strength inside her. "*Huh*, way too early," he said huskily.

He buried himself deeply within her, his hips thrusting hard.

Chapter Thirty-nine

"Today I begin my life as a Comanche," Jae said, stretching her arms above her head as she sat up in the bed of soft pelts beside Night Hawk. "Lois begins hers. Or should I say she began it last night. She spent her first full night with Crying Wolf."

"It is good to see my old friend's eyes come so alive of late, since he discovered his feelings for my adoptive mother," Night Hawk replied. He gently grabbed Jae's wrists and lowered her back down to the bed. "It is good to feel so alive inside, myself, since having discovered my feelings for you."

He slid his hands down her arms, then across to her bare breasts. He cupped them, then lowered his tongue to a nipple and flicked it across the tight, pink nub.

Jae closed her eyes and sighed. "Will it be this way every morning?" she whispered, placing her hands on his bare sinewed shoulders, reveling in the touch of his muscles. "Will you always want me like this? Even when I look a fright from having slept all night?"

Night Hawk gazed up at her, his eyes hazed with desire. "I shall always want you, early in the morning, late in the night, and any time of the day should you ask me to come to you," he said throatily.

"Please do it again," Jae murmured. She twined her fingers through his thick, long flaxen hair, urging his mouth back to one of her nipples. "Flick your tongue over my nipples. It feels so wonderful. It makes me feel as though I might just float away."

She smiled devilishly down at him. "But I must know something first," she said, watching his eyebrows arch as he questioned her with his eyes. "How do I taste?"

"Like the fresh, new morning itself," Night Hawk said, then drew away from her with a start when he heard the thundering of hoofbeats outside his lodge.

Jae sat up quickly.

Night Hawk turned to her.

They questioned each other with their eyes, then bolted from the bed and hurried into their clothes when they realized that the horses had reined in just outside their lodge.

In a doeskin dress that was more fully gathered and comfortable than the one she had worn during last evening's celebration, Jae followed Night Hawk outside.

When she saw who was there, their faces drawn, their expressions weary, she took a step back, stunned. The cowhands had headed back to the ranch as soon as the fight against Black Crow had been won. Why then, had they returned?

"What has happened?" Night Hawk asked, looking at one cowhand, and then the next. "Why have you returned to the Comanche village?" He gave Crying Wolf a quick glance when he rushed over and stood at his side, then looked up at Jake Martin, the cow-hand who was the closest to him.

"I don't know how to tell you," Jake said, then grew silent when Lois came from a tepee and ran over to stand beside Crying Wolf.

Lois paled when she saw how Jake looked at her with eyes filled with a strange sort of remorseful apology. "Jake, what's happened?" she asked, stepping closer to him. "Why are you here? Shouldn't you be back at the ranch, helping to catch up on the chores?"

Jake lifted his sweat-stained, wide-brimmed Stetson hat from his head. "Ma'am," he said, resting his hat on his lap. He then looked at Night Hawk. "I think you'd best go and stand beside your ma. She might need you. The news we've brought ain't a bit good."

"I'm fine and I can take whatever you have to say without anyone's help," Lois said, boldly lifting her chin. "Now tell us what you've come to say."

"Ralph is dead," Jake said, noticing how the news came like a bolt of lightning to both Lois and Night Hawk.

Night Hawk stood as though in a spell for a moment. He gazed at Jake, his mouth parted in disbelief. Although Night Hawk had left his adoptive father, thinking he could learn to hate him, he knew that he could never truly have felt hatred for the man. He had loved him as a father for too many years. Those memories were not cast aside so easily.

"How did it happen?" he asked. Out of the corner of his eyes, he saw Jae holding Lois steady as she broke down in a sudden torrent of tears.

"When we arrived at the ranch, we found the massacre," Jake said, almost choking on the words. He lowered his eyes, swallowed hard, then continued with the morbid tale. "Everyone, even the last cowhand, was dead. They had been massacred in their sleep, then . . . then everything had been set afire." He slowly shook his head back and forth. "No one had a chance in hell of escapin' the fiery inferno of your father's house, nor the bunkhouse."

Feeling ill as he envisioned everything in his mind's eye, Night Hawk turned his back to the cowhands, wiping tears from his eyes.

Night Hawk willed himself to regain control. He turned and faced Jake again. "Could you tell who was responsible?" he asked.

"There was no way to tell," Jake mumbled. "All's I can say is that from those bodies we could inspect, bullets were used to kill them. So it could have been the work of Indian renegades, *or* fugitive outlaws."

"For everything to be done so heartlessly, I would say it was done by someone filled with much hate," Night Hawk said, welcoming Jae as she returned to his side. He turned his head and watched Crying Wolf lead Lois to his tent.

Then, his jaw tight, he glared at Jake. "What of the cattle?" he asked shallowly.

"That's the strangest thing of all," Jake said, kneading his chin contemplatively. "Only those that were trapped by the fire died. The others were left in the pasture."

"That proves that the murders were done out of pure vengeance," Night Hawk said, his teeth grinding together in his building rage.

"Black Crow?" Jae asked, gazing up at him, drawing his eyes back to her.

"I would have to think that he might be responsible," Night Hawk said, nodding. "He had to have found out, somehow, where the ranch was located."

"Is he a good tracker?" Jae asked softly.

"He is a great scout and tracker," Night Hawk said. "Why do you ask?"

"When my father's cowhands came to help your people, they left many tracks behind," she said softly. "Black Crow and his three warriors could have followed them back to the ranch."

Night Hawk clenched both of his hands into tight fists at his sides. "*Huh,* perhaps . . . perhaps . . ." he said, his nostrils flaring angrily.

"I feel so guilty," he then suddenly blurted out. He hung his head. "Had I not sent for the cowhands to come and help me here, our father would not have become a target of hate, left vulnerable by his lack of cowhands to help protect against raids."

Jae slipped her arms around his waist and laid her cheek on his chest. "Darling, please don't blame yourself," she whispered. "Remember that if you had not sought help from the cowhands, your people would still be led by that tyrant. You can't blame yourself for doing what was right. Please don't do this to yourself."

"I will have my own vengeance," Night Hawk ground out, then eased Jae from his arms. "But first I must return to the ranch. I—we—must see to my . . . your father's burial. We must give all of the men a Christian burial."

"Yes, but Night Hawk, by returning, might we be stepping right into a trap?" Jae asked, searching his eyes as he gazed down at her.

"Do you not remember? There were only four Comanche and one of them, Black Crow, was wounded. It would not take much to fight off so few." He lifted his chin proudly. "And always remember this, my woman. Never do I run from a fight." He glanced over his shoulder at his father's lodge and saw Brown Bull standing in the doorway.

Then he looked at the cowhands. "I want to thank you for bringing the news," he said, reaching to shake Jake's hand. "But you can go on your way now. I hope you can find a new life elsewhere. There are many ranches. They always need cowhands."

Jae grabbed at Night Hawk's arm. "But, Night Hawk, if we are going to ride back to the ranch, wouldn't it be better if we did not travel alone? These men could ride with us until we reached the ranch, then go on their way."

"Their lives have been disturbed enough by me," Night Hawk said solemnly. "I will ask no more of them." He smiled slyly. "And I have my own plans, anyhow."

He shook Jake's hand again, then stepped aside and watched the cowhands ride away.

"I hope you have made the right decision," Jae said, her eyes filled with worry.

"I must go and meet with Eagle Wing," Night Hawk said. "Please go to my father and explain what has happened."

Jae watched him walk away. She suddenly was more afraid than she had ever been in her entire life.

Chapter Forty

"I feel so vulnerable," Jae said as she rode straight-backed in her saddle.

Her fingers clung tightly to the horse's reins as she glanced around her. They had just left the perimeters of the village. She felt as though she and Night Hawk were sitting ducks as they headed out on the trail with no more than their few firearms to fight a possible battle with Black Crow and his warriors.

"Why didn't you have someone ride with us?" she then asked. She felt foolish for showing him just how frightened she was, for until now, he had always seen and admired the strong side of her character.

"We are not totally alone," Night Hawk said, glancing over his shoulder, smiling. "Eagle Wing and several warriors follow behind us, far enough away so that no one but us will know they are there. If a trap has been set for us, it will backfire."

Jae looked over her shoulder, seeing nothing. Then she gazed over at Night Hawk again. "Why didn't you tell me your plan earlier?" she asked softly.

"Because until now I was not aware of how afraid

you were," Night Hawk said, giving her a slow stare.

"Yes, I'm afraid." Jae squared her shoulders. "And I am not ashamed to say it. I . . . am . . . damn scared!"

"It is good to see that you are not ashamed of your fear," Night Hawk said. "You would not be human if you did not fear this journey home to our father's ranch." He reached over and circled his fingers around one of her hands. "I, also, do not like the uncertainty of what lies ahead. But I do take comfort in knowing that I will have my vengeance. Nothing will stop me from having my vengeance."

They rode on, stopping only long enough to eat, water their horses, and stretch.

As they stopped to make camp their first night out from the village, a noise in the nearby thicket caused them to tense and stare suddenly at one another.

Jae dropped her horse's reins and gasped when suddenly they were surrounded by a gang of outlaws. When their leader rode up, sneering at Jae, her insides grew cold in recognition.

"Good Lord," she gasped out. "Jonas Adams."

"It's been awhile, ain't it?" Jonas said, his eyes crinkling. He gazed at Night Hawk as one of his outlaws disarmed him. "I didn't think you and Jae'd be foolish enough to leave the Indian village alone. My, oh, my, I thought we might have a big fight on our hands. But you've made it easy for me to kill you. You rode right into the trap I set for you."

Jonas glared at Jae again. "You should've stayed at your papa's house where I could've burned your carcass along with his," he said, laughing throatily. "This way, by bein' with the Injun, you've brought him in on my hunger for revenge. I knew that once you were told about your papa's massacre, you'd come runnin' to bury him."

Jonas threw his head back in a fit of laughter. "You, who roamed the Thicket like some wild animal, ended up havin' two pas?" he choked out between his laughs. Then he glared at Jae again. "Well, wild thing, they're both dead now. And *you* will soon be dead as well. Then I can go on about my business without havin' you on my mind ever again."

"You . . . killed . . . my true father?" Jae gasped out.

Night Hawk glared at Jonas. "And so I was blaming the wrong man," he growled. He looked all around him, at all of the fugitives on their horses. "Seems you had no trouble finding enough outlaws to join your lust for blood." His eyes narrowed as he glared at Jonas again. "I should have made sure you were dead long ago."

"Seems your mind was too much on a certain wild thing to think straight," Jonas said, nudging Night Hawk in the chest with the butt end of his rifle. "Well, 'breed,' I'll make sure you two share the same grave."

Jonas laughed throatily. He waved his rifle in the air as he looked back at his men. "Place two ropes in those trees over yonder!" he shouted. "We're going to have us a hanging! It might not be as exciting as watchin' the white man's ranch house and bunkhouses burning, but anyhows, it will be somethin' fun to watch."

The air was suddenly rent with the noise of war whoops. Like a black cloud, a shower of arrows were discharged upon the enemy from the hidden brush on all sides. The outlaws' horses reared and plunged and fell upon each other as gunfire burst out from all around. First one outlaw fell from his horse with mortal wounds, then another; the others were trampled by their crazed steeds.

And before they were able to see whom to shoot at, most were disarmed, wounded, or dead.

Stunned, and still on their horses, Jae and Night Hawk stared disbelievingly around them. Jonas lay dead on the ground, having been downed by several arrows as he had tried to run for cover.

Jae's mouth dropped open and fear grabbed her at her heart when she saw that it had not been Eagle Wing and his men who had come to their rescue. Suddenly Black Crow and his warriors appeared on their horses.

As Black Crow stopped close beside them, his eyes met Night Hawk's. Slowly, deliberately, he slipped his bow over his shoulder.

"Do not think I have come to kill the whites so that I can massacre *you*," Black Crow said, his face void of expression as he gazed at Night Hawk. "I can now go onward with peace in my heart. I can enter the land of the hereafter when I die without fearing being rejected. I have saved your lives. I now ride on and make another life for myself elsewhere."

Black Crow glanced down, then looked slowly up again. "My time of raiding is over," he said solemnly. "I wish now only to live the rest of my days out in solitude. Without my people, I have no reason to plunder the whites. Without my people, I . . . am . . . nothing."

Suddenly Eagle Wing, Crying Wolf, and many more Comanche warriors appeared behind Black Crow and his warriors, their weapons drawn.

Eagle Wing stared at the dead white men, and then at Black Crow. He leveled his rifle at Black Crow. "Step down from your horse," he flatly ordered.

"Allow him to ride onward," Night Hawk said solemnly, his eyes still locked with Black Crow's. "He is no threat to anyone."

"But, Night Hawk . . ." Eagle Wing said, raising an eyebrow.

"He has earned the right to be free." Night Hawk's eyes were still locked with Black Crow's. "Allow it."

Eagle Wing edged his horse away from Black Crow's. He lowered his rifle and watched as Black Crow and his warriors rode away, then he questioned Night Hawk with silent eyes.

"Black Crow is responsible for this," Night Hawk said, gesturing toward the dead outlaws. "He saved my life and Jae's. His life must now also be spared."

Jae reached over and took Night Hawk's hand.

When he looked her way, he saw tears in her eyes as she smiled at him.

Chapter Forty-one

Several Months Later

It was the time of the Green Corn Ceremony. Now married to Night Hawk, and with Snoopy snuggled against her drum-tight pregnant belly, Jae sat beside Touch the Sky, who was also married and pregnant.

Lois sat with them, radiant in her own marriage and just as content, even though she and Crying Wolf had never considered having children, for Crying Wolf was in the sunset days of his life. He did not want to leave a wife with a child when a father would not be there to nurture the child into adulthood. Their love for one another was enough.

Numerous fires had been kindled outside the village short distances from each other around a large circle. Each family had its own separate fire, and by each fire had been placed a quantity of green corn, piled high on buffalo skins.

The corn was now roasting in the fires, while everyone sat in the center of the two-acre circle.

Singing their green-corn song, the dancers whirled

and swayed and danced around the fires. Jae listened carefully to the words of the song and how it was sung, for at this time next year, when she wouldn't be swollen with child, she planned to be a part of the dance.

She leaned forward, absorbed in the music that was being sung.

"Ahow, aho, aho, ahow," the singers sang over and over again, their bodies and feet keeping time to music being hammered out of a dry skin drawn over a hoop. The dancing continued for a long time, and then the dancers sat down on the south side of the circle.

Jae watched Chief Brown Bull rise slowly to his feet. She gasped when she noticed how he faltered, his knees almost buckling beneath him.

She sighed with relief when he finally stood straight and proud, yet she could not help but notice that something was wrong with him. His face had a gray pallor. His eyes looked tired. And as he began to address his people and slowly walked around the circle, she saw that he was doing this with much effort. His voice trembled; his shoulders swayed.

Jae looked quickly at Night Hawk. She saw that he was also concerned about his father. More than once, he looked as though he might get up to go to Brown Bull, then he would sit back down to watch him some more.

Jae saw the deep concern in her husband's eyes. She watched his hands reach out for his father, then he would rest his hands once again on his knees.

Jae turned slowly back to Chief Brown Bull. His health had improved in great measure these past weeks, yet everyone knew that the poison that had been fed him had taken its toll. He had not been able to regain his full strength.

Night Hawk had even urged his father not to join in the Green Corn Ceremony today, to let War Chief Eagle Wing take charge. But his father had stubbornly said that he had never missed a Green Corn Ceremony. Nor would he today!

Jae watched Brown Bull walk around the circle, raising his hand above the separate piles of roasted corn as he passed them, talking all the while, invoking a blessing.

After he sat down, and everyone had taken a roasted ear of corn, Night Hawk leapt to his feet and went to his father.

Night Hawk knelt down before Brown Bull. He reached a hand to the vein in his father's throat, and he swallowed hard when he found his pulse very weak.

Night Hawk turned frightened eyes to Eagle Wing. "Come, friend!" he cried. "Help me get Father to his bed!"

The whole band of Comanche rose to their feet. They were mute as they watched their longtime, beloved chief being lifted from the ground and carried between Night Hawk and Eagle Wing.

Jae dropped Snoopy to the ground. She and Touch the Sky ran on ahead of Night Hawk to Chief Brown Bull's lodge and prepared his bed for his arrival.

As he was carried into his tepee and placed on his bed, Brown Bull's eyes opened slowly.

Night Hawk knelt down beside the bed. "Father, why did you not listen to me?" he said, his voice filled with despair. "Why did you not stay home today and rest? You have overtaxed your heart by involving yourself in the ceremony."

Little Horse came into the lodge, breathless. He knelt down beside Night Hawk.

"My sons," Brown Bull said, his voice barely a whisper, "I love you both so much." He looked past them at Touch the Sky as she came and knelt down on Night Hawk's left side. "My daughter, the flower of my wigwam, I have always been so proud of you." He reached a trembling hand to her swollen belly. "And I would have been as proud of the child born of yours and Eagle Wing's love."

"Father, you are not going to die," Touch the Sky stammered out between deep sobs. "Please do not talk like you are."

"Send for my wives," Brown Bull said. "Tell them I send for them in my last moments. Have them bring my other children. I must say good-bye to them, and then I have words for my son Night Hawk alone."

Touch the Sky went for his wives and children. Everyone stood back as good-byes were said.

The wives and children left again. Chills rode up and down Jae's spine as she heard the women moaning and wailing in their private lodges.

"Night Hawk, please stay," Brown Bull said, then looked around at everyone else. "Understand this time I must have with my older son. Things must be said. He who inherits my war shield will share my last moments on this earth."

Everyone began to file silently from the lodge, Jae with them.

When she heard her name spoken by Brown Bull, her heart lurched. Scarcely breathing, hoping that he was going to allow her to stay with her husband, she turned and gazed at Brown Bull.

"Wife of my older son, and mother of my unborn

grandchild, stay and hear what I say to your husband," Brown Bull said, gesturing with a weak, trembling hand toward her.

Touched by his kindness, Jae smiled at him, but Brown Bull did not see the smile. His eyes were closed. His breathing was shallow; death rattles were rumbling from his lungs.

Jae crept to Night Hawk's side. She knelt down beside him, reached over, and took one of his hands.

They both waited for Brown Bull's eyes to open again. They hoped they *would* open. The death rattles were worsening, filling the air like some ancient ghost rattling chains.

Brown Bull sighed. He choked. He wheezed.

Then he opened his eyes and smiled, first at Night Hawk and then at Jae. "Although she is white, this woman has made you a good wife," Brown Bull said between gasping, weak breaths. "She has earned an Indian name." He gazed up at Night Hawk. "I have one chosen for her. Or would you rather give her a name of your own choice?"

"She shall carry your chosen name proudly," Night Hawk said, slowly stroking his father's brow.

Brown Bull nodded. He smiled at Jae. "Wife of my firstborn, from now on you will be called Searching Heart," he said. "The name was chosen because of the way your heart searched until you found a husband in my son."

Moved deeply by his affection for her, Jae wiped tears from her eyes. "The name is so beautiful," she murmured. "Thank you for giving it to me." She smiled at Night Hawk. "And doesn't the name sound so feminine?"

"The name Jae has never fit the woman I have

known in you," Brown Bull said, drawing Jae's eyes back to him.

Brown Bull again closed his eyes, but still he talked. "Night Hawk, get my war shield," he said softly. "Hold it. Let us talk about it. There is then something else I wish to give you. Then my talking will be over. I will rest until my spirit is ready to rise from inside me."

Jae choked back a sob. She covered her mouth with a hand.

And when Night Hawk came and knelt down beside the bed again with the beautiful shield, she turned soft eyes up at her husband and smiled.

"My son, my shield is now yours," Brown Bull said, reaching a trembling hand to trace the designs on the shield. "Do you see the painted bull?"

Night Hawk nodded.

"That is my design, painted the day after the shield was passed down to me by my dying father," he said, pride in his voice. "What design will you choose, my son?"

Night Hawk found it hard to talk when he knew that his father was dying. Yet he found courage in his father's bravery and sat square-shouldered beside the bed, his gaze now on the shield. He thought for a moment, then smiled over at his father.

"Tomorrow I shall paint the design of a hawk on the shield," he said proudly. "Then the shield will rest again beside the lodge entrance until *my* son chooses what he will paint on the shield beside your buffalo and my hawk."

"That is good," Brown Bull said, his voice growing weaker as he spoke. Then he looked more seriously into Night Hawk's eyes. "There is something more I need to say."

"What is it, Father?" Night Hawk's heart ached to see his father's failing strength.

"I have it in my power to name chiefs for our village," Brown Bull said, placing a gentle hand on Night Hawk's arm. "I, who have born the title of Civil Chief *and* Head Chief since Black Crow's expulsion from our tribe, pass the title of Head Chief on to you now, my son. And, my son, do not give this title away as you did War Chief!"

Night Hawk's eyes widened. He swallowed hard. He felt so honored by his father's belief in him that he found it hard to say anything.

But seeing that his father was waiting, he laid the shield aside and hugged Brown Bull. "I shall proudly accept the honor of being Head Chief for our people," he said. "Thank you, Father. I shall never fail in my duties to my people."

"I know that to be true. And it is in your power now to name the one who will be Civil Chief. Give the title to Crying Wolf, my son. He well deserves the honor."

"*Huh,* I agree," Night Hawk said, smiling at how his old friend would beam with the special title of Civil Chief! "And I will tell him that it was your dying wish that he should be our people's Civil Chief."

Brown Bull nodded and smiled, then gently shoved Night Hawk away from him. He nodded toward the back of the lodge. "My son, now it is time for you to get something else that is soon to be yours," he said, his voice so weak it was barely audible.

Night Hawk followed his father's gaze and saw what he was talking about—his father's wardrobe case.

He dutifully placed the buffalo-hide shield back in

its proper place, then went and got the wardrobe case in which his father kept his prized clothes. It was a rawhide case, envelope shaped and laced together at the edges. It had a tie-down, fold-over flap. In this case, Night Hawk knew he would find his father's best leggings, moccasins, blankets, and braid wrappers. Such a case was also handed down from father to son.

"My son, this case is now yours," Brown Bull said, his eyes closed as he spoke. "Keep the treasure that is in the case, all but what you choose to place on this old man for his grave."

Night Hawk struggled to keep his emotions at bay. Then suddenly he could not last any longer. The tears welled from his eyes. He laid the wardrobe case aside and leaned over his father, desperately hugging him.

"We have not had enough time together," Night Hawk cried. "Our years together were stolen from us. Father, do not die! Stay! Let me love you longer, Father! Let *my* son give you *his* love!"

Jae sobbed and turned her eyes away, then turned back around when she heard the gentle, comforting voice of Brown Bull as he tried to ease his son's pain.

"My son, do not be sad over my death," Brown Bull murmured. "Do you not know that I do not fear death? That I welcome it? The good Comanche who has been brave in battle and who walks upright among his tribe is transmitted to a valley ten thousand fold longer and wider than the land we live on today. The climate there is always as mild as it is in the Moon of Plants."

Brown Bull stopped and caught his breath.

Then he continued in a soft voice. "Where I am going, there is cool water and pounded corn and mustangs forever at hand. Buffalo and deer abound, and the horses are fleeter than the wind."

He gently patted Night Hawk's back with his trembling hand. "My son, I will be happy there. I will wait for you to join me. No one will ever separate us as we were separated before. We have missed so much by not being together long enough on this earth. When we are reunited in the heavens, we will live together for eternity!"

"All of those things are true and beautiful," Night Hawk said, easing from his father's arms. "But this is now, and I cannot help but want you longer with me."

"My son," Brown Bull said, now gasping out the words, "grass and sky go on forever, but not Brown Bull." He smiled from Jae to Night Hawk. "I will be dust . . . you will be dust. . . ."

Jae held back a gasp when she saw Brown Bull take a deep, shuddering breath. He showed no fear in dying. There was peace in his eyes; there was a smile on his lips.

Night Hawk's heart lurched, for as he heard an owl's mournful cry, followed by the whisper of wings as they stroked the air just outside the lodge, his father drew his last breath.

Jae turned to her husband and welcomed him into her arms. She held him tightly as he buried his face against her bosom.

"He died peacefully," Jae tried to reassure. "Feel blessed that you were here with him. It was so touching to see you together, to see the love, to feel it."

"He . . . is . . . gone forever," Night Hawk said, clinging to Jae. "I can hardly bear his loss."

"But you must," Jae whispered to him. "There are those who wait for you outside the lodge. They will want to come and see your father before he is prepared for burial."

"*Huh*, there are so many who love him," Night Hawk said, straightening his back as he eased from her arms.

He reached a gentle hand to his father's eyes and closed them. "He was such a regal, powerful, yet loving man," he said, finding courage to face the next few days by recalling so much that his father had said in the last few moments of his life. "So many will miss him."

"You have the strength for all of them to carry them through their grief," Jae said softly. She took him by the hand. "Come. You have duties to see to as Head Chief. Your people await the sad news about your father."

Night Hawk smiled at Jae, then rose away from the bed and stepped outside the lodge. All eyes were on him. Everything was silent. Everyone waited the news.

"My father's spirit has left his body," Night Hawk said, then gestured toward the heavens. "Do you not feel his presence, though? He is here with us. He will always be with us."

Firelike pains rippled through her belly. Jae grabbed at it and looked quickly up at Night Hawk. She hated disturbing him at such a time as this, but there was no denying the pains that were suddenly almost tearing her apart.

She was going to have the baby today!

Being so upset over the death of Brown Bull had brought the pains on prematurely!

She had one full month left before the child was supposed to be born!

Another pain ripped through her abdomen, almost

doubling Jae over. She moaned and sank to her knees.

Night Hawk looked quickly down at his wife. When he saw what was happening, how much pain Jae was in, he swept his arms beneath her and quickly carried her to their lodge.

Touch the Sky and Lois ran after them and moved beside the bed as Night Hawk gently laid Jae across it.

"The child . . ." Jae panted out, sweat streaming from her brow. She reached for Touch the Sky's hand. "The child is coming!"

Normally only the medicine man and medicine woman, and Indian women attendants, were allowed in a Comanche lodge where a woman was in labor.

But now was different.

It was a joint effort.

Everyone moved frantically into action and time seemed to lose its meaning as the hours passed.

Just as Jae felt she couldn't bear any more, the baby's head began to emerge. She screamed and grabbed Night Hawk's hand, squeezing it as she grunted, groaned, and shoved. She felt as though she might faint, but fought against it.

Then she felt a sudden surge of relief when the baby slid from inside her into Lois's waiting hands.

Tears flowed from Jae's eyes when she heard the first cries of her child.

"It is a son," Touch the Sky said as she cut the umbilical cord and handed it to the village medicine woman, who would wrap it up in buckskin and hang it in a hackberry tree. If it was untouched before it rotted, the child would live a long life.

The medicine woman would also be required to

carry away the afterbirth and throw it in a running stream.

Touch the Sky took the child from Lois and wrapped him in rabbit skins, then handed him over to Night Hawk. "Big brother, is not your son beautiful?" she asked, sighing as she continued to look at the baby.

"*Huh*, so beautiful," Night Hawk murmured.

Incredulous at how small a baby could be, so tiny the child fitted snugly into the palm of one of his hands, Night Hawk continued to gaze proudly down at him. His son looked totally Comanche, from the dark shock of hair on his tiny head to the copper color of his skin. And when he opened his eyes and gazed up at Night Hawk, he saw the same deep black gaze his father had had.

"Today I lost a father but have gained a son," Night Hawk said, gently placing the child in Jae's arms. "Searching Heart, is he not perfect? Is he not a beautiful child?"

Jae gazed at the tiny baby lying next to her, so taken by him that she was choked with happiness. She ran her fingers over his tiny body. "It is a miracle that he was born today," she said, smiling up at Night Hawk. "Does not his birth help ease your sadness over losing your father?"

"*Huh*, and so shall we name him Brown Bull in honor of my father?"

"Brown Bull is a beautiful name for our son," Jae murmured. "And he will carry it proudly when he is old enough to know who he was named after."

When little Brown Bull began to cry, Night Hawk knelt down beside the bed and watched his wife place their child's lips to her breast for the first time.

"What a beautiful sight," he said, then looked heav-

Cassie Edwards

enward. "Do you not think so, Father? I feel you here. You are seeing your grandson before taking the long ride on your steed to the afterworld!"

A great gust of wind suddenly shook the buckskin lodge.

Night Hawk and Jae gazed at one another, then smiled knowingly.

Chapter Forty-two

Three Years Later

The Eagle Dance was in progress for Little Horse, held in his honor for a young brave turning warrior. White Fire, the village medicine man, had been offered a smoke by Night Hawk, who was now Little Horse's acting father.

White Fire had accepted the smoke to show that he approved of the Eagle Dance to be held in Little Horse's honor. The decision was a serious one, because he would lose some of his power to the Eagle Dancer.

After White Fire had accepted the smoke, he had announced the time and place of the ceremony. He and Little Horse had risen before daylight and gone to the river to bathe. They stripped to their breechclouts, put on war paint, let their hair down and put eagle feathers in it, and rubbed themselves with sage.

The hours since then had passed quickly.

The Eagle Dance was now in progress.

It was just turning dusk.

One huge fire was burning in the center of the village, its flames leaping heavenward.

Everyone was there, sitting on blankets in a semicircle, with the opening to the east, watching the young brave acting out what was necessary for him to be a proud warrior.

Little Horse and many of his friends, who soon would participate in the same dance, danced around the fire in their brief breechclouts and war paint.

Jae, with Night Hawk at her side, and their three-year old son Brown Bull sitting on her lap, watched as one of the most important parts of the ritual began to be acted out.

The drums continued to pound out their steady rhythm as Little Horse left the dancers and ran toward a brush lodge that had been erected especially for this event and placed where everyone could watch.

All eyes were on Little Horse as he crept stealthily toward the brush lodge. The drummers ceased playing their music. Inside the lodge was a young maiden favored by Little Horse, and her family.

As the Comanche people gasped out their pretended outrage, which was also a part of the ritual, Little Horse rushed into the lodge and then came out with the girl, her family following them outside, pretending to be afraid of the young brave.

Little Horse raised a fist in the air and shouted several phrases taught him by White Fire. Little Horse had captured a girl! The family had been overwhelmed by his prowess. They had no choice but to give their daughter up to the brave.

The victorious raider walked the young maiden over to the fire, where he proudly showed off his prize.

The girl, Sweet Bird, sat down on the ground, facing Little Horse. Six drummers played. The women of the village began to sing victory songs.

Tears came to Jae's eyes as Night Hawk rose and went to Little Horse. As everyone became quiet, Little Horse was named a warrior by his brother. He was then given his adult name, White Horse. The name had been chosen because of the dream that had come to Little Horse in his vision quest.

As he had fasted four days and nights in the hills, he had dreamed of a sparkling white horse that came to him, first prancing, and then sprouting wings and flying away across the sky.

The horse had returned to Little Horse in the dream. He had allowed Little Horse to mount. The brave had then ridden the sleek white mount all across the heavens, soaring low as he gazed upon his village, where he had seen the girl who would be a part of his Eagle Dance ceremony.

He had returned to the butte on which he had spent the past four days and nights, and had awakened feeling older and wiser. He had fled home and told only his older brother what he had experienced. He told Night Hawk that he wished to be named White Horse. It was a more adult name than Little Horse! It was a name brought to him during his vision quest!

The ceremony now over, White Horse ran to the river to bathe. Everyone watched him as he dove into the water and swam upstream four times, then came out of the river bathed, proud, and ready to be a man.

As the crowd dispersed and everyone went to their lodges, Jae and Night Hawk paused long enough to watch White Horse run away toward the nearby butte with Sweet Bird.

"He is now a man," Night Hawk said. He placed a finger to Jae's chin and drew her eyes away from White Horse and Sweet Bird, who were snuggled close together as they now walked more slowly, their hands clasped. "She is turning into a woman. It is all right for them to be together."

"Sexually?" Jae gasped, paling.

"No, not sexually." Night Hawk chuckled. "They will just sit and talk. There might be some kisses exchanged. But that is all. White Horse has much respect for the young Comanche maidens. He would never want to dishonor them by wrongly touching their bodies."

Jae gazed down at little Brown Bull. He was sound asleep in her arms.

She then turned smiling eyes up at Night Hawk. "I am no longer a young maiden, and you are no young warrior," she said, giggling. "And our son is very much asleep. Would you do more than kiss me, my darling, in the privacy of our lodge?"

"Have I ever denied such a request by my wife?" Night Hawk said, chuckling low. He took Brown Bull from her arms and hastened on to the lodge as Jae walked more slowly to absorb the magic of the stars that were now popping out overhead like miniature lanterns being lit.

And when the moon came out in its full splendor, Jae gazed at it and smiled. "Mr. Moon, I have never been so happy," she whispered.

When she arrived at the lodge, Brown Bull was already in his cradle, a buckskin blanket drawn up to his chin. Snoopy lay just beneath the cradle. The raccoon had become Brown Bull's shadow. He adored the child.

Jae stood over the cradle. She reached a gentle

hand to her son's brow, then leaned over and kissed him.

Strong arms swept around her waist, then slowly drew her around, and she laughed softly when she discovered that Night Hawk was already undressed.

Her gaze swept over him, smiling to see that he was more than just undressed. He was aroused and eager for their private, sensual time together in bed.

Night Hawk wasted no time undressing Jae. Then he swept her up into his arms and carried her to their bed. He laid her down on a thick cushion of furs and blankets. He knelt over her, his hands touching, caressing, and arousing her every sensitive place.

As he touched her, surges of warmth flooded through her body. Each stroke promised so much. She tingled with the aliveness of it.

"Kiss me, my Comanche husband," Jae whispered, her face flushed with sexual excitement. "Fill me, my darling, with your heat. Make . . . love . . . to me."

Night Hawk braced himself with his arms over her. He twined his fingers through hers and took her hands and held them slightly above her head as he shoved his throbbing heat inside her.

She wrapped her legs around his waist and thrust her pelvis toward him, giving him easier access to her throbbing woman's center.

Tremors cascaded down her back as his lips came down on hers in a frenzied kiss. Her body moved with his as desire raged and washed over her. She felt the promise he offered her in each thrust inside her. She was delirious with sensations. She knew that this would not be a long loving. She could already feel herself growing close to that edge of ecstasy that would give her the fulfillment she sought.

She could tell that Night Hawk was entering that

same realm of passion by the way his body was tightening with each of his bold thrusts inside her.

He slid his mouth from her lips. He laid his cheek against hers and closed his eyes. He let the magic take hold. He let it guide him close to the brink of rapture.

Then he kissed her again and made one final, deep thrust inside her. His body trembled violently against hers.

Jae's body shook as she clung to him. She was only vaguely aware of making soft, whimpering sounds as the pleasure spread through her like warm sunshine.

And then they lay side by side, their fingers intertwined. "I wish it could be like this forever," Jae murmured. "But I feel things closing in on the Comanche, and because of only a few renegades who make it hard for the rest of the tribe."

"If I ever discover that Black Crow has gone back on his word and is responsible for the havoc being spread among the white community, I shall hunt him down like an animal and be less merciful to him than I would a dog gone mad," Night Hawk said solemnly.

"He did seem genuinely apologetic the last time we saw him," Jae said, turning over on her stomach. She rested her chin in her hands as she gazed at Night Hawk. "Let's talk about something else. I was wrong to mention problems after we have enjoyed such a wonderful day honoring Little Horse, and now, after we have shared our hearts again so fully."

"You must remember to call him White Horse from now on," Night Hawk corrected as he brushed fallen locks of Jae's hair back from her brow. "As you are called by a name other than that which you were born with." He placed a soft kiss on her brow. "My beautiful Searching Heart. How I love you."

"You make life so wonderful," Jae said, snuggling next to him. "Thank you for saving me from the life I was forced to live in the Big Thicket. Thank you for saving me from Jonas Adams, and even my*self*. If not for you, I doubt I would be alive now."

"Destiny led me to you," Night Hawk said, hugging her close. "I shall always protect you. I shall always cherish you."

He gave her a gentle kiss, then once again only lay with her, holding her. "Let us not talk anymore of the savage shadows of life. Let us talk of what we have together now, and what we have found with my true people, the *Ner-mer-nuh*, the Lords of the Southern Plains, the Comanche!"

He sighed. "*Huh*, yes, it is good to have found my rightful place in life with my people, and with you," he said softly. "Let us be thankful, my wife, for the goodness of the Wise One Above."

"*Huh*, yes, I feel so very blessed." Jae twined her fingers through her husband's flaxen hair and drew his lips to hers.

Their kiss was soft and sweet, as was their love for one another, a love that would endure forever.

Letter to the Reader

Dear Readers:

I hope you enjoyed reading *Savage Shadows!* The next book in my "Savage" series, which I write exclusively for Leisure Books, is *Savage Longings*. *Savage Longings* will be in the stores six months after the release date of *Savage Shadows*.

I'm really excited about *Savage Longings!* This book is the sequel to *Savage Secrets* and is the story about my Cheyenne great-grandmother, Snow Deer. *Savage Longings* will be filled with much excitement and adventure, but most of all it will have much tender sweetness between Snow Deer and her white husband, my great-grandfather.

For those of you who are collecting my Leisure Savage Series and want to read about my backlist and my future books, please send a self-addressed, stamped envelope for my latest newsletter to the following address:

Cassie Edwards
Route 3, Box 60
Mattoon, IL 61938

Always,
Cassie Edwards

THE Savage
S E R I E S

SAVAGE SECRETS
CASSIE EDWARDS

Winner Of The *Romantic Times* Reviewers' Choice Award For Best Indian Series

Searching the wilds of the Wyoming Territory for her outlaw brother, Rebecca Veach is captured by the one man who fulfills her heart's desire. But can she give herself to the virile warrior without telling him about her shameful quest?

Blazing Eagle is as strong as the winter wind, yet as gentle as a summer day. And although he wants Becky from the moment he takes her captive, hidden memories of a long-ago tragedy tear him away from the golden-haired vixen.

Strong-willed virgin and Cheyenne chieftain, Becky and Blazing Eagle share a passion that burns hotter than the prairie sun—until savage secrets from their past threaten to destroy them and the love they share.

__3823-4 $5.99 US/$7.99 CAN

SAVAGE PASSIONS

CASSIE EDWARDS

**Winner Of The *Romantic Times*
Lifetime Achievement Award
For Best Indian Romance Series!**

Living among the virgin forests of frontier Michigan, Yvonne secretly admires the chieftain of a peaceful Ottawa tribe. A warrior with great mystical powers and many secrets, Silver Arrow tempts her with his hard body even as his dark, seductive eyes set her wary heart afire. But white men and Indians alike threaten to keep them forever apart. To fulfill the promise of their passion, Yvonne and Silver Arrow will need more than mere magic: They'll need the strength of a love both breathtaking and bold.

_3902-8 $5.99 US/$7.99 CAN